PRAISE FOR

THE SHARK

"This romantic thriller is tense, sexy, and pleasingly complex."

—*Publishers Weekly*

"Precise storytelling complete with strong conflict and heightened tension are the highlights of Burton's latest. With a tough, vulnerable heroine in Riley at the story's center, Burton's novel is a well-crafted, suspenseful mystery with a ruthless villain who would put any reader on edge. A thrilling read."

—RT Book Reviews, four stars

BEFORE SHE DIES

"Will keep readers sleeping with the lights on."

—*Publishers Weekly* (starred review)

MERCILESS

"Burton keeps getting better!"

—RT Book Reviews

YOU'RE NOT SAFE

"Burton once again demonstrates her romantic suspense chops with this taut novel. Burton plays cat and mouse with the reader through a tight plot, credible suspects, and romantic spice keeping it real."

—*Publishers Weekly*

BE AFRAID

"Mary Burton [is] the modern-day queen of romantic suspense."

—Bookreporter.com

NEVER LOOK BACK

ALSO BY MARY BURTON

I See You
Hide and Seek
Cut and Run
The Last Move
Her Last Word

The Forgotten Files

The Shark
The Dollmaker
The Hangman

Morgans of Nashville

Cover Your Eyes
Be Afraid
I'll Never Let You Go
Vulnerable

Texas Rangers

The Seventh Victim
No Escape
You're Not Safe

Alexandria Series

Senseless
Merciless
Before She Dies

Richmond Series

I'm Watching You
Dead Ringer
Dying Scream

NEVER LOOK BACK

MARY BURTON

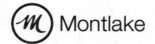

Text copyright © 2020 by Mary Burton
All rights reserved.

Published by Montlake, Seattle
www.apub.com

Amazon, the Amazon logo, and Montlake are trademarks of Amazon.com, Inc., or its affiliates.

ISBN-13: 9781542009843
ISBN-10: 1542009847

Cover design by Caroline Teagle Johnson

Printed in the United States of America

NEVER
LOOK
BACK

PROLOGUE

Nashville, Tennessee
Monday, August 17, 10:30 p.m.

Heat and humidity punched up the bleach's faint scent in the van's dark interior. It made his eyes water, his throat burn, and his palms itch under the latex.

Scrubbers and fine brushes cleaned surfaces well enough, but disinfectants seeped into unseen crevices and obliterated pesky droplets of blood. Trace evidence sowed the seeds of a cavalier man's downfall.

Perhaps the second dousing of cleaner had been overkill, but his belt-and-suspenders approach never failed him. He had many faults, but carelessness was not one of them. Better this temporary irritation than a lifetime in a jail cell.

He rolled down the driver's side window, knowing next time he would rinse out the vehicle with more water after the bleaching. He turned his face toward the warm, fresh air. He inhaled and closed his eyes, pretending the whoosh of cars on Interstates 24 and 40 was the ocean. Some of his best Date Nights had been on secluded beaches.

He had enjoyed traveling up and down the East Coast because he had decided long ago the women at the beach were the prettiest.

Accustomed to warm air and sunshine, they tended toward short skirts and revealing tops and, for the most part, stayed in shape.

As much as he loved the ocean, he had sensed it was time to move on to new territory. Maybe it was because he was getting older, but he had felt a pull toward Nashville, his hometown. His parents were long dead. Any friends he'd once had would not recognize him. Repatriation was good for the soul. It reinvigorated the senses. Challenged the mind.

Nashville, Tennessee. Music City. Home of the Country Music Hall of Fame. He had forgotten that it was such an exciting, bustling city filled with beautiful ladies who did not disappoint.

What Nashville lacked in beaches it made up for with out-of-the-way spots. The houses he had found were all located at the end of winding roads on the tops of hills. Their views were amazing. In the five weeks he had been back, he had enjoyed two Date Nights with women he had chosen from the streets. Online shopping for a date was efficient, but it also left a digital trail. Old-school cruising left less evidence.

Once he'd made his selection, it was off to his hilltop, where he and his Lady Loves had had all the time in the world to get to know each other.

Good relationships needed privacy. They could not be rushed.

Yes, sir. He had enjoyed two very fine dates recently. He should have been satisfied by now. But instead he remained ravenous and craved a third date.

He blinked and then rubbed his nose. The smell was fading, which was good. First impressions mattered.

The strong scent was due to two cleansings in as many days. Generally, he allowed more time. But he was not getting any younger. And each day he realized how precious time was becoming.

He had parked his van in the shadow of an abandoned South Nashville warehouse in an area called the Bottom. This industrial section was nestled between the Nashville airport and the juncture of

Interstates 24 and 40. It was the workmen's world by day and the playground of prostitutes and johns by night.

A couple of miles north, the skyscrapers shimmered over Music City's business district. Nestled among the tall buildings was Lower Broadway, where red, white, and blue neon lights charmed tourists into cowboy boot shops, honky-tonks, and the Grand Ole Opry.

Only a stone's throw separated Nashville's vibrant downtown from the Bottom, but the worlds could not have been more distant.

In the Bottom, revving cars, shouts, and gunfire replaced the sound of live music. The air carried the odor of fetid garbage rather than smoky barbecue. Instead of smiling tourists strolling Lower Broadway, junkies needled heroin into exhausted veins while hookers slid into an endless supply of cars.

This was his tenth trip to the Bottom in the last month. Down here the lineup changed from day to day, week to week. Always a fresh face. Familiarity could make a man sloppy, but he approached each trip as if it were his first, careful to avoid aggressive pimps or the very rare cop.

Most of the women down here had a hard, worn look that did not appeal. He did not care for the experienced ones. Too jaded. Tough like gristle. Not just any gal would do for Date Night.

Tonight, he felt lucky. In control.

On the corner across the street stood two women. They had arrived about a half hour ago and seemed to know the area well. The women were constantly adjusting their outfits and scanning the area. A third girl arrived. She spoke to the duo, and the other girls did not appear to welcome her.

New Girl was not tall, but she was slim and very fit. Long black hair draped shoulders clad in a white button-down shirt. She had twisted the shirttails around her narrow waist and tied them into a knot above a brass belt buckle. The top four buttons were unfastened to the edges of a lacy white bra filled with ample, perky cleavage. Some men liked legs. Others, ass. He was a breast man.

Skinny jeans perfectly hugged legs rising out of red cowboy boots studded with silver rhinestones. She had a fresh look that was pleasing. His Date Night girl needed to have some experience, but he also did not want rode-hard-and-hung-up-wet.

This one looked young. Body of a teenager, but her demeanor suggested she was a few years older. Hard to tell. The streets aged girls like her.

This was not the first time he had seen this one down here. Three nights ago, he had glimpsed her laughing with several of the girls, but before he could make his move, the priest who operated the Mission had engaged her in a lengthy discussion.

He leaned forward, resting his forearms on the steering wheel. The glow of the streetlight shadowed Date Night girl's angled chin. Her back was straight. Tits out. Good posture. This girl was self-assured and would do nicely.

He imagined the sound of bones crunching. Screams. The feel of warm blood on his face.

The strong and healthy ones could sustain a great deal of abuse. It was always disappointing to go to the trouble of finding a date, arranging a first outing, and then having them die too soon.

He had had thirteen girlfriends in all. A couple of girls had made it beyond a week, but the others had barely survived a few days. His longest relationship had lasted sixteen days.

New Girl ran long fingers through her hair, arching her back seductively as if she knew he was watching. His attention focused on the trim waist and then roamed over her full breasts and slim neck. He imagined her stripped down, her tanned skin glistening in the moonlight and a tight collar around her throat. Dangling from the collar was the key to unlock the cuffs that restrained her.

He had high hopes for this one. He imagined her breaking, submitting to him.

Growing hard, he palmed his johnson. Anticipation crept through him. "Ready to play in my van, Ms. Perky Breasts?"

He was tempted to walk up to her, but with the other girls close, he did not. Moving in the open was a recipe for trouble. Even if the other girls did not remember him, there were unseen cameras or witnesses lurking. Lots of traps in the game he played. And he knew them all.

He scratched above his ear where some of his real hair had slipped the confines of the blond wig. Tugging at his gloves, he was anxious to be done with it, as well as the colored contacts and glasses, but he could not reveal himself until he and his girl were alone. It was the belt-and-suspenders approach.

New Girl fished in her purse, pulled out a cell phone, and raised it to her ear. She ducked her head, as if in deep conversation. Pimps kept a tight leash on their girls. Most texted every half hour and expected a quick response, or there would be hell to pay. Always better to avoid the pimps. The priest was also a problem. She watched out for the girls like they were her flock.

Date Night girl ended her call as a black early-model Cadillac pulled up. It had chrome wheels and a white convertible top with Tennessee plates. The first two girls approached the car and leaned inside to chat with the driver.

"Don't you leave me, girl." He whispered the words over and over as anxiety crawled up his back.

As Date Night girl lingered back, the two women laughed at something the driver must have said. The passenger door opened, and the two women slid inside, nestling close to the driver. His Date Night girl took a step back and watched the vehicle drive off.

Ms. Perky Breasts was now alone. Another sign.

It was just the two of them.

Now or never.

He glanced in his rearview mirror, catching the reflection off the leg restraints bolted to the floor. He checked his driver's side door for the syringe taped to the vinyl. Three other needles just like it were taped strategically throughout the van. All were loaded with enough ketamine to drop a linebacker. And even if she screamed, the van was soundproof. He had tricked out the vehicle specifically to ensure everything was contained until they reached his place in the woods.

He turned the ignition key. The van's engine started. He kept the headlights off as he inched his vehicle out of the shadows toward her. His gaze swept the area one last time, and when certain it was just the two of them, he pulled up beside her.

She held back a moment, eyeing him. Brown eyes glinted with street smarts. No one lasted long on the street without survival sense.

He got his first close look at her. She was older than he had first thought. Late twenties maybe, but her skin had a healthy glow that he liked. Her lips were full and her cheekbones high. Exotic.

She sniffed, rubbed her nose, and swayed slightly as if she were a little drunk.

Caution checked him briefly. Something felt off about her. What was it? His gaze slowly roamed over her again, but as soon as he got a good look at her breasts, he swatted away his worries. A small cross dangled on her chest, and when she shifted, he was sure he glimpsed pink nipple.

She was exactly his type. Better than he had hoped for. She was already one of his top picks, and they had not even started partying yet.

The streets may have smartened her up, but he was about to teach her lessons she had never learned.

She rolled back those shoulders like she was the one in charge. For a moment he hesitated, reconsidering his choice. He tended toward the docile but always enjoyed the ones with a little fight and spunk.

Risk versus reward.

He rolled down the passenger-side window, careful to keep his gloved hands in his lap and out of view. The scent of her spicy perfume reminded him of a previous date. He took it as a good omen. No signs of track marks on her arms. And if she did meth, it had not been for long.

She glanced from side to side and then stepped forward. That direct brown-eyed gaze made him anxious for the takedown. Transitions were always tricky.

"Looking for a party?" he asked.

She studied him with intense eyes. "Not tonight, pal. Calling it early."

Despite his desire for a challenge, her rebuff irritated him. She was supposed to say yes and get in the car. That was why he was in the Bottom. The hunting was easy.

On the passenger side of the van, there was an automatic door that opened with the push of a button. Modifications ensured it snapped open fast. Repeated practice guaranteed he could be between the seats and grabbing her wrist in less than two seconds. She would have to be on her game to get away.

He mentally raced through the steps, already excited about the risk of grabbing her.

Door open.
Grab the girl.
Toss in back.
Door close.
Syringe.
Cuffs.
Drive.

His record was three seconds.

"I'm looking for a date," he countered. "And I'll make it worth your while."

She wobbled again and then stepped a little closer. Anticipation burned inside him. But she halted before she reached the strike zone.

"How long you looking to party?" she asked.

"All night, and I can afford it." Greed always shifted the odds to his favor.

Large round hoop earrings shifted as she regarded him. Her eyes narrowed. She sniffed again. "That's a couple grand."

"Of course."

"I've got to clear it." In a blink, she texted her pimp.

Time was slipping away. She should have been in the van by now. He removed a roll of singles with a Benjamin on the outside. He had brandished this same wad before and had even handed it over once or twice. But he always got it back. It was his lucky lure.

She studied the roll but did not reach for it.

He smiled. "Time is wasting. There are other fish in the sea, sugar."

She tightened her hand on her purse strap.

One gloved hand slid to the syringe. Seconds slowed to a crawl. He was anxious to touch her skin. "Let's get this party started."

She glanced at her phone and slowly shook her head. "Sorry, boss man says no."

Fucking pimp. He could feel her slipping away. "We can keep this between us."

She took a step back. "And then my guy beats the hell out of me."

His smile froze in place. He had tried to be nice. Tried to do this the right way. But she was being difficult. He would show her *difficult*.

He pushed the button and the automatic door crashed open. His heart pulsed as he ripped the syringe free and bolted between the seats. The needle's tip rose, glittering in the streetlight's glow. He reached for her arm and manacled his fingers around her wrist. He jerked her forward, brought the needle down, thumb on the plunger.

But she pivoted, twisting her arm up and around and breaking his hold. The needle skimmed along her jeans and the tip broke off. She bounded back so fast that her ankle rolled before she righted it.

He tossed aside the useless syringe and lunged toward her. With his right hand, he grabbed a handful of her hair, and she howled. He yanked her toward the cab. She dug in her heels. But he was stronger. The boots slid over the concrete, leaving black scuff marks as she tried to pry his hand from her hair.

As he reached for the waistband of her jeans with his left hand, she released her grip. He mistook it for surrender. A jolt of triumph coaxed a smile. "We're going to have some fun tonight."

That short-lived victory incinerated as a rush of pain seared his right thigh. The unexpected pain caught him off guard. What the hell?

He recoiled automatically. His grip slackened as he looked down at the knife embedded in his leg. He scrambled to regroup. The second syringe was taped to the back of the passenger seat. If he could just get her to the van . . .

With a grunt, he tightened his hold on her hair, closing the distance to the door. His first Date Night girl had also given him trouble, but he had been inexperienced in those days and she had gotten away. It had taken him weeks to find her again. This one would not escape.

Screaming, she gripped the blade handle, rotated it, and tore into fresh flesh. His blood was on her hands, her face, and his chest.

He dragged her toward the car as rage raced through his veins like liquid lava. Punishment! She needed to learn her place.

A set of headlights appeared and raced toward him. He was four feet from the van. Four feet separated him from freedom. From fun in the mountains.

Date Night girl drove a knee into his crotch. Reflex had him turning but not fast enough to avoid a glancing blow to the jewels. He caught his breath. His fingers slackened. She jerked free, pulling the knife with her and leaving him with only strands of her hair and his own pain and fury.

She stumbled back. Her eyes locked on him as she gripped the handle.

Go after her, or get away?

The question repeated in his head over and over as the headlights grew brighter. A horn blared.

Beep! Beep!

He growled his frustration. He hated relinquishing control but knew he had to cut his losses. The hairs on the back of his neck rose, just as they had when dear old Dad's mood had shifted. He had survived at this game long enough to know when to fold. Always another day to fight.

He jumped into the van and slid behind the steering wheel. He put the van in drive and looked toward the woman, now illuminated by the headlights.

Date Night girl stumbled backward, teetered in her red heeled boots so wildly her right ankle bent sideways and would have snapped if she had not corrected quickly. Those perky breasts heaved up and down as she gripped the knife.

There was always a tomorrow.

Revenge was sweet.

He punched the gas and drove. Tires peeled against the asphalt. The automatic door banged closed. A rushed glance in the rearview mirror caught the girl one last time. She had pulled a gun and stared at the van as if trying to memorize his plates.

He rounded the corner as his brain fixated on staying free. He had altered his appearance enough, so if she got a cop to listen, they would have no idea what he looked like. Still, it might not be long before a BOLO went out on a windowless white van.

He did not drive far before he pulled into a preselected warehouse. He jumped out of the van, inhaled the scent of bleach, and hobbled to another vehicle. He would come back for the van soon. He glanced down at his leg and the blood soaking his pants. The wound was throbbing.

Belt and suspenders.

Sitting in his car, he gripped the wheel with gloved hands. He winced as he started the engine. The van's seat was wet with blood, but it was hidden well enough.

He drove out the other end of the warehouse, took another side street, and ten minutes later pulled into a crowded parking garage near one of the chain hotels. Another car switch and he was on his way to freedom.

He slowly tamed his breathing and racing heart. His thoughts doubled back to Ms. Perky Breasts.

No one got the better of him. He would find her, and she would feel his fury in every bone and nerve in her body. By the time he was finished with her, she would beg him for mercy.

CHAPTER ONE

Monday, August 17, 10:45 p.m.

The van's wheels screeched around the corner and as its headlights faded, Melina tightened her fingers on the SIG's grip. She shifted the weapon's sights away from the now-empty road toward the second vehicle. In the pregnant moments filled with blinding light, adrenaline, and pain, she could not determine if the driver of this second car was the cavalry or a friend of Lover Boy's.

The car's front door opened, and a female driver rose up, hands held high. "It's me—Sarah."

Panic sharpened Sarah Beckett's characteristically serene voice as she stepped forward. In her midthirties, Sarah ran the Mission, a kind of halfway house for prostitutes. The girls on the streets called her the Mother of Lost Souls.

Headlights silhouetted Sarah's shapeless blue shirt, worn capris, and god-awful Jesus sandals. Red hair coiled into an unruly topknot already ringed by too many escaped curls.

"Are you all right?" Sarah demanded.

Melina's hands trembled as she lowered her gun. "Yeah, I'm fine. You saved the day."

Sarah reached for her, but Melina pulled back. "You're bleeding. Let me help."

"It's his blood. Not mine." Her scalp hurt. Her ankle throbbed. She had lost a chunk of hair, and in a day or two her wrist would be bruised. But otherwise, no worse for wear.

"Where the hell did that van come from?" Sarah asked.

"Parked in the shadows. No one saw him. Where are the other girls?" Melina scanned the streets for any sign that he might return.

"Back at the Mission. They're fine."

"Good."

"You shouldn't have been here alone."

"I called you, didn't I? I figured a minute or two out here would be fine."

"It wasn't fine." Sarah raised a trembling hand to Melina's hair. "What did he want?"

"To kill me."

Sarah fisted long fingers more accustomed to cupping a chalice or playing the piano at Sunday service than throwing a punch. "This was a stupid idea."

Melina tamped down the adrenaline swelling in her throat. "Dangerous, maybe. Not stupid."

"Jesus, Mary, and Joseph. You're covered in blood."

Blood coated her skin and her clothes. She hoped the guy did not have HIV or hepatitis. "I need to call the cops."

"My assistant already did," Sarah replied.

"Sam knows about this?" Melina asked.

"He was there when the other girls came back without you. He was furious. He was on the phone with the cops before I could get out the door."

As if on cue, blue lights bounced off the nearby warehouses. "How did he get the cops to the Bottom so fast?"

"Friends in high places, I suppose," she said.

It was Sarah and Sam's favorite joke. She not only ran the Mission, but she was also an ordained Episcopal priest.

Two police cars rolled up, and immediately two officers were braced behind their open driver's side doors. Weapons pointed in her direction.

The cops were young, fresh faced, and she would bet neither one of them had been on the streets more than a year. She knew adrenaline made rookies extra jumpy. Everyone wanted to go home at night.

"Drop your weapon!" one officer shouted.

Melina gently knelt on the concrete sidewalk, laying her SIG and knife near weeds jutting up through the sidewalk cracks. She stayed down on both knees, hands locked behind her head, and Sarah followed suit.

One cop held back, weapon trained on them, while the other approached. "Identify yourself," he said.

Her ankle was really throbbing. Thankfully, it did not feel broken, but a sprain was the last thing she needed. "My name is Melina Shepard. I'm an agent with the Tennessee Bureau of Investigation. My badge is in my purse."

The cop approached and kicked the gun and knife away from her.

"Be careful with that knife," she said quickly. "It's covered with the suspect's blood and needs to be bagged. Better yet, get a forensic van down here."

Silent, the young officer grabbed her purse, stepped back, and dug until he retrieved the leather wallet. He flipped it open. The badge's gold glittered.

"Agent Shepard, are you injured?" the officer asked.

The adrenaline rush was fading, leaving her with an unsettled feeling. "No."

"And who is this?" the officer asked.

"Reverend Sarah Beckett."

The officer eyed Sarah's long arms still suspended above her head. "You run the Mission?"

"That's right," Sarah said.

"I've heard about you. You can put your arms down." He extended his hand to help Melina up, but she refused it. "Thanks, but I'm covered in the suspect's blood, and I don't want to contaminate the evidence."

"I'll radio for an ambulance," the officer said.

"It's really not necessary," Melina said.

"Yes, it is," Sarah said. "She's been through a lot."

The officer returned to his car as the two women stood.

News traveled fast, and this unsanctioned adventure/fishing expedition by Melina meant an ass chewing was headed her way. She had come to the Bottom at the behest of Sarah, who was worried about two girls who had gone missing from the streets in the past couple of weeks. Missing persons reports had been filed, but so far, the police had not spent much time on either case. Sarah knew the girls and had begun making headway with both toward getting them off the streets.

Melina had suspected she was chasing a pimp who did not want to lose his best moneymakers. They were likely being held in a run-down crack house. A smart pimp would not kill a working girl, but instead would lock her in a room and bring johns to her.

The smell of bleach lingered in her nostrils, as did the memory of the van's padded walls. She mentally cataloged details about this assailant, including the syringe, the perpetrator's blond wig, and his efficient, practiced assault. This was not his first attempt to kill. The setup was sophisticated and clearly reflected very dark fantasies.

She stared at the scuffed tips of her boots and thought about the missing girls. A shiver ran over her scalp.

"Who attacked you?" the officer asked.

"I don't know. I wasn't expecting that kind of trouble." A sigh shuddered through her. "The driver was a white guy. Clean cut. Blond hair, but it was a wig. Gloves. Dark jacket. Jeans. Boots. Not the type you would expect to meet in a place like this."

Sarah snorted. "Rich or poor, married or single, religious or atheist . . . all kinds troll these waters."

"I need that evidence bag," Melina said. "The knife needs to be secured."

The second officer pulled on latex gloves and retrieved an evidence bag from his cruiser.

"What are you doing out here alone, Agent Shepard?" the officer asked.

Doing the exact thing training officers told them not to do in the academy. "Reverend Beckett was worried about two missing girls. I was trying to find them."

"Alone?" the officer asked, his voice sharp.

"With me." Sarah spoke clearly, as if confessing her sins.

The officer's attention shifted between the two. He shook his head in disbelief. Even as a rookie, he knew it was a crazy stunt.

"I was wrapping up my questioning with the girls," Melina said. "I then called Sarah and was preparing to leave. Then the van started moving toward me." She recounted her remaining observations of the attack. There was no masking that she had been reckless.

"Where did you get the knife?" the officer asked.

"It's part of my belt buckle." She rubbed her hand over the red scratch marks now marring her olive skin. The second officer bagged the knife that had been a gift from her dad when she'd graduated the academy. "Be careful with that." Again, she recalled the scent of bleach. This guy was no amateur. "It's got a killer's DNA on it."

CHAPTER TWO

Monday, August 24, 6:00 a.m.

Head pounding. Ankle faintly throbbing. Alarm clock blaring.

Melina grabbed the phone charging on her nightstand and shut off the buzzer that had yanked her from a deep sleep that had only come after too many hours of staring at the ceiling. She had seen 1:00 a.m., 3:00 a.m., and finally 4:00 a.m. before she had drifted off. She had barely slept in the last seven days.

She sat up, pushed back thick strands of hair. Her scalp was still tender to the touch, but thankfully, her attacker had not ripped out massive clumps as she had first feared.

She closed her eyes, immediately picturing the inside of the van. Handcuffs. The syringe. The sharp scent of bleach.

The images had haunted her all week, as had the threats from her boss, Agent Carter Jackson. Jackson's normally controlled southern drawl had sharpened with anger as he had watched the doctor examine Melina's ankle in the hour after the attack.

"You're lucky!" he yelled. "And the reverend is no smarter! Protocols are in place for a reason!"

"It was worth it," she countered.

"You do not speak, Agent Shepard. You listen." He began to pace the room. *"You're confined to your desk while I decide if I reassign you to Records Division for the remainder of your career!"*

She understood Jackson had been so upset because he was worried. She only hoped in a week or two he would cool off.

Yesterday, she had stopped at a coffee shop and picked up a triple espresso for him. She had set the peace offering on his desk and dawdled, hoping he would look up from his computer. He had not acknowledged her.

She was not only way up Shit Creek, but Jackson had snapped her paddle in his big bare hands.

She swung her legs over the side of the bed while staring at the digital time. "Fifteen more minutes of sleep." She whispered the words like a prayer, mentally calculating how fast she could dress and be out the front door.

Handcuffs. Syringe. Bleach.

Her heart thumped faster in her chest. Who was she kidding? Sleep, if that is what she had attempted last night, was not returning anytime soon.

As she scooted to the edge of the mattress, her oversize T-shirt twisted around her waist. Bare feet skimmed a cold hardwood floor, and she remembered the shag carpet was still waiting in the virtual shopping cart, along with a dozen other items she could not afford until payday.

She was slow to put weight on her right ankle. She could walk now without a limp, but there was still some swelling.

She stood, padded down the long hallway to the galley kitchen, and turned on her coffee maker. No matter how tired she was or how late she got home the night before, she always set up the coffee. One-quarter cup of grounds to four cups of water. The perfect blend that soothed her cranky morning self.

Melina grabbed almond milk from the fridge and poured a small amount into an oversize UT mug. The handle was a little too big for her hands, but the twenty-ounce capacity saved her return trips. She dug a frozen bagel out of the freezer and put it in the toaster oven. Ten minutes at 350 degrees promised what would taste like an almost freshly baked bagel.

A scratching sound at her back door had her turning to see a cat peering under the edge of her blinds. She retrieved a can of tuna fish from the cupboard and tried not to get the contents on her hands as she placed it onto a clean plate.

She unlocked the patio door secured with three locks her father had installed. She tiptoed barefoot toward the patio table, where the small calico cat patiently waited for her daily meal.

"It's the good stuff, Wild Kitty," Melina said. "I promise no more generic brands of tuna." She had learned that lesson when the cat had taken one sniff and pushed the plate off the table. Snob.

The cat now took a nibble, as if testing. Satisfied, she began to eat, growling as she bit into large chunks of tuna.

How did the saying go? "Dogs have masters and cats have staff." She carefully ran her hand down the cat's back once or twice, knowing any more displays of affection would not be appreciated.

"Eat up, kid. See you tomorrow."

The cat did not even look up. Melina retrieved yesterday's dish and went back inside and set the plate in the dishwasher. She filled her mug to the brim with coffee and headed toward the shower. She switched on the tap and, as it heated, sat on the side of her bed and read emails on her phone.

Agent Jackson had sent her a text last night, demanding an early-morning meeting. Shit. This was day seven since her encounter, and she had no idea what Jackson had planned for her next.

She pressed the hot mug to the side of her head.

Melina rose, dug a clean white shirt and black pants from her closet. The good thing about desk duty was that she had time to go to the dry cleaner and linger in the grocery store. It was nice to have a stocked kitchen and a dresser full of clean clothes. The extra workouts had been a bonus, too.

If her schedule got any more consistent, she was going to go insane.

She shrugged off the T-shirt and stepped into the shower. Carefully, she dunked her head under the spray while avoiding the sensitive spots.

Stupid stunt. Juvenile. Dangerous. Agent Jackson's words rattled in her head, until finally she tuned out the sound of his voice.

She had screwed up.

Time to move on.

He would get over it.

Out of the shower, she gently dried off her thick hair, wrapped herself in a towel, and wound a second towel around her head. It smelled of lavender, and she liked it better than the lemon scent.

"Oh, God." She caught herself before she shifted to a critique of cinnamon bagels versus poppy seed. "I'm already turning soft."

Time to get dressed and face the music. Agent Jackson was still aloof. When he passed her office, he sometimes stopped and shook his head, but he did not bother to engage.

As she buttered her poppy seed bagel, her thoughts shifted to her attacker.

Who the hell was this guy? His little horror-show-on-wheels had not been thrown together on a whim. It had been the fulfillment of years of fantasy and countless hours of work. The slight smell of bleach she had detected still made the hair on the back of her neck stand up.

She walked to the back window and noted that Wild Kitty had vanished. She had places to go, mice to kill. The $1.29 of tuna was gone.

As she turned from the window, her thoughts went to the girls who worked the streets around the Mission. During Melina's very predictable lunch hours this week, she had visited Sarah. There had been no sign of the two missing girls nor of the white van modified to inflict pain.

"Where the hell are you?" she muttered to herself.

She filled a travel mug with the remainder of her coffee, grabbed her backpack, and headed out the front door. As she twisted her key in the dead bolt, a man called out to her. It was her neighbor Travis. Or Trey. Some name that ended in *s*. Or *y*.

"Hello, there!" he shouted.

Melina tightened her hand on her backpack's strap and turned to face the man who lived on the other end of her unit. In his late fifties, he had told Melina his life history. A resident in the complex for ten years. Former schoolteacher. Was married but divorced for the last six years.

"Melina!"

"Yes." Melina could hear her mother's voice, dipped in its southern charm, warning her to be nice. "What can I do for you?"

"Have you seen my cat, Simba?"

"Simba?"

"She's calico and has a white patch on her chest."

Ah, so Wild Kitty was not as orphaned as she pretended. Her fat cheeks should have been the dead giveaway. "I saw her this morning."

"And she seemed fine?"

"Yes, sir."

"She didn't come in last night. When the weather gets warm, it's hard to keep her inside."

"She looked like she could take care of herself."

Travis or Trey held up a ringed pink collar with a heart-shaped name tag jingling from the front. "She slipped her collar again."

"Maybe she doesn't like pink."

"What?"

"Never mind."

"She's a little too independent for her own good," he said. "I'm afraid a wild animal is going to hurt her. If you see her, bring her home to me. I've a bag of dried kibbles for her."

"I'll let her know."

When Melina reached her car, she noticed a trio of cigarette butts. They were behind her car and she imagined someone leaning against her bumper, staring toward her unit. There was a faint hint of pink lipstick on each filtered edge. The guy next door dated a lot of women. Maybe one had been out here waiting for him to return from his bartending shift.

She leaned against her trunk, staring toward the line of town houses. It took time to smoke three cigarettes. Fifteen or twenty minutes if rushing, longer if killing time. "So, who's being watched?"

Frowning, she slid behind the wheel of her car. The engine fired, and she backed out of the spot and headed toward the office. At least the white-van driver had not been wearing pink lipstick.

Fifteen minutes later, Melina arrived at the Tennessee Bureau of Investigation's offices on R. S. Gass Boulevard. The road into the complex wound over a lush, rolling landscape past modern buildings that contained TBI's Nashville offices. The Tennessee Bureau of Investigation was the state's primary criminal investigative agency. Agents investigated crimes related to drugs, corruption, organized crime, terrorism, and fraud. Down the road was another building that housed the state medical examiner's office.

Juxtaposing the modern buildings was a third building. The Freemasons had built the colonial revival stone structure circa 1915 to house their widows, orphans, and elderly. Later incarnations included a tuberculosis home and a foster home for boys.

She parked, showed her badge at the front desk, and made her way to her office. She dumped her backpack in her chair and glanced at her clean desk. She missed the chaos of reports and files piled up and around her desk, as well as the dust on shelves filled with well-worn technical manuals and the odd certificate of merit. This organization stuff had to stop.

A sharp knock on her door had her looking up. Her boss, Carter Jackson, filled the doorframe. A full, dark mustache matched thick hair threaded with silver at the temples. He was wearing his customary charcoal-gray suit, light-blue shirt, and red tie, but he never looked fully comfortable in it. She imagined when he got home at night, the tie was the first to go.

He was nearly forty and divorced and had made a name for himself a decade ago when he had broken up a nasty human trafficking and drug ring. For his efforts, he had been awarded a promotion, which came with a desk job. He never made a comment about leaving the streets, but she knew he missed the work.

"Shepard, you were born with a lucky horseshoe up your ass." Jackson's gruff comment was a welcome change from the stony silence.

"Only one?"

"That knife you stuck into your attacker delivered a nice DNA sample. I had the DNA testing fast tracked."

She had detailed all her recollections of the van's interior. Jackson might have been pissed at her reckless actions, but he had been listening. "Really?"

"I was on the phone late last night with the head of an FBI profiling unit. He's coming out here to investigate the case himself."

The FBI didn't investigate cases unless there was good cause. "FBI interaction sounds great, sir."

"Agent Ramsey will be here in about an hour."

"That soon?"

"He just called me from the Nashville airport."

"Of course." She was not fond of FBI intervention, but on the bright side, she was not going to be confined to the bowels of TBI for the remainder of her career.

As if he'd read her thoughts, he said, "Like I said, lucky horseshoe. You should buy a lottery ticket."

***

For the last seven days, all he could think about was Ms. Perky Breasts. He pictured her stripped naked and begging him for mercy as her blood flowed freely onto the floor of his van.

He slowly unwrapped the bandage from around his thigh and inspected the ten neat stitches. He had sewn up the wound himself, knowing the cops were looking not only for his van but also for a man with a leg injury.

Fragments of the gauze caught in the wound. Gently, he tugged as strand after strand peeled away from his skin until the strip released from the jagged wound. It was not infected, and he could now stand and walk with only a small limp. As much as he had wanted to retrieve the van, the injury would not allow him to leave his home in the woods.

Gingerly, he spread more antibiotic ointment on the wound and wrapped it again. He carefully tugged up his pajama pants.

He had stayed away from the Bottom for seven days and nights now. There had been no news reports about the incident or of the two other missing girls. The prostitutes and their problems did not merit any airtime in the crazy news cycle.

His luck was also holding in regard to the van. According to the transponder he had affixed under the front axle, it remained in the warehouse.

Coffee in hand, he stepped out onto the porch of his cabin and stared out over the woods that ringed the edge of his property. He loved the woods. And staring at them never failed to calm him. He took a sip and settled back into a rocker and then glanced toward the empty one beside him.

Ms. Perky Breasts should be sitting there with him. He had cooled off a lot in the last week, and he no longer dreamed of peeling her skin from her body.

His phone rang, pulling his attention from the woods. He recognized the number and smiled. "Hey, sweetie."

"Hey to you, Grandpa. How are you doing?"

"I'm doing just great." He rose and walked to the railing. "You packed and ready for boarding school?"

"Yeah, can't wait. Mom is driving me crazy."

"Give your old mom a break. It's hard seeing someone you love leave."

"I'm grown up. What's the surprise?"

He chuckled. "There's a lot you need to learn about the world, Sue."

"I guess. How are you feeling? Are you taking your medicine?"

He had been diagnosed with cancer months ago. The pending surgery promised to leave him neutered and possibly incontinent. He would no longer be the master of his life. He was not going down that path.

"Like clockwork."

"When do you go into the hospital?"

Never. "Soon."

"Are you coming to parents' weekend?"

"I wouldn't miss it for the world."

"Great. I've got to go, but I just wanted to call and let you know I'm thinking about you."

"Love you, kid."

"Me too, Grandpa."

They ended the call, and he refocused on the woods. He had loved a lot of women in his life, and he was sad to see them all leave.

He pictured Ms. Perky Breasts standing on her corner. He was destined to dominate her. She was ordained to submit to him. But sometimes destiny needed a hard shove.

He would give it another day or two before he retrieved the van from the warehouse. When he did, he would change the plates and slap on one of the half dozen bogus business signs. Like him, the van was a chameleon. Then he would go looking for his girl.

It was just a matter of time before Ms. Perky Breasts returned to her corner. A girl had to make a living. And everyone, including a hooker, was a creature of habit.

He smiled, then sipped his coffee. "This Date Night is going to be extra special, baby."

CHAPTER THREE

Monday, August 24, 11:00 a.m.

FBI special agent Jerrod Ramsey waited as the airport's rental car clerk checked for his reservation. Her name tag read **SALLY**. This was her first day on the job, she had said several times, and she was having trouble with the computer. She looked to be in her early twenties and had freckles scattered over the bridge of her nose, and her hair was tied back in a neat ponytail streaked with several strands of blue. Triple ear piercings in the left ear, and she had suntan marks from a halter top. Her right thumb was calloused, and the nail was longer than her others. He guessed musician. A guitarist. Making ends meet until the big break.

"Can you spell your last name again for me?" she asked with a halting smile.

"R-A-M-S-E-Y. First name Jerrod. With a *j*."

"Thank you." The longer she tapped on the keys, the pinker her cheeks grew. Finally, she called over her manager, a short doughy man with thinning brown hair, who glanced at him cautiously and then quickly dropped his gaze to the screen. "We're sorry for the wait."

Ramsey fished his phone out of his pocket and scrolled for the confirmation email. He had traveled countless places, and most trips came with a snafu. "I have a confirmation number."

The manager was Fitz, according to his name badge. He brushed the girl's hands away. "I told you how to do this twice this morning." He punched more keys. "Here it is, a black SUV."

"That's it."

"Do you have this?" The manager's voice bit with sarcasm, and he lingered a fraction too close to the female clerk's personal space.

Sally shifted a step away.

The manager was likely in his late forties, and Ramsey guessed he had spent his career processing thousands of car rental orders. The yellowing of his fingertips suggested he was a heavy smoker, the bags under his eyes hinted at poor sleep, and bloodshot eyes implied a hangover. No hint of a wedding band. This job was his fiefdom, and bossing women like Sally around made him feel better about his miserable existence.

Ramsey handed over his credit card to Sally and lifted his gaze to ol' Fitz. "Thanks, Fitz. She's got this now."

Fitz held his ground for a beat, mumbled, "Have a nice day," and then retreated back to another computer station.

Sally rang up the order. "You here for business?" Her conversational tone had a nervous edge, but her smile was bright.

"Yes."

"Music or banking?" she said with a smile.

"Troubleshooting."

Curiosity sparked in her gaze as she handed him his credit card and car keys. "Have a great trip."

"Thanks." If he had to bet, Sally would take less than six months to discover this job was not worth the paycheck.

He grabbed his roller bag filled with case files and headed toward the rental car bus. Ten minutes later, he was walking down a line of cars. He always rented the same make and model whenever he could. It cut down on the confusion that came with unfamiliar surroundings.

His phone rang as he tossed his roller bag and briefcase in the back seat. He recognized his niece's phone number. "Kylie."

"Uncle Jerrod. Where are you?"

"Nashville." He shrugged off his jacket and draped it over his bag before closing the door.

"I got your text. What's up?"

Kylie was his older sister's child. At twenty-two, she had graduated from college and was beginning her first year of Columbia Law School.

"Checking in on Grandma. How is she doing?"

"Okay. She's always grumpy."

"When is your mother coming in to help?"

"I don't know. She's in Paris. Don't worry, I've got the Grandma shift covered."

"How long can you stay?"

"A week."

"Good. That helps. I should be back in Washington by then."

"I don't do much. Tracy takes care of everything."

Tracy had been his mother's caregiver for five years. She was one of the very few people his mother listened to these days. "It's good to have family around Grandma this time of year."

"I hear ya. Grandma does keep asking for Grandpa. Tracy and I are going to take her to the beach."

He glanced at his watch and checked the date. "It's always a bad day for her." The air blowing from the vents slowly cooled. "It's the anniversary of Grandpa's death."

"I remember. I just can't believe she does. She's forgotten so much."

Forgetting his father's suicide would have been the one act of kindness Alzheimer's could have done for his mother. But there was nothing kind about the disease.

This was not the first time he had been away from home at a critical time. He had missed Kylie's college graduation. That had caused a blowup with his sister and renewed her complaints about his job. "Can I talk to Grandma?"

"Let me check." Silence and then muffled conversations between Kylie and his mother. "She doesn't want to talk to you or anyone."

Six years ago, he had walked into the family home and greeted his mother, and she had started screaming. She had called the cops. That was when he'd realized she was really sick. Her memory had flickered on and off until finally it had not returned. He had been one of the first people she had forgotten. "I'll be home in a few days. Can you hold down the fort?"

"You know I can," she said.

"Thanks, kid."

"Back at you, old man."

"Touché."

She was laughing when she hung up.

He locked away thoughts of home and shifted to the task at hand. It was never a good day for anyone when Ramsey or one of his crew left their Quantico headquarters and visited their jurisdiction. He chased the worst of the worst serial killers. The type of monster he and his team chased was not the garden-variety gangbanger. Their prey included predators who ate their victims' flesh, sold children for sex or murder, and dismembered and mutilated bodies of the living and the dead. No one wanted to believe the creatures Ramsey hunted were real. He knew better than anyone that evil lurked in the darkness and was waiting for its chance to claim a new victim.

Now he was back in Nashville, Tennessee. It was home to a thriving economy and a growing population, which meant the city attracted the best and worst of humanity.

While in law school, he had thrown in an application to the FBI on a lark. It sounded like an interesting job, and he had dreams of carrying a gun and badge and screening for the Hostage Rescue Team. Chase a few bad guys, sharpen his shooting skills, and then eventually head to Wall Street, make bank, meet a smoking-hot wife, and raise a couple of kids. When he was old and gray, he could retire to the family estate on the shores of the Chesapeake Bay and maybe write his memoir.

Then fate stepped in and punched Ramsey right in the mouth. Ramsey's old man, who had been a gentle soul more interested in his birds than the boardroom, had trusted the wrong man. Stuart Kline, a talented lawyer and accountant, had lured his old man into a quagmire of investments that toppled a fortune that had taken three generations to build. Ramsey's father, unable to face his son and his board of directors, shot himself in the head two weeks after Ramsey graduated law school.

Kline earned only seventeen months of jail time in a minimum-security prison with cable television and conjugal visits.

Newly minted law degree in hand and more pissed off than Ramsey could put into words, he joined the bureau's white-collar crime division. He knew numbers, understood the legal system, and had grown up in the rarified world of old money.

He had a natural talent for reading people, dissecting their moves, and hearing the meaning behind their words.

Ramsey's success in white-collar crime had caught the attention of his supervisors, and he had been transferred to the criminal division. He recognized the transfer for what it was. He was a chess piece in a game bigger than white-collar crime. The best press followed the sexier hunt for serial killers, and he had the chops for the work.

The killers he and his handpicked team chased were soulless, narcissistic sociopaths who did unforgivable things to a human body.

Ramsey drove across town and wound his way toward the TBI offices. He found a spot close to the entrance. He shrugged on his coat, brushed the sleeves smooth, and checked his tie in the reflection of the vehicle's glass. He grabbed his briefcase before entering the building.

He showed his credentials to the TBI officer stationed at reception. "I'm here for Agent Melina Shepard and her supervisor, Agent Carter Jackson."

The officer called up to the investigative offices and informed him Shepard would be right down. A few minutes later, elevator doors dinged open and a trim woman stepped off. She wore black fitted pants and a white shirt, and her dark hair was pulled back in a tight ponytail that brushed her shoulders. Slim hips, muscular thighs and arms, and full breasts all caught his attention in a less-than-clinical way.

In her early to midthirties, she was attractive with deep-olive skin and sharp brown eyes alight with curiosity and hints of annoyance. She was someone who appeared wary by nature and who would have let the facts unfold before she fired the first question. He guessed a deliberate pause had been part of the reason she had survived her attacker last week.

She extended her hand, and he stepped forward to accept it. Long fingers wrapped around his hand and squeezed with surprising strength. "Agent Ramsey. Agent Melina Shepard."

He held her hand tight, noting the subtle callus likely earned with weight training. "Pleasure."

"I hear my DNA sample brought you here?" Hers was a husky, rich voice.

"It did."

"It's been less than a week. That's a fast turnaround for the FBI."

"Your boss is a hard man to ignore." Jackson had staked his reputation on Shepard's assessment of the van's driver, who she believed was a practiced killer. Quantico, Jackson had warned, had better pay attention.

"Yes, he can be." She was already walking toward the elevators and pressed the button. "Agent Jackson is waiting for us upstairs. He's finishing up a call."

"Good."

The doors opened and they stepped in. She selected the third floor. "Are you going to tell me who I stumbled across?"

"I'll save the show for when we have Jackson. Will cut down on repetition."

She regarded him closely. "I stumbled onto a bad one."

Ramsey had a file filled with pictures of dead women killed by this man. "One of the worst."

Silent, they rode to the third floor, and when the doors opened, she introduced him to the receptionist and pointed him in the direction of the bathrooms. When he shook his head no, she knocked on a corner door. The nameplate read **JACKSON**. She poked her head in the door. "Boss? Agent Ramsey is here."

"Come on in."

She stepped back, motioned for him to go in first. He stood his ground and waited for her. Annoyance in her gaze appeared again, but she clearly decided there were bigger battles to fight than outdated chivalry.

Carter Jackson ended his call, stood, and unrolled shirtsleeves over muscled forearms that suited a former UT quarterback. Midforties, Jackson had been with TBI over twenty years. He had a solid reputation in the state and at Quantico.

Jackson extended his hand. "Welcome to Nashville."

Ramsey was met with a strong grip. "Wish it were under better circumstances."

"Likewise," Jackson said. "There's coffee in the conference room."

Ramsey's doctor had once mentioned he should cut back on the brew and take more vacations. It was laughable. Ramsey had a better chance of taking up knitting.

Agent Shepard led the way toward the conference room. They passed several open doors, and a glance in each found a curious agent finding a reason to hover.

The conference room was well lit with a bank of windows that overlooked the surrounding compound. Melina stood back as the two men filled cups. Her move didn't appear to be deferential but strategic. She was assessing him, taking note of the small details that he knew could yield insight into any man.

Ramsey sat at the end of the table and set his briefcase and coffee cup down. He clicked open the locks as Jackson sat and Shepard closed the door.

She sat to his left, and though she kept her gaze downcast, Ramsey sensed her curiosity. From what Jackson had said on the phone, Shepard was good at what she did. She had worked the entire state doing mostly undercover and human trafficking cases, but she could be reckless. That trait was her best asset but also her Achilles' heel.

"Agent Shepard, how do you know"—he glanced at his notes— "Reverend Beckett?"

"Our parents are neighbors. She's two years older, and we knew each other growing up. She knows the women who work the streets around her mission. When she learned two were missing, she asked me if I could ask around."

"And you figured you could handle it alone?" Ramsey asked.

No hint of apology softened her grim expression. "Yes, I did."

"And when did you realize the driver of the van wasn't your ordinary john?"

"As I said in my report, when I smelled hints of bleach in the van."

"Consider yourself fortunate," Ramsey said.

Darkness shadowed her eyes. "I do."

"This individual's DNA is linked to at least ten murders across the country. But I believe there are more victims."

"Ten?" No missing the anger tightening her words.

"That we know of. If you hadn't stabbed him, you would have been the next victim. Who gave you a belt buckle with a knife?"

"My father. He's a retired Nashville homicide detective."

Points for Dad. He opened his folder and pulled out a series of crime scene photos. The images were all of nude women at various stages of decomposition.

Agent Shepard studied the first image with keen interest. Ramsey had seen the pictures so many times that he could describe them without looking. The image she studied now was of Nikki Smith, Victim #6. She had been a runaway who at seventeen had started selling herself on the streets. She had been twenty-one when she was murdered. "Cause of death was strangulation, but as you can see from the cuts and puncture marks on her body, she was tortured before she was killed."

"Is that a handcuff key on the chain around her neck?" Shepard asked.

"Yes. All the victims were found with similar keys on their bodies. We think he was toying with the women. The key that could have set them free was dangling from their neck out of reach."

Agent Shepard nodded as she studied another picture. "Are those drill marks on the body?" Her tone was an odd blend of curiosity, anger, and some horror.

"We believe so," he said.

She passed the images to Jackson, whose stoic gaze shifted from sadness to anger. "When was she killed?"

"2005. Her body was found on the side of a rural road in Maryland; however, she worked the streets in Baltimore. She'd been missing for a week. The next victim was found two years later in South Carolina. Again, young woman, tortured and strangled."

"Does he have a type?" Shepard asked.

"He goes after the prostitutes," he said. "The ones he chose weren't on the streets long."

"Inexperienced. Not yet hardened by the streets."

"Yes."

"They were easier targets," Shepard said. "The experienced ones might have avoided him."

"Exactly."

"Does he have a physical preference?" she asked.

He searched in his file for a one-page compilation of a series of photos that was of all the victims' faces taken within one to two years before their deaths. Some were high school yearbook pictures, others were DMV, and a few were grainy snapshots.

Agent Shepard's gaze moved from face to face, methodically scanning the images. "Dark hair, olive skin, brown eyes."

"You fit his profile perfectly," Ramsey said.

"He didn't choose me at random?"

"No."

"Lucky me."

"If it hadn't been you, it would have been someone else."

"The two missing girls that Sarah Beckett has been searching for look like these women," Jackson commented.

"Do you think the van driver is connected to the two missing women?" Ramsey asked.

"Since I'm not a fan of coincidence, I'd say yes," Jackson said.

"If that's true, we've got a much bigger problem than I originally thought," Shepard said.

"Reverend Beckett does serve women he targets," Ramsey said.

"How long did it take to find the bodies of the other victims?" Jackson's frown had deepened.

"Anywhere between one week to nine months," Ramsey said. "He's not interested in credit or being noticed. He dumps them in secluded locations and moves on with his life."

"He wants to keep doing what he's doing," Jackson said.

"Correct," Ramsey said. "Which makes him even more dangerous and harder to catch."

"And now he's in Nashville," Jackson said.

"He was seven days ago," Ramsey said. "Agent Shepard, you're the first person we know of who has survived direct contact with him and has seen how he operates."

She sifted slowly through all the images one more time. If she were worried about her near-fatal mistake, her cool expression gave no hint of it. "What can we do for you?"

"Have there been any sightings of his van?" Ramsey asked.

"We put out a BOLO as soon as Agent Shepard called in her attack," Jackson said. "We also went through all the street cameras in the area in the days after the attack. There was no sign of the van."

"No one has seen it. We are assuming he ditched it somewhere close to the Mission."

"I've spoken to Reverend Beckett several times in the last few days," Shepard said. "She hasn't heard anything about him appearing again, and all the working girls are on notice."

Jackson closed the file of images. "We'll assist in any way we can."

"I'd like to work with Agent Shepard and interview the women who were working that night, along with Reverend Beckett."

"What do you think the chances are that he's still in the area?" Agent Shepard asked.

"I'm not sure he is. But this is as close as I've gotten."

"How long have you been chasing this guy?" Agent Shepard asked.

"Seven years. I picked up the case when we crossed paths in Wilmington, North Carolina. He killed three prostitutes there."

"He's not worried about leaving DNA on his victims," Agent Shepard said. "But he's obsessed with leaving none in his van. Thus, the bleach."

"Control is important to him, especially in the van, which is his workshop and domain," Ramsey said. "He spends a lot of time in it. Agent Shepard, you noted that the side door opened with astonishing speed."

"Correct," she said.

"He's spent time modifying it to reduce the abduction window to an acceptable risk."

"And he doesn't want his kills to be attached to it," Jackson said.

"Not to the van," Ramsey said.

"But he wants his DNA to link the victims," Agent Shepard said. "Like an artist signs his work."

Ramsey was impressed by her insight. "Agreed."

"He must be certain he's not in any databases," Jackson said.

"So far, he's not," Ramsey said.

"He's a clean slate and likes his van the same way," Agent Shepard said, more to herself.

"Exactly," Ramsey said.

"I looked at dozens of van pictures this last week," she said. "I'd say this one is at least ten years old."

"I'd like to drive to the corner where your attack occurred, Agent Shepard," Ramsey said.

"What if I return to the corner tonight? If he's out there, he could see that I've gotten back to work."

"No," Jackson said.

"It might eventually come to that," Ramsey said. "For now, I just want to see the area."

"I can take you now. We can also pay a visit to Reverend Beckett."

"Good," Ramsey said.

Agent Shepard tapped her fingertips on the open file. "If this killer ditched the van, he'll be back for it. He has to have stowed it close to the Mission. I could go through surveillance footage of the area. It has to be on a private security camera somewhere."

"I've had officers doing exactly that for the last three days," Jackson said.

"And?" she asked.

Jackson's phone rang. He glanced at the number, his face tight with annoyance. "I have to take this."

"Sure," Ramsey said.

Jackson nodded as he listened to the person on the phone, his scowl softening as he ended the call. "We might have gotten lucky. Officers located the white van in a warehouse twenty minutes ago."

"Where?" Ramsey asked.

"Five blocks from where Agent Shepard encountered him."

"I want to see it before it's moved or disturbed," Ramsey said.

"Be my guest. Agent Shepard will drive you."

A glimmer of excitement caught in her brown gaze. "Yes, sir."

Jackson left them and Ramsey followed Shepard to her office. The walls were bare, which he thought odd since he knew she had been in this office for two years. If not for the neat piles of papers along the wall behind her desk and the dust covering the shelves crammed with used investigative books and the odd certificate of merit, he would have assumed she had just moved in. She had not bothered with formalities like diplomas or the standard grip-and-grin photos taken with dignitaries at award ceremonies. He had read her jacket and knew she had been awarded two accommodations, which were nowhere in sight. He was not sure yet if she saw them as an unnecessary bother or if she was making a statement. He guessed the latter.

"Why were you out there alone?" Ramsey asked.

"I wasn't alone until the last couple of seconds."

"I don't consider an Episcopal priest proper backup."

"You haven't met Sarah."

"Does she have law enforcement experience that I'm not aware of?"

"No. But she runs a halfway house in the Bottom. That's not for the faint of heart."

He had read her report multiple times and had almost memorized it. "Why didn't you leave with the other two women?"

She raised her chin. "Sarah was very concerned about the missing women. I was on the street hoping to get a lead from one of the pimps or the girls. If I couldn't find out where they were, I wanted to identify any individual that might have seemed off to them. I thought I'd give it just a few more minutes. And then your Key Killer rolled out of the shadows."

"Key Killer?"

"Not the best name, as far as violent killers go, but the name seems to fit." She grabbed her backpack and walked past him. He noted the slight limp. The rolled ankle must still hurt.

"I can drive," she said.

"I'd rather take my vehicle. It's my mobile office."

"Like the Key Killer."

He liked his creature comforts and he missed his own vehicle. "We'll take my car."

"Whatever works for you."

They crossed the lobby and went out the main door to a black SUV.

"I bet it's identical to the car you drive in Virginia," she said.

"If you want to play the profiling game, I have a few assessments of you I can share."

She met his gaze. "In due time, Agent Ramsey."

CHAPTER FOUR

Monday, August 24, Noon

The last thing Melina needed was Ramsey rooting around in her brain. She sensed he already had several accurate observations to share. Looking in a mirror was not top of her priority list.

Still, curiosity had her stealing a quick glance into the back seat of his rented vehicle. There was a black roller bag, small enough to carry on. He would not have checked it because his files were too important to risk with baggage handlers. She imagined it contained a second set of socks, a few clean shirts still in their dry cleaner bags, and workout gear. He did not want to be here long, but he was prepared to stay as long as he was effective.

He was not wearing a wedding band, but a lot of cops did not. The less the bad guys knew about them the better. His suit was top quality and the stitching appeared custom. The gold watch on his wrist was a Rolex, expensive but old. Ramsey did not flaunt what he had, and she decided he had grown up with money. One did not measure success by material things if one always had them. She would bet a paycheck he could trace his lineage back generations.

She sat in the front seat of the rental car and clicked her seat belt. He slid behind the wheel, put on dark glasses as the soft scent of his aftershave mingled with rental car air freshener. The thick pine scent, like the bleach, was designed to mask the presence of previous occupants.

As Melina read off the address of the warehouse where the van had been found, Agent Jackson texted indicating he would meet them there. She acknowledged his message before punching the street number and name into the GPS.

This was the part where she was probably supposed to make small talk. Nope. She was going to let him go first.

"How long have you been with TBI?" Ramsey asked.

His tone was smooth, but the words were as practiced as a concert violinist's notes. She imagined the honed script that came with an FBI badge. He was close to forty, which suggested he had worked with countless local law enforcement officers just like her.

"Seven years," she said. "Most of it was in the Knoxville office."

"Where are you from?"

She had one foot in the doghouse with Jackson and the other ready to race into this investigation. She reminded herself that her goals did not involve staring at the four blank walls of her office. "Nashville. My parents still live here. As I mentioned, Dad's former law enforcement and Mom's a retired schoolteacher. I have an undergraduate and master's in psychology. I thought I wanted to be a social worker but found I didn't have the temperament to hold hands and talk about feelings."

"Nice to be back home?" He almost sounded sincere.

"It is," she said honestly. "Mom makes enough food at Sunday dinner to fuel me for a week." When he did not comment, she asked, "What's your story? Your accent has a very slight southern drawl."

A small smile tugged at the edge of his lips. "I thought I'd lost it."

"Nashville has a way of reenergizing the faintest southern accents."

He nodded as if making a mental note. "I'm from Virginia. Grew up near Alexandria."

"Lots of tourist stuff. A lot of traffic, even then."

"It's worse."

They wound their way around the beltway and soon found themselves headed toward the industrial south side. He moved down a series of side streets until they rounded a corner and came upon the collection of police cars.

"Are you sure no one else survived the Key Killer?" she asked. "Guys like him don't come out of the womb knowing all the tricks of the serial killer trade."

Killers evolved. Initial crimes were generally petty. Peeping Toms. Small fires. However, over time they honed their skills, graduating to animal cruelty, rape, and murder.

Like everyone else, killers practiced and learned by trial and error. Modifications to the Key Killer's van had likely been ongoing as the killer learned, adapted, and evolved.

"If we can identify him," Ramsey said, "we'll most likely find someone who got away."

"Catch-22. The woman could lead to this killer, but we can't find her until we find him."

"I had an agent search the crime reports in Georgia, South Carolina, Maryland, and North Carolina. We were looking for prostitutes who had escaped a violent john. There were many, but none mentioned a van."

"You said ten victims. So far, I count five. Where were the other women killed?"

"Three in Atlanta between 1999 and 2004. And two in Savannah, Georgia, in 2002."

"That's a rather defined area," she said.

"Serial killers often have geographical preferences. Even truckers, pilots, and salesmen have territories or routes."

Yellow crime scene tape now roped off a generous area around the open bay of a gray warehouse dotted with signs reading **FOR SALE**.

Ramsey parked behind a marked car and the two got out, meeting in front of his vehicle before walking toward the uniformed officer controlling access.

Each showed their badge.

The officer noted both of their names in a log that tracked everyone coming and going beyond the tape that Ramsey now held up for her to duck under.

The warehouse was dimly lit, but she could see the outline of the windowless van shadowed in the far north corner. It looked just as it had when it had emerged from the shadows toward her. Her nerves tightened as she imagined what would have happened if she had not broken free.

Melina handed Ramsey a fresh set of latex gloves, and then she slid on a pair as Jackson walked up. She offered him a set and he did the same. Their footsteps fell in time, echoing up toward the rafters of the large room.

Standing beside the van was Matt Piper, head of TBI's forensic department. He was a tall, lean guy in his early thirties. He wore khakis and a blue button-down with the department's emblem over the right breast pocket. He wore his hair short and neatly combed, and his shirt's and pants' creases were sharp, the laces of his shoes double knotted, and his nails neatly trimmed.

"Agent Ramsey, this is Matt Piper, head of the forensic team," Jackson said.

Ramsey extended his hand. "Good to meet you."

A spotlight in the corner switched on, illuminating the van. The plates were missing and judging by the screws that lay on the concrete floor, they had been removed hastily.

The cleaned tires and the exterior glistened in the new light. The vehicle was older than she had imagined. There was not anything about the vehicle that would have caught a cop's attention. Bland vanilla. But that was the point. He wanted to go unnoticed.

A camera flashed as another technician moved around the vehicle snapping pictures. Melina studied the passenger side, imagining the sliding door catapulting open with alarming speed. Whoever this guy was, he knew his way around a toolbox.

"Piper, have you looked inside yet?" Jackson asked.

"No," Matt replied. "We just arrived ourselves. Uniforms cordoned off but didn't inspect it, per your orders."

"Appreciate that," Ramsey said.

Melina moved up to the driver's side window and peered in. It was neat, no signs of anything out of the ordinary.

More pictures were taken, and finally a uniformed officer arrived with a slim jim, which he wedged between the driver's side window and the rubber casing. The door lock clicked. He lifted the handle and opened the door.

The faintest scent of bleach wafted out. Most of the scent had dissipated in the last seven days, but it had enough punch to direct her mind back to a fear she refused to acknowledge.

Her stomach turned and sweat formed at the base of her spine. Absently, she touched the section of her hair that he had nearly ripped out. Her mind flashed back to the adrenaline-fueled moments when she had fought desperately for her life.

In the hours after the attack, she had replayed the attempted abduction over and over. She prided herself on being alert, but that night she had let her guard slip.

Ramsey pressed the van's power door button. The door snapped open with an uncommon speed, making Melina flinch slightly enough to bring her back to the moment.

"He was out the door in a matter of seconds," she said clearly.

"Ten confirmed kills," Ramsey said. "It takes practice."

"Yes. Every move was choreographed," she said.

Another light in the warehouse switched on, and this time she had her first fully illuminated look at the cargo bay.

"You did retrieve the syringe from last week's crime scene, correct?" Ramsey asked.

"Yes," Melina said.

"The contents are being analyzed," Jackson said. "We should know in a day or two."

Four O-rings were screwed and welded into the metal floor. Cuffs linked to long chains were attached to each ring. The walls were padded. Hanging on the driver's side wall was what looked like a toolbar complete with hammers, small saws, and a drill. On the driver's side door were remnants of duct tape, where she guessed he had kept the syringe.

It was a do-it-yourself torture van. And she had been less than four feet away from being trapped inside here.

Melina smoothed her hands over her pant legs. Her father had always told her a good cop kept their emotions in check no matter how bad it got on the streets. *Don't ever let them see you squirm. Do whatever you need to do to hold it together, and later in private you can deal with it.* When she had asked him how he dealt, he had laughed and pointed to his garage filled with woodshop equipment and lopsided handmade furniture her mother refused to let him bring in the house.

"We know this killer has been active for at least twenty years," Ramsey said. "And over that time, he's moved between at least five jurisdictions. The only jurisdiction to give him a nickname was Atlanta. There he was the Riverside Ripper because the bodies had been found near rivers or bodies of water. All collected evidence and did their investigations, but no one came close to catching him."

Jackson shook his head as he reached for the backdoor latch. "I can only imagine what he did to them. This setup is a house of horrors."

Melina glanced up and caught Ramsey's reflection in the rearview mirror. Tension etched his features. She held his gaze a beat and then looked away, hoping her complexion was not too ashen.

"I saw the sketch you created with the forensic artist," Ramsey said.

"It's not very detailed," she said. "I'm frustrated I didn't remember more. I'd have thought I would be the perfect witness, but not so much."

"It was less than a minute of high-adrenaline interaction," Ramsey said. "Not conducive to memory."

"For the average citizen," she countered.

Ramsey's frown deepened as if he understood her frustration. "Mr. Piper, I want you to dismantle this van. I don't want one square inch left untouched. No one cleans up all the evidence."

"Understood," Matt said.

"Agent Jackson, you said you studied the security footage of this area?" Ramsey asked.

"We did," Jackson said. "We have the van rolling into this warehouse three minutes after Reverend Beckett's 911 call."

Ramsey crossed the warehouse to a section where tire tracks imprinted the dust. "Do you have footage of a car leaving the warehouse?"

"Not on the same camera," Jackson said.

"There're two entrances to the warehouse," Matt said.

"He had a second car stashed here," Ramsey said.

"That's a lot of work on his part," Melina offered.

"He has won every time," Ramsey said. "It's why he's operated for so long. Check the cameras on the west side of the warehouse. See what vehicles were traveling the area minutes after the initial time stamp."

"Will do," Jackson said.

Melina shifted her attention back to the van. "It's not a cheap vehicle. Even used, it would have cost some money."

"But it's older. I'd say a 2007," Ramsey said. "He's comfortable with it. It's part of him. There's a lot of sick history between the two."

"He clearly didn't use it in the early murders," Melina said.

"I think he settled on it after some practice."

"That makes sense," she said. "A used van is cheaper and doesn't stand out as much. It also doesn't have GPS."

"He has to have some serious mechanical skills," Matt said. "The modifications are professionally done."

"Very likely," Ramsey said.

"Does he strike in any particular season?" Melina asked.

"Spring and summer," Ramsey said.

"Not fond of the cold?" Jackson asked.

"All evidence suggests victims vanished in the warm-weather months," Ramsey said.

She stepped back from the van, feeling a familiar tension ripple through her as she walked around to the driver's seat. "You said he's not in CODIS. Have you uploaded his DNA to an open-source site and traced him through a possible relative?"

"When we matched the DNA on your knife, that idea came up for discussion," he said.

Tracing criminals via DNA and family lineage was a new technique and still required a judge's approval before a law enforcement agency could traipse through family trees. "Ancestry is a hot topic these days," Melina said.

As an adoptee, she had always had an interest in ancestry sites. However, she rarely discussed this with anyone, because she was never comfortable sharing anything more personal than her favorite football team, barbecue joint, and country music band. The real personal stuff stayed locked away.

"It's worth a try," Ramsey said. "I have an agent at Quantico who's used this technique on another case."

The ideal match in an ancestry search was a sibling, half sibling, first cousin, or parent. That was the DNA equivalent of hitting gold. The further back the matches went, the more family trees branched and would have to be built out. But it was a start. Melina had had her

DNA analyzed about a year ago but could not force herself to look at the results.

"As far as we know, this guy has not struck for almost five years," Ramsey said. "We thought he might have died or just gotten too old. Now we know he's still active and in your backyard. And thanks to you, we just might catch this guy."

"Tell that to my boss," Melina said.

A faint smile tipped the edges of his lips. "I'd like to meet Reverend Sarah Beckett."

"The Mission is right around the corner."

"Perfect."

CHAPTER FIVE

Monday, August 24, 2:00 p.m.

Fatigue born from endless cases stacked up back to back was settling into Ramsey's shoulders. He would power through today and get enough shut-eye tonight to fuel him for the cases waiting for him back at Quantico. But right now, it was one foot in front of the other. This kind of fatigue was worrisome because it led to mistakes and missed leads. He was too close to catching the Key Killer to make a mistake now.

Ramsey and Shepard left Jackson with the van. The two walked back to the vehicle and climbed in.

Shepard removed sunglasses tucked in the side pocket of her backpack, and within minutes they were headed toward South Nashville. Ten minutes later, they parked in front of the one-story community center.

The board-and-batten siding was a faded blue and looked in need of a fresh coat of paint. But the small patch of grass bordering the front was neatly trimmed with two planters filled with yellow marigolds. The Mission did not have a lot of financial resources, but it made the most of what it had.

"Sarah started her ministry about three years ago. Like I said, she gets women off the streets. As a group, they make herbal soaps and scrubs and sell them in town. The products are quite popular."

"What's the percentage of women under her ministry who stay clean and off the streets?" Ramsey asked.

"Over seventy percent."

"Impressive."

They got out of the car and walked to the double front doors. He deliberately reached it first, pulling it open.

"You might have to stop doing that," she said as she passed.

"Opening doors?"

She paused as she raised her gaze to a large cross hanging on the wall. "If any of the guys see you treat me as a prim and proper lady, I'll never live it down."

He cracked a small grin, and for the first time in a long time felt a lightness of spirit. "I'm not worried about you. My guess is that you can eat the lunch of anyone at TBI."

"True. But they can turn into a bunch of middle school kids. And that gets annoying." She walked up to a bell hanging on the wall and rang it.

Seconds later a petite woman appeared. In her midthirties, she had a thick shock of red hair tied up on her head, ivory skin, and freckles that splashed over the bridge of her nose. Her jeans and sweatshirt were covered in speckles of blue paint. She was wiping the same hue from her hands with an old rag.

"Melina," she said, smiling.

"Sarah, I'd like you to meet FBI agent Jerrod Ramsey. Agent Ramsey, Reverend Beckett. She runs the Mission."

Ramsey extended his hand. "Pleasure."

"I'd shake your hand, but you don't want to be near me. I know a good suit when I see one."

His hand remained extended. "I'm not worried."

She wiped her hands on a rag and grasped his. "Can I get you two some coffee? We just put a big pot on. You can ask me anything you want."

They followed her into the kitchen where a tall stocky man dressed in jeans and a white apron was setting up a row of plates on a stainless steel counter.

"This is Sam Jenkins," Reverend Beckett said. "He's my right-hand man."

Sam was in his late thirties and was carrying an extra twenty pounds on his frame. Dark brown hair brushed the top of his collar. He wiped his hands on his apron and extended one to Ramsey. "I hope you're keeping Melina out of trouble?"

Shepard shot him a look that was both familiar and irritated. "Sam."

Grinning, Sam held up his hands. "I get it. Official business."

Shepard's cheeks burned as her shoulders stiffened.

"Agent Shepard is the reason I'm here. She tangled with a man I've been chasing for years."

Frowning, Sam poured three cups of coffee. "We all heard about it. Some of the residents are still upset. Hell, I'm still upset."

Shepard cleared her throat. "What are you doing now?"

Sam's brow rose, as if he knew she was trying to divert the conversation. "We're setting up for a catering class. The goal is to teach the residents practical job skills. In this town, someone's always looking for food-service workers. Melina's one of our best instructors."

"What do you teach?" Ramsey asked.

"Self-defense," Shepard said.

"And cake decorating," Sam added. "She makes one hell of a sugar flower."

Shepard groaned. "You're killing me."

Sam winked. "What? Can't wield a gun and a piping bag?"

Ramsey did not comment as they all took their coffees and left the kitchen, finding their way to a small conference room. The walls were decorated with large snapshots of residents in the kitchen, in Bible study, and in self-defense class. His gaze was drawn to the latter, keying in on a picture of Shepard wearing sweats and a determined grin as she flipped a man nearly twice her size.

Reverend Beckett closed the door and sat. "There's been no sign of the two missing women. Melina has called twice a day to check."

"Are you sure they didn't leave town?" Ramsey asked. "It's not unusual."

"Both women have children, which I know doesn't necessarily mean they'll stay. But both were making progress toward getting clean."

"Easy to fall off the wagon," Ramsey said. "Failure rate with addicts is high."

"I've considered that. But I don't think that's the case. Something feels really off about this," Reverend Beckett said.

"Do you have pictures of the missing women?" Ramsey asked.

"I do." She reached in her pocket and pulled out two images printed onto computer paper. "I take a picture of every woman who enters the program here. It's not only for identification purposes, but I also document it as their 'before' picture. You'd be amazed at some of the transformations."

"Yes, ma'am," he said.

"Anyway, I also try to collect a full history, but they aren't always forthcoming at first. And others tend to tell you what they believe you want to hear."

Ramsey studied the unsmiling, drawn faces. Both women had shoulder-length dark hair and appeared to be in their early twenties. "Did any of the women mention the man in the van?"

"A few girls remembered seeing it two weeks ago. They all joked that he was a virgin, meaning he's never paid for sex in the Bottom before. I didn't even remember the van until Melina's encounter with its driver," she said. "All of them thought there was something off about the guy."

Ramsey wondered how many of the women really remembered the van after Agent Shepard's attack by the Key Killer. Memories were a tricky thing. They were easily suggestible and not wholly reliable. The women's fear of a killer hunting women like them could easily inject itself into their subconscious and taint their recollections.

"And you think the missing girls got into that van?" he asked.

"I'm not entirely sure. I do know the usual girls on the streets are present and accounted for as of yesterday."

That was because the killer did not have his van. It was his base of operations. Without it, he might be sidelined until he found another. That might have bought them a little time. "What did the girls say about the van?" Ramsey asked.

"Like I told Melina, it was driving around the Bottom. This van never stopped, but it passed by enough that it was noticed."

"You said they considered him a virgin. Anyone get a look at the driver?" he asked.

Reverend Beckett lifted her cup to her lips. "They described a man with black hair."

"The guy who came for me was wearing a blond wig," Shepard said.

"Reasonable that he's altering his appearance on a regular basis," Ramsey said.

"Some thought he might have been a businessman or a 'nice guy' from the suburbs." She made air quotes with her hands. "They get types like that. Men who want to try the forbidden fruit but haven't quite summoned the nerve to cross the line."

"The women have seen this behavior before. What bothered them about him?" Ramsey wanted specifics, which generally supported real memories.

Reverend Beckett cradled her cup. "He stared at them for a long time. Gave them the creeps," she said.

"They've all been stared at before," Ramsey said.

"My boss said the same thing. The ones who survive life on the streets develop a sixth sense. They know when something is off. Without it they don't last long."

"Can you clarify?" Ramsey asked.

"One girl said he was wearing gloves and sunglasses. It was hot and dark."

"Did anyone see his face?" Ramsey knew he was likely repeating Jackson's interview, but sometimes a day or two could jog something loose. Even if the memories were not wholly accurate, they could have enough elements of truth to lead to something more substantial.

"Not that I know. But I'll keep asking."

"Where did they see him?"

"Seven blocks from here. He was on Southside Avenue across from the tire store."

A clatter from the other room had Reverend Beckett rising.

"I've got it," Shepard said. "Be right back."

"We're mixing up the oils for the new line of hand soap," Reverend Beckett said.

"How long has Agent Shepard volunteered here?" Ramsey asked.

"For a couple of years. Did she tell you we grew up in the same neighborhood?"

"She did."

"Both our moms were teachers and both our dads cops. She's genuine. She'd do anything for you, but she takes too many chances."

"Does she say the same about you?" he countered.

Reverend Beckett grinned. "Two peas in a pod."

"What are the names of the missing women?" Ramsey asked.

"Delia and Joy. Each uses the last name Smith, but I doubt it's either of their real surnames."

"Has anyone been by their residence?"

"Delia lives on the streets. Joy stays in a small room over her sister's garage. I did contact Joy's sister, but she's not seen Joy in two weeks."

"What's the sister's name?" he asked.

"Emily Ross. I can pull up her contact information for you."

"That would be appreciated."

Shepard reappeared. "It was Sadie. She dropped a tub of coconut oil. Some spillage. Sam is cleaning it up. I asked Sadie if she would talk to Agent Ramsey."

"Sadie takes our mission work to the streets, literally. She's out there almost nightly making sure the girls are eating and getting medical attention if they need it. She was out there the night Melina was attacked."

Steps echoed in the hallway moments before a short, heavyset woman with short-cropped hair appeared. The woman appeared to be in her midthirties. She had blotchy skin, and discolored teeth indicated a prior meth habit. Her eyes were clear, but Ramsey had no way of knowing if she was totally clean or for how long.

As if reading his thoughts, Reverend Beckett said, "You can't work in my shop if you're using. I have mandatory random drug tests for everyone. If you pull a positive, then you have to leave until you can prove you've been clean for ninety days."

Sadie tipped her chin up as she reached for a rumpled packet of cigarettes in her back pocket. "I've been clean for five years, two months, and seven days."

"We're very proud of her," Reverend Beckett said.

"Why were you on the street with Agent Shepard?" Ramsey asked.

"My friend Fiona and me used to work the streets with the missing girls, and because we still know all the players well, we offered to stand on the street corner with Melina."

"Did you see the van?" he asked.

"No, we left right before he approached her."

"You left Agent Shepard alone." An intended accusation rumbled under the statement.

Sadie shot Shepard a hard look that looked more sad than angry. "She said she had it under control."

"I told them to leave," Shepard said. "I just wanted a few more minutes out there. Like I said before, I had a feeling."

"Describe it," Ramsey said.

"There are nights when the vibe feels off. Like when the air shifts before a storm comes."

"Not very scientific," he said.

"You've never operated on a hunch?" Shepard asked.

Ramsey didn't respond. "Facts, Agent Shepard."

"Turns out I was right," she said. "Only the storm wasn't the one I was expecting."

"What were you expecting?"

"To see Joy or Delia, I guess. Maybe their pimp."

"Reverend Beckett, did you see the van?" he asked.

"All I saw was the man trying to pull Melina into the van," Reverend Beckett said. "I was too busy freaking out and blaring on the horn to get a good look at him."

"Was this your first time out there alone, Agent Shepard?" Ramsey asked.

She shifted. Took a sip of coffee. "No, it was my third. I'd met up with the gals twice the week before, but we never saw the van."

"Does Agent Jackson know this?"

"No," she said.

Whether it was that last night or the week before, the killer had noticed Shepard. And Ramsey could see why she would be noticed. Despite her edgy street vibe, there was something about her that was hard to ignore.

"Have you seen any signs of a man loitering around since that time? Anything that felt off?" he asked.

"Not around here," Sadie said. "Rev, what about you?"

Reverend Beckett's brow furrowed. "I've seen no odd men, at least no more odd than usual."

It had been seven days since the van driver had made his move. He was injured and without his van. He was likely feeling angry and frustrated over the failure.

All the prep in the van's interior told Ramsey he had been challenged by women before. But instead of giving up, he had adapted and changed strategies—the handcuffs, the drugs he had ready for Shepard, and the bleach.

This killer would not let a setback stop him. He was modifying his tactics. He was always looking for an advantage while also being careful. The chances of finding usable evidence were slim.

Until his aborted abduction of Shepard, this killer had played his cards perfectly. Now that he had failed and been injured, he was not likely to forget the woman who had caused both.

CHAPTER SIX

Monday, August 24, 4:30 p.m.

Melina was back in her office, free to return phone calls, while Ramsey did the same from the conference room. She was grateful to have some distance from him. He was intense and not easily approached, and small talk was not her friend. Ultimately, he would evaluate her work on this case and report back to Jackson.

She scrolled through the messages and returned her mother's call first. "Mom," she said, trying not to sound impatient.

"A little bird told me you've been on desk duty."

"Who?" She rose and looked around the office. No one was watching, but she did not doubt her mother had connections.

"Like you, I don't rat out my confidential informants."

Melina heard the smile in her mother's voice and decided to dial back the tension in her own tone or her mother would lock in like a guided missile. "How's Dad?"

"On the mend."

"Did you throw away the old ladder?" Her newly retired father had decided he was perfectly capable of putting siding on their thirty-year-old house regardless of his seventy years. He had fallen off the rickety ladder two weeks ago and broken his foot. His doctor had said he would fully recover unless he pestered his wife too much and she killed him.

"I tossed it in the garbage the day after the fall. I wanted to set it on fire, but we're in a drought."

"Good call. Can I do anything?"

"Nothing time and a little bourbon for me won't fix."

Quirky inside jokes brought down Melina's blood pressure because they reminded her that she had family behind her. Despite a couple of moody teenage years, she had always cherished her place in the Shepard clan. Her mother understood all this, and clearly suspected that desk duty meant something had gone down.

"I'll be by on Sunday," Melina said.

"If you can manage it. I know work gets busy."

"Never that busy."

"Bring a few good war stories home to your dad. You know how much he enjoys them."

This current case was right up his alley. Well, except for the small part that included the near murder of his only child. "Will do, Mom."

"Love ya, kid."

"Love you." She hung up, knowing she had hit the jackpot when Molly and Hank Shepard had adopted her.

Twenty-eight years ago, when Hank Shepard had been a uniformed officer for the state police, he had received a call that a little girl had been spotted on the side of the northbound lane of Route 25. He had been five minutes out and had responded.

He said he had almost not seen her the first time because she was huddled by the guardrail. In fact, it was her yellow jacket flickering in his rearview mirror that made him turn around.

He found her dressed in shorts, a white T-shirt, red boots, and the yellow raincoat. Most of her thick black hair had escaped her ponytail, and her eyes were red from crying. Her hands had been trembling, and when he had gotten out of the car, she had taken several steps back.

"It's okay. I'm here to help. My friends call me Shep," her father said.

To this day, Melina barely remembered the moment. She recalled his bright headlights shining on his frame, blinding her to only the outline of a giant. But she also recollected a soft, soothing voice that chased away some of the fear.

"What's your name?" he asked.

Too rattled to lie or give the other name she was told to use, she spoke the truth. "Melina."

"That's a pretty name. Melina, are you hungry?"

She nodded.

"I thought so. I can take you back into town, and we can get something to eat and maybe find your mom and dad."

"They're dead," she said.

"Your mom and dad are dead?"

She nodded.

His smile only hardened for a split second. "Who left you out here?"

She had never told him the woman's name. She was not sure if she had not recalled it or was too afraid to say. And when she was old enough and no longer afraid, the name had already faded from her consciousness.

She wished now she had spoken to the big man as his rough hands had wrapped gently around her own fingers. If she had not been so afraid to talk, she could have told him about the person who had left her, and he could have dug deeper into her past. But she had remained silent, even when he had called his wife, Molly, who had come to the station armed with blankets and peanut butter and jelly sandwiches. The opportunity to find her biological family was gone.

The Shepards had pulled strings and gotten social services to release her into their custody. There had been an exhaustive search for her birth family, but no information had materialized. Some surmised that, given her dark hair and olive skin, she had come from Mexico or Central America. She did not speak Spanish, so if she had been brought over the border legally or illegally, there was no way of determining her nationality. Her past had simply vanished.

A knock on her door had her looking up. Jackson stood in her doorway. "I have a case for you."

"I thought I was working one."

"This one's more up your alley. Missing persons case."

She had been assigned to her first one five years ago in Knoxville. The missing boy, Johnny, was eight years old and autistic, and he had vanished from his backyard. A scent dog was summoned but was two hours away.

She walked across the property toward the woods behind. With the temperature dropping, she had no time to waste. Knowing autistic children often walked in straight lines, she did the same for almost an hour before she heard the rustle of leaves. She turned around and saw something moving. She called out the boy's name. That's when she saw the red shirt and the crop of blond hair. She had found him, cold, hungry, and scared.

She wished she could say that all her cases had turned out so well, but too many, as far as she was concerned, had ended up unsolved. But somewhere along the way, she had earned a reputation as a solid investigator.

"Who's missing?" she asked.

"There's been a car accident. There's a child on the scene, but the driver is missing, and I need you to check it out."

She rose, reaching for the jacket slung over the back of her chair. "Is the Key Killer involved in the accident?"

"No. This has nothing to do with him. There's not much you can do with that case at the moment, and I need you now."

Her heartbeat kicked as her mind instantly filled with dozens of questions about the child, the absence of an adult, and the condition of the car. She pulled in a breath, taming the rush of adrenaline. "What is the child's medical condition?"

"She appears to be fine but is confused and upset."

"Is she talking?"

"No."

"Why is TBI being called in? This should be a case for local police."

"There's something the local police want us to see in the trunk of the car," Jackson said. "Since we rarely have a genuine profiler in our office, I thought it would be helpful if Ramsey is on scene as well."

They passed the conference room's glass wall where Ramsey had set up temporary shop. He was standing, a cell phone pressed to his ear as he stared out the large tinted window overlooking the former Freemason foster home. Melina knocked on the glass to get Ramsey's attention. Turning, he held up an index finger, signaling her to wait.

Annoyed at the delay, she turned to Jackson. "What's the something?"

"I'm going to let you both see it for yourselves. If it's really what they say it is, we'll need Ramsey."

Ramsey ended his call and rose, pushing down his shirtsleeves as he crossed to the door. "What's going on?"

"There's another case," Jackson said. "I'm going and so is Shepard. I'd like you to come along."

Ramsey frowned as if he were mentally shifting priorities with the flip of a switch. "Sure."

He shrugged on his coat, carefully collected his files, and arranged them in his briefcase. His suit coat gently flapped as he approached.

"What are we headed into?" Ramsey said.

"I'm not sure I believe it myself," Jackson said.

"Boss wants us to see it for ourselves," Melina said.

"Understood," Ramsey said.

"I'm in a white SUV," she said to Ramsey. "Separate cars might be more efficient this time."

"Roger."

The three divided, each moving at a clipped pace. Ramsey had his phone to his ear again as he angled into his car, and Jackson headed toward the exit as she jogged to the far side of the lot lovingly known as Siberia.

As Melina started the engine, Jackson was gone, but Ramsey's vehicle waited at the parking lot exit. When she drove up behind him, she caught his gaze as he glanced in his rearview mirror. The intensity in his eyes was direct and cutting. He shifted his attention quickly back to the road, but as he drove and she followed, she knew he was as keen a hunter as the Key Killer.

CHAPTER SEVEN

Monday, August 24, 5:15 p.m.

Ramsey saw Shepard in his rearview mirror, gaining on him and then taking the lead as they merged their cars onto the interstate. She wove in and out of traffic, moving quickly toward the accident site. There was no quit in this woman.

When he was not trying to keep up, he recognized some of the scenery, but found the metro area had changed since his last visit seven years ago. More buildings, strip malls, and people on the road than he remembered, but a growing local economy drew more residents who strained roads and local infrastructure. He missed the slower pace of yesterday. But as his dad used to say, nothing stayed the same.

Shepard skated through a yellow light that turned red quickly. He stopped, watched her car turn left and out of sight. A text from her hit his phone. It contained the location of the accident.

He plugged it into his GPS and when the light finally changed, he followed the prompts, which guided him into a residential neighborhood.

The houses were small but stylish. Many had front porches deep enough for two rockers. The yards were filled with tall, mature oak trees and green lawns faded by the August heat. He guessed this neighborhood had been built in the late 1940s.

He spotted Cox Road, the location of the accident, and took the left despite the GPS's warning to reroute. He savored a moment of superiority over the machine until the road dead-ended into a wooded cul-de-sac.

Cursing, he threw the car in reverse and was ready to rush back to the main road when he caught the flash of blue lights on the other side of a bank of trees. GPS had been right. The road was divided by a narrow stand of thick trees.

GPS reactivated, he turned the car around, got back out on the main road, and this time allowed the GPS to take him around the block until he spotted the other side of Cox Road.

After a curve in the road, flashing blue lights signaled the collection of cop cars up ahead. He nosed his car in at the back of the line behind Shepard's, shut the engine off, and got out.

He clipped his credentials to his waistband and strode toward the group of uniformed officers standing by a late-model Ford SUV that had slammed right into a collection of mature trees. The front end had taken a direct hit, totaling the car. Smoke and steam hissed from the engine, but there was no fire.

He squared his shoulders and headed toward a big burly man dressed in a brown-and-tan sheriff's uniform. The officer was talking to Shepard and Jackson.

There was more salt than pepper in the sheriff's hair. A paunch and deeply lined tanned skin placed him in his late sixties. Judging by the way the sheriff glared at the wrecked car, he was counting his days to retirement.

Shepard cleared her throat as she looked at Ramsey. "Glad you could join us."

"Got turned around a bit," he said with a slight grin.

"Ah." She turned to the man beside her.

"Agent Ramsey, I'd like to introduce you to Sheriff Alan Jones."

The sheriff's scowl deepened as he took Ramsey's hand.

The old man arched a brow in a way that was supposed to make Ramsey feel like a rookie fresh from the academy, an outsider, take your pick. Ramsey had seen it all.

"Agent Ramsey is working with TBI on another case," Jackson said. "He's here to offer his expertise."

"Lucky for us," Sheriff Jones said.

"Agent Jackson said something about a missing driver." Shepard's tone was crisp.

Sheriff Jones shook his head. "Correct. No sign of the driver. The minor has been transported to the hospital. The EMTs took the girl away about fifteen minutes ago. She suffered only minor cuts and bruises, but the EMTs wanted the doctors to do a full workup just in case."

She glanced toward the mangled gray car. "How old is the girl? What's her name?"

"She says her name is Elena Sanchez. Says she's six but she looks younger."

"Did she say who was driving the car?" Ramsey asked.

"She won't say. We barely got her to tell us her name. She doesn't seem to trust cops too much."

He looked around at the cul-de-sac with the car jacked up on a two-foot-high stump covered in tall grass. The front section was molded around a big oak.

"Who called it in?" he asked.

"Neighbor closest to the crash," Sheriff Jones said. "The woman heard a car screeching past and then a loud bang. She said they get a lot of traffic even though the neighborhood prevented the road being cut through to the other side. Mother with kids raised holy hell when the Department of Transportation started clearing trees because she didn't want it to become a major shortcut to the interstate, which is blocks away."

"This can't be the first time this has happened," Ramsey said.

Sheriff Jones nodded. "Neighbor said a half dozen drivers have tried to make it across in the last year alone. Forensic guys estimate the speed was at least forty miles per hour based on the damage done to the engine. Way I see it, the driver was distracted, complacent, and speeding. No surprise here."

The other side of Cox Road led to the main highway. "Did anyone see the driver?" he asked.

"No." Sheriff Jones flipped through a notebook. "The neighbor, Pam Piercy, said that by the time she reached the car, the driver was gone. The kid was crying so she shifted her attention to the child."

Shepard removed a small notebook from her pocket, flipped to a clean page, and wrote down the name. "Which is her house?"

"The first on the right as you're leaving. The street address is 2317."

"Thanks. Mind if we have a look at the car?" Shepard asked.

"Be my guest."

She crossed to the back of her SUV and fished out latex gloves. As she handed a set to him, he noted she kept the trunk of her car equipped with basic forensic equipment, MREs, flares, extra shoes, and rope.

Shepard walked past Ramsey, Jackson, and Sheriff Jones, her focus squarely on the vehicle. Her expression had shifted and sharpened with even more intensity. If the Key Killer case had been out of her wheelhouse, this one was not.

After looking inside the car's driver's side window, she circled around to the opposite side of the car. The airbags had deployed. The front passenger seat was covered in discarded fast-food wrappers, bags of half-eaten snacks, a few empty soda cans, and a few rumpled receipts.

A fine dusting of black powder on the steering wheel, door handles, and radio buttons told them the forensic team had started working the scene.

"Sheriff Jones, I see your guy has dusted for prints. Any luck?" Shepard asked.

"The steering wheel, dashboard, and door handles were wiped clean," he said.

"What about the buttons on the side of the driver's seat?" Shepard asked.

"Checked and also clean," Sheriff Jones said.

He glanced back at the car seat. The harness was unhooked, done no doubt by Ms. Piercy or EMTs when the child was removed. Still, the driver would have handled the seat multiple times. "He should dust the sides of the car seat, as well as its underside."

"I'm sure he did both," the sheriff said.

"I don't see powder on the car seat," Shepard said. "Better check, Sheriff."

"Will do."

"Why not take the child?" Ramsey asked.

"Driver was injured and couldn't carry the child," Shepard theorized. "Maybe the girl was crying and making too much noise. Maybe the driver isn't far from the scene now and is watching us. Or the driver is already at the hospital."

"Hospital security is on notice to monitor incoming calls," Sheriff Jones said. "We've also notified hospital staff to keep everyone other than immediate hospital staff away from the child."

"Good," Shepard said. "She's alone, hurt, and frightened. She's vulnerable to any kind of suggestion."

Among all the clutter in the back seat were blankets, stuffed animals, and well-worn toys. In the car seat's cup holder was a juice box with a straw. She touched the box, shaking it gently. It was still half-full and felt slightly cool to the touch.

"When was the crash called in?" she asked.

"Less than one hour ago," Sheriff Jones said.

Shepard picked up a floppy stuffed dog covered in Goldfish crumbs. One of its eyes was missing, and the fur was worn off the ears. She brushed off the crumbs. "Sheriff, did your people find any signs of drugs in the vehicle?"

"A spent joint on the passenger-side floor," he said.

"The driver was worried about the cops," Ramsey said.

"Over a roach?" Shepard asked. "The driver was worried about something bigger than that. Sheriff, we're out here because Agent Jackson said we needed to be. Time to tell us why we're really here."

"I heard you were a real charmer," Sheriff Jones said. "What's your nickname again? I forgot."

"There are a few, but my favorite is Glinda, the Good Bitch."

Jones sidestepped the comment and wrestled on a fresh pair of his own gloves and walked around to the driver's seat. "We opened the trunk earlier, fearing someone might be inside. You never know. Once we determined what we had back here, we closed it right up."

Tension rippled through Ramsey's body as he braced. "Open it."

***

Melina took a step back from the trunk and, out of habit, slid her hand to her weapon. She hated surprises.

The last time she had found a surprise in a car trunk, she was responding to a call from the Virginia State Police. A Staunton man had abducted his three children and was believed to be en route to Tennessee. When she received word that the car had been spotted, she caught up to the deputies just as they pulled the man out of the vehicle. They then opened the trunk and discovered the three children, ages two, three, and four. All three girls were badly dehydrated and had to be rushed to the hospital. The youngest did not survive. To this day, she could still smell the combined stench of urine, vomit, and cheese crackers.

The latch popped and the wide trunk lid slowly opened. The large interior was crammed full of an assortment of junk just like the car's interior. There were a couple of large black roller suitcases, a small red cooler, a few garbage bags, and what looked like a large jar underneath a quilted blanket. A strong chemical smell emanated from the trunk and was enough to make her raise her hand to her nose.

"It smells like formaldehyde," she said.

"I noticed it as soon as I opened the lid." Sheriff Jones nodded to his forensic tech and asked him to start snapping pictures. "Once I took a look under the blanket, I called TBI."

The sheriff gingerly lifted the quilt soaked in the chemical solution. The jar lid was not screwed on tightly. Someone had taken the jar lid off and not replaced it properly. The sheriff carried the damp blanket to a tarp.

"As soon as the deputy got a peek in the trunk, he hustled the child away from the car and halted the investigation. I got a good long look before I called TBI."

In the right corner of the trunk was a large old pickle jar with the label still attached to the front and back. The top lid was green, and the glass was clear. At first, she thought what she saw floating inside the jar was some kind of pickled vegetable.

The sheriff grabbed the jar and, turning his face away from the contents, held it up for Melina and Ramsey. The sunlight caught the jar and reflected off the dusty glass, forcing her to refocus. When she did, she realized why she was here, as well as the FBI.

"May I?" Ramsey reached out for the jar.

"Be my guest," Sheriff Jones said.

Ramsey tilted the pickle jar back until the dusty glass caught evening light that illuminated the interior. The murky liquid made it difficult to identify what was floating in the jar until he leaned it forward and one of the objects settled on the glass.

It wasn't filled with pickles. Floating inside were human fingers.

"Jesus H. Christ!" Jackson said.

"Sheriff, have you asked the child about the jar?" Melina asked.

"Not the kind of topic I want to bring up with a kid. That'll be your job," Sheriff Jones said.

"Got it."

The digits appeared to be all ring fingers, and they floated as Ramsey moved the jar from side to side. Several were shriveled with a pale, ghostly gray color and appeared to be from different individuals. Only one had nail polish on it, and it looked relatively fresh.

"Six," Ramsey said. "Six fingers in the jar."

"Six females? Six males? Both?" Melina asked.

"The fingers are small and appear to be female, but DNA testing will confirm that," Ramsey said.

"Are they trophies?" Jackson asked.

"That's exactly what they are," Ramsey said. "Some killers collect their victims' jewelry, underwear, driver's licenses, or shoes. This individual keeps fingers."

Her breath trickled through her clenched teeth. She stepped back and looked at the car's California plates. "Sheriff, have you run these?"

"Of course. The car was reported stolen sixteen days ago from San Diego, California. I've put a call in to the local San Diego police and have asked them to locate the owner."

"We need to get the fingers to the medical examiner's office and have them determine if there are any usable prints," Ramsey said. "We might get a hit in AFIS."

Identifying the victims was a vital first step, but her priority was finding the driver and talking to the child.

"What's your impression, Agent Shepard?" Ramsey asked.

His deep baritone voice sounded professorial. She straightened, tightening her grip on the stuffed animal at her side. "At this stage, I don't know what to think."

"Come on, you have thoughts and impressions. I can see it in your expression. Any thoughts about the driver, the child?"

"The child didn't lack for snacks. The food isn't nutritious, but standard fare for children. Snacks keep a child quiet."

"True. But I sense the driver has genuine affection for the child," Ramsey countered.

When she'd been about six, she had been famous for her meltdowns. Her mother had quickly started carrying Goldfish crackers and juice boxes. Even to this day, her mother knew a handful of Goldfish made her happy.

"This driver abandoned the child," she said. Something her mother had never done. "The driver values self-preservation over the welfare of the girl."

"Assuming the driver knew about the pickle jar's contents, he or she is familiar with violent behavior."

"Cuts fingers off people, but is careful to keep the child fed."

"Some violent offenders can care about family and friends and draw a line between their two worlds," Ramsey said.

Yeah, it was called compartmentalization. Keep a firm line between light and dark. Some killers could manage it for decades. For others, a simple trigger shattered the illusion and was usually their downfall. "But even for the most hardened, those worlds often collide eventually."

"Yes, they do."

She hoped for Elena's sake the wall had been firmly in place until the accident. "The driver's sense of self-preservation trumps any of the snacks and toys. Cheap food is easy to come by. Freedom is not."

"Did anyone see the driver run away after they heard the crash?" Jackson asked.

"No," Sheriff Jones said. "We'll check with the residents and see who has private security footage."

"You might get lucky," Ramsey said.

"I'll put a couple of deputies on it," Sheriff Jones said.

She stared at the jar of digits floating in the viscous liquid but discovered she had no words. Many of the victims murdered by serial killers were faceless, nameless women who worked in the sex trade. They were women who had left home a long time ago, and if they went missing, family rarely noticed, nor did they care.

"I want to get to the hospital and speak to Elena," Melina said.

"I'll follow," Ramsey said.

"If we all go, she's sure to clam up." Melina looked at Ramsey and Jackson. "You both can be a little overwhelming."

Ramsey and Jackson looked at each other.

"I can be charming," Ramsey said.

"I have two kids of my own," Jackson said.

"No," Melina said. "I'll talk to the girl."

Jackson released his breath, seeming to concede to her on this. "I'll escort the fingers to the medical examiner's office."

"I want to see the child," Ramsey said. "She's our only witness right now."

"All right, but let me do the talking," she said.

He attempted a smile as if to prove he could soften his image. "Done."

"Don't do that," she said.

"What?"

"Don't smile at the kid. It will terrify her. Just be quiet."

"What's wrong with my smile?" he asked with genuine curiosity.

"You're the detective. You figure it out."

CHAPTER EIGHT

Monday, August 24, 6:00 p.m.

Melina lost sight of Ramsey as each drove toward the hospital, but she was not concerned. He was a big boy and perfectly capable of finding the right address.

His presence unsettled her, which was a rare occurrence. Since her rookie days, she had dealt with her share of tough cops who expected her to prove her worth. Those days were long past—until Ramsey, who was in a different league of cop. He noticed more than the average bear, and there was a hint of ruthlessness that was keeping her on her toes.

For now, she was grateful for the time alone in the car. She needed to process the scene without enduring his scrutiny.

She arrived at the hospital and parked. As she crossed the hospital lot and strode toward the front doors, she spotted Ramsey approaching from her left flank. His long even strides ate up the distance quickly, and by the time she reached the front door, he was at her side.

"You made it," she said.

He grinned and paused, allowing her to walk through the sliding doors first, but he was the first to reach the information desk and show his badge. She held up hers as he said, "FBI agent Jerrod Ramsey and TBI agent Melina Shepard. We're here to see Elena Sanchez."

The older woman with white curly hair wore a blue smock over her street clothes and sported a badge that read GINA, VOLUNTEER. Brown eyes widened as she checked her computer screen and then, squaring her shoulders, said, "Third floor. She's on the pediatric wing."

"Thank you," Ramsey said.

They stepped into the car, and Melina pressed three. A tall man in a white coat entered the car and leaned past her to press four. The three stood in silence until the doors opened on the third floor.

"Remember, I do the talking," she whispered as they stepped out.

"I'm here to not smile," Agent Ramsey said.

"Exactly."

At the floor station, she got the attention of a young nurse, Nora, and each showed their identification badges and made introductions.

"Any calls from family?" Melina asked Nora.

"Nothing."

"Has anyone called the hospital about a young child brought into the emergency room?" It was not beyond the realm of possibility for the driver to worry about the child or, more likely, what she would say.

"No calls. You're her first visitors."

"That might change when the media gets this story," she warned. "Just keep everyone off limits to the girl for her own safety."

"Of course."

Melina reached in her backpack and pulled out the stuffed dog. She straightened the crooked eye and arranged the ears so that they dangled neatly around its furry face.

Her mind tumbled back to before the Shepards had adopted her. To the faint outline of a similar stuffed furry companion. She could not say if it had been a dog, cat, or bear, but she knew it had been soft and that when she'd held it close to her nose, the smell had given her comfort.

She rolled her shoulders and head from side to side and practiced a smile before she opened the door to the private room. The overhead light was dim and the shades drawn. A television mounted on the wall broadcast an episode of *SpongeBob SquarePants*. The girl lay in the middle of the bed, her eyes closed. Dark hair framed her small olive-skinned face. Small lips were pursed, and her brow was wrinkled into a frown.

Melina struggled with the same anger that always threatened to get the better of her when she worked a case involving a child. It was one thing for her to have her abandonment issues. The damage had been done, and she had found a way to make it work for her. But that did not mean every kid had a coping mechanism and everything was going to be all right. She looked forward to meeting the driver of the car and locking his or her ass up.

She pulled up a chair beside the bed as Ramsey stepped back into the shadows. She took the little girl's hand in hers and for several seconds said nothing as she simply sat.

The girl's eyes began to roll back and forth under her closed lids, and her body began to twitch. She was dreaming, and judging by the deepening frown on her face, it was not good.

"Elena," Melina said softly. "Elena, shhhhh."

The girl shook her head, and a soft cry escaped her lips before her eyes popped open and she looked around the dimly lit room. Her gaze was panicked, reminding Melina of a cornered animal.

"It's okay, honey." She heard Ramsey shift, but hold his ground. "You're safe, Elena. You're in the hospital."

The girl turned toward Melina, her eyes still as her grip tightened around Melina's fingers. She was a stranger to the child, and in any other circumstance the child might have drawn back. But in this moment, she sensed the child was drowning, scrambling to stay afloat. Melina was her life raft.

"You're okay," Melina said softly.

The tiny girl was silent, panic turning her liquid-brown eyes brittle. No tears glistened, suggesting this was not the first time she had been left on her own.

"My name is Melina." Given the girl's probable bias against cops, she planned to leave that detail out for now.

"I want my mom," the girl whispered.

"I'm trying to find your mom, but don't know where to look. What's her name?"

Elena's mouth bunched into a frown.

"I'm not mad at your mom. I just want to find her," she said.

Tears now welled in the girl's eyes, and several spilled down her cheeks. "You can't find my mom."

"I'm pretty good at finding people." She held up the stuffed dog. "I found this guy."

"Petey!" Elena released Melina's fingers and grabbed the dog, closing her eyes as she held the toy close.

"I found Petey," Melina repeated. "Help me find your mother."

"You can't," she whispered. She hugged the dog close, burying her nose in the soft fur.

"Why not?"

Silence stretched. Melina could feel the girl's tension, as well as Ramsey's behind her. The child sensed the agent had suspicions about her mother's fate.

"Why can't I find your mother?" Melina asked.

The girl didn't open her eyes, and when she spoke, her voice was so faint it was hard to understand her. "My mom is dead."

It was Melina's turn to be silent for a moment as she digested the words and juxtaposed them against the image of the glass pickle jar and its ghoulish contents. "Honey, what is your mother's name?"

"Christina."

"And where did your mommy live?"

"California." That tracked with the plates on the car.

"Where in California?"

"1040 Litton Lane, Imperial Beach, California. 619-555-1212."

"That's your home address and phone number?" She quickly scribbled down the information.

"Yes. Mama made me learn it."

"That's very smart of you to remember. When did your mom pass away?"

"On my birthday."

"When's your birthday?"

"August twenty-two."

"That was a couple of days ago," Melina said. "What happened to your mom, honey?"

"She never woke up that morning."

"Why not?"

"BB said it was the needle in her arm. It would make her sleep forever."

"Who's BB?"

"My friend."

"Was BB driving the car?"

"Yes."

"Was BB in a hurry to get somewhere?"

"She was mad."

"About what?"

"Sonny yelled at her. She yelled back. Mama always said don't make BB mad."

"What does BB look like?"

"I dunno. Like BB."

"Does she have blond or brown hair?" Melina asked.

"Blond. But it's black on top."

Melina continued with more questions until she had a fuzzy profile of a middle-aged woman with bleached-blond hair and a taste for fast cars and flashy clothes. "Who is Sonny?" she asked.

"I don't know."

"Is Sonny a boy or girl?"

"A boy."

"Did he seem to know BB?"

"Sonny is her friend."

"Was Sonny in the car when it crashed?"

"No."

"Do you know Sonny's last name? I'd like to call someone that knows you or BB."

"Don't call Sonny. He's scary."

Her lips flattened into a small grim line, and whatever sense of calm the girl had started to enjoy vanished. "That's okay. We won't call Sonny. I promise."

The girl shook her head. "Promises break."

"Not mine." Melina's clear, direct tone did not allay the child's fear. "Where is BB?"

"She had to run for help. She told me not to worry and she would be back." The girl twisted the fur on the dog's floppy ear.

"Do you know why the car wrecked?"

"BB was driving really fast."

"Did she try to stop?" Melina asked.

"I dunno. We just hit something hard."

Who left a kid in a wrecked car? BB sure as hell had not called the cops or paramedics. Melina smiled at the girl. "BB was right. Help did come. She sent me."

The girl studied her, and though there was no hint of a smile, some of the tension straining her face eased.

"I'm tired. I want to go home."

"I'll find BB, okay?"

The girl nodded.

"Until I do, you stay here with Petey and watch *SpongeBob*."

"Will you come back?" Skepticism and hope both flashed in the young gaze.

"I will be back. And remember, Elena, I always keep my promises."

The little girl's lip stuck out and trembled. "I don't believe you."

Six-year-olds should not know that kind of distrust. But too many did. Melina tugged off her watch and handed it to the girl. "Keep this for me, and you can give it to me when I get back."

"It's mine?"

"Until I get back. Then I'll need it."

Elena traced the clock's face with her small index finger. "I'm going to keep it if you don't come back."

At this stage, she did not want to ask the child about the jar of severed fingers. If the forensic team and medical examiner couldn't tell her more, then she might have to ask the child about them. "I know. You're a smart girl. But I'll be back tonight."

"Okay."

Melina patted the girl on the hand, smiling even as she pushed back fresh waves of anger and frustration. She rose, and as she turned, the girl grabbed her hand.

"See you soon, Elena," Melina said.

As she moved closer to the door, Ramsey ducked out of the room and waited for her in the hallway.

"You okay?" he asked.

"I'll be better when I get my hands on BB and Sonny." She lived for the moment when she could lock handcuffs around the wrists of scumbags like them.

Melina strode to the floor's station and asked for Elena's doctor to be paged. She and Ramsey waited less than a minute before a woman dressed in scrubs appeared. In her early thirties, she wore her blond hair in a french braid that accentuated a strong jaw. Wire-rimmed glasses magnified green eyes reflecting annoyance and fatigue.

The doctor crossed to Melina and Ramsey. "I'm Dr. Savannah Lawrence. I'm Elena's doctor."

Ramsey extended his hand and introduced himself. Melina followed suit. "Can you give us an update on the girl's health?" he asked.

"She sustained a contusion on her chest, but it was likely caused by the seat belt at the time of impact. MRI showed no head or back injuries."

"What about signs of sexual assault?" Melina asked.

Anger climbed up Dr. Lawrence's face, bringing color to an otherwise pale complexion. "I did examine her. From what I can see, she's never been sexually active."

She hoped the doctor's assessment was totally correct, and they had gotten to the girl in time.

"The police forensic technician came by earlier and took her fingerprints. Do you know more about the girl's identity?" Dr. Lawrence asked.

"The prints are still being processed," Ramsey said. "As soon as we do, we'll let you know."

Dr. Lawrence shook her head. "She's a sweet kid."

"At that age, they all are, or would be if they had a decent parent or guardian." Melina recalled her mother's stories about how she had been holy hell in the months after her adoption. It was as if she had been testing her parents' promise to raise her.

"I can keep her here a couple more days, but the hospital will discharge her once she's medically cleared. They'll need the bed. I've already placed a call to social services."

"Understood." Melina handed Dr. Lawrence a business card. "But do me a favor and don't move the girl without calling me first."

The doctor read the card and carefully tucked it in her breast pocket. "Of course."

It was not lost on Melina that Elena's story was so similar to her own. She acknowledged her instant dislike of BB and would find a way to lock it away. When the time came to interview BB, she needed to maintain distance and perspective. Her emotions could play no role in the interrogation.

After the doctor left, Melina and Ramsey walked to the elevators. He reached for his phone. "I'll text the FBI office and see if we can find the address the child gave us. I'll also have them search for the child's birth certificate and the mother's death certificate. We might get lucky."

Melina glanced at her wrist and remembered she'd left her watch with Elena. She fished out her phone and checked the time. "It's almost six thirty. The car BB was driving will be towed to the TBI forensic bay this evening and gone over tonight, but I'm not expecting much of a preliminary report until at least tomorrow morning."

"The prints from the severed fingers should be processed fairly quickly," Ramsey said, "but may take a little longer."

The medical examiner would feed the usable prints into the Automated Fingerprint Identification System, or AFIS. From there they would be cross-checked against a database containing millions of prints in a matter of hours.

"I have a couple of hours of daylight, so I'm headed back to the crash site to start knocking on doors. I'll also call Sarah and see if any of the girls on the street have any news about our guy."

"Understood. When I have an ID on the victims, I'll contact you," Ramsey said.

"Thanks." Absently, she rubbed her bare wrist adorned only by the faint tan line left by her watch.

No time for a quick session at the gym tonight, which was too bad. Nothing like driving a roundhouse kick into a punching bag to work shit out.

"Why'd you give your watch to that child?" Ramsey asked. "It looked expensive."

Her mother normally would not have been thrilled to know she had handed off her college graduation present. But given the circumstances, she'd understand. "Trust always comes with a risk."

A ghost of a smile tipped the edges of his lips, but it looked rusty. The deep lines around his mouth and the crow's-feet feathering from the corners of his eyes suggested frowning was his default expression. "You don't strike me as the trusting soul."

That coaxed the day's first and likely only real smile. "Oh, I'm not. I'd hate to lose that watch, but in the big picture, it's a small risk."

CHAPTER NINE

Monday, August 24, 7:00 p.m.

By the time Melina left the hospital, her stomach was grumbling, and she was craving a burger and fries. Some cops drank when they were stressed. Others smoked. Some worked out. Breaking a sweat did wonders for her, and it was her go-to vice. But when she could not work out, she ate. Thankfully, her fast metabolism burned through the high-fat calories found in a cop's standard takeout meal. Her metabolism still worried her mother, who warned Melina that one day she would not be able to wolf down a second burger or have a late-night bowl of ice cream.

Today it was a burger, fries, and a vanilla shake from a drive-through. She flattened the burger's wrapper in her lap, balancing the burger between her thighs as she drove to the crash site. She alternated sips of the shake with bites of burger without a second thought. Fifty percent of her intake was consumed on the go. A meal at a table with no interruptions was a thing to be cherished. At least this grub was warm and did not come from a vending machine.

She had polished off the burger and sucked on the straw—always important to end the meal on a sweet note—as she pulled onto the correct side of Cox Road.

Ramsey had made a wrong turn and ended up on the other side. Had BB done the same, but was traveling too fast?

She drove to the crash site. The car had been towed away, and all that remained were the red flares that had burned down to black ash. She shut off the car and stepped outside.

The air was thick with a coiling humidity, and the evening sun still tipped the mercury well over ninety degrees. The summer heat in Nashville could be brutal. Most visitors pictured the cooler temperatures of the Smoky Mountains, which were a couple of hours east.

She shrugged off her jacket and tossed it on her driver's seat before locking the car door. The fresh strand of yellow crime scene tape stood still in the motionless air.

She ducked under the tape and looked again for skid marks. There appeared to be none. BB had been rushing. Maybe worried about her encounter with Sonny? Had she been talking on the phone? Yelling at Elena? Distracted by the jar in the trunk? Whatever was going through her mind, she had not seen what was coming.

She reached the edge of the woods and looked back. Twenty feet away she spotted very faint tire marks. Melina walked heel to toe along the length of the faint skid mark. Less than ten feet long. This had not been a frantic stop.

She studied the distance to the woods. It was maybe twenty feet. There were equations that could determine how fast the car had been traveling based on the distance and the damage to the car.

Mr. Brewer, her ninth-grade math teacher, had always warned her that there were real-world applications for algebra and geometry. His terse you-will-be-sorry lectures had not motivated her beyond a B minus, but now she might concede she owed the guy an apology.

She got in her car, pulled around, and nosed the front of her car toward the marks. Guessing that BB might have been rushing, she punched the gas until her speed reached forty miles an hour. When she reached the existing tire marks, she hit her brakes, stopped.

She parked her car on the side of the road, got out, and walked to the tire impression she had made. Next, she studied the tread left presumably by BB. They were almost identical, suggesting BB had been traveling at about forty miles an hour. It was not an excessive amount of speed, and she had stopped well short of the woods. There was no way she could not have seen the dead end.

Maybe she had been spooked. Maybe she was being followed and knew she could not turn back. Cornered, she had chanced driving through the woods, never expecting the tree trunk.

She looked down the tree-lined street to the houses. Had BB been visiting someone on the street?

She walked to the end of the skid marks and nudged the burned-out police flare with the tip of her boot. She followed the tire marks off the road into tall grass and surrounding stumps. From the road, she could understand why someone desperate to get away would try to cross it when the other side was visible one hundred feet away.

Pushing through waist-high grass and scrub, she followed the tent markers left by the forensic tech and trailing BB's escape. Sweat collected between her breasts and shoulder blades. She shoved up her sleeves and kept walking.

It took almost a minute before she reached the final yellow marker. She found herself standing on the cul-de-sac where Ramsey had dead-ended earlier. This street, like the one on the other side, cut through a middle-class neighborhood made up of small clapboard homes.

Unless someone had seen BB running or a security camera had picked up her escape, she was in the wind.

Time to knock on doors. She picked the first house on the right. There was a blue Chevrolet parked in the driveway. The house was one level and had an exterior porch running its length. There was a planter filled with bright-yellow pansies. Both the yard and house were well cared for. The porch was swept and the windows clean. This person was meticulous, which made them a better witness candidate. She rang the bell.

Inside the house, the steady clip of footsteps drew closer before the door snapped open. The woman standing on the other side of the screened door appeared to be in her late sixties. She wore a floral sleeveless dress, and her gray hair was pulled back into a neat ponytail.

"May I help you?" The woman's rusty voice was laced with a deep Tennessee drawl.

Melina held up her badge. "My name is Agent Melina Shepard. I'm with the Tennessee Bureau of Investigation. There was a car accident nearby, and I was hoping you'd let me ask you a few questions."

"I'm Caroline White. I spoke to the Nashville police this morning. I didn't have much to say."

"Did the officer ask you about the accident?"

"He did. I saw the police sirens and lights. Sounded like it was quite a big fuss. We have cars get fooled by Cox Road all the time. Both sides were supposed to be connected, but the folks on either end protested, myself included, because we didn't want it to turn into a speedway, which is exactly what it would be. Anyway, there are maps that show it connects."

"Ms. White, were you home this morning?"

Ms. White pushed open the screened door. "I was. But why don't you come in so I can pour you a glass of water or tea? It's blazing hot out here, and you look like you're about to burn up."

"Thank you, ma'am." She stepped inside, cool air chilling her skin as she scanned the small living room. It was decorated in a kind of country charm decor that included overstuffed furniture, lots of ruffled pillows, and more pictures of children and grandchildren than she could count. All these kids had plump faces and wide grins. The images stood in stark contrast to Elena's drawn features.

She looked toward a kitchen as she also noted there was a hallway to her right. "Do you live alone?"

"I do," she said as she waved Melina toward the kitchen. "I've been in this house for thirty-six years. My Silas and I raised our four children here."

The air-conditioning was still cooling her skin as Melina walked into the kitchen. A pot rack hung over a small island made of the same brown wood as the cabinets. Most of the beige countertops were covered with rows of cookbooks, an Elvis cookie jar, and an assortment of appliances.

Ms. White offered Melina water or tea, and Melina opted for the former. When she accepted the glass and drank, she was amazed how good it tasted. "Thanks. That hit the spot."

"Good. Got to take care of our police."

"Did you hear the accident?"

"I might have. I had the news on, but I didn't have my hearing aids in yet. The television was turned up. Used to drive my husband nuts but he's gone, so I turn it up as loud as I want now. Anyway, I thought I heard a thump around 11:00 a.m. I should have gone to look, but they were doing a story on the Prince and Princess of Wales and I do love that British royalty."

"You didn't see anyone run past?"

"No, I didn't, but I can tell you that Jordie Tanner across the street has one of those security cameras."

"On his doorbell?"

"No, Jordie has a camera in his trees. He points it right at the cul-de-sac. We've had kids park down there, and they can create quite a fuss."

Melina set her empty glass on the island, pulled her notebook from her back pocket, and jotted down the man's name. "Do you know if the officer spoke to Jordie?"

"I'm sure he knocked on his door, but Jordie is a long-haul trucker and he won't be back in town for a couple of days. I didn't think about the camera in his tree until just now. I should have told the officer, but it completely slipped my mind."

"Do you have Jordie's phone number?"

"Sure." She walked to a wall-mounted phone. Taped to the wall beside it was a list of numbers. "Ready?"

"Shoot." As Ms. White recited the number, Melina scribbled it down. "Great. I'll give him a call today."

She tucked her notebook back in her back pocket. "Thank you for the water. I want to get across the street and have a look at the camera. Anyone else on the street who might have seen the accident?"

"That, I don't know. I'm the only one on the block who's retired. Most of these folks work jobs that get them up and out the door before the sun. Many take overtime or work a second shift."

"Thank you again," Melina said.

"Of course, honey. Stop by anytime."

When Melina stepped out into the heat, it felt twice as hot and thick as it had moments ago. Amazing what your body could become accustomed to in such a short amount of time.

She jogged across the street into Jordie Tanner's yard and looked up into the trees until she spotted the camera. It was painted green and brown and reminded her of the cameras used by hunters to monitor game. She took a few pictures with her phone and then, with her line of sight, followed the angle of the lens. If BB had come running through this area, that camera had caught her.

As she walked back to her car, she dialed Jordie's number. The call went to voicemail. She left her information and asked him to return her call as soon as possible.

She knocked on four more doors, but as Ms. White had suggested, no one was at home. An hour after, the sky had fully darkened as she headed back to the other side of Cox Road. Then she knocked on more doors but noted the local officer had left his card wedged in several of them.

By the time she was behind the wheel, her skin was broiling. The car's AC first blew out only hot air as it cranked up, so she kept her car door open until it slowly cooled off the interior and her. She sat and reached for her phone. Curious about Agent Jerrod Ramsey, she typed his name into the search engine. She had been intrigued by the guy since she had seen him waiting for her in the TBI's lobby. Tall, dark, and imposing.

Ramsey had left few digital footprints. Not surprising. She was careful about that as well. Piecing together the bits of information, she learned he had been with the FBI for almost fifteen years and now headed up a team that worked a variety of violent crime cases across the country. Most recent included a series of cold cases near Austin, Texas; in the Blue Ridge Mountains of Virginia; and in his own backyard of Alexandria, Virginia.

She found only two images of him, and both were official FBI portraits. He looked like he had ten years ago, only his face had filled out a little and there was now some gray hair.

There was nothing about the man or his personal life. Made perfect sense. A guy like that did not want nor did he need the attention.

Habit again had her glancing toward the watch that was not there. She dialed the hospital and spoke to the charge nurse, who reported that Elena had had no visitors. She thanked the nurse, turned the car around, and pressed the accelerator.

"BB, you didn't just vanish, girlfriend. Someone saw your ass running from that accident, and it's a matter of time before I catch you."

As she approached the stop sign, her phone rang. She saw Ramsey's name on her phone. "Yes, sir."

"Please, no *sir*." Normally, his voice was rough like sandpaper rubbing against wood. Nothing like the polished suit, tie, and shoes that cost more than she had spent on rent last month. This time, he sounded almost chagrined by the title.

"Sorry. Force of habit. I just canvassed the homes on Cox. Located a security camera and have put a call in to the owner but for now, nothing."

"We'll definitely want that camera footage."

"I'm on it."

"I'm at the medical examiner's office. Can you stop by?"

The state medical examiner and the Tennessee Bureau of Investigation offices were on the same campus and were less than a few blocks apart.

"I'm about fifteen minutes out. Have you pulled prints?"

"We have been able to get readable prints on two of the fingers so far, and they have been submitted to AFIS. Hope to have an identification when you arrive."

A jolt of excitement zipped through her like it always did when a piece of the puzzle fell into place. Having the name of a victim would likely tell them something about the killer and maybe lead them to BB. "I'm on my way."

CHAPTER TEN

Monday, August 24, 9:00 p.m.

Ramsey did not need to see Agent Melina Shepard to know she was approaching the autopsy suite. Her defined footsteps, like her voice and mannerisms, were clear and direct. Even the slight southern accent that wove through her husky tones was not willowy or soft but strong and sharp like barbed wire.

Her face and body were angled and honed but with enough curves to turn heads. She might not have noticed the men at the crime scene stealing glances at her, but he had. If she had caught them, her direct stare, which had a way of dissecting layer by layer, would have challenged them until they had the good sense to look away.

The one time her expression had softened had been when she had spoken to Elena. Then, genuine concern and empathy had warmed her voice. Most cops, especially those with children, could not escape the emotions of an injured child. Whether she had a kid, or she had been hurt as a child, she'd had a real connection to Elena.

Shepard rounded the corner. She still wore the dark jacket over a fitted blouse, long black slacks, booted heels, and her badge clipped to her belt. Her olive skin had a faint glow of sun likely picked up while canvassing the neighborhood.

"Agent Ramsey," she said. "Secured an identification yet?"

No small talk. Which in all honesty, he did appreciate. Talking about the weather, music, or whatever bullshit people filled the airways with at times like this never sat well with him. Shepard did not play politics. She simply did not care whose feelings got hurt. That was noble but shortsighted if she had any ambitions to rise through the ranks.

He understood strategy and looked upon office politics like a necessary evil. He was good at it. And for that, he was able to get whatever his team needed.

"We now have two identified," he said. "The doctor has given us the use of his conference room. I can brief you, and then we can meet with him."

"Perfect." She moved away from him and opened the conference room door in her habitually expedient way. She flipped on the lights and crossed to a small refrigerator and plucked out two bottled waters. As he entered the room, she held one up for him, but when he declined with a shake of his head, she replaced it. She twisted off the top and was drinking greedily as she sat.

He took a seat and pulled the tablet from his briefcase. "I've been in contact with my agents at Quantico, who fast-tracked the identification of the prints."

She removed a notebook and a pen from the backpack slung over her shoulder. "I suppose we're lucky this killer opted to save fingers and not ears. And why ring fingers?"

"Other than the obvious symbolism of love and romance?" Ramsey asked.

"Left ring finger is supposed to be a direct line to the heart."

"It's not a random choice, Agent Shepard."

"He's arrogant or a fool. Otherwise why save such telling evidence?"

"He preserved mementos precisely because they can be easily identified."

"Taunting the law?"

"I think so."

"Jesus." She shook her head, then finished off the bottle. "What do you have?"

He pulled up emails from Agent Andrea "Andy" Jamison, who worked on the ViCAP database. "These are from Andy Jamison at the bureau. She tracks monsters with her computer."

"That's efficient."

"Andy is good at her job. When I told her that we have six severed fingers, she dug into her database and found one hit immediately." The ViCAP system relied on local law enforcement to input the data from their local violent crimes.

"Does she have any cases involving missing ring fingers?"

"No cases submitted with that particular detail. If this killer moved from jurisdiction to jurisdiction, a cop might not find it odd enough to bother with a ViCAP application."

Shepard frowned. "I get it. Especially if it's a small locality with minimal staff."

"Andy identified Cindy Patterson, age thirty-eight, as one of the victims who has an arrest record. Patterson was murdered December 2007. She vanished after a concert at the arena in Kansas City, Missouri. According to statements, her friends saw her leaving the venue about 11:00 p.m., and she was walking toward a parking garage. She insisted she was meeting her date and would be fine."

"Did they ever ID the date?"

"No. None of her friends reported ever meeting the guy. He apparently was from out of town, and Cindy hooked up with him in a bar. Bottom line, she never made it to her car, which was found by police in the parking garage after she had been reported missing."

Shepard tapped the side of the empty plastic bottle. "Was her body found?"

"Two days after Patterson vanished, the area was hit by a wicked ice storm that dropped two inches on the area. Over a quarter of a million homes and businesses were without power with downed trees everywhere."

"Meaning the search didn't really get off the ground."

Ramsey heard the frustration in Shepard's voice. "Delayed at best. Nothing really thawed out until the following spring, when her body was found thirty miles outside of the town. Remains were badly decomposed, but the medical examiner did get DNA from the teeth that eventually identified Patterson."

"Were the police able to determine if the ring finger was missing? Out in the open, animal activity does a number on a body."

"The remains were badly compromised. We might not have connected Cindy to this if not for her arrest record."

"What was she arrested for?" Shepard asked.

He pulled up the mug shot. Cindy had been blond, with blue eyes and a long narrow face. Full lips turned down in a frown. "Drug dealing and fraud."

"She wasn't a Girl Scout, which meant she also wasn't on anyone's priority list."

"Medical examiner was able to find the hyoid bone in the neck and determined it was broken."

"Although strangulation isn't quick or easy, it's personal and doesn't leave ballistics traces."

"Cindy's sister, Robin, stayed in contact with police and tried to keep the case active," Ramsey said.

"But it's impossible to compete with the growing caseloads and budget constraints."

"Exactly."

"We get to tell Robin Patterson her sister was murdered by a serial killer." She rose and grabbed another water from the refrigerator. One quick twist and the bottle top opened. "Anyone else in Cindy's life other than that mystery date who might have been a suspect?"

"She ran with a rough crowd according to her file." And as Shepard sat down, he said, "There's a second identification. Her name is Nina Hall, age thirty-nine."

"Maybe we'll get lucky and see a connection between the two women."

"That might be difficult. The victim was last seen in Portland, Oregon, in November 2009 leaving a popular nightspot called Sugar."

"Our boy has a thing for musicians?"

"Maybe." He pulled up her picture, revealing a blond woman with a round face, bright smile, and sparkling eyes.

"He likes blondes?" she queried.

"Perhaps. Two is enough to hint at a pattern, but not enough to confirm it. Nina Hall was the same age, height, and build as Cindy. And like Cindy, she vanished from a gathering of friends after midnight."

"Was she found in a field?"

"No, in her own bathtub." He swiped to a collection of crime scene photos. She leaned forward. Her eyes narrowed as she studied the woman lying in her tub, head tipped back, dull eyes peering out of drooping lids. Her left hand draped over the side sans the ring finger.

"There isn't a tremendous amount of blood," Shepard observed. She widened the image with the swipe of her fingers and enlarged the woman's neck. "She was strangled. Her heart stopped beating, and when the finger was removed postmortem, only a small amount of blood was involved."

"Correct. The single amputation struck the local homicide detective as odd, and he made a note in the file. He even called around to other jurisdictions in his state and asked if they'd seen a similar case. The general consensus was no, so he didn't submit a case to ViCAP."

"He was assuming this killer only operated in Oregon."

"It's flawed logic. But nothing to be done about it now."

Drawing in a breath, she sat back. "Which leaves us with several women yet to be identified."

A knock on the door had them both shifting attention from the tablet to the newest arrival, Dr. Josh Connor. Tall and lanky with a runner's build, Connor was in his midthirties and had a pleasant face. Brown hair offset inquisitive green eyes.

Shepard rose and extended her hand. "Agent Melina Shepard. We met last year. I was working a child abduction case."

The doctor wrapped long fingers around her hand, studying her face a beat. "I remember. Tough case. Father was involved."

"He was convicted and sentenced to fifty years. Too bad it couldn't have been longer."

"That's what hell is for," Dr. Connor said.

"I'd rather not wait for hell," Shepard said. "Justice in this world is far more satisfying."

Ramsey agreed but kept his thoughts to himself.

Back in the autopsy suite, an overhead examination light shone down on a stainless steel table that butted up against a station equipped with a sink, a series of swing spouts, hoses, and electrical outlets. Lying on the counter was a sterilized blue pad and an open pack of autopsy equipment including scalpels, bone cutters, scissors, a basin, and a bone saw. A full complement to dismantle a body.

Normally, there was a sheet covering the body. Today, it was a disposable blue pad covering six wrinkled ring fingers lined up in a neat row.

Dr. Connor handed out latex gloves, and once he'd donned his pair, he pulled back the covering. The strong scent of formaldehyde lifted into the air. The fingers looked remarkably small.

Dr. Connor knitted his hands together. "As we all know, six examples of digitus medicinalis, or fourth fingers. They're all from left hands." He picked up the first finger and pointed the severed edge toward the light. "Note that the skin and bone are slightly pinched, but the actual bone is smooth. This suggests something sharp, perhaps bolt cutters, which compress and then slice. If the killer had used a different implement, such as a saw, it would have left a much different impression."

"More jagged," Shepard said.

"Exactly." Dr. Connor held out the finger. "This kind of clean cut would also have required some strength. A weaker person would have worked the handle of the cutters repeatedly, leaving more tears and marks."

"Our killer is a physically strong man," Shepard said.

"I'd say so," Dr. Connor said.

Ramsey inspected the severed digit. Over the years he had seen dozens of ways humans could mutilate and dismember each other. The only way to professionally process and then proceed was to remain distant from the fact it was a human.

The doctor placed the finger back in its original position on the table.

"Symbolically, the right hand is considered the physical hand and has greater visibility," Ramsey said. "The left hand represents character and beliefs. Romantic promise. Chastity."

"Isn't there usually a sexual element with serial killers?" Shepard asked.

"In most cases, yes," Ramsey replied. "And if not sexual, gratification is attained through the victim's suffering or death."

"This guy has a complex with the ladies," she challenged. He could see her cheeks flush as if she were trying to control her temper. Most would not have noticed the subtle change, but he did. "What kind of sexual fantasy expresses itself this way?"

"It's important not to prejudge," Ramsey said. "If you get angry, it could cloud your judgment."

"Funny, I find anger fuels me," she said.

"Anger is easy," Ramsey said carefully. "Dispassion takes practice."

Shepard shoved out a sigh. "You're saying if our killer quacks like a duck and walks like a duck, he might not be a duck?"

"If you mean he's not sexually motivated, then yes."

"Fair enough." She shifted her attention back to the doctor. "Which two fingers belong to Cindy and Nina?"

"Cindy Patterson's is the one I just showed you," Dr. Connor said. "And Nina Hall's is the one to the right of it."

"And the other four?" she asked. "What can you tell me about them?"

"The next three appear to be a little more recent. Maybe in the last five or six years. And the last finger is very recent, as in the last couple of weeks."

Shepard rocked back on her heels. "Could it be Christina Sanchez?" she asked. "According to Elena, her mother just died."

"I don't know," Dr. Connor said.

"Hopefully we have a missing persons case on file. Were all the fingers removed postmortem?" Shepard asked.

"Yes," Dr. Connor said.

Shepard reached for her cell phone. "Though two similar victims are not enough to establish a firm pattern, we can still reference their profiles. Given that set of guidelines, we're looking for a deceased Caucasian female, potentially blond and in her late thirties."

"Can't speak to the hair color, but age sounds right," Dr. Connor said. "I can tell you this office has had no female victims that were brought in with missing fingers for as long as I can remember."

"If the victim hasn't been brought here, then area cops don't know about her either. Doesn't mean there wasn't a missing persons report filed." As Shepard tapped the phone against her thigh, it chimed with a text. She glanced at the number and frowned. "Excuse me." She opened the phone. Agent Shepard, this is Richard Barnard, Elena Sanchez's caseworker. The hospital wants to release her by Wednesday to one of my foster families. Call me at your convenience.

She read the text aloud, straightening her shoulders and rolling her head from side to side. If he had not been paying attention, he would have missed a series of expressions implying distaste for social services. As a cop, she clearly understood foster care was a better alternative than BB. However, he believed she personally loathed the option.

"The girl needs to be with people who can care for her," he said.

"I realize that." She shoved her phone in her pocket and refocused on their case. "Anything else you can tell us about these women?" Shepard asked.

"Not at this time," Dr. Connor said.

"You identified two. That's a start," she said. "We have two families to notify. Maybe when we talk to them, we'll discover more information about the women." She ripped off her gloves and tossed them in the trash can. "Thanks, Doc." Without another word she walked out of the suite and into the hallway.

Dr. Connor shook his head. "She's upset."

"She's not upset. She's pissed."

"How do you know?"

"Death notifications put cops in a foul mood."

***

As Melina stared out the large glass window that overlooked the parking lot and the rolling land beyond it, she pulled in a couple of deep breaths. What she would not give for a few rounds in the ring right now. She just wanted to pound something.

The autopsy suite door opened behind her, and she heard Ramsey's steady, methodical footsteps. If she had to wager, she would bet the guy had ice water in his veins. He studied everything with such an exquisite detachment that she found herself envying him.

"Were you ever in foster care?" he asked.

That one-two punch of a question brought her thoughts into sharp focus. "Where'd that come from?"

"I'll take that as a yes?"

"It's a none-of-your-damned-business kind of response."

"A yes."

She readied a couple of verbal jabs but caught herself. Agent Ramsey was the senior officer, and the last thing she needed was a pissing match with him. "I was only in for a couple of weeks, but that was enough."

"How old were you?"

"I was five."

"Almost the same age as Elena."

"Yeah."

"Where were your biological parents?"

He had the good sense not to refer to whomever had brought her into this world as Mom and Dad. Those titles she reserved exclusively for the Shepards.

"I have no idea. My mother left me on the side of a dirt road about twenty miles outside of Nashville in the middle of November."

"Who found you?"

"Local sheriff."

"What are the chances?"

"Pretty damn slim. But he found me." She remembered the cold and the fear burrowing into her bones. She'd hated crying, even then, but she could not stop bawling as she'd stared up and down that dark road. And then there had been the sight of headlights. All in the space of a second, hope had collided with terror. What if it hadn't been her mother coming back for her? Even then, she'd understood not to trust everyone.

She often looked back and wondered how she could have missed that monster who had given birth to her. But a child, alone and afraid, would have given anything to be back with the devil she knew.

"And he turned you over to foster care."

"Yeah. What I didn't realize was that he went home and told his wife about me, and the next day the two were at the courthouse petitioning the judge to release me into their custody. A day later, they picked me up."

"Elena's case touches a nerve."

"You could say that." She managed a slight grin. "But don't worry. I'm dialed in. I'll find BB, the killer obsessed with fingers, and the Key Killer, even if it means turning over every rock in Nashville."

***

It was nine thirty when BB arrived at the East Nashville bar. She was glad for its stale, smoky air and the scent of booze. Her body ached as she angled her lean frame around the tables and sat in a back corner booth. A sigh leaked over her lips as she relaxed back against the worn red leather. She had been lying in her motel room for the last several hours and could no longer stand the four walls. They were starting to remind her of prison.

She raised her hand, motioning to the gray-haired, tatted bartender with a smile. She adjusted her silk top and reached for lipstick in her purse.

He looked her way as he finished wiping down the bar and then signaled a waitress to the table.

"What'll it be?" the woman asked.

"Bourbon. Neat, sugar," she said. "Your bartender is going to be pouring a lot tonight."

"You got it."

She glanced in a small compact mirror and smoothed on fresh pink lipstick. She had screwed up, but that did not mean she had to look the part. Smoothing her blond hair back with manicured fingers, she pressed her lips together.

Aching ribs told her the damn airbag had left her chest bruised and battered. She fished out a bottle of aspirin from her purse as the bartender set her bourbon in front of her. "Thanks, doll. Might as well get me another round."

"That kind of day?" It was a halfhearted attempt at conversation that she had heard one too many times.

"You have no idea." She winked, popped the aspirin in her mouth, and chased it with a gulp of bourbon. The blend burned her throat, and she would have coughed if her damn ribs hadn't hurt so bad. But as the fire subsided, soothing warmth began to spread through her body.

"Sonny, what the hell have you been doing?" she muttered.

She gulped down what remained in the glass. The second glass arrived right on its heels. This time she sipped. She stared into the amber liquid. Neon lights from the front window sign reflected in the tawny drink as she tipped the glass slowly from side to side.

Hitting that stump had been a stupid mistake. She'd had no idea it and a dozen of its friends were hiding in the tall grass, waiting to pounce on the dumbass who thought she could run the gauntlet. But she had been rattled. Images of the pickle jar flashed in her mind. What the hell kind of monster had Sonny turned into?

BB's hand trembled slightly as she raised the edge of her blouse. The initial redness on her belly was turning blue. Fucking stump.

"Shit." BB pulled out a packet of smokes from her purse. Lighting the tip of one, she inhaled deeply, savoring the burn in her lungs.

When she had seen him face to face a couple of days ago, she had been startled by how big he had become. He had always been tall, but now he was muscular, and any hints of the boy she had known were gone.

"I told you when you called last week that I didn't want to see you," Sonny said.

"Honey, that hurts. After all we've been through." She had always been able to sweet-talk him. *"I want to make things right between us."*

"Get out. I don't ever want to see you again. And stop calling me." He looked as if he was going to hit her, but Elena called out from the car. He looked past her to the child and stilled.

"I want us to be a family."

He blinked and shook his head. "Go!"

Irritated, she spoke before she really thought. "I'm not giving up on you, Sonny. You and me and the kid can be a family."

That seemed to piss him off. "You're not my family."

"We are family. Give me the key so I can get the money out of the safety-deposit box. Once we have that, we can do anything."

He shook his head, a bitter smile twisting his lips. "You came for the money."

"I came for you."

"Really? Well, I threw out the key."

A smile tugged the edge of her lips. "You never throw out anything. Especially stuff I give you. Still have that gold key chain I bought you in Reno the night you got your cherry popped?"

Hints of color rose in his cheeks, and he shoved her back. "Fuck off, BB."

"BB!" Elena shouted.

The kid had gotten out of the car and followed her. "I'm right here, baby."

As Elena came closer, Sonny looked as if he'd seen a ghost. "Who the hell is that?"

BB smiled. The kid was the trump card she would play next. She wrapped her arms around the girl's thin shoulders. "Elena."

"Elena?" he said softly.

"Looks just like the other little girl we both loved. Remember?"

Sonny stumbled back, his gaze locking on the child. "Go away."

"My key, please."

He slammed the door in her face.

BB and the kid had found a motel and cooled their heels for a couple of days. That gave her time to figure out Sonny's habits and schedules. On the third day, when he left for work, she broke into his house.

As a kid, Sonny had had a habit of hiding his money in his shoes. She went straight to his closet and searched among the high-dollar country-western boots. She quickly found a few hundred bucks rubber banded around several credit cards shoved in a boot. Shuffling through the cards, she realized none had his name on them. Ol' Sonny was stealing just like Mama BB had taught him. It made her proud.

She'd been pocketing the cards when she had spotted the jar. One look at the grisly contents, and she'd known Sonny was far more dangerous than she had realized.

She ground her cigarette into an ashtray. The bartender brought over another drink, and she gulped it down in one swallow. "I like your style, baby. I'll take another."

"I'll need a card to keep this tab running."

She handed him a credit card. "There you go, doll."

As the booze soothed her nerves, her thoughts slowed so that she could process them.

She had wiped the car clean of her prints, so the chances of a cop identifying her quickly were slim to none. She had wiped the jar down as soon as she'd placed it in her trunk. And if she had not been in such a damned panic after the crash, she would have taken it with her. The little trinkets were her path back to the key.

Leaving Elena behind had not been a choice but a necessity. There was no way she could drag her own battered body away from the wreck and have a kid in tow.

Jesus, that kid could scream.

Elena was a pain in the ass, but BB liked her. The girl was tough and was going to be a ballbuster one day.

It was not like she had abandoned Elena or left her to face a pack of wolves. As she'd fled through the tall grass and shrubs, the distant sound of police sirens had mingled with the kid's cries. The cops would see her right away and take her to the hospital to get checked out. There might be a foster home, but BB would find a way to track the kid. She no longer had the jar, but if she could get the kid, there still might be a chance to trade with Sonny.

When she reached the bottom of her glass, she was tempted to order another drink. She pushed the glass away and asked the bartender for the tab. Drunks got sloppy and ended up in jail.

The bartender brought her a slip to sign. The card had worked. Hopefully she would get a few more hours' use out of it before it popped as stolen.

The bartender picked up the slip, glanced at the tip, and smiled. "Thanks, Dee."

A crooked grin tipped the edges of her lips as she freshened her pink lipstick. "No, thank you, baby."

CHAPTER ELEVEN

Monday, August 24, 11:00 p.m.

Fear had been a part of Sonny for as long as he could remember.

As a small boy, he was always terrified that his world would shatter. Day after day, he would conjure imagined scenarios that cast him alone in an empty, cold house or running down a dark, lonely road, chasing headlights that vanished into the night.

The last few days had been particularly jarring. It should have been business as usual, but the foundation under his feet was crumbling.

A girlfriend had once announced he had abandonment issues as she packed her things and left his house for good. She accused him of holding on too tight. That he needed to trust. "Not everyone is out to screw you over," she had screamed as she'd slammed the door on her way out.

But she had been wrong. Hell, his last girlfriend, Jennifer, had left him not even a week ago. He had moved on, of course, but as he sat in the tub with his new girl, Tammy, he made a point to savor this perfect moment, which he knew would not last.

In the background, the country music playlist finished the last of twenty songs and reset to the first song. Roger Miller snapped his fingers in a steady beat, strummed his guitar strings, and launched into "King of the Road." The smooth melody conjured memories of riding down back roads in a blue Cadillac, top down, with the sun warming his face as his outstretched hand tried to catch the wind blowing over his fingertips. But today, he resented the uncomfortable reminder that his time was up. Time to move on. Nothing lasts forever.

The bathwater was turning cold, and the light was fading. The tall candles had melted down to nubs, leaving only a faint glow and a puddle of wax pooled on the vanity. He shifted and tightened his hold around her soft, supple shoulders as he pulled her closer to him. "It's time."

She was silent. Undaunted by the chilling waters. He knew she enjoyed it as much as he did. Maybe more.

He leaned her forward, rose out of the tub, and stepped onto the ice-blue bath mat that matched the towels on the rack and the paint on the wall. He gently laid her back against the edge of the tub and smoothed her blond hair off her face.

The music's novice chords of A, D, E, A, A, D, E repeated as the song rolled on like a trucker's wheels.

Nothing lasted forever.

He dried off and dressed in dark jeans, a V-neck sweater, and worn cowboy boots that he had bought in Kansas City thirteen years ago. He glanced back at the woman with her arched back, which exposed the delicate curve of her neck. So beautiful.

"I know you want me to stay, baby," he whispered.

Silent, Tammy ignored him. He had seen the same look on Jennifer's face.

Sighing, he reached in a small duffel and pulled out a favorite pair of bolt cutters. The sharp tip of the shears caught the fading candlelight.

He knelt by the tub and gently removed Tammy's hand from the water. "I want to remember you, like this, forever."

His fingers skimmed over the slim wrist. The pulse that had beaten so furiously when he had first met her had stopped. She felt no more fear. She no longer had to make the rent or worry about her ex finding a prettier version of her or about her crap boss pinching her ass when no one was looking. He had released her of her burdens.

Carefully, he dried off Tammy's fingers. They were long and sensual. Her nails were beautifully manicured and painted a dark blue. "You have lovely hands. It was one of the things I noticed about you."

Sonny reached for the bolt cutters and angled the sharp edges on either side of her naked ring finger. He drew in a deep breath and then with a hard squeeze clamped the handles closed. The blades cut through the flesh and bone, snipping the finger off in one neat cut. The finger fell to the ground beside his knee.

There was little blood. Her heart had stopped pumping hours ago.

He gently laid the hand on the surface of the water and watched as a fine ribbon of blood followed the fingers to the tub's porcelain bottom.

He fished a plastic bag from his duffel and placed his new trophy inside. He rose and leaned forward to kiss the woman on her lips.

"I'm sorry I can't stay," he said. "Darlin', it's been real nice."

As the dimming candles flickered lazily on the blue walls, he rose and wiped down all the surfaces he might have touched before he grabbed his duffel bag and placed his trophy inside. He picked up his iPod, waiting until Miller sang his last note before turning the device off and shoving it in his pocket. Her chin had dipped forward as her torso had begun to slump closer to the water.

Sonny left her house and drove home. As he made his way through the streets, he felt relaxed and unhurried. The killing always brought a rare, if fleeting, sense of peace. Though the serenity would not last forever, he took comfort knowing that today would be with both of them forever.

He had absorbed her fear and then her last breath. His face had been the last she had looked upon. What they had shared was rarer and more intimate than sex. They were one.

He walked through the small house and into the kitchen. He opened the refrigerator and pulled out a beer. He popped the top and took a long drink. He foraged in a cabinet and found a bag of potato chips. Taking both, he walked into a small den, clicked on the television to a game show host declaring he had a winner.

Sonny grinned. He felt the same way.

CHAPTER TWELVE

Tuesday, August 25, 6:00 a.m.

Melina had slept like shit. After she had knocked off work, she had gone by the hospital to see Elena. Although the child was sleeping, she had sat with her awhile.

When her head hit the pillow at 2:00 a.m., she spent the next two hours staring at the ceiling. When sleep did come, she dreamed about deserted roads, cold, and fear.

Finally, at five she rose, showered, and made a strong cup of coffee. When Wild Kitty scratched at the back door, she made a plate of albacore tuna and sat out on the patio drinking coffee while the cat ate. Through the fence, she heard her neighbor call for his cat. Neither she nor Wild Kitty spoke up.

She checked her phone. No updates from Ramsey on the Key Killer or Mr. Ring Finger. She should not expect one, but that did not stop her from checking twice more. She read the local news on her phone, and when the cat finished eating and left, she collected the plate and went inside.

By the time she had dressed, it was after six and she had headed to the office.

As she crossed her apartment parking lot, she noted the collection of three cigarette butts by her car. She had made a point to park in a different spot. And again, the lady with the pink lipstick had chosen to stand by her car and smoke.

The beauty of being a cop was that her natural suspicions could be satisfied fairly easily. She fished a latex glove from her pocket and picked up the butts, carefully wrapping them up.

When she arrived at the office complex, most of the individual office doors were open, and she could hear the tap of keys on keyboards mingling with hushed conversations. Ramsey was already set up in the conference room working.

Fatigue scraped her nerves and sent her in search of more coffee to make her more fit to be around humans. Coffee first. Ramsey could wait.

But as she passed the conference room, he rose and opened the door. "Mr. Piper is ready with an update."

She kept walking. "Let me grab a second cup of coffee, and I'll be right there."

After Melina tanked up her to-go cup, she saw Ramsey waiting in the hallway. Silent, she followed, sipping as they cut across to the forensic lab. After showing their badges, they rode the elevator down to the first floor, where the crashed car had been towed.

In the open bay on a concrete floor, the mangled metal appeared more snarled and torn than it had on the street. Distracted by Elena and the jar, Melina had not fully absorbed the extent of the damage.

The center of the front grill and fender was bent, and the frame was angled out of alignment. The front passenger side was scraped, and the hood was crumpled.

"I'll say it again," she said. "I can't believe BB was able to run."

"Adrenaline was pumping. And given the surprise in the trunk, BB didn't want to talk to the cops."

The echo of footsteps brought their attention around to a young woman in her early thirties. She was tall and slim with short light-blond hair. Sharp gray eyes stared out from behind thick-rimmed glasses.

"Agents Ramsey and Shepard, I presume?" the woman asked. When both showed their badges, she thrust out her hand. "I'm Agent Henrietta Wagner. Henri to the crew around here. Matt worked until about 5:00 a.m. and has run home for a shower. But I've been working with him along the way."

After an exchange of a few pleasantries, Henri walked them to the front of the car. "Not the worst crash I've seen. If the vehicle had struck the tree on the driver's side, she or he would have been more seriously injured. But as luck would have it, this individual's side of the vehicle was fairly intact."

"Too bad. It would have saved us the chase," Melina said.

"I've spent the last couple of hours dusting the car for prints, and needless to say I've pulled many. However, as we learned at the crime scene, none were pulled from the steering wheel or any of the normal places you would expect the driver to touch. But as Agent Ramsey suggested, we did dust the car seat and pulled up several good impressions from the side and the back buckle. Prints were fed into AFIS about an hour ago, so we are hoping for some kind of hit."

Henri walked them over to a table filled with a variety of belongings that Melina recognized from her earlier look in the trunk. "Whoever packed the trunk used every available square inch."

"Their entire life was in that trunk," Melina said. She walked along the edge of the table, looking at the contents of one of the suitcases: eight sets of high-heeled shoes, sparkling tops and dresses, and a collection of black and red lace underwear.

"Looks like it. The driver enjoyed high heels, designer jeans, and sequins. There was also a stash of credit cards in one of the bags. They were all reported stolen. There was also a sling and a cane."

"Our driver is a grifter or con artist," Melina said.

"And likely has an arrest record," Ramsey said.

Henri received a text. "Looks like you're right. Our driver does have an arrest record. Just got back the AFIS results. Her name is Bonnie Lynn Guthrie. She's fifty-nine years old and was born in Dallas, Texas." She tapped on a link and turned the phone toward them. "This mug shot was taken in 2014. Arrested for credit card fraud and possession of heroin in Ventura County, California. After the fifth arrest, she was sentenced to ten years in prison. California cut her loose after five years, time served. She's been out on parole the last year."

"Has she checked in with her PO recently?" Ramsey asked.

"She missed her last appointment with her parole officer. Until then, she had checked in faithfully," she said. "His contact info is in the text."

"Can you text me that?" Melina asked.

"Number?" Henri typed as Melina recited the digits. "Done."

Melina pulled up the image as soon as it hit her phone. A flicker of recognition tickled the back of her brain. She enlarged the face with the swipe of her finger. Old memories reached out from the shadows, and the odd sense of déjà vu grew stronger. She scrolled through Guthrie's priors but did not see any connection to Nashville.

"Do you see something familiar about her?" Ramsey asked.

"Not really." She turned off the screen and tucked the phone away. "Henri, anything else you can tell us about the car?"

"No evidence of decomposition fluids," Henri said. "I checked after the discovery of the jar and fingers. I did find a small bag of pot. No firearms."

Melina glanced at the time on her phone. "I have time to swing by the hospital and check on Elena and show her the picture of Bonnie to confirm it's BB."

"Mind if I tag along?" Ramsey asked. "I'd like to hear what she has to say."

"Sure. Suit yourself." She thought about the pink-tipped cigarette butts in her pocket. "I need to make a quick stop at Matt's office before we go."

***

It took a couple of tries, but Ramsey was able to convince Shepard to let him drive both of them to the hospital. He was certainly interested in what Elena had to say, but his focus was on Shepard. She had stared at Bonnie Guthrie's picture as if she had seen a ghost. Her eyes had widened and the color had faded from her cheeks. However, when he had asked, the agent had quickly cloaked whatever had been going on in her head.

Perhaps Guthrie reminded her of her foster days. Maybe she had arrested someone like that linked to a horrific crime. Whatever the reason, Bonnie Guthrie had made an impression on Melina Shepard.

He swung into a convenience store and gassed up his vehicle. "Can I get you anything?"

She reached for her wallet. "I'd love a soda."

"Keep your money."

He jogged inside to pay for the gas and grab her soda and a few PowerBars to tide him over between meals. While Ramsey was at the checkout, armed also with wintergreen gum and a bag of nuts, his eye caught the display that read **A BAZILLION BUBBLES. ONE PUFF AWAY.** He questioned the statement's truth but still chose a pink container decorated with white and blue flowers. Ignoring the clerk's raised brow, he placed the bubble mixture into the pile and paid for the lot.

Back in the car, he handed her the soda as he tossed his paper bag in the back seat.

"Thanks."

He started the engine and switched on the radio. A country music song played softly as she twisted off the top of the soda and took a long drink. She dropped her gaze to her phone and retreated into her own thoughts, as if entering a private, windowless chamber. He could almost hear the door closing behind her.

Normally, silence suited him just fine. In high-stakes cases, he took moments like this to examine and reexamine the fractured pieces of the case's puzzle.

"I'm trying to get used to the country music. It's not my regular fare," he said.

She looked up from her phone, blinked as if shifting mental gears. "I'm betting classical. Or whatever kind of music people raised with old money listen to."

Old money sounded a little tainted when she said it. "Why do you say old money?"

"Your cuff links and watch look vintage, and you don't strike me as the type of guy who haunts antique stores. Your precise use of the King's English is another giveaway. And the cut of your suit. It's handmade, isn't it?"

The sharp assessment hit home. "And all that says old money? Newly rich can adopt all those traits."

"You don't seem to acknowledge any of it. New money cares; old money grows up with the good stuff and treats it like a second skin."

"What else do you notice?"

"You have a house on the water. Potomac River is close to Northern Virginia, but so is Chesapeake Bay. Your skin is tanned, and your hands are weather beaten. I'm guessing they've been exposed to a lot of sun. Crew or sailing."

A smile tugged the edges of his lips. "I sail."

"And you have a dog," she said. "Golden retriever? Just a couple of hairs on your pants, which I bet you don't bother to brush off because you like remembering him. My father's dog, Axel, can do no wrong."

"You should be a profiler," Ramsey said.

She closed her phone. "Don't all cops have to be to some extent? We have to identify genuine versus deceptive behavior almost every day."

"True." He slowed as he approached the hospital. "You said your mother cooks Sunday dinner?" he asked.

"Mom expects my presence unless I'm in a shoot-out or tracking a missing person. Arterial spray is also acceptable."

He pulled into the hospital parking lot, slid into a spot, and shut off the engine. "Nothing wrong with a hot meal."

She laughed. "You haven't tasted my mom's cooking. Heart of gold but hide the can opener and dinner is going to be late."

"Your dad cook?" he asked.

"Yeah. He's pretty good at it. He took a fall recently and is recovering, so she's back in the galley. And if that's not an incentive to get well, I don't know what is. What's your deal—now that we are making small talk?"

"You summed me up pretty well. Harvard undergraduate, Yale Law."

"Blood's bluer than I thought. Who takes care of the dog?"

"The dog lives with my mother on the Chesapeake Bay. I visited this past Sunday, and he and I went sailing."

"His name?"

"Romo."

"After the Dallas Cowboys quarterback? Christ, that's treason in Washington Redskins territory."

"No truer words." As he got out of the car, he grabbed the brown paper bag from the back seat, and the two crossed the lot to the hospital entrance. He could not say he had broken the ice with Shepard, but there was a small crack. Normally, he did not bother beyond basic politeness when working with local law enforcement. But Shepard stoked his curiosity.

The elevator doors opened, and they stepped inside, joining a doctor and a couple of nurses. The nurses were discussing an upcoming wedding, but he quickly filtered out the details.

When the doors opened to the pediatric ward, the nurse on duty offered a quick update on Elena. The girl had had a fair night, but there had been some crying. Still, physically she was fine and would be released soon.

They found the little girl sitting up and watching a cartoon. Ramsey did not recognize the characters, but judging by the child's face, she did. She was not really animated, but any child in a stressful situation would be the same. She appeared less lethargic and scared. He sensed she had lived a transient life and accepted change as a matter of course.

"Hey, Elena," Shepard said. The lightness had returned to her voice. "How are you doing?"

The girl kept her gaze on the television and tightened her hold on the stuffed dog as if she sensed another change was coming. Shepard's watch dangled from the girl's tiny wrist. "Good."

Shepard pulled up a chair. "I came by last night, but you were asleep. Sorry I was so late getting by. Been trying to figure out a lot of things."

"Okay."

The monotone, almost dismissive tone was a coping mechanism. This kid was very wary of emotional connections. He bet she had been burned enough times before.

For several minutes, Shepard watched the cartoon, laughing in a few spots. "I love this one. It's when Papa Smurf builds a house."

"Yeah." This time the girl tossed a side-glance at him. "Do you want your watch back?"

"You keep it for now," Shepard said.

The girl rubbed her other hand over the watch's face. "Okay. Who's he?"

"He's a sailor and has a dog named Romo. His name is Jerrod, and when he's not sailing or playing fetch with Romo, he works for me."

Ramsey shifted, amused at Shepard's assessment. It was designed to soften up the girl's fears but revealed a few of Shepard's inside thoughts about him. He grinned, but the girl shifted and dropped her gaze.

"I did stop by a store today, Elena." Ramsey held up the paper bag. "Want to see?"

She did not answer, but he had her attention.

He removed the pink plastic vial from the bag. When her expression turned quizzical, he explained, "I used to play with this when I was a kid. It says on the label that if you blow once, it will make a million bubbles. I'm not sure you'll get a million, but you'll get a lot."

"I don't know how to make bubbles," Elena said.

"It's easy enough," he said, moving slowly toward the bed. He twisted off the top and handed it to Shepard, then, removing the wand from the container, held it up and blew into the hollow circle at the end. A large bubble materialized, broke free, and then floated toward the girl.

Elena looked amazed.

He blew a few more bubbles, and by the third time she was smiling. "Do you want to try?"

"Yes."

Ramsey came around the side of the bed and handed her the plastic container. "Dunk the wand, hold it up, and blow."

She blew hard, but the thin coating of liquid popped before it became a bubble. "It didn't work."

"Dunk it again, and this time blow very gently."

Her second try was also a fail, but her third worked, to her great delight. The three sat there for another five minutes while the child created bubble after bubble.

Finally, she grew tired and handed the bubble mix to Shepard, who carefully screwed on the top. "I'm putting this over here so you can play with it later."

"I like bubbles," Elena said.

Shepard removed her phone from her back pocket and found the picture of Bonnie Guthrie. "Elena, can you look at a picture and tell me if this is BB?"

The girl shrugged.

Shepard showed her Bonnie's picture, and Elena took the phone, studying the face closely.

"Is BB coming for me? She said she would come get me if I stopped crying," Elena said.

"I'm still trying to find BB," Shepard said. "Does BB have friends or family in Nashville? Did you two stop and visit anyone?"

Elena stared at the picture of BB. "She said don't talk to cops. They'll put you in jail."

"I'm not going to put you in jail," Ramsey said. "Neither is Melina."

"BB says cops lie." Elena laid down the phone and shifted her gaze back to the Smurf cartoon.

"I don't lie," Shepard said. "I said I'd come back, and I did."

The girl glanced down at the watch and the stuffed dog. Absently, she twisted a piece of the fur between her fingers. "BB has a friend."

Slight traces of tension rippled through Shepard's shoulders. He knew the feeling. It was exciting when a piece of the puzzle presented itself.

She did not rush to comment, as if seeming to understand that gaining more of the girl's trust needed to be slow and steady so she would not spook the kid. "I know we've talked about the man BB talked to before. You think maybe we can talk about him again? I'm trying to figure this guy out."

The girl was silent a moment before she said, "Okay."

"Where did you see Sonny?" Shepard asked.

"At his house."

"What did the house look like?" With children, interview questions had to be specific.

"Brown."

"Brown paint. Brown bricks?"

"Bricks," Elena said.

"Did the yard have green grass or pretty plants?"

"Yeah. There was also a bath for birds."

This information suggested to Ramsey that Sonny kept up appearances. That was not surprising, considering his killings went back so long. He was accustomed to masking his behavior.

"You said he had a mean face," Shepard said. When the girl appeared to tense, Shepard scrunched up her face. "Did his face look like this?"

A ghost of a smile teased the girl's lips. "Meaner."

Shepard tightened her face another notch. "Like this?"

"You don't look mean," Elena said, smiling now.

She jabbed her thumb toward Ramsey and stage-whispered, "I bet he can make the right kind of mean face."

The girl cupped her hand close to her mouth. "He can."

Ramsey scrunched up his face and looked in a mirror across from the bed. "I don't look mean. Melina looks mean."

"I do not," Shepard said lightly.

The girl's eyes widened with amusement, and then she giggled softly.

Shepard was smiling, and he sensed a genuine amusement that he found was very satisfying. "Did something make Sonny mad?"

"Sonny didn't like it when BB called him Sonny. He said it wasn't his real name," Elena said.

"Did he say what his real name was?" she asked.

"No."

"What does Sonny look like when he doesn't have the mean face?" Shepard asked. "What color is his hair?"

"Black. Like yours. And his eyes are brown like yours," the girl said.

They went through a series of questions until they had a rough description of Sonny. He was likely in his midthirties, tall, not fat but not thin, brown hair and eyes, and he had several guitars in his house. It was a start, but with no last name or an address, Sonny would be impossible to trace.

"When you were at Sonny's house, did he give anything to BB?" Ramsey asked.

"No."

"Did she go back to Sonny's house?" Shepard asked.

The girl shrugged. "I don't know. We went to the motel and I fell asleep."

Which did not rule out the possibility that BB had left the girl and returned to Sonny's house.

The girl yawned. "BB takes stuff all the time from everyone."

Did the preserved fingers belong to Sonny? Had BB taken them for some kind of leverage? He made a mental note to check past known associates for Bonnie Guthrie.

"You've been a big help," Shepard said.

The girl yawned again and blinked slowly. "Okay. When you find BB, can I leave?"

"You get to leave here really soon. I'll talk to your doctor again when I come back later. I should know more this afternoon."

The girl's eyes widened with panic before she seemed to catch herself. "Do you have to leave?"

Shepard smiled at the child. "I can't find BB if I don't leave for a little bit. And we need to find her."

The girl frowned. "Okay."

Shepard smiled at the girl, but as she turned to leave, the girl grabbed her fingers in a surprisingly tight grip.

Shepard seemed to tense, as if absorbing the child's desperation. She leaned forward and hugged the girl. The child's arms clutched her neck, and her small frame melted into the agent's.

Shepard patted the girl on the back. "I'll be back. I won't leave you hanging."

"Promise?" Elena whispered.

"Promise. And don't lose my watch."

"Okay. I won't." She giggled.

Finally, Shepard was able to peel the girl's arms free, and with one last squeeze of the hand, she and Ramsey left the room.

Shepard reached for her cell and dialed. After an extended pause, she said, "Mom, this is Melina. Call me back when you can. I have a favor to ask."

Ramsey did not speak as the two strode toward the elevator. He pressed the button. "You okay?"

"Sure. I'm fine."

"You don't look fine."

"Save the profiling for the suspects."

"It doesn't take a profile to recognize your expression is tight and your face is pale."

"Don't," she warned.

As the elevator doors opened, Ramsey was already texting. "I'm having Andy cross-check BB's arrest records with the name Sonny."

"Bonnie Guthrie definitely knows the guy from way back. She gets out of prison and stays in California for a year, and then something happens, and she ends up stealing a car, a kid, and body parts. My guess is the guy has access to money or something of value to Bonnie."

"Agreed."

The doors closed and she pressed the lobby level. "She just didn't happen to find herself in Nashville. She had a plan. I went back and looked at the crash site. There are no skid marks."

"I noticed that. She was hell bent on making it to the other side. But why?"

***

When Melina and Ramsey reached the first floor, her phone buzzed with a text from her mother. Back home. She and her mom had a system. If Melina called, her mom would text back. Given Melina's job and schedule, texting was the only option that worked.

"I'm going to swing by my folks' house and check on my father. If there's an update, contact me."

"Will do."

They drove back to the TBI offices. Melina could ask him about what he was doing next, but she did not care right now. "I'll be back in an hour."

"Understood."

She settled into the front seat of her car, letting the heat from the seat soak into her chilled skin. She was grateful for the solitude.

Old, latent fears long suppressed grew stronger and crawled from the shadows. They swirled and then joined to create a picture of another little girl standing on the side of a deserted country road. Her heart was racing with fear and dread, and her body was drenched in sweat.

Melina raised her fingertips to the base of her throat. Her pulse thrummed under her skin. Unwanted fears of abandonment and loss tangled together and wrapped around her chest.

"Nope. Not doing this now," she said. "And fuck you, BB."

She fired up the engine and then texted her mother, alerting her she was coming by for a visit.

CHAPTER THIRTEEN

Tuesday, August 25, 11:45 a.m.

Ramsey returned to the hotel room he had used last night. He had reserved the room for three nights, but there was a good chance he would be extending his stay.

The **Do Not Disturb** sign remained on the door, and when he entered, he was glad to see the maid had not come. Though he carried all sensitive files and his laptop in his briefcase, he still did not like the idea of anyone invading his space while he was gone. Better to have a rumpled bed and day-old towels. If he needed anything, he'd have the front desk send it up while he was present.

He could have returned to the TBI offices but had opted for the seclusion of his hotel room. Loosening his tie, he dialed the hotel restaurant and ordered the steak and potatoes, just as he always did when he was on the road.

He shrugged off his jacket, hung it up in the closet, and removed his tie, which he also draped over a hanger. He removed his gun from the holster on his hip and placed it in the nightstand drawer between the two double beds, next to the Bible. Threading his fingers through his hair, he sat on the edge of his bed beside his briefcase, which he knew was loaded with a dozen files of open cases he was monitoring across the country.

He did not have to open any of them to recall the horrific details of each. There was a killer in Maine who had stabbed six prostitutes and mutilated their bodies. An offender purported to be female in Miami was hunting couples walking along the beach at night. In Denver, there was a man who kidnapped young women and held them for months as he sexually assaulted them. Only when the killer tired of his victim did he stab her to death and dump her body on a mountain roadside.

Each on their own would give normal people nightmares. In the early days of his career, pictures of mutilated bodies had wormed into his dreams and bothered him, but slowly over time, he'd hardened to the images. Now, he had been chasing monsters for so long he did not flinch over the myriad of ways a human could be murdered.

He had once worked with a senior agent who had reminded him that the best way to boil a frog alive was to put him in cold water and then slowly turn up the heat. The frog did not notice the temperature change until it nearly boiled. And by then, it was too late for the poor bastard to jump free.

In retrospect, he knew that senior agent had been talking about himself and the toll the job took. Ramsey had never imagined he would suffer such a fate. He would know when the time came to get out. Now, he was not so sure. Whatever desires he had to call it quits were always silenced by the screams of the next victims demanding justice.

Needing to connect to someone, Ramsey dialed his mother's home number. The phone rang three times before his mother's caregiver, Tracy, answered. "Ramsey residence."

"Tracy, it's Jerrod. I'm checking in."

"Hello, Mr. Ramsey. Your mother is doing fine. She's actually up."

He glanced at his watch and allowed for the one-hour time difference. "She normally naps this time of day."

"You know she doesn't sleep when you're out of town. I don't know how she knows, but she does."

"Can I speak to her?"

"Sure can."

He heard Tracy's muffled voice as she seemed to speak to his mother. And then finally, "Jerrod."

His mother sounded clear and happy, which was now a rare combination. "Mom. How are you doing?"

"I'm doing just fine."

"How is your morning going?"

"It's a lovely day here. No humidity, and the breeze off the bay is amazing. I have Romo right here with me. He's sleeping." She chuckled. "He's getting older and likes to sleep more, whereas I'm just the opposite."

"As long as you feel good." His father used to say his mother had been one of the smartest minds he had ever encountered. She had earned her PhD in English literature and could speak five languages.

"I'm wonderful. How are you?"

A smile tipped the edge of his lips. "I'm great. Working."

"Make sure you take care of yourself. I know how you get when you work too hard. Are you eating?"

"Yes."

"A good meal will always help with your studies."

"My studies?"

"Starting your senior year in college. I can hardly believe you're so grown up."

He rubbed the back of his neck with his hand and glanced up in the hotel mirror. There was more graying at the temples, and the frown lines around his mouth were deeper. "It happens to us all."

Romo barked in the background. "Looks like the old boy is up. Time to take him for his walk. Are you doing all right, son?"

"Just fine, Mom. Can I talk to Tracy?"

"Sure."

Seconds passed and then, "Mr. Ramsey, don't worry. She's not taking the dog for a walk. I've got this."

"Thanks, Tracy."

"Sure thing, Mr. Ramsey."

The call ended, and a second later his phone rang again. He cleared his throat and accepted the call. "Andy."

"Boss man," Andy said.

He rubbed the back of his neck as he walked toward the drawn curtains of his window and glanced out at the parking lot. How many parking lots and dumpsters had he had the pleasure of overlooking the past fifteen years?

"I did a search of Bonnie Guthrie as you requested. She's had quite the career." Andy was always cheerful. It should have been annoying, but it was not.

"Stands to reason the charges in California weren't her first."

"Not by a long shot. Her first arrest was in 1976. She was fifteen and picked up for shoplifting. It was a first offense, so she was let off. It was another two years before she was caught stealing again. This time she did a few days in jail."

"Give me the abbreviated version."

"She likes to steal. She's made a career of it. She was married for a short time while she was in Texas, but her husband died of natural causes in 1990. After his death, she took off."

"What about Sonny? Any known associates by that name?"

"I was on the phone with each jurisdiction where she had a record and asked that same question. The only mention of a Sonny came from her most recent California parole officer. He said she referenced Sonny a couple of times and said as soon as she was clear to travel, she was going to see him in Nashville."

He stilled. "Any other information about Sonny?"

"No. The parole officer said he asked but she wouldn't say."

Nashville had been Bonnie's destination. "What about the child? Elena. The girl said her mother's name was Christina Sanchez. Was there a record of Bonnie having a relationship with Ms. Sanchez?"

"Bonnie never mentioned Christina or a child to her parole officer."

"Was Christina or Bonnie living at the address Elena gave us?"

"Yes. The address is in East LA. Not the best part of town. Not surprising. Ms. Sanchez was arrested several times for prostitution and possession. Her offences were small-time stuff, but she got picked up regularly. Sanchez never did hard time, but she was in and out of jail several times before her daughter was born."

"Find out who owned the residence where Sanchez lived. Maybe the landlord can tell us something about Christina, Elena, or Bonnie."

"Might take me a day or two, but I'm on it."

"Thanks, Andy."

"How much longer will you be in Nashville?"

"A couple of days. I want to see what's going on with this case; then I'll turn it over to TBI. Anything on the Key Killer?"

"Who?"

"The killer who murdered ten prostitutes."

"The Key Killer? Who came up with that moniker?"

"Local PD."

"I was reviewing the victim case files we have on the Key Killer, a.k.a. the Riverside Ripper in Atlanta. As you know, the first victim was killed in June 1999. What I'd forgotten is that she'd filed a police report a week before she vanished for good. In her report, she claimed a strange man driving a white van approached her. She said he tried to coax her into it with a wad of bills, but her street radar went off. He tried to drag her inside, but her pimp showed up. A week later she was dead."

Shit. He had forgotten that detail as well. Too many damn cases. They were all starting to blend. "The killer doubled back?"

"Appears so. Tell Agent Shepard to keep her eyes peeled."

"Will do." He hung up.

A knock on his door had him reaching for his gun and tucking it under his belt at the base of his spine. He looked through the peephole and saw the hotel room service guy. His name was Benny, and he had delivered meals the last two nights.

Ramsey fished a twenty-dollar bill from his pocket and opened the door. "Hello, Benny."

"Good day, sir. I have your lunch."

Ramsey handed him the folded bill and took the tray. "Thanks, Benny."

Benny rubbed the bill between his fingers as if touch might confirm this tip was as good as he hoped. "Thanks."

"Sure."

The kid gave him a once-over, his bright eyes narrowing a fraction. "Are you FBI?"

"What makes you ask that?"

"I dunno. I heard some of the guys in the lobby talking."

Fresh face and bright eyes were typical of those on the other side of the thin blue line. They only saw excitement and all the shit that was on TV. If he showed this kid his files and told him what he really saw, he would ruin the kid's year.

He defaulted to a practiced half grin that tipped the edge of his lips. "Don't believe everything you hear. Have a good day."

Before the boy could ask a second time, Ramsey stepped back and pushed the door closed.

He set the tray down on the desk and rolled his head from side to side. He reminded himself that his kind of work needed to be done. The world needed men like him, women like Shepard, just like they needed garbage collectors.

Everyone agreed that someone had to clean the mess up. They just did not really want to know the particulars. It made for a lonely life that took a toll not only on personal relationships but also on physical and mental health.

Years ago, he'd had a fiancée. She was beautiful, bright, and truly kind. But the more he had confided in her about his work, the more distant they became.

He was never sure if she had pulled away from him or he from her. Whatever the cause, neither could stop, and eventually they only spoke about the weather or social gatherings. There had been no drama or hard words when it had ended. It simply did. He'd heard she was now married to an ob-gyn and was expecting her second child.

It all went back to the question asked by his mentor. How did you boil a frog alive? Slowly.

In Shepard's dark eyes, he saw the isolation. The loneliness. In her, he saw his own anger mirrored back. She was not as subtle about her frustrations as he was, but then he doubted she cared if she offended anyone.

If Ramsey shared his files with Shepard, she would not run away from it. They had more in common than either was willing to admit.

CHAPTER FOURTEEN

Tuesday, August 25, Noon

"Mom!" Melina shouted as she pushed through the front door of her parents' house. She removed the key from the lock, rattling the ring in her hand as she crossed the living room and headed down the back hallway toward the kitchen. The light of a television glowed, and the sound of the midday news mingled with her parents' voices. "Mom!"

"In the den, honey! I heated up a plate for you. It's in the kitchen."

Her stomach grumbled. "Be right there!"

"Mom made meatloaf, buttercup. Your favorite," her father shouted.

It was the one dish her mother made well. "She's a goddess!" She hurried into the kitchen, pulled a warm plate from the oven. She peeled off the foil and grabbed a fork and a soda before making her way to the den.

Her father sat in his recliner, his legs elevated, a slipper on his left foot and a cast on his right. He wore a favorite pair of khaki work pants and a T-shirt smudged with paint colors from last summer's renovation project. She kissed him on the forehead, and he patted her on the arm as he muted the news. Axel, their nine-year-old rescue pit bull mix, lay on his dog bed. He thumped his tail as he looked up at her.

Melina kissed her mother, who peered up over half glasses, smiling as she sat in another tufted chair. "How's it going?"

"Just watching a game show, kiddo," her mother said.

"You haven't killed Dad yet, I see."

"A few close calls but he still lives to tell the tale."

She sat and cut into her meatloaf. "She's dangerous, Dad."

"I know," he said. "Never a dull moment in this house, but Axel keeps me in line."

The dog lumbered to his feet and sat in front of her. He had the pitiful look down pat when food was involved. She pinched off a piece of meatloaf, and he eagerly accepted it.

Her mother sighed. "The vet says he's fat."

"He's husky," her father said. "Big bones."

Her parents argued often about the dog's weight. He was their second child, the son they never had. "Speaking of bones, have you broken any lately, Dad?" she asked.

"Better to break bones than sit on my ass all day and watch the world go by," her father countered.

Hank Shepard had been in law enforcement for over thirty-five years when he'd retired the year before. Since then, he had spent the better part of the last year rebuilding the house from the outside in. She had no doubt, once he had the all clear from the doctor, he would be back on a ladder like nothing had happened.

Meanwhile, he was doing a fantastic job of driving his wife insane. Lately, she had been talking about selling the house or taking a long vacation. All her plans had fallen on her father's and Axel's deaf ears.

"You're going to owe her that vacation," Melina said. "Give me enough notice and I'll watch Axel."

"Seriously?" her mother asked.

"I promise."

"I might consider it." Her father patted Axel on the head.

Her mother ignored her father's vague promise and shifted narrowing eyes on Melina. "You don't like to babysit Axel. What's going on?"

Melina took a bite of the meatloaf and savored the mix of vegetables, spices, and ground beef. "This is why I moved back to Nashville. To be close and help."

Her mother's face stilled as if she were waiting for a second shoe to drop. "I thought you said it was the promotion."

"And the meatloaf. And Axel." She took several more bites, not realizing how hungry she had been. "This is amazing."

"Glad you like it." Her mother put her book down. "What brings you by in the middle of the day?"

"Do I need a reason?" Melina asked.

"No, but you have one," her mother countered.

She stabbed one more bite, swirled it in the butter mashed potatoes. Her mother knew her too well. She ate the last bite and placed the plate on the floor for Axel to finish off. He began lapping up the scant remains immediately.

"We have a six-year-old child in the hospital. She was in a car accident." She saw the worry darken her mother's eyes. "The child is fine, but the driver abandoned the vehicle and the child."

Her mother hissed in a breath and sat a little straighter. She said nothing, but both her mother's and father's attention was laser focused. "Social services has the case, and she'll be moved to a foster home likely by tomorrow afternoon."

"What do you know about the driver?" her father asked.

"This is confidential, guys," Melina said.

Her father's gaze warmed with interest. "You know we're a vault."

Melina had no doubt. "The driver's name is Bonnie Guthrie. She did time in California but missed her last appointment with her parole officer. She's not the child's mother, according to the child."

"And?" her father prompted.

She popped open her soda and took a long pull. She skipped over why Ramsey had originally come to Nashville. "FBI got involved when an officer found a pickle jar filled with severed fingers in the trunk of Guthrie's car. All the fingers appear to be female. The medical examiner has pulled prints. We have identification on two of the victims."

"It's not like you to discuss your cases with us," her mother said.

And here came the part that dug into uncomfortable feelings. "The kid kind of reminded me of myself. The way she was just left."

"Aren't the scenarios fairly different?" her father asked.

"You always gloss over how you found me. And I've never pressed for details. Now, I'm pressing."

Her father glanced at her mother. And when she nodded, he sat a little taller. "A call came in that there was a child on the side of the road."

"Who called it in?"

"We know the call came from a pay phone at Stella's Diner. Back in the day, no cells."

"I get it. Old school," she said. "Did anyone ever talk to the folks at the diner?"

"I did, after I picked you up," he said. "You were standing on the side of the road hiding behind a guardrail."

"I remember that part of the story."

"No way I would have found you if someone hadn't told us to look near mile marker one twenty-five." His voice grew quiet. "I drove past you twice and saw no sign of you. I decided the third time would be the charm. That's when I saw your yellow jacket. You reminded me of a frightened animal."

Her mother rubbed Axel's head in a soft, loving way, as if she were calming that lost version of Melina.

"When I reached for you, you took off running," her father said.

"You said I came straight to you."

"No. I had to move quickly to snatch you up. You started kicking and screaming, and I held you tight until you calmed down. Must have taken a full five minutes. Finally, I think all the trauma just wore you out, and you collapsed against me."

"That's when he called me," her mom said. "I met him at the station."

"Foster care took me," Melina said.

"For seven days," her mother said. "Took that long for your daddy and me to pull every string we had to get custody."

"When you went to the diner, could anyone tell you who called the police?" Melina asked.

"The call came in at 10:05 p.m. on a Thursday night," her father said. "The restaurant manager didn't have surveillance cameras, and it had been a busy night. There'd been an event at the local high school, and the place was packed full of kids and parents. But Brenda, the woman working that night, did remember a woman coming in with a boy. She remembered thinking the woman wasn't a regular customer and the boy looked upset."

"Did Brenda say what the woman looked like?"

"Blond. Dressed kind of showy. Drove a big car."

A faint memory of a car flashed. The vehicle had a wide back seat and was stuffed full of suitcases and garbage bags filled with clothes. "Did the woman or boy call?"

"She's not even sure if either one of them made the call. In her words, it was busy as hell and she didn't know up from down."

"Anything else about this woman?" Melina had pushed aside this story for so long she had almost convinced herself that it did not matter. Now, the scant details teased her with a past that suddenly felt as if it mattered very much.

"Any names? Credit card receipts?"

"None. Paid cash. Didn't leave a tip. They each ate, used the restroom, and left. No one saw them before or since."

"How do you know they haven't seen them since?"

"For a few months, I checked in at least once a week. Social services searched for your birth family but stopped after a few months. I kept looking just in case there was someone who might make a claim on you."

"Your father knew I wasn't going to let you go without a fight," her mother said.

"Whoever the woman was, she never came back to Nashville." Her father studied his daughter with the keen eye of a veteran cop. Every so often she caught a glimmer of the badass cop he had been back in the day. "Has this case brought all this up?"

She sighed. "I suppose it has. I had a dream last night."

"What kind of dream?" her mother asked.

"Being in the back of that oversize car and then getting yanked out and being left on the side of the road."

"You used to have nightmares when you were little, but they stopped when you were about ten or eleven," her mother said.

"They never really stopped. I just stopped talking about them."

Her mother frowned. "You always had the same dream?"

"Yes." Melina did not like seeing her parents' deepening frowns. She had never liked seeing them worried, especially about her. Maybe that was why she had stopped talking about the dream, excelled in school, and been a model student at the academy. Somewhere buried in her subconscious was the idea that if she was not perfect, they would not want her. "But it's nothing like it used to be, and these days, the dream doesn't bother me that much. I think seeing Elena today just reminded me of how I ended up."

"Who's overseeing this child's case with social services?" her mother asked.

She checked her phone. "The guy's name is Richard Barnard."

"I don't know the name," her mother said.

"I could make some calls," her father said.

"That's kind of what I was hoping, Dad. Better I stay out of it since this is an active homicide investigation."

"Homicide?" her mother asked. "That poor girl."

"Yeah," she said.

"I'll look into it." Her father's tone had shifted from dad to cop. "I'll see to it she gets the best foster home."

"Thanks, Dad."

"Any time, squirt."

***

Sonny was glad to be home. It had been nice spending the night at his lady's house, but it was time to get back into his routine. There had been a season when he could be on the road for months and be content. But as he had gotten older, he'd liked sleeping in his own bed. Liked having his stuff around him.

Restless, he shoved the key into the lock and pushed open the door. He dropped his small duffel bag and flipped on the light.

The instant his gaze scanned the small living room, he knew something was wrong. He quietly closed the front door behind him and reached for the SIG in his waistband under his shirt. He chambered a round and very slowly crossed the pine floor toward the couch and collection of photos he had taken on the road for over fifteen years.

The house was silent except for the slight hum of the refrigerator. He flipped on the kitchen light and confirmed that the space was as neat and clean as he had left it. He liked a clean house. Liked knowing the scent of pine waited for him when he came home.

He jiggled the back doorknob and discovered it was locked. Still, the hair on the back of his neck rose, and he could not shake the feeling that someone had been there.

"Bonnie," he muttered.

She had been calling him for weeks, but he had ignored her. He had no idea how she had gotten his number but knew damn well how clever the woman could be.

Seeing her had been a kick to the gut. It had taken everything to remain calm. Once he'd checked his emotions, he'd recognized that familiar hangdog expression on her face. She'd had a sob story and when that had not worked on him, she'd cut to the chase. She wanted the key, but once he gave it to her, she would realize he had spent the money.

His fingers itched as he imagined wrapping them around her pencil neck and squeezing until she died. Then the kid had gotten out of the car, looking for Bonnie.

If not for the kid, he would have strangled Bonnie right there. He had sure dreamed of it often enough. But the kid had gotten to him and twisted his heart in ways he had thought were not possible anymore.

She was a cute little thing. She needed a real parent and protecting, something he had never really had. But all that was drowned out by the deep sense of betrayal he still felt toward Bonnie.

He had been a teenager when the cops had cuffed Bonnie's hands behind her back and led her to the squad car. She was all he had in the world and was the closest thing he had to a mother. When she was taken away, he was scared shitless. He scrounged enough money for a bus and rode it to the city jail. Bonnie had always gotten out of scrapes, and he prayed she'd find a way out of this one.

When he arrived at the city jail, his hands were trembling as he sat in the visitors' room and waited for Bonnie. When she'd appeared, he'd been so glad to see her.

"Baby, you came to see me," she said through the thick glass.

"What do I do, Bonnie?" He scooted closer on his seat, wishing he could hug her.

She sniffed and leaned forward a fraction. "Is all our stuff still at the motel?"

"Yes."

"Pack it up and find a place to live. There's money in the bottom of the black suitcase. That will do you for a while. There's also a key. Hang onto it. It'll take care of us when I get out. In the meantime, you know how to get money. Don't worry, Sonny."

She had taught him how to pick pockets, shoplift, and extort money, but she had always been there to distract the mark. And because they had moved around so much, he had no friends, and whatever real family he might have had was long gone. Now he would have to survive by himself. He was alone.

Bonnie was not out soon. Despite her pleas of innocence, she was sent away for seven years. He cried the day she left for prison, and for weeks he barely got by, living on the streets. And then a local minister took him in, fed him, and gave him a warm place to sleep. It was about that time that he was going through the black suitcase again, looking for more money. When he found the key hidden in a side pocket, he threaded it through a chain and wore it around his neck for years.

There were GED classes at the center and people who encouraged him to figure out what he wanted. He had no more excuses not to live a clean life. A job as a roadie with a band followed. He took the key, found the duffel full of money, and used it to build up a pretty damn good life.

He walked toward his bedroom, passing the rows of pictures taken of him on the road. More places than he could remember, but all damn good times.

He carefully pushed open his bedroom door and turned on the light. His gaze swept the room, which at first glance looked intact. He almost thought he had imagined the home invasion stuff when he saw the closet door ajar.

Sonny was a creature of habit and always closed the closet door. His heart beat faster as he moved toward the door and opened it wide. Dropping to his knees in front of the pair of boots, he knew in his gut what he would discover. Bonnie had come back, and she had remembered his habit of stashing cash.

He shook out the pair of black Tecovas boots, and when nothing came out, he shoved his hand into the boot and fished around with his fingers. It was empty.

"You stupid, stupid moron."

Heat rushed to his face as blood rose in his cheeks. He had been a fool even to answer the door.

Once Bonnie set her sights on someone, they could resign themselves to being screwed every way to Sunday.

He slammed the boot down. It was not the cash that really bothered him but the credit cards. None were his, and they could be traced back to his lady friends.

He ran his hands along the wall and felt for the pickle jar hidden under a blanket. His fingers skimmed over dusty plywood flooring, finding no blanket or jar.

"Shit!"

His heart galloping, he reached for his cell and turned on the flashlight app and searched the darkness. No jar. The space was empty.

"Bonnie," he hissed.

She had taken his jar of memories, knowing she could use it against him. With the jar, she could easily shatter the life he had built.

He glanced at his phone and double-checked his incoming calls. There was no number that he did not recognize.

He rose and walked to the window and discovered it was unlocked. There were scratch marks along the metal frame. Bonnie had pried it open, climbed in and out with his treasures.

It was Tuesday afternoon. The cops had not come knocking on his door, which meant Bonnie had not gone to the police. Yet. She also had not contacted him, which was not like her. Patience was not one of her virtues.

Whatever game she was playing, she had underestimated him this time. He was no longer a naive young boy desperately seeking her approval. Bonnie did not have a clue who she was fucking with.

He went to the trash in the kitchen and fished out the number she had scribbled on the piece of paper. He typed in the cell number and was ready to hit send when he paused.

There was no tracing the jar back to him. It was her word against his that she had stolen it from his house, and he was always careful to wipe his prints clean from the jar each time he handled it.

Bonnie was running low on money. Otherwise she would not have broken in and taken his cash. And if she used any of the credit cards in the stolen stack, she would bring the cops down on her, not him.

He fished a Ziploc bag from his pocket and opened it. He removed the bloodied wad of paper towels and carefully folded back the layers.

Nestled inside was the severed finger. Gently he stroked the cool pale skin. It would not be smart to save this one. If Bonnie talked, the cops would come knocking and they would tear his place apart.

But he could not bear to part with his girlfriend's gift. He had to find a better hiding place, and if Bonnie came at him again, he would add her finger to his collection.

CHAPTER FIFTEEN

Wednesday, August 26, 11:30 a.m.

Melina called Matt for an update on the white van, but the forensic team was still taking it apart. Another call to Jackson told her Bonnie Guthrie remained in the wind.

She drove to the Mission and parked. It did not take long to find some of the regular girls roaming the streets looking for a john. She crossed the street to where two women stood. They were older, late twenties, and both wore very short skirts and halter tops that barely contained their breasts. Both wore wigs and high heels that made her own feet hurt just looking at them.

"Morning, ladies," she said. "I'm Melina."

The taller of the two women eyed her carefully. "You're that cop."

"That's right. I'm friends with Sarah."

"Just about got your ass dragged in a van, I hear," the woman said.

"Correct. Speaking of the van, anyone seen any odd men lurking around?"

Both laughed. The shorter of the two lit a cigarette. "They're all weird, honey."

"Point taken," Melina said. "Anyone hear from Delia or Joy? They turn up?"

The women looked at each other and then shook their heads. "We haven't seen them," the tall woman said.

Melina handed each her card. "If they turn up, call me, okay?"

"Should we be looking for the van?" the short woman asked.

"No. The cops have impounded it. But the driver is still on the loose. So be careful, okay?"

Melina spoke to several other women, but the story was consistent. No one had seen Delia, Joy, or the Key Killer.

"Where the hell are you?" she muttered. She started her car and drove toward the hospital, grabbing a couple of Happy Meals on the way. Her phone rang as she pulled into the parking lot.

"Agent Shepard."

"This is Agent Ramsey. Nashville police arrested Bonnie Guthrie in an eastside motel. The credit card she was using was reported stolen last week."

Her heart kicked into high gear. "Have you interviewed her yet?" Melina asked.

"No. Thought we could both share that pleasure."

"She's at the Metro-Davidson detention center?"

"That's right."

"I can be there in thirty minutes."

"I'll be waiting."

She quickly pulled onto the road toward the detention center. It was a quarter after twelve, which put her ahead of any afternoon commuter tangle of cars filling the roads. She merged onto Interstate 24 and headed south. She ate both meals as she drove and saved the toys for Elena.

Melina pulled into the fenced parking lot of the brick facility and parked. She grabbed her bag and was out of the car, looping her identification around her neck. She found Ramsey standing in the lobby, phone in hand and reading.

"Agent Melina Shepard," she said to the guard on duty.

The sound of her voice had Ramsey raising his gaze as the guard waved her through.

Without a word, the two passed through another set of doors, checked their weapons in lockers, and then made their way to an interview room.

"You said she was picked up in a motel?" Melina asked.

"A dive next to a bar called Max's. The clerk said she stumbled in about midnight and wanted a room. He asked for a credit card and she produced an American Express Gold Card."

"How did she pay for the drinks at the bar?"

"Officers spoke to the bartender at Max's. Her card worked there."

"Was it the Gold Card?"

"No."

"She was too buzzed when she showed up at the motel to use the card that worked," Melina said.

"When Bonnie's card was declined, she handed the clerk another. It was declined. When the third came back stolen, she got an attitude. That's when he called the cops."

"So, three's the charm with this clerk," she said.

He smiled. "She put up quite a fuss. Took two officers to get her cuffed. When they searched her purse, they found a stack of credit cards an inch thick and bound together. Nashville PD is checking the cards right now to see when they were stolen."

"With her record, she's looking at more prison time."

He opened a door. "That's the least of her worries. If she can't prove she has legal custody of Elena, she's facing transporting a minor over state lines, which is a felony."

"She's been around the block enough to know what that means." Bonnie would not see daylight for two decades if both those convictions held. "That kind of time might get her to open up about the pickle jar and Elena's family."

"That's the plan," Ramsey said.

"Do you want to take point in the interview?"

"You're being polite. You want it," he said.

"FBI trumps TBI, and my boss told me to play nice. But yes, I want first crack at Bonnie Guthrie."

"She's all yours then."

They were met by a deputy who escorted them to an interview room furnished with two chairs in front of a glass partition. They each took a seat. When Melina heard the rattle of cuffs and keys on the other side of the door, she sat straighter, feeling an odd sense of nerves.

The door opened to a guard escorting a female inmate dressed in an orange jumpsuit. Her hands were cuffed in front of her while her head was high, with no signs of contrition in her direct gaze. Blond shoulder-length hair draped over narrow shoulders, the edges reaching the top of full breasts.

Bonnie approached the chair and looked first at Ramsey. She did not appear impressed and slowly shifted her gaze to Melina. A flicker of interest darkened the woman's green eyes, and a crooked smile tugged the edge of her lips. She sat down, leaned back in her chair, and folded her hands in her lap.

"You two don't look like local cops. TBI?" she asked Melina.

Ramsey answered. "FBI special agent Jerrod Ramsey."

"And you, doll? You FBI, too?"

A grating sense of familiarity scratched the underside of Melina's skin. "Agent Melina Shepard. Tennessee Bureau of Investigation."

Bonnie's head cocked as she studied Melina's face. "Melina. That's an unusual name."

"Really?" Melina asked. "I never gave any thought to it." But of course, she had thought about her name a great deal. The night she met her father, he had asked her name. Melina. It was the one link she had to her past.

Bonnie's smile widened as she settled back in the chair. "I used to know a kid named Melina. But that was a long time ago."

Most would not consider Bonnie beautiful, but she was striking. Square jaw, sharp nose, and full lips that curled into a wide smile.

Tension coiled in Melina's belly as she stared at Bonnie's face. It was unsettlingly familiar. She suddenly had no patience for nice words or rapport building. "You were driving a 2007 gray Ford sedan."

"Was I?" Bonnie asked.

"We pulled your prints from the underside of a child's car seat," Melina said.

"Did you?" Bonnie had played this game so many times she could keep this going for hours.

Melina was not known for her patience. "Can you tell me how you came by the pickle jar?"

"What pickle jar, honey?" Bonnie asked.

Melina sighed. "The pickle jar in the trunk of the car you wrecked on Cox Road on Monday afternoon. We found it and the little girl strapped in her car seat."

Bonnie shook her head. "I don't know what you're talking about."

"The prints found on the underside of the car seat match those belonging to Bonnie Lynn Guthrie. The officers here identified you by your prints. You're one and the same Bonnie Lynn Guthrie."

Bonnie glanced at her long nails, painted a dark red. The ring finger and thumbnails were chipped. "I don't know what you're talking about. And I think I'm entitled to a lawyer, if I'm not mistaken?"

"The county has contacted a lawyer," Ramsey said. "He should be here soon."

"Well, doll, I tell you what. Why don't you come back and see me when I have my lawyer? Not smart to talk to the cops without one." She wagged an index finger at them. "You folks can be so sneaky. Can take my words and twist them all around."

"We've already identified the prints on two of the fingers of the murderer's victims," Melina said. "It's a matter of time before we identify the others, but two will convict just fine."

Some of the humor dimmed in Bonnie's gaze. Absently, she clicked nail against nail and stared back.

"Your prints are also on the jar," Melina lied.

Bonnie smiled as she rose. "I think it's time we ended our little chat."

"Where did you get the credit cards?" Melina asked.

"I still don't know what you're talking about."

"The card you gave the bartender was stolen, but it's not been reported yet. The name on the card is Jennifer Brown."

"You can keep talking all you want," Bonnie said, "but I don't have anything to say."

"You haven't asked about Elena," Melina said. "She's been asking for you, BB."

This time her smile looked more pained than amused. "I don't know an Elena."

"Elena is small for her age. And when you see her lying in her hospital bed holding that stuffed dog, it's kind of heartbreaking," Melina said.

Tension stiffened Bonnie's shoulders, but Melina sensed it had nothing to do with missing the girl. Bonnie was worried about what the girl would say.

"I don't know any kid named Elena." Bonnie pounded on the door.

"She's been talking about Sonny."

Bonnie shook her head. "Sorry, can't help you."

"DNA will tell us if you and Elena are related, but I'd say not."

Bonnie faced the door but did not speak.

"If you can walk away from Elena this easily, makes me think you have a habit of leaving children. What other children have you abandoned?" Melina wanted to worm her way under Bonnie's skin so that she would drop her guard just for a second or two.

Bonnie slowly turned and studied Melina with narrowing eyes. Then very slowly the smile returned. "Baby, sounds like you aren't talking about Elena anymore, are you?"

The room felt as if it had dropped from underneath her feet. An unwanted edge crept into her tone. "Who would I be talking about?"

"I don't know, baby. You tell me."

"Did you wreck your car intentionally?" Melina asked.

"Who would do such a thing?"

The guard opened the door and Bonnie stepped through it, glancing back and winking at Melina before she vanished. The door slammed behind her.

Melina sat back in her chair, her fingers curling into fists. "Don't say it."

"Say what?" Ramsey asked.

"I let my personal feelings get the better of me," she said.

"Maybe. But you did get under Bonnie's skin. Tension in the eyes and a slight flattening of her lips suggested stress."

"She looked pretty comfortable to me," she said.

"BB puts on a good show. That's what she does for a living."

"She can try to look as cool as possible, but she won't be able to talk her way out of forensic evidence. We have her prints on the car seat but not on the steering wheel or front seat. There's also credit card fraud."

"That should be enough to hold her," Ramsey said. "But I've been surprised by judges before. She's safer in jail right now," he said. "One thing to sell out a kid. Quite another to betray a serial killer."

***

As Ramsey and Shepard retrieved their weapons from the jailhouse lockers, he glanced down at her. Her lips were compressed, and her brow was knotted. As she shoved her gun in its holster, he was close enough to see the fast pulse of her carotid artery. She was still shaken by her encounter with Bonnie.

He opened the door for her and followed her across the lobby to the front steps. "Bonnie Guthrie has returned to Nashville not just because of Sonny, but because she has been here before. She's familiar with Nashville."

Though Shepard's face appeared outwardly stoic, he noted the microexpressions, the shift of her stance and her breathing, which all pointed toward her unsettledness.

"I agree," she said.

"We can assume she has been using Elena as a means to an end. The child is likely a good distraction that enables Bonnie to manipulate and steal. She might also have some kind of appeal for Sonny."

She raised her chin a fraction. "Agreed."

"Bonnie tilted her head to the left slightly when you mentioned Elena's name. She knows the girl, but she's calculating if the child is still of use to her."

Shepard removed her sunglasses from her backpack and slid them on. "No argument here."

"Bonnie has used other children just as she has Elena. Do you think Sonny might have been one of those kids?"

"It's very possible."

"The mother figure is a powerful force in a child's life, and children naturally want to please," Ramsey said.

Shepard remained silent.

Ramsey added, "Bonnie pointed out that your name is unusual."

"I picked up on that. She was trying to get into my head. She's not the first."

"I can dance around this a little longer, but I don't have the patience." He dropped his voice a notch. "Is there any way you and Bonnie are connected from back in the day? Was she the woman who left you on the side of the road?"

Shepard stared at him from behind her dark glasses. "I don't know. Maybe."

"Did she seem familiar?"

"Yes. But this isn't the first time I've looked at a woman and wondered if we were related or if she were the one who abandoned me. It's common for adopted kids to wonder about their birth parents."

"I don't think she's your birth mother," he said.

He sensed her interest had sharpened to a fine point. "A DNA test would answer that question. I'm game to provide a cheek swab."

"Have you ever had your DNA tested?"

"Yeah. About a year ago, I sent it off to one of those sites that promised to tell you about your ancestry."

"Did you ever follow up and look for family matches?"

"No. I can tell you that I'm sixty-seven percent European, and the remaining thirty-three percent is Native Mexican."

"I would think you would want to know. Investigating people is what you do."

"Easier to peel back the layers of a suspect's life than my own. I decided to let sleeping dogs lie."

"Does meeting Bonnie make you curious? A lot of cases are getting solved via DNA these days."

"Yeah, I hear you," she said.

"And?"

Shepard laughed, but it sounded joyless and hollow. "Honestly? Meeting Bonnie makes me want to bury my test results. I'm not sure if I want a personal connection to her or her little pal Sonny." She shoved out a sigh. "But you're right. I need to think like a cop."

"If it helps, Bonnie isn't in town for you. She's here for Sonny because he has something she wants. Safe bet it's money."

"I hope it is just about money for her. I don't want to be connected to Bonnie or Sonny."

His phone rang. Irritated by the interruption, he glanced at the number and recognized it as his contact with the Nashville Police Department. "I better take this."

She looked relieved. "Certainly."

"Jeff, what do you have for me?" Detective Jeff Granger was with Nashville Homicide and had worked with Ramsey a couple of years ago on a case.

Ramsey watched as Shepard pulled her phone from her back pocket and dropped her gaze to it.

"We did a search on the credit cards that were found with Bonnie Guthrie. We contacted one of the victims and found something you're going to want to see."

"That was fast," he said.

"There was one card that was not reported missing. We started with that one."

"And?"

"Like I said, you better come and have a look for yourself. I'm texting you an address."

"I'll leave now." When he hung up, he noted the slight shift in Shepard's posture. She'd been listening. She was inquisitive by nature. That made her avoidance of her own past even more curious. "Nashville police have located the owner of one of the stolen credit cards. They want us to come and have a look."

"Interesting," she said.

"Care to join me?"

"You couldn't keep me away."

Shepard stayed close on his bumper as the two made their way north up I-24 toward the west side of Nashville. GPS guided him off the interstate and then down a collection of roads until he found himself in a small neighborhood filled with clapboard houses that looked as if they had been built in the twenties and thirties.

When Ramsey rounded the final neighborhood corner, he spotted a half dozen cop cars parked in front of a small one-level blue house. Yellow crime scene tape marked off the front and side yards.

Cops did not trick out a crime scene like this for a stolen credit card.

CHAPTER SIXTEEN

Wednesday, August 26, 3:00 p.m.

So far, there was no sign of a forensic van, but it was just a matter of time before half the Nashville police force was on scene. Ramsey parked a half block beyond the house and then strode back to meet Shepard at the edge of the tape.

"Things are heating up." She removed her sunglasses and swapped them for a set of latex gloves in her jacket pocket. She handed him a pair and threaded her fingers through her own set.

They introduced themselves to the uniformed officer, who directed them inside, where Detective Jeff Granger was waiting.

"You worked with Granger before?" she asked.

"On a task force," Ramsey said. "He's solid. Professional."

"I agree."

Ramsey's and Shepard's paths had come close to crossing several times in recent years, and he was sorry they had not met sooner.

They ducked under the tape and, at the edge of the front porch, slipped on paper booties. As soon as they reached the front door, he stopped.

"Jesus," Shepard muttered.

No one ever got used to the smell of decaying flesh. Some cops developed tricks to beat the stench, but he found rubbing Vicks on his upper lip just coated the rot with a menthol flavor. Eventually, the odor receptors in the nose stopped sending messages to the brain.

He stepped over the threshold and paused in the living room. The thermostat was set to sixty degrees, and the house felt like a meat locker.

"Killer turned down the AC so no one would smell the body," Shepard said. "The heat's been brutal the last few days." She searched the premises. "Jeff!"

"In the back bathroom," Jeff called back. "I'm down the hall. Last door on your right."

Ramsey noted the framed wall posters of various country-western and rock bands. Given that Nashville was the hub for country music, the town had more than its share of touring bands pass through.

Detective Granger stuck his head out of the bathroom door. In his late fifties, he had gray hair and a full mustache that made him look a little like the actor Sam Elliott. "She's in here. We believe her name is Jennifer Brown."

Ramsey moved past Detective Granger and looked into the bathroom. The woman was lying in a tub filled with water. Her blond hair was tied up in a neat topknot with tendrils flowing down over her shoulders. Large breasts bobbed on the water.

She stared sightlessly up toward the tin-panel ceiling, her mouth agape. Purple bruises shaped like fingers ringed her pale neck. Her eyes bulged and her lips were bloated.

Most of the crime scenes Ramsey had seen in the last five years had been via photographs. He had always considered himself an active participant but now realized he had become far more removed.

As repulsed as he was by this aftermath of violence, a surge of energy shot through his body. It had been too long since he had felt the rush of adrenaline that came with an active crime scene. He missed it.

Shepard stood behind him and asked, "Ramsey, when's the last time you worked a scene like this?"

"It's not been that long, if that's what you're asking," he said.

"It's been a while for me, too. I find people. And if they turn up dead, I turn the case over to homicide investigators," she said.

His gaze dropped to the victim's left hand. The ring finger had been clipped away with a sharp instrument. He guessed shears. "This finger didn't make it into our jar."

Ramsey motioned her forward. "The medical examiner will confirm time of death, but I estimate she has been dead at least a few days."

"Jeff," she said. "Do we know anything about Jennifer Brown?"

"We've only just begun to piece together her story. DMV tells me she's thirty-nine, five foot eight, one hundred and thirty pounds, green eyes, blond."

"Another blonde," Shepard said. "We know the first two victims were blondes. Coincidence is turning into a pattern."

"Ages are all about the same," Ramsey added. "So are the heights and weights. Our guy has a definite type."

"Don't they look a little like Bonnie?" she asked.

"The forensic team is pulling up," Jeff said.

"I'm not sure Bonnie was even in town when this woman died," Shepard said.

"Maybe she was in contact with the killer, and her text or call set him off," Ramsey said. "Sonny is not going to want to be found."

"Believe me, there are plenty of missing persons praying not to be found. It's certainly harder to locate them, but they usually leave a trail."

The sound of voices and technicians carrying equipment into the house signaled the arrival of the forensic team. Ramsey and Shepard both headed outside.

The air was hot and there wasn't a cloud in the sky. Shepard closed her eyes and tipped her face to the sun, and he noted the long, graceful line of her neck. She was a beautiful woman.

She straightened and opened her eyes, scanning the street. "I can start knocking on the doors of the neighbors and see if anyone has seen anything." Her phone buzzed and she glanced at the display. She let the call go to voicemail. "A call from the correctional facility."

"Who?"

She played back the recording and held it out so he could hear. The message was from the sheriff, informing Shepard that Bonnie Guthrie wanted to see her again. "Interesting."

"Wonder what game she's playing?" he asked.

"I'm not sure." She closed her phone and tucked it in her back pocket. "She's messing with me again. She's a grifter. They manipulate people."

"Why you?"

"She sees me as the weak link in this investigation. And for the record, she would be wrong," Shepard added.

"I can have a uniformed officer knock on doors. Better if you talk to Bonnie and see what she has to say. We need to find Sonny soon."

"I owe a visit to Elena first. It won't take me long. The girl might have something more to share. Bonnie can wait."

He liked her style. "Call me after your visit."

***

It was close to dinnertime when Melina knocked on the hospital room door and poked her head inside. Elena was sitting in her bed watching the nurse take her blood pressure. Set in front of her was a plate of nearly untouched food. The watch still dangled from her wrist.

"Knock, knock," Melina said.

The girl's eyes brightened, but there was no smile. "Melina."

"How are you doing?" Melina asked.

The nurse glanced up from the blood pressure gauge. "She's doing just fine. MRIs came back, as well as the blood work. She doesn't show any sign of injury."

"That's fantastic." The news meant that Elena would be leaving the hospital today or tomorrow at the latest. But with no custodial parent, Elena would be placed in foster care. Though the foster parents might be well meaning, they were still strangers. This little girl had seen far too much upheaval in her young life.

The nurse removed the blood pressure cuff and stepped back. "Maybe you can get her to eat."

Melina lifted the covering over the large plate. "Mashed potatoes? Who doesn't like mashed potatoes?"

"I love them," the nurse said.

Elena shrugged but didn't respond.

Melina set down her backpack by the bed. "Let me try."

"She's all yours," the nurse said.

When the woman vanished out the door, Melina walked to the small sink in the room and carefully washed her hands. She dried them with a paper towel and then balled it up. Raising her hand high in the air, she tossed it toward the trash can. It bounced off the rim. "Rats. No points for me."

She did not speak, but Elena regarded Melina as she picked up the discarded towel and held it out to the girl.

"Do you want to try?" Melina asked.

"No."

She tossed it in the trash. "Where are your bubbles?"

"Gone."

"You used them up?"

Another shrug. "Yeah."

"Well, I'll have to mention that to Jerrod. He might be able to pick up more." Using the plastic fork and knife, she stirred the melted pool of butter into small bites before she opened the packet of salt and poured it on the potatoes.

"It's okay," Elena said. "I don't need any more bubbles."

"Why not?"

"It's better to travel light."

"Is that what BB told you?"

"And my mommy."

Elena twisted Melina's gold watch around her slim wrist. She remained quiet, and Melina was willing to let the silence stand while the child processed her choices. Trust could not be forced.

Finally, Elena whispered, "I miss her."

"I know you do, honey." She swirled the potatoes and the butter. "Did you and BB leave while your mother was asleep?"

"Yes."

"Is your daddy looking for you?"

Elena glanced at the watch's face. "I don't have one."

"You left your home right after your birthday, right?"

"Yes."

"And that was August twenty-second?"

"On my birthday."

Elena's eyes did not fill with tears. The girl was accustomed to coping with absences, including her father's and now her mother's. "BB told Mommy needles were bad. Mommy said she was sorry and promised to stop."

"I'm so sorry."

"BB said not to be sorry. Sorry is for losers."

"That doesn't mean your mother didn't love you," Melina said.

"BB said she was weak."

"I bet she couldn't help herself," Melina said. "She was sick."

"With what?"

"Some grown-ups can't stop. They want to, but they can't." Melina laid her hand softly on Elena's arm. "None of this is your fault."

Elena closed her eyes. "Okay."

"It's going to be okay," Melina said.

The girl's narrowing gaze suggested otherwise. But she nodded as if she had been taught not to show her true feelings.

"Honey, I'm going to see BB this evening," Melina said.

The girl reached for her stuffed dog.

"Is there anything you want me to tell her?"

"No."

"What about Sonny? Do you want me to tell him anything?"

"No. I don't like Sonny. He has a mean face," she said.

"Did Sonny live near where BB's car crashed?"

Elena shrugged and kept her gaze down. "I don't know."

Frustration nipped at Melina, but she kept her tone calm. "That's okay."

Elena picked at the fur on the dog's paw. She had worn a bald spot. "Am I going back with BB?"

"No, honey."

"Why not?"

"Because BB is in a little trouble right now. She's in time-out."

"She's been bad?"

"Yes."

There was a knock on the door, and Melina turned to find her mother standing in the doorway. She was holding a bag from the local box store that she would bet her last dollar was stuffed with toys, clothes, and packets of Melina's favorite flavor of Goldfish.

"Can I come in?" Molly asked.

"Sure." After rising, Melina stepped aside so her mother could get a good look at Elena. "You must be Elena."

The girl looked at her with more curiosity than fear. She nodded.

"Elena, this is my mom, Mrs. Shepard."

"Oh my word, don't call me Mrs. Shepard. That makes me sound all old." She scrunched her face as she set the bag down by the bed. "You can call me Mimi. That's what my little grandnephew calls me."

Her mother took the seat by Elena's bed. "Have you not eaten your lunch?"

Elena shook her head.

"Melina was the worst eater when she was your age." She scooped up a small bite of mashed potatoes and swirled it in the melted butter. "Her daddy and I didn't meet Melina until she was five. She was such a scrawny little thing, and all she would eat was white bread and ketchup."

"I like ketchup," Elena said.

"It's as good as mashed potatoes. Try and see."

Her mother leaned forward, coaxed the girl's lips open, and put the food in her mouth. Elena ate, staring at Molly in a way that reminded Melina of herself.

One of her first memories of her mother was in a room like this. She had been in the hospital just a couple of hours and was chilled to the bone despite the layers of blankets put on her by the nurses. The bottoms of her feet had been raw from walking barefoot. She'd felt all alone and tried to hold back the tears.

And the room door had opened, and her mother had swept in, bringing with her the scent of a rose perfume. Melina inhaled the same fragrance now. It never failed to ease the world's stressors.

Melina folded her arms and watched as her mother coaxed another bite and then another into the girl. Soon Elena was drinking milk from a straw.

"See, Melina, Elena is a very good eater," her mother said. "I knew she would be." Molly cleared away the empty plate and set it off to the side. "I have coloring books. Would you like to color?"

Elena frowned. "I don't know how."

"Well, then you're in luck." Molly set a *Frozen* coloring book featuring the Disney princesses on the table. She rummaged in her bag and pulled out a twenty-four pack of crayons. "Other than Melina, I'm the best at coloring books."

As her mother began to leaf through the black-and-white pages, Melina said, "Elena, do you mind staying with my mom? I'll come back."

Her mother tossed Melina a bright smile. "Don't you worry about us. We're going to be fine. I have some books for Ms. Elena. I also heard that she likes bubbles—and guess what? I have bubbles."

The girl nodded as she selected a blue crayon from the box.

"Good choice." Her mother rose, kissed Melina on the cheek. "Do what you need to. I have this covered," she whispered.

"Thanks, Mom."

"Are you kidding? I couldn't sleep last night because I was so excited to meet Elena."

Melina hugged her mother. "See you soon, Elena."

The girl scooped up another crayon. "Are you coming back?"

"I will. Soon."

The girl nodded and began to color.

Out in the hallway, Melina shrugged her shoulders, tossing off an invisible weight she hadn't realized she had been carrying. Elena was in good hands. She could not say the same for Bonnie.

***

Sonny had learned her name was Sandra Wallace, and she worked as a bartender and waitress in a local honky-tonk several blocks north of the Lower Broadway strip. The bar was off the beaten track and was frequented by locals before 5:00 p.m., though the occasional tourist stumbled across it.

More importantly, Sandra had the look Sonny liked. Tall, buxom, with brassy-blond hair, she was known for tossing back her head and laughing loud. It was an infectious laugh that made everyone in the room turn and look in delight and sometimes annoyance. Sandra Wallace never entered a room unnoticed.

She liked the attention.

Craved it.

And she had gotten his attention.

As he watched her standing behind the walnut bar mixing a Manhattan, he could feel himself growing hard. He wrapped his hands around the cool glass of his beer bottle, imagining that it was her slim neck.

"Baby, what are you doing over there alone?" Sandra asked. She had shifted those blue eyes in his direction, and for just a split second, he imagined it was just the two of them in the world.

Sonny grinned, knowing ladies liked the look of him. A little bit of effort and he could have them eating out of his hand. "You look mighty pretty tonight, Sandra," he said. "But then you always do."

Her grin widened and a chuckle rumbled in her chest as she arched her back slightly. Her breasts pulsed out, drawing his attention away from her neck for only a moment.

"What are you doing after work?"

She shrugged. "What do you have in mind?"

"When do you get off?"

"Midnight."

To have a date scheduled so soon after the last two was not really smart. Time and distance between his dates had always been a strategy that kept him off the law enforcement radar. But since Bonnie's first text almost two weeks ago, his well-cultivated control had abandoned him. In its place was a bone-deep sense of loneliness that had made the four walls of his bedroom oppressive. "If I'm out back at, say, 1:00 a.m., you'll be ready?"

"Sure will."

He leaned forward, smoothing his fingers up and down the bottle's neck. "Sandra, do you have a bathtub?"

She moistened her lips. "I do, doll. Why?"

He took a swig of beer. "Wait and see."

Her eyes darkened with desire, and she would have lingered if not for another patron calling for another beer. She winked at him and slowly turned, sauntering toward the other side as if knowing he was watching her leave.

His phone rang, lighting up the number as **Blocked**. He let the call go to voicemail. A tickle of worry tightened his gut and reminded him loneliness was the least of his problems now. He finished his beer and, grabbing his phone, left the bar. In his car, he played back the voicemail.

The sound of Bonnie's voice grated over his nerves, and as tempted as he was to hit delete, he listened.

"Baby, you know who this is. And you know where I am. You need to help me."

He sat for several minutes before he played the next message. *"This is Ralph Hogan. I'm a bondsman who has been contacted by Bonnie Guthrie. She's asked me to contact this number. She says you will cosign for a bail bond."*

He could almost hear her smile as she gripped the phone and leaned toward it to whisper.

She was savvy enough to know the calls were recorded, so she hadn't called him directly. But for her to give this man his number implied an unspoken threat. *Help me, or I give you to the cops.* When Bonnie was cornered, she always came out swinging.

His heart kicked into high gear, and he replayed the message. Drawing in a breath, he reminded himself that he had some time. She would not play her cards until she ran out of options. She was a survivor and knew the best long game was to stay under the radar. If she turned on him, she would likely get tagged as an accessory after the fact.

She did not want to tell the cops what she knew, but she would. She never made idle threats.

He shoved his phone in his pocket and glanced into the bar's front window. Sandra was laughing and pouring beer from a tap. Already, she was smiling at another man.

Sonny had a couple of buddies that were bail bondsmen like Ralph Hogan. Working with bands and musicians for so many years meant he knew not only where to find the best drugs and food at 3:00 a.m. but also which bail bondsmen were quick and discreet. He did not know Ralph. But he had a friend who would.

Sonny checked his watch. As much as he wanted to go on a date with Sandra tonight, she would have to wait. He would deal with Bonnie first and then make time for his new girlfriend.

CHAPTER SEVENTEEN

Wednesday, August 26, 6:00 p.m.

Melina sat in the prison interview room, reminding herself that Bonnie Guthrie was nothing more than another con and thief. Just because Bonnie had remarked that she had once known a Melina did not mean she was telling the truth or that they were connected. Time to shake off her own emotional baggage and get on with the job of being a cop.

The knob twisted and the door opened. Bonnie entered the room and stared at her through the glass partition. She looked comfortable. Her shoulders were squared, her chin angled up like she was queen of this realm.

Melina doubted the relaxed demeanor. Bonnie had been around the block enough times to know she was facing serious jail time. She had also learned that no one better ever see you sweat in prison.

Bonnie grinned at Melina. "You got my message?"

"I'm here," Melina said.

"What took you so long? I called a few hours ago."

"Things to do, people to see."

She watched as Bonnie shuffled over to the chair and sat. Grinning up at the guard, she winked. "Thanks, doll. You can leave us now."

Scowling, the guard closed the door behind him. She sat back. Melina waited for Bonnie to speak.

"I don't suppose you can arrange for me to get some smokes? I've been craving one since they picked me up."

"I don't smoke."

"No, I don't suppose you do. I bet you're a health nut."

"What can you do for me, Bonnie?" Even to Melina's own ears, her tone sounded terse.

Bonnie shook her head. "Exactly."

"Are you going to tell me about the pickle jar?"

"I don't know anything about that. It must have been shoved in the trunk long before I got ahold of the car."

"Your prints were on the jar."

"Were they? If they were, which I doubt, it's because I was shuffling crap around in the trunk to make room for my own stuff."

"Who owned the car?"

"Belonged to a woman I knew back in LA."

"Does this woman have a name?"

"I have no idea. I gave her fifty bucks and she gave me the car. I know, bad deal on her part, but junkies do all kinds of dumb things when they need a fix."

Melina was tempted to call bullshit on Bonnie's story, but she decided to play along. "Okay, you don't know anything about the jar. Why were you in that neighborhood? What was the rush?"

"I had to pee really bad."

Melina shifted, tamping down a stab of frustration. "Tell me about Elena."

Bonnie's grin faltered a second. "What do you want to know?"

"She's not your kid." Melina looked Bonnie up and down. "No offense, but you're a little old to have a six-year-old."

Bonnie's eyes narrowed a fraction. "None taken, doll."

Melina did not smile but enjoyed some satisfaction knowing she, too, had found a soft spot. Bonnie was getting old and did not like it one bit. "Did Christina Sanchez own the car before you?"

Bonnie leaned forward, her gaze locking on Melina's. "Who?"

"Elena's mother. The junkie who overdosed."

"I don't want to talk about the kid or her junkie mother. I'd rather talk about you."

"For now, we'll stick with Elena. Where is Elena from? Where is her mother?" Melina would not allow Bonnie to redirect the conversation.

"Christina was a drug addict. When I got out of prison, I rented a room from her. That was a year ago, and she was barely making it then. I started taking Elena with me more and more while her mother turned a trick or slept it off."

"And you took the child so she could help you steal."

"We had outings. Little girls need sunshine, and we lived so close to the beach."

"What beach?"

"Imperial Beach in Southern California."

"Where is Christina Sanchez from?"

"I don't think you'll find any records of her. She came over the border about seven years ago. Had Elena in California, though."

"Does Elena have a birth certificate?"

"I doubt it. Christina was as afraid of the doctors as she was the cops. She was sure if she asked for help, she would be back home across the border."

"So how did you end up here in Nashville?" Melina asked.

"To find you, of course."

Melina's heartbeat jumped into high gear. Likely, Bonnie was lying to get under her skin, but it still took all her control to keep her tone steady. "Me?"

"There's a few things I could tell you about yourself."

"I doubt that."

Bonnie ran long fingers through her hair. "Oh, come on. You don't remember me? After all I did for you?"

"What you did for me? We've never met before." Deep down, she sensed Bonnie was telling the truth, but she could not bring herself to admit it out loud.

"Don't you remember anything before you were adopted?"

Melina rarely discussed her adoption, so there was no way Bonnie could have picked up that information in the jail or on the streets.

"It's hard to ignore the past," Bonnie continued. "God knows I've tried, but it has a way of rearing up and biting us on the ass."

Melina folded her arms, cultivating a bored, disinterested look. Cops needed to know when to shut up and listen. Allow the silence to coax free the truth. Her heartbeat ramped up as a fine sheen of sweat formed at the base of her spine.

Bonnie traced her index finger in small circles on the stainless steel table. "When you were little, your eyes were as big as saucers and you cried all the time."

Melina remained still. Bonnie was playing her. She had to be because if she was not and she was telling the truth, then the lid on her entire past was about to blow wide open.

Bonnie grinned almost as if she were recalling a memory. "You were a clingy little thing, too. Fussy eater."

Melina calculated their age difference. "How did we meet?"

"I was married to your granddaddy, baby. Howard and I had been hitched for about six months when we got a call that his daughter, Lizzie, had overdosed. She was your mama, child."

Melina swallowed. Something in Bonnie's words resonated with truth. "Lizzie?"

"That's right. Lizzie was in her late twenties when you were born. That was all before my time. According to Howard, she was always a troubled kid, and then she hooked up with a guy that was dealing drugs. Fast-forward a few years and she had dropped two kids and was shooting heroin."

The name Lizzie rang a distant bell in her memory. "What was Lizzie's last name?"

"Guthrie, baby. She never married. You were born Melina Guthrie."

Melina felt light headed. All her life she had wondered where she'd come from, and now the answers were coming at her faster than she could process them.

Two children. She had a sibling. There was another someone out there like her? "You said she gave birth to two kids?"

"You have an older brother. His name is Dean Guthrie, and if I had to guess, he's your half brother. Lizzie never stayed with any one man long."

"Does Dean go by the name Sonny now?" The pieces of her past nudged closer together, and she struggled to hide her hopes and fears.

"No. Sonny is my nickname for him."

Melina remained silent as she processed. Her half brother was in Nashville, and there was a good chance he was a killer. Her mouth felt dry. "Is Dean using his real name?"

Bonnie grinned. "No, and I have no idea what name he's using now. I just call him Sonny. But none of that is important to this story."

"I'd say the name of my half brother is very important." Melina tapped an index finger on her thigh, careful to keep the twitch hidden from Bonnie. "According to your police record you're quite the con."

"Oh, I'm the best," she said, smiling. "But cons don't always lie. At least the good ones don't."

"Okay. I'll bite. How did I end up staying with you?"

"Your mama overdosed when you were five, and Howard was not too keen on taking in a couple of kids." Bonnie did not take her gaze off Melina. "But I've always had a soft spot for children. I could never have any of my own and taking the little ones under my wing fills a part of my soul."

"You took Sonny and me."

"That's right."

"Howard and you didn't live happily ever after. Otherwise I'd not have ended up in Nashville." She stopped short of mentioning she had been abandoned. Melina could not know for sure yet how much of her story was bullshit.

"We were a nice little family for a few months. But Howard had a bad ticker. He dropped like a stone one day, and it was just Sonny, you, and me."

"How'd you get to Nashville?" Melina asked.

"We were headed east. I had friends in Virginia." Bonnie laced her fingers together and leaned forward. "One thing I've never been able to figure out."

"What's that?"

"We stopped on the side of Route 25. It was the middle of nowhere. In fact, the next stop was a few miles east. I got out to pee, and when I came back to the car, you were gone. I searched for hours. Who found you?"

Images of a darkened road edged to the front of her mind. She imagined the bright stars in the sky, the gravel cutting into her slippers, and the hoot of an owl. Raw terror had stolen the wind from her lungs, and she could not bring herself to scream. She countered Bonnie's question with, "You're saying you didn't leave me?"

"I'll admit you were screaming like hell and would not stop. That's part of the reason I pulled over. Hard to reason with a little girl when you're standing in the way of what she wants. I never had much luck winning over those of the female persuasion. Men I can handle, but not women."

"You abandoned me because I was crying."

"No. That would be criminal. I came back to the car and you were gone." Bonnie shook her head. "But to this day, I still don't know how you were found. I asked Sonny, but he said he never knew."

Bonnie was lying. The woman had abandoned her on the side of the road. And because she had not mentioned a call to the police from the diner pay phone, Melina realized the only other person who would have known she'd been dumped would have been the brother—Sonny, or Dean, or whatever name he was using now.

"I'm sorry I lost track of you. I was so tired, but that's no real excuse. I should have been more careful."

"And just like that you kept on driving."

"Good Lord, no. I drove around looking for you. I was coming up on the spot where I left you when I saw the flash of the cop's car. I knew you were in safe hands and thought you'd be better off if you weren't living on the road."

Blood rushed to Melina's temples, and her heartbeat nearly drowned out her own voice. "What about my brother? Did you desert him, too?"

"We stuck together for a long time. Like I said, I can handle men."

A memory, like a snippet of film, suddenly flashed. A little boy handed her half of a peanut butter and jelly sandwich. *"I made it with extra jelly,"* he said softly.

Melina shifted in her seat.

"I know I failed you both in different ways and taking care of Elena reminded me of my mistakes. But when I saw that picture of you in the paper and read the story about you finding those poor children locked in the trunk of a car, I knew I had to come see you. I knew if I found you, Sonny would be close. He always looked out for you. I was hoping we all could make amends."

She remembered the cigarette butts clustered by her car. They'd all been tipped in pink lipstick. Bonnie had been watching her apartment for a couple of days. "You sound sure of Sonny."

"I *know* Sonny better than anyone."

A part of her wanted to believe Bonnie, and another part prayed she was lying. "No one has ever identified himself to me as my brother."

Bonnie looked oddly satisfied with her new captive audience. "He wouldn't do that."

"Why not?"

"He knows himself well enough to realize you would be safer if he kept his distance."

She thought about the fingers in a pickle jar. If Sonny had been the one who had collected them, then her half brother was a serial killer.

Melina made a note to do a search on Dean Guthrie, who she guessed was in his midthirties. Whether or not Dean or Sonny was family, he was likely a killer. "What name does he use now?"

Bonnie shook her head and the grin returned. "You asked me that before. But I can't give away all my secrets, baby. I have to keep some of my cards close to the vest until we can make a deal."

"If I start digging, I'll find out if you're lying to me."

"Oh, I'm not lying. You'll find birth certificates for you and Sonny. Consider this the first of many meetings, baby. Go on and check on Elena's history, and find out what you can about Howard Guthrie. He would be seventy-six now if he had lived. And when you realize that I'm telling you the truth, then we'll talk again."

Frustration bubbled up in Melina. "Who put the pickle jar in the back of the car?"

"I don't even like pickles." Bonnie rose, walked to the door, and knocked. "Do your homework first and then we'll visit again." The door opened and Bonnie vanished into the back halls of the jail.

Melina sat back and closed her eyes. Her cheeks flushed with heat. Slowly she rose, grateful she could stand straight and at least appear pulled together.

***

Melina returned to the TBI offices and found Ramsey again camped out in the conference room. On the table next to his laptop was a collection of files in a neat row. He had removed his jacket and rolled up his sleeves and was wearing a pair of tortoiseshell glasses.

She knocked on the open door. He looked up at her, and the swirl of emotions, chasing her since the jailhouse, slowed. "Nice little setup you have here," she said.

He removed the glasses and carefully set them down beside his laptop. "I used to pride myself on being able to work anywhere. Back of car, hotel room, fast-food restaurant. But the last few years since I've been overseeing the team, I stay in Quantico mostly. It's a challenge to concentrate without the creature comforts."

From her perspective, he looked focused. "You seem to be adapting well."

"Managing." He studied her closely as he sat back in his chair. "How did it go with Bonnie?"

She pulled out a chair and sat. So much for small talk. "She's either one of the best con artists I've ever met, or she just blew my past apart."

His eyebrows knitted with curiosity. "How so?"

Melina began to unpack Bonnie's statements. Even as she recited the facts about Lizzie Guthrie, she could not believe that she was talking about her own life.

Ramsey sat quietly, absorbing each word. If not for this case, Melina would never have shared any of this with a colleague. This man now knew more about her life than the parents who had raised her.

"You've never heard of any of this before?" he asked.

"No. Nothing."

"Would your parents have kept it from you to protect you?"

"No. They have always been straight with me. What they know, I know."

"Are you sure?"

"I'm not sure about a lot of things right now, but that is one of them. It explains why social services couldn't find anything on me. There was never a missing persons report filed. No birth certificate was found. Even my birthday was fabricated. My parents made it official when my adoption was finalized."

"This is all assuming that Bonnie is telling the truth."

She stabbed her fingers through her hair. "Oh, I considered that. But, I, too, am good at sniffing out liars."

"Do you believe her?"

"I do."

"Do you believe her because you want to? It's very common for adoptees to hunger for knowledge of their past, even if it's not corroborated."

A devil's advocate's job was to challenge statements and debunk theories. "I considered that. But she knew I was left on the side of the road."

He tapped his finger on the edge of the polished table. "I'll run Lizzie's and Dean Guthrie's names through the FBI databases."

"Thanks."

As he typed a text message, he asked, "What does Bonnie want?"

"I think she's going to angle for a deal. She'll soften me up with the missing pieces of my life and then trade what she knows about the pickle jar for immunity."

"You believe she knows the killer."

"I'm convinced she does. She came back to Nashville to see him. She calls him Sonny, but that's not his real name. His birth name is Dean Guthrie, but he doesn't use it."

"Oh shit."

"And before you ask, I have no clue who the guy is. However, Bonnie says he knows who I am." The creep factor on this case had certainly kicked up a few more notches.

"Bonnie comes to town to look up Sonny, and somehow figures you're nearby," Ramsey says. "She asks him for help. He refuses. She gets pissed and takes the evidence of his dirty work. Only Bonnie screws it all up when she wrecks the car. And you're the cop that lands the case. Is that the gist of it, Agent Shepard?"

"Did she screw it up?" Melina asked. "That's a hell of a coincidence."

"You think she staged the accident?"

"I don't know. I found cigarette butts near my car. There were several, and each was tipped in pink lipstick. I dropped them off at the lab, so I'll know soon enough if they belong to Bonnie."

"How did she find you?"

"My name was in the paper on a child abduction case."

He reached for a folder, pulled out a sheet of paper, and pushed it toward her. "We've identified two more pickle-jar fingerprints."

She glanced at the sheet detailing the unsolved homicides. The other two women had vanished in 2014 from Denver and 2015 from Dallas. "Neither had ties to the Nashville area."

"So far, we know this killer targeted his victims from all over the country in four different major cities: Kansas City, Portland, Denver, and Dallas."

"Accessible, large populations. Easy for a serial killer to move around unnoticed."

"I have also located the sister of our most recent victim. Jennifer Brown's sister lives in Nashville," he said.

"Has she been notified of her sister's death?" Melina asked.

"No."

"What's her name?"

"Kelly Brown. She's forty-one and works as a bartender."

Melina had made death notifications before, but they never got easy. Nor forgotten. "Give me her contact information and I'll visit her."

"I'd like to come along, if you don't mind."

"Sure. Ready?"

He rose and grabbed his jacket draped across the back of his chair. "I can drive."

"Sure."

In the car, she dialed Kelly's number as he pulled out onto the main road. The call went to voicemail. She considered identifying herself but thought better of it. Better to see her reactions and hear the tones in her voice when she received the news. Until she could prove otherwise, everyone attached to any of her cases was suspect.

Ramsey crossed town in twenty minutes and followed the GPS to a small neighborhood. The houses were modest and one level, dating back to the turn of the last century. Their best days were long gone, and their residents were not likely far behind.

He parked in front of a white clapboard home with a small front porch. The summer heat had baked out the grass to a light brown, giving it the texture of straw. There were three vehicles in the driveway, including a low-riding black four-door and two trucks. On the side of the house was a rusted bike with a flat tire and a collection of stacked clay flowerpots that looked as if they had not been used in years.

Out of the car, Melina stood shoulder to shoulder with Ramsey as they studied the dwelling. Ramsey unbuttoned his jacket, and she pulled back the front of her jacket to slightly expose the holster and weapon underneath.

Cops could tell a lot about people by their homes. They all had to make snap judgments about the occupants based on a hundred different details all processed with each step toward the front door. Home visits could be surprisingly deadly. A warrant for unpaid parking tickets could lead to a shoot-out because the occupant was hiding drugs. Domestic disputes could also turn deadly, and cops had to worry not only about the abusive spouse but also about their codependent victim, who did not want to see their loved one in handcuffs.

She walked up the slate sidewalk knitted together with weeds and scrub grass and stepped up the two porch steps. Ramsey remained a couple of feet behind, one foot poised on the bottom step and the other on the ground.

On both sides of the door were windows, each draped in thick dark curtains. She rang the bell but did not hear the chime echoing in the house. She pressed it again and then banged hard on the worn screened door. It took several harder knocks before she heard footsteps moving toward the front of the house. A flutter of curtains to her right had her standing back and just to the left.

The door opened to a woman with tangled, long blond hair, a pale round face, and bloodshot eyes smudged with yesterday's mascara. She regarded Melina as she swiped back hair from her face. An oversize red T-shirt hung over faded jeans.

"What's this about?" she asked.

Melina held up her badge and identified herself. Ramsey did the same. "This is about your sister, Jennifer."

"Oh, shit. What's she done now?" Kelly asked.

"Your sister was found dead in her home," Melina said.

Kelly pulled off a rubber band ringing her wrist and tied up her hair. "What? How could Jennifer be dead? She's been clean for five years. Shit, did she have a relapse?"

"She did not die from an overdose," Melina said. "The circumstances are suspicious." Details about the homicide scene and especially the removal of the ring finger would not be released until the killer was caught.

"How did she die?" Kelly's gaze sharpened, cutting away all traces of fatigue.

"We can't say right now. Was there anyone in her life who could have harmed her?"

"Shit, are you saying it was murder?" Kelly demanded.

"Yes, ma'am."

Kelly opened the door wider. "Want to come inside? The house is a wreck but seems I should invite you in."

"Are you here alone?"

"No, my boyfriend, Gus, is here. He's a bartender like me, and we both worked double shifts yesterday. We only got home a few hours ago."

Melina crossed the threshold, pausing as her eyes adjusted to the dim light and her gaze swept the small living area. The thick scent of cigarettes and Mexican takeout lingered in the air as she examined the lone worn leather couch, wide-screen television, and coffee table stacked with used paper plates. In the corner was a makeshift bar covered in two or three dozen liquor bottles.

"Can you ask Gus to come out here?" Ramsey asked.

"Sure." Kelly walked into the bedroom. "Gus. Cops." She opened the door. "Shit."

"What is it?" Ramsey asked.

"He's gone. Out the bathroom window."

Ramsey's jaw tightened as he moved past Kelly into the room. When he returned, he asked, "What's Gus's last name?"

"Gaines."

Ramsey scribbled down the name. "Is he wanted for anything?"

"No doubt." Kelly picked up a few of the paper plates and dumped them in an overflowing kitchen trash can. "I can call Gus and get him back here?"

"Do it," Melina said.

Kelly dialed the number. She sniffed. The phone rang. She held out the phone so they could hear. "It's going to voicemail."

Ramsey took down the phone number. "Where does he work?"

"Pete's Bar, like me." She shoved her phone in her pocket. "Can I get you a coffee?"

"No, thank you," Melina said. "When is the last time you saw your sister?"

"About two weeks ago," she said. "We had lunch."

"Do you keep up with her?"

"Yeah, I mean we try. Busy lives get in the way."

"Was Jennifer dating anyone?" Ramsey asked.

"She dated Kyle about six months ago, but he moved back to California. He wouldn't have hurt her. He's such a stoner I don't think there's an aggressive bone left in his body."

"What did your sister do for a living?" Melina asked.

"She was a tour guide when she wasn't following one of her favorite bands."

"She was a groupie," Melina said.

"Yeah. Though she thought of herself as having higher standards."

"Who did she follow?" Melina asked.

"I'm not sure of the latest band. It changed with her mood."

"You said she'd been on the road?" Melina wasn't fooled by Ramsey's silence. He was processing every detail about Kelly and her house.

"Yeah, she'd been on tour for most of the spring, traveling around the country. She'd only just gotten back a few weeks ago. She told me the tour went fine. Sometimes groupies can cause trouble for the band, but she said this go-around it was pretty smooth. No troubles. And like I said, she has been clean and sober for the last five years."

She and Ramsey would be meeting with the medical examiner in the morning. It was standard to run toxicology tests, which would determine if Jennifer had been truthful with her sister.

Kelly sat down on the couch and rubbed her face with her hands. "I'm still trying to wrap my brain around what you just told me. I mean, she was only thirty-nine. Shit. Can I see her?"

"I can arrange a viewing with the medical examiner," Melina said.

Moments like this could be the most telling. Shock caught people off guard, and sometimes the masks dropped for just a few seconds, revealing the true person underneath.

Kelly reached for a crumpled packet of cigarettes on the coffee table, fished out a lighter tucked inside, and lit one. She took a long pull. "You haven't told me how she was murdered."

"We have to wait for the medical examiner's report."

"Are you telling me you won't tell?" Kelly demanded. "You must have some idea."

"I'd rather have the official story and let the medical examiner explain it to you," Melina said.

Kelly inhaled and shook her head as she blew out smoke in a quick breath. "Shit. Shit. Shit."

"What was the name of the tour company where Jennifer worked?"

"Nashville Tours. She gave guided tours of the city. She could tell you anything and everything about the area."

"Anyone on the tours give her trouble?" Ramsey asked.

"Not that she mentioned."

"What about parents or friends we could talk to?" Melina asked.

"Dad's been MIA since we were kids, and Mom died a few years ago. Cancer. It's just the two of us. Me, now." She raised a trembling finger and pressed it against her brow as if her head was throbbing.

"Do you have the name of her boss?" Melina asked.

She rose, and with the cigarette perched between her lips, she rummaged through the junk drawer of a desk until she found a dog-eared pamphlet. She handed it to Melina. "I'm not sure of his name, but you can find their offices at the end of Lower Broadway facing the Cumberland River. They're in a small trailer, and if you arrive early or late in the day, the two red tour buses are parked out front."

The killer they were chasing had already proven he had a particular type that Jennifer perfectly matched. Whether he had first spotted her on the tour or somewhere else, Jennifer had landed in his crosshairs and was now dead.

CHAPTER EIGHTEEN

Wednesday, August 26, 9:00 p.m.

Melina stared at her phone, trying to read emails as Ramsey drove from Kelly Brown's house to the active crime scene at Jennifer's residence. She was having a hard time concentrating. Her mind kept returning to Bonnie and Sonny.

"You said earlier you had your DNA tested?" Ramsey asked.

His deep voice pulled her out of spiraling thoughts. "What?"

"DNA. Tell me again why you haven't analyzed your results?"

"You mean why does the missing persons agent find everybody but herself?"

A half smile tugged the edge of his lips. "Basically, yes."

"I could say that I've been really busy the last year, which would be true. But I'd be lying to you and myself. I didn't want to know. My life is really good as it is."

"You aren't curious about your past?"

"Sometimes. But I made it a habit a long time ago after a very frustrating ancestry assignment in elementary school not to look back." She shook her head. "All the teacher wanted us to do was build out a family tree, and I couldn't do it."

"When you see a mother and child and note the physical similarities, do you wonder who you look like?"

"Sure, I do. I don't look like my parents, who are fair skinned. I also don't share their temperament. They are fairly laid back while I'm high strung. I wonder why I like to chew ice or can't sleep more than six hours."

"Yeah. All that."

"We can't choose our family, Ramsey."

A very slight shrug lifted his shoulder. "Knowing your genetic history isn't always a blessing."

"How far can you trace your family back?"

"No more than most."

"Bet a paycheck you can go back at least three hundred years."

"Give or take."

She laughed. "I'm picturing a portrait gallery in some dusty home in the Hamptons."

"It's not dusty. We have a staff that cares for it."

"Jesus, do you have portraits of ancestors hanging on the walls?"

"Yeah, a few. My mother is the keeper of the family tree. I've not had much interest in it."

"Because it's right there and you can see it anytime. It's not a gnawing unknown that will always be out of reach."

"That's the way it is for you?"

She shrugged. "Don't ever tell my mother, but yeah, sometimes."

"Look at the DNA test. You might get a hit."

"If I get any more hits like Bonnie or Sonny, I'm not sure I could stand the excitement."

"What about genetic questions? General medical health history?"

"All important questions. But you're searching for logic in my emotional quagmire, Agent Ramsey."

"Logic isn't the root of the problem."

She pressed her fingertips to her temple. "And what is?"

"Fear. Fear of the unknown. You don't mind the unknown in general or in other people's lives, but you don't like it for yourself."

She nodded. "Makes me feel a little out of control or as if I'm standing on a shaky foundation."

"For what it's worth, you're handling all this well."

She liked the deep, rich timbre and the way the creases at the corners of his eyes deepened. "I know you're not married. What else can you tell me about you?"

"You tell me, Agent. What do you see?"

"You want me to profile you, FBI man?"

"I can dish it out, so I better be able to take it."

She regarded him for only a couple of seconds before saying, "You're worried about losing your edge. It's why you're here. You could have sent another agent, but you came instead. Are you approaching a big birthday? What, fifty or sixty?" she teased.

"Ouch. Thirty-nine and one hell of a promotion. Means moving to the Washington office."

"But you aren't going to take it, are you?"

He was silent for a long moment. "No. Though that information is not public yet."

"I'm a vault," she said. "What is plan B after the bureau?"

"No idea. Which scares me almost as much as the idea of years filled with politics, congressional hearings, and budgets."

"I have the unknown past and you have the unknown career future. Aren't we the pair?"

"If you decide to look into those results and need help with the genealogy charts, Andy from my team is good at that kind of thing."

He had flipped the conversation back to her, steering it away from feelings he would rather not think about. "Thanks, I'll keep that in mind."

"Tackle the genealogy from a different angle," he offered. "It's not about you right now. Find out more about your history, prove or disprove Bonnie's claims, and hopefully figure out who the guy is with the pickle jar."

"I see the logic," she said.

"And?"

"I'll have a look at it tonight. If I have questions, I'll reach out to Andy."

"Glad to be of assistance."

They pulled up to Jennifer Brown's home and angled the car behind the state forensic van and a couple of cruisers.

During her first trip to the house, Melina had not had the time to study it closely as she had processed the controlled mayhem of the forensic team and uniformed officers doing their jobs.

Yard work and general home maintenance had ranked low on the priority list for Jennifer. The recycling bin full of wine and beer bottles suggested she'd liked to have parties. Her five-year abstinence had likely never actually made it past one year.

Melina and Ramsey both pulled on rubber gloves and stepped into the foyer. All the blinds were drawn, and the faint scent of death still lingered. The ashtray on the coffee table was full of cigarette butts. Some were cupped in lipstick and others not. The brands varied between Virginia Slims and Marlboro. There was one wineglass, lipstick matching the color on the cigarettes, and a pile of cheese crackers. No signs of pets and only a few photos encased in dollar store frames. Furniture appeared secondhand and worn, and the couch was covered in unnaturally orange cracker crumbs.

Ramsey walked into the kitchen and opened the refrigerator and then slowly looked around the small galley space. He picked up a collection of travel brochures that looked like newer versions of the one Kelly had shown them. Hanging on a hook was a red vest and pinned over the left pocket was a gold brass nameplate that read **Jennifer**.

Matt Piper, dressed in a hazmat suit, looked out of the bedroom and raised his hand. As she moved toward him, she noticed the death scent grew stronger. "Any luck?"

"We're still working our way through the bathroom and bedroom. I have dozens of prints. I can tell you there is no forced entry and no signs of a violent struggle."

"Anything else you can tell us about her killer?" Ramsey asked.

Matt motioned for them to follow him into the bedroom and the adjoining bath. "I think our guy got into the tub with her."

"Why do you say that?" Ramsey asked.

"Two things. First, the hair found in the tub includes hers and someone else's. Second, there are signs that the tub's water spilled over, and what didn't dry up pooled under the tub. However, when she was found, the waterline ringing the inside of the tub only reached the halfway mark."

"Any signs of his DNA?" Melina noted scented lotion and more lipstick beside the sink.

"I've collected multiple hair and skin fibers," Matt said. "At this point we don't know if it's the killer's or someone else's."

"He knows her," Ramsey said. "She invites him into her house, and he strangles her and then places her in the tub. Why does he get in the tub with her?"

"He isn't ready to leave her," Melina said. "He's lonely and wants to spend time with her. Bathing together is very intimate."

"He doesn't have to worry about expectations or unnecessary conversation from her. She's totally his and exists only for him."

"It's not the violence that attracts him, but the need for connection," Melina said. "I've seen a similar character profile with pedophiles. The sick bastards want the emotional connection."

"And he takes the fourth finger on the left hand," Ramsey said.

"Which is supposed to be the direct line to the heart." She glanced at her hand and traced her naked ring finger. Bonnie had been in

188

Nashville to find Sonny. And though Bonnie had not admitted it, it wasn't a huge leap to assume she had stolen the jar filled with fingers from Sonny. And if anything Bonnie had said about Sonny was remotely true, he was her half brother.

"I would bet he's charming," Ramsey said. "He woos his victims. Why force them when you can coax them into your arms? He's moderately, if not very, attractive. The lack of struggle with his victims is a big part of the reason he has stayed under the radar."

"If he sticks to his pattern, then he'll only kill once in the Nashville area," Melina said.

Ramsey shook his head. "If he keeps to his pattern."

"A half sibling hit in the ancestry world is akin to hitting gold. Whatever DNA we pulled from the crime scene that we think belongs to this guy should be compared to mine. If we can confirm he's my brother, we might be able to use that to our advantage."

***

Resting and meticulous wound care had paid off for him. Though the gash was still tender, he was now mobile and ready to make his next move.

Now, nine days after nearly snagging his dream date, he drove to the Bottom in a rented dark-blue four-door sedan ready to get his van. But as soon as he approached his warehouse, he spotted the notice on the front door. CRIME SCENE.

"Shit!" he shouted.

As he drove past, he was careful to keep his head ducked. There were always cameras watching. How the hell had they found his van?

Angry now, he blamed this mess on Ms. Perky Breasts. She had hurt him, and she must have told something to the cops about his van and they had found it.

He needed to figure out who Ms. Perky Breasts was, find her, and make her pay.

He circled the block for almost an hour, but he found no sign of the girls she had been with last Monday night. A week was a long time for girls like Ms. Perky Breasts. He dreaded the thought that she had moved on or found a new corner to work.

He drove around the block again and decided any girl at this point would do for now. The sex was boring when there was no pain, but he might get lucky and find out something.

Three girls stood on the corner just ahead. They huddled close. All were wearing high heels and short skirts. One had a cigarette dangling from her hand. All the women were blondes, or at least wore blond wigs. Not the look he wanted. None of this felt right.

He slowed his vehicle to a stop in front of the women. He lowered the passenger window as the tiniest blonde approached his car. "I need a date."

She tossed her cigarette aside. "How long?"

"Half hour. Get in and we can go around the corner."

Her smile told him she liked the idea of staying close. A quick turnaround meant she could find another client quickly. He bet she thought her evening was looking up.

They agreed on a price and she slid into the front seat, locking in her seat belt. As promised, he drove to a darkened alley. He shut off the engine and killed the lights.

"Take the wig off," he said.

She hesitated and then pulled the blond wig off. Dark hair tumbled out. It was not as lush as Ms. Perky Breasts', but it was better.

"You like it?" She tousled her hair with her fingers.

"Yeah."

She unhooked her seat belt and twisted in the seat toward him. Her gaze dropped to his lap, and, not seeing signs of an erection, she licked her lips and rubbed her hand over his crotch. The sensation was pleasant enough, so he nodded, giving her the go-ahead to unzip his pants. She pulled his cock free and took just the tip while looking up at him.

He imagined Ms. Perky Breasts chained to the floor of his van. An electric prod to her breast would make her scream. Or maybe a solder gun to her belly. He could burn his initials into her pale tight skin.

"There you go, baby," she said. "Nice and hard. Want me to climb on top?"

"No."

As if understanding, she wrapped her lips around his cock and began to suckle. He fisted a handful of her hair and drove her face down hard. She gagged and shifted her hand to his thigh to steady herself. Her fingers brushed his wound and he hissed in a breath as pain cut through him.

"Careful!" he shouted. He released the pressure on her head.

She instantly sat up and stared at him with wary eyes. No doubt her instincts were telling her to run. "Did I hurt you?"

He ran his hand lightly over his thigh. "No. Finish it."

She moistened her lips, hesitated, and then went down on him again. He grabbed her hair with both hands this time and twisted the strands until he knew it hurt. A whimper rose in her throat.

Her suffering excited him, and he gave in to the pleasure and coiled his hand tighter around her hair. Finally, he came in her mouth. She choked, trying to catch her breath. If he kept her like this, she might suffocate.

Suffocate. It was too easy a death.

"Swallow it," he ordered.

When she complied, he let her up. She drew in a deep breath and pressed her back to the passenger door. She was smart enough not to complain.

He zipped up his pants and then fished a couple of twenty-dollar bills from his pocket. "I'm looking for someone. Tall, lean, dark hair.

Doesn't dress like a hooker. She was on your corner Monday night a week ago."

"I don't know her." She eyed the bills. "I could ask."

"I can do my own asking."

"You a cop?"

"No." He folded the bills neatly in half, creasing the edge to a fine point. "Who else would know about this woman?"

"The best person to ask is Sarah. She runs the Mission. She knows almost all the girls."

He handed her the bills. "Get out."

She quickly opened the door and stumbled into the alley. His headlights turned on with the engine, catching her slim frame pressed against the wall. Even if she remembered him, he had altered his appearance enough to throw any cop off.

He backed out of the alley, turned, and headed back toward the city. He needed to get a van.

Buying a van in the Nashville area was not a smart idea. He decided to return to Atlanta, Georgia, to the dealership he had used when he had bought his old van. Maybe it wasn't smart to repeat past moves, but he was willing to risk it.

The rental car created a digital trail, but he was not worried. In all his years, the cops had never come close to finding him.

CHAPTER NINETEEN

Thursday, August 27, 6:00 a.m.

Bonnie Guthrie smiled as she signed her name on the bail bondsman's paperwork. The bail bondsman's name was Ralph, and he reminded her of a guy she had dated when she'd lived in New York during a summer of decadence after leaving home for good.

Ralph stacked his papers into a neat pile. "It shouldn't be much longer, Ms. Guthrie. I'll deliver this check to the magistrate now, and you should be out real soon."

"You're amazing, doll." She ran her fingertips lightly down her breasts.

"Do you need a ride?" Ralph asked.

"A ride? That's full service."

"We're accustomed to transporting our clients to a destination within twenty miles."

"Well, that would be lovely." She winked. "Remind me to write an online review for you."

"Always appreciated. The judge wants you back in two weeks for a preliminary hearing."

"I'll be here," she lied. The truth was she planned to find Elena. Sonny did not know it yet, but his future was tied up with Bonnie and that little girl. And once he had Bonnie and his "sister" back, he would stop doing whatever it was with the severed fingers. The boy had never been right after she had dumped Melina, but she had never figured he was this messed up.

All Sonny had to do was produce the key, and the three of them would have enough money to live in style in Mexico. She could have told Melina the name Sonny was using now, but she had kept quiet to protect him. They could search Dean Guthrie all they wanted, but it wouldn't lead them to Nashville.

She might be partly responsible for his messed-up mind, and she had a chance to help him, the kid, and herself. Win-win for everybody.

Ralph escorted her to his car and opened her door. She slid into the front seat, showing him the full length of her tanned legs. She was glad to be out of jail.

"Doll, I'm starving," she said. "What say I treat us to breakfast?"

***

Melina hustled back to her town house after an early-morning run. It would have been smarter to catch some shut-eye in the few hours she had, but she had to burn off steam. Her mother used to say Melina needed to run to get the wiggles out.

She kicked off her shoes and opened a can of tuna fish. She set it out on the patio table for the neighbor's cat.

She switched on the television to a weather channel that offered the right amount of background noise so that she did not feel alone. As coffee brewed, she opened her laptop; then she poured herself a cup and dumped in two teaspoons of sugar.

As she sipped her coffee, she clicked on the DNA website and logged on to her account. Her name appeared, and beside it in red letters were the words *New Information*.

"New. That can't be good," she whispered.

If her job had taught her anything, it was that the situation could always have more surprises. She held her breath as the icon bounced back and forth before the section opened. She scanned the list and saw that she had several fourth-cousin matches. The initial burst of excitement faded as she calculated that tracing those relatives would mean going back to their shared great-great-grandparents. It was possible but would take a ton of man-hours.

Still, she clicked on the cousin located in Ohio. He did not have a picture attached, but she noted he was sixty-two years old. The next cousin was not much more promising. She lived in North Carolina and was in her early seventies. No picture attached to her profile either.

She fished out her phone and pulled up Andy's contact information. She wanted to ensure that Andy was cross-checking her DNA against the killer's.

She took another sip from the coffee cup, copied the link to her test results, and attached it in an email to Andy. She paused for a moment and then hit send.

An email response from Andy came back almost immediately. I'm on it.

"Ready or not," Melina said.

One way or another, she was going to learn something about her past.

Her phone rang and she half expected to see Andy's name. Realizing it was her mother, she wondered if this woman had an inkling of what she had done. She felt like a traitor and closed her computer screen.

"Mom."

"Don't go by the hospital to see Elena today. She's not there anymore."

Melina sat forward. "Where is she?"

"She's with Dad and me. Dad pulled a few strings, and social services agreed to let her come home with us. We picked her up late last night."

Relief washed over her. "Isn't that going to be a lot on you with Dad laid up?"

"Nothing I can't handle." Her mother's voice sounded buoyant, as if she welcomed the challenge.

"What can I do to help?"

"Nothing you can do, honey. I've got this under control. She's sleeping in your old bed now."

"Did you turn on the purple night-light?" Her mother had bought it for her when she was about six, and it still remained in her old room.

"Of course. Put a fresh bulb in yesterday."

"Thanks, Mom."

"Just wanted to let you know so you can focus on the job." Her mother dropped her voice a notch. "The poor thing was exhausted when we got her home. We watched a movie and ate dinner. She fell asleep as soon as her head hit the pillow. But a dream woke her up within the hour."

Melina remembered how the fatigue had always mingled with the fear of dreams. "Has Elena said anything that might help me?"

"Not yet, but if she does, I'll pass it on."

"Good." She sipped her coffee. "I look forward to catching this guy."

***

Ramsey met Melina at the TBI offices. He had two coffees waiting, one for himself and the other for her. He had already learned Agent Melina Shepard was more approachable if caffeinated.

"Thanks," she said, prying off the lid. "I can really use this."

"Didn't sleep well?"

"I dabbled on the genealogy website, trying to trace my family tree. I had very little luck. I emailed off what I had to Andy. She's already on it."

"Good. Your time is better spent with me."

"I came to that conclusion very quickly."

Ramsey drove Melina to the medical examiner's office. They showed their badges, though the guard recognized Melina. "Agent Shepard, we meet again," he said.

Melina tucked her badge in her pocket. "No offense, but I can't say I'm glad to be back," she said with a smile.

The guard nodded with a slight grin. "No offense taken."

As Melina and Ramsey walked toward the elevators, she said, "I was here a few times over the winter. A van filled with undocumented workers was found. All the occupants were dead. It took several visits here to sort out identities and causes of death." When he arched a brow, she added, "Asphyxiation. The truck had a faulty exhaust system and the occupants kept it running to stay warm. They all expired from carbon monoxide poisoning."

"How did missing persons get involved?" Ramsey asked.

"I tried to match up the dead to their families. I was able to locate families for three of the victims."

She had worked days, fearing some of the women and men had left behind children and loved ones. In the end, she had been forced to stop and move on to a new case.

They rode the elevator down to the lower level, where the medical examiner performed his autopsies. They gowned up and met the doctor in his autopsy suite.

He stood by the badly decomposing body of Jennifer Brown. Her skin had loosened and drooped from her arms and her abdomen. The decaying process had also darkened her skin and shrunk her cuticles, which gave the impression that her nails had grown. Her left ring finger was missing.

Her head rested above the block tucked under her neck, arching her bruised chin upward. Her blond hair was brushed back, and her eyelids were closed.

"We were just about to start," Dr. Connor said.

"Thanks for waiting on us," Ramsey said.

"After seeing that jar full of fingers, I'm happy to expedite this investigation," Dr. Connor said.

"How long has she been deceased?" Ramsey asked.

"I took her liver temperature, and I estimate she died last Monday to Wednesday."

"Over a week," Melina said. "She died before Bonnie stole the pickle jar. Are her prints a match to one of the unidentified fingers?"

"Yes," the doctor said.

"Cause of death?" Ramsey asked.

Dr. Connor moved to the top of the table. He tilted the head, angling it so that the bruised neck was exposed. "Unless I find evidence to the contrary, I'd say strangulation."

"The bruising around her neck is defined," Melina said. "It's consistent with a choke hold."

"Yes, that's exactly what happened," Dr. Connor said. "Sometimes you see shadow bruising that indicates the killer had to adjust his grip because he didn't have the strength to maintain the initial choke hold. But in this case, I see none of that. I suspect this killer is physically fit and strangled her without hesitation."

Dr. Connor then repositioned the head and reached for a scalpel. He positioned the sharp blade at the top of the breastbone and made the Y incision between and under the breasts.

For the next hour, Melina and Ramsey watched as Dr. Connor inspected and weighed the organs, took tissue samples, and then examined for signs of sexual assault. As he had theorized, the victim had been healthy, and there were no signs of intercourse.

When Melina and Ramsey walked out of the medical examiner's office, she craved the warm sunshine on her face. "I need to call the tour company," she said. "I want to talk to her boss." She wondered how Elena was doing with her mother.

Ramsey checked his watch. "It's eight thirty. They should be open by now."

"I'll head straight over and try to catch the crew before too many tourists swamp the place." Next to learning about any potential stalkers, she wanted to establish a timeline for Jennifer Brown's last days.

"I'm going to meet with the forensic department and see what evidence they were able to pull from Jennifer Brown's house," Ramsey said.

"We'll reconvene later today."

"Perfect." Ramsey dropped Melina off at the TBI offices down the road. As he drove off, she shifted to her car and sat still for a moment, letting the day's heat warm her chilled bones.

She dialed her mother's number. "Mom, how's it going?"

"Elena is still sleeping."

"She's doing all right?"

"The poor kid is exhausted. I wonder when she last had the chance to sleep this well. You were much the same when you came to live with us."

"About that. The woman who had custody of Elena, Bonnie Guthrie, said she knows me." Melina pinched the bridge of her nose, focusing her energy on a calm, even tone. "She said she was the one that left me on the side of the road outside of Nashville when I was a kid."

The line was silent. "I don't understand."

"That's my point. I think she's telling the truth."

"What kind of monster does that to a five-year-old girl?"

"Believe me, the world has plenty of them."

"I'd like to meet this woman face to face." A sharpness honed the edges of her mother's words.

"You'll have to stay clear for now."

"Just let me know when I can."

"Unsettled business, Mom?"

"Damn right."

***

Using the same car dealer was not really smart. But it had been almost ten years since he had bought from the dealer. If a cop should come across this place, no one here would remember him from all those years ago.

He walked into the dealership as soon as it opened. A car salesman was at his side in minutes. An hour later, a deal was sealed, and he was driving off the lot in his new van.

It would take a smart and determined cop to connect all the dots, and so far, he had not crossed paths with any cop who had the staying power to track a guy like him. Cops were somewhat lazy by nature. Most were looking to get home alive and make it to retirement. They had no skin in the game.

Feeling confident, he pulled into a Hardee's drive-through and ordered three burgers, a bucket of large fries, and a jumbo soda. He had not eaten much in the last few days. Worry always stole the appetite right out of him, and now that he had his van, he was feeling more like himself.

When he pulled up to the window, a pretty young girl with dark hair and a bright smile took his order and handed him back his change. Too bad his van was not ready for her yet.

"Thanks, darlin'," he said.

"Have a nice day."

"Always do."

He drove to the center of a large retail parking lot and sat, eating his burgers first. Second, he ate the fries one by one, and then he drank the soda. It was a quirk of his and never varied.

One food at a time. One woman at a time. Undivided attention was the best.

He dumped his trash in a grocery store trash can and then used their restroom. He washed his hands carefully and bought several protein bars and waters before sliding behind the wheel. He started the engine, savoring its hum. He had had his last van for over ten years.

A lot of good memories, and if he thought too hard about it, he got emotional.

"No looking back."

He switched on the radio and pulled out onto the highway, following it toward the interstate. He could have gone anywhere in the country. He had never hunted in the Southwest, and he imagined they grew more wholesome girls out there. He would not mind finding himself a big-busted beauty with full, round hips. A man needed something to hold on to.

As he was considering driving north versus south, he felt a pull west back to Nashville. His thoughts turned back to the brown-eyed girl who had taken one of his punches and come out swinging. Ms. Perky Breasts. She was unfinished business. He would start his search with the Mission.

Feeling excited, he cranked up the radio and turned northwest on I-75.

"Hang on, darling. Daddy's gonna fix up his van just for you. And once I find you, we're going to have the best party you ever did attend."

CHAPTER TWENTY

Thursday, August 27, 10:00 a.m.

Melina made her way back across the Cumberland River into Nashville and down to Lower Broadway. Warm summer days brought tourists out in droves, and today was no exception. The streets would be filled within the hour with people dressed in shorts and newly purchased Nashville T-shirts, eating ice cream and carrying bags filled with their latest souvenirs.

She drove down the center of Lower Broadway until it fed into First Street, which skimmed along the Cumberland River.

Melina found parking across the street and jogged quickly to the Nashville Tours address. As she drew closer, she saw the red, white, and blue trailer. **OPEN** flags flapped by the front sales window occupied by a guy who looked too old to be summer help. Gray hair swept back in a ponytail with a matching handlebar mustache made him look like a walrus.

She waited as a couple of women dressed as tourists paid for the ten o'clock tour. When they were done, she held up her badge. "I'd like to ask you a few questions about Jennifer Brown."

"I have a few questions myself," the man said. "She didn't show up for her scheduled tours and I haven't seen her since."

"What was the last day you saw her?"

He shoved out a sigh as he stared at a paper calendar in the booth. "Sunday, August sixteenth. She worked double shifts that day. She was supposed to work a big tour the following Monday afternoon but didn't show. So if you see her, tell her she's fired."

"Your name, sir?" she asked.

"Sean Terrell." He dropped his gaze and shuffled through the morning receipts. "I own Nashville Tours."

"Sean, Jennifer was murdered."

Sean's sour face softened as he lowered the slips of paper. "Dead? Shit. I thought she just blew the job off."

"We believe she died sometime around August seventeenth or eighteenth. And you're sure you saw her on the sixteenth?"

"Yeah. She picked up her paycheck." He rubbed his hand over his mustache in what she guessed was a common expression of frustration. "She could be a flake but was nice to everyone. Who would want to kill her?"

"That's what I'm trying to find out. How many tours did Jennifer take the week leading up to the sixteenth?"

"Close to twenty. She was my busiest tour guide. She's real popular with the guests. They liked it when she sang. She had dreams of making it big like half the other folks in this town."

"I understand she liked to travel with bands."

"She used to do it a lot, but in the last year not as much. Money and tips are too good giving tours and she's getting a little old."

"She was thirty-nine."

He held up his hand. "I'm not saying she's old, but on the concert circuit a lot of those girls are barely eighteen. Hard to compete. And don't get your back up with me. Just relaying what she told me."

"I get it. Did anyone on the tours take a particular interest in her?"

"I don't follow our buses."

"If a woman is going to tell you she's washed up at thirty-nine, she's going to say something about a customer hitting on her."

"We have a strict no-touching policy. All our guides are instructed to call the cops if a guest gets handsy."

"I get it. But I'm thinking this guy's attention would have been welcomed. If I had to guess, I'd say he was in his late thirties and a big guy. Strong. Maybe even charming." One of the tour buses pulled up.

"Let me get this group unloaded and the next tour going."

"Sure. Go ahead."

Sean jogged over to the bus and exchanged glances with the tour guide as she readied to board the bus. The woman was tall, lean, and appeared to be in her midforties. She was dressed in country-western garb and reminded Melina of vintage Opryland.

Melina held up her badge. "Got a second? Ms. . . . ?"

"Jefferson. Dolly Jefferson. This must be about Jennifer." She reached in her back pocket and pulled out a packet of cigarettes and a lighter. She lit the tip and inhaled.

"Why do you say that?"

"I know Jennifer. What's she done now?"

"She's dead. Murdered."

The woman drew in a breath but didn't seem too torn up about the news. "I'm sorry to hear that."

"You good friends with Jennifer?"

"We worked together. Got along well enough. Look, I don't want to be a witch, but I have exactly ten minutes to have a smoke before I go out again."

Melina felt no sense of urgency. Her questions would take as long as she wanted. "Do you know who she was dating?"

"There was a guy, Billy, who worked as a bartender, but they broke up about three months ago."

"Where did he work?"

She hesitated, as if searching for the name. "Red's, I think. I remember because he treated me to a round of drinks. Jennifer hung out there a lot."

"Her sister said she was sober five years."

"She didn't do drugs, but she still drank. In her mind that was sober."

Melina scribbled more notes. "Anyone recently?"

"She met a guy at Red's a couple of weeks ago. Jennifer liked him and said he had asked her out. He knew music and some of the bands. They had a lot in common."

"Did they hook up?"

"Yeah. She was like a schoolgirl after their first date. He said he was in the music business and could introduce her to people."

"Did she believe him?"

Another puff of smoke crossed her lips as she shrugged. "If I had a nickel for all the faux music producers I've met, I'd be rich. I don't think she really believed him, but they were having a good time."

"Your boss said she worked her last shift on Sunday, August sixteenth. Did she have a date with her guy that night?"

"Yeah, I think she did."

"And do you recall his name?" Melina asked.

"I'm not sure. It was a young-sounding name. The kind a little boy uses."

"Sonny?"

Her gaze brightened. "Yeah, that's exactly right."

"Thanks."

Sean trotted toward them, and the woman dropped her cigarette and ground it onto the pavement. "I've got to go."

Melina stood still as the woman grabbed a water bottle and then jogged back toward the open-air bus.

"Well, good morning, Nashville!" she shouted. The bus engine roared as it pulled away onto First Street.

"I'm going to need to see your receipts, Sean," Melina said.

"Sure. Whatever I can do. How far back?"

She would bet money this Sonny guy had not just appeared. He either frequented Red's or had taken several tours and gotten to know the guides until he'd found the one he wanted. "Take it back a month."

"That's a long time. It's going to mean at least a thousand tickets."

"Thanks." She handed him her card. "The sooner the better."

***

Sonny knew from his surveillance operations that in the late afternoons the residents of Melina's Nashville town house complex had not arrived home just yet. They were packing up at their downtown offices and getting ready to call it a day. For the next hour or so, the parking lot would be fairly free of traffic.

He was dressed in a maintenance uniform that mimicked the crew who serviced the building. His shirt and pants were not an exact match but close enough to convince anyone he belonged there.

He touched his ball cap and crossed the lot. As he approached her door, a cat meowed from the bushes. He did not like cats. They creeped him out, the way they were always lurking around.

He knocked on the door, and when he heard no answer, reached for the pick set and worked the instruments into the lock for several seconds before the lock and dead bolt clicked open. He quickly pocketed the set and, grabbing his toolbox, hurried inside.

"Maintenance," he shouted.

No answer came, but he still moved cautiously, peeking into the living room and beyond it to the galley kitchen. He moved up the stairs to the second floor. There were two bedrooms on this floor. One housed two road bikes and some camping gear and served as a makeshift storage room. Steps away was the second room.

He set his toolbox down and crossed to Melina's unmade bed. He raised her crumpled pillow to his nose and inhaled the faint scent of jasmine shampoo. It was a nice soft scent that he never would have put with a woman like her.

Carefully, he replaced the pillow exactly where he had found it. He knew she was the type of woman who noticed the small details.

He was the same. They shared the same quirks and mannerisms. So much alike. So much shared past.

Crossing the standard beige carpet, he lifted his toolbox and headed down the stairs to the kitchen and opened the refrigerator. She kept a small bottle of milk, a carton of eggs, and a few apples. The pantry was filled with a few staples, including a dozen cans of tuna fish.

When he closed the door, his gaze was drawn to a picture of Melina taken with an older man and woman. She called them Mom and Dad, but they were not her real parents or family. He was her family. He snapped a picture of the image. He took a video of the entire residence.

He had been keeping tabs on her for years, but this was the first time he had stepped into her space. Not wanting to intrude was important to him. But until Bonnie left town, it was best he kept a closer eye on his kid sister.

He sat down on the leather couch, glanced over the article in the open *Forensic Magazine* and then toward the television. A click of the remote brought up a home decorating channel.

She was not any more interested in picking up a paintbrush or making curtains than he was, but images of cozy homes comforted her. He was exactly the same. Stress always sent him into furniture stores, where he wandered from room to room, imagining what each piece would look like in that nice cozy home he was building just for the two of them.

He leaned back on the couch, closed his eyes, and smoothed his fingers over the plush leather. They had been apart for too long, and it was time their family reunited. Only then would he feel whole.

The complication now was Bonnie. So far, she was keeping her mouth shut and had not told the cops about the jar. But he was too smart to believe that Bonnie was finished with him. She had said she wanted to help him and to make things right. He did not believe her. She would never leave until she had what she wanted.

Bonnie was also enjoying jerking him around. She had always gotten a kick out of hearing him say he needed her right before she took off. A part of him still wanted her to stay. Still savored the way she kissed his cheek when he had been good. And a part of him wanted to be a family again.

Sonny cursed. He knew women like her broke men's hearts for sport. And he was finally smart enough not to let it happen again. He should have killed her when he had the chance, but the kid had stopped him. He did not know where Bonnie had found the girl but damned if she was not a carbon copy of Melina.

"Fuck you, Bonnie," he muttered. "You're not going to play me."

This time would be different. He was in control.

He drew in a breath, smoothing his hand over the sofa's creased, worn leather. He shifted his thoughts back to Melina. His sister. His blood.

This is where Melina sat when she was home. He imagined for a moment what it would be like to sit beside her like he used to.

The sense of peace was fleeting. Because, as always, images of Bonnie crept back into the dream. Bonnie had ruined everything in his life he had loved, and this time it would be different.

Pushing to his feet, he removed a small camera from his toolbox. Carefully, he crossed to an air vent in the wall, unfastened the screws, detached the grate, and placed the camera just inside. He checked his phone to make sure the camera was transmitting and, when he confirmed it, replaced the covering. Taking an extra moment, he wiped up the few specks of dust that had fallen out and scooped the particles up and dropped them into his box.

Standing at the threshold and looking back, he inhaled, drinking in her scent one last time, and then closed the door behind him. The cat was gone. The curtains in the unit next door were still, and there was no activity in the parking lot.

With a renewed sense of purpose, he strode toward his car. For the first time in years, he did not feel lonely.

***

Bonnie tugged her sheer blouse over her black bra and glanced over her shoulder at Ralph. He lay on the motel bed, as naked as the day he was born and passed out cold.

When she had coaxed him back here, she had stripped and slid her hands down his pants and taken that man to places he had only dreamed about. If Bonnie could do anything well, it was screw a man silly. When he had fallen asleep, she had dug a few tranquilizers from her purse and ground them into a fine powder. She then made coffee in the motel coffee maker and waited for him to stir at the aroma. He took two sugars and two creamers. She had smiled when he'd said he had to get back to work. To buy time for the sedatives, she had taken his nearly empty cup and given him a blow job. Five minutes later, he was out.

She had done the same with her late husband. There were times when he had gotten drunk and had been ready to whale on her, Sonny, or Melina. She had protected those kids then, not only because she liked them but also because they did not need the cops on their doorstep. All in all, she had done a good job until she had fucked up with Melina and then later Sonny. Maybe she was getting sentimental in her old age, but she had a chance now to make it right for both of them.

She rummaged in his pants pocket and dug out his keys and wallet. She fished out the bills and a credit card and left the rest for him. She liked Ralph and did not want to put the old boy through a trip to the DMV for a replacement license. That was just plain cruel, even for her.

She figured he would be out for twelve hours before he woke up and reported it. Smiling, she tucked the card in her back pocket. Bonnie could do a lot of damage in twelve hours.

CHAPTER TWENTY-ONE

Thursday, August 27, 3:00 p.m.

Melina sat in her car checking emails outside of Red's, waiting for it to open. She had barely scrolled through a couple when her phone rang. It was Ramsey.

"Yes," she said quickly.

"The driver of the white van removed the VIN numbers from the dashboard and the door and the engine block," he said without fanfare.

She relaxed back against the headrest. "You sound a little too happy. Something tells me this story doesn't end here."

"The former owner also took the initiative to etch the VIN number on the underside of the engine block."

"That's my kind of paranoid."

"A trace of the vehicle shows it was purchased in Atlanta, Georgia, ten years ago from a used car dealership."

She waited for the punch line.

"Long story short, the van was traced to a man by the name of Edward Mecum."

"And who is Mr. Mecum? Assuming that's his real name."

"That's what we're trying to determine, but according to an FBI database search, he has no criminal record."

"I don't hear dejection in your voice." She ran her fingers over the steering wheel, watching as a group of middle-aged tourists entered one of the landmark cowboy boot shops on the street.

"I contacted the car dealership in Atlanta."

"And?"

"No record of sale for the older van, but the manager did say that he sold a similar white van this morning to a man who paid cash. The buyer's name was Edward Mecum and he had a limp."

She had jabbed that knife hard into his thigh and twisted it for good measure. She took some satisfaction knowing she had hurt him good.

"I don't suppose Edward Mecum gave the dealer an address?"

"He was required to."

She leaned forward. "And?"

"I have an address of a property that's located thirty miles outside of Nashville."

"You know how to make a girl's day." A man flipped the CLOSED sign to OPEN in the Red's window.

"How soon can you meet me?" he asked.

"Give me a half hour," she said. "I'm on Lower Broadway. Just spoke to Jennifer Brown's boss and want to follow up on a lead. I'll update you when I see you."

"I'll pick you up at the office."

"Bring burgers. I'm starving."

He chuckled. "Will do."

She grabbed her bag, slid out of the car, and strode toward the bar's entrance. She was greeted by the faint scent of beer and cigarettes. There was a long bar covered in a thick coat of polyurethane. Behind it, rows of liquor bottles peered down from terraced shelves. Above the bottles was a collection of red cowboy hats.

"Hello?" she said.

A man pushed through swinging doors, wiping gnarled hands on a bar towel as he approached her. A sweep of his gaze seemed to be enough to tell him she was not here for a drink. "What can I do for you?"

She held up her badge and identified herself as TBI. "Came to ask you about a customer. Her name is Jennifer Brown. She dated a bartender by the name of Billy."

He nodded. "Blond. Big boobs."

"She's in her late thirties."

"Yeah, I remember her. What do you want to know?"

"Was there anyone here who hassled her or maybe paid her too much attention?"

"She was a flirt. Knew how to use those tits to get men to pay attention. But she was dating Billy and stayed close to the bar."

"And after they broke up, did she keep coming around?"

"Yeah. Saw her in here about two weeks ago. She left with a guy, but I couldn't tell you who he was."

"You have surveillance cameras in here?"

"I do, but the recording only lasts two weeks."

"She was last seen on August sixteenth. That will put us in that two-week window. I need you to pull it for me."

"What's the deal? Is Jennifer in some kind of trouble?"

"Someone killed her," she said.

"Shit."

"Yeah, shit is right." She removed a business card from her wallet. "Call me when you have those recordings later today."

"Sure."

She stepped outside into the bright sunshine, her gaze skimming the businesses around Red's. How many had surveillance cameras?

In her car, she started the engine and called Agent Jackson and updated him on both cases as she drove through town. He pledged to send officers to the businesses around Red's. If there was footage, it would be recovered.

Ten minutes later, Melina pulled into the TBI parking lot, where Ramsey waited in his black SUV. She locked her car, got into the passenger seat, and placed her backpack between her feet.

He handed her a cup of coffee, which she gratefully accepted. It tasted sweet, like two-packets-of-sugar sweet. She checked the burger. No cheese. "And how did you know I don't like cheese?"

"Because I'm not a fan," he said.

"Lucky guess, then?"

"Yes."

"Good. Your powers of observation are a little too keen for me." As she sipped her coffee, she updated him on Red's and the hunt for camera footage.

"We might get lucky with the video surveillance at Red's. Most killers like the two we are dealing with are creatures of habit," he said.

"Wouldn't that be nice?" She bit into the hamburger. Not bad. If she had had her way, she would have adjusted the relish-to-ketchup-to-mustard ratio, but she was too hungry to complain.

"Andy did a quick search on Edward Mecum. I can tell you he comes from money. He was married twice and has two children and several grandchildren with the second wife. He lives off his investments. He has several properties north of Nashville. As tempting as it is to reach out to his family, I don't want to spook him now. Better to learn all we can about him before we approach the family."

"Agreed."

"According to county utility records, the house account billing is current."

She plucked a fresh napkin from the stack. "There are areas north of Nashville that are very isolated. If a woman were held there, no one would ever know it."

Images of the van's interior appeared in her mind and then quickly switched to the pictures of the dead prostitutes' wrists. All were ringed with red marks left by too-tight handcuffs.

"What happened to the first wife?" Melina asked.

"She divorced him in 1999."

"Divorced in 1999? The killings started in '99, correct?" Melina asked.

Life stressors for an individual with homicidal fantasies could send them over the edge. In Mecum's case, the stress was not money but perhaps a divorce.

"Do you know anything about the ex-wife?" she asked.

"I haven't been able to locate her yet," Ramsey said. "We're working on it."

"It's been twenty-one years since the divorce and there's no record of her?"

"No."

In Melina's experience, women living normal lives did not generally fall off the radar. "Any children in the relationship?"

"Not according to public records."

Confirming for her that blessings came in all forms, and a childless marriage for a guy who liked to cut up prostitutes was one.

"Mecum does have a law degree, but he never practiced," Ramsey offered. "Family money meant he didn't have to work."

"What about his parents or siblings?" she asked.

"No siblings. Mother died of cancer fifty years ago and father died in a car crash when the boy was fourteen."

She shifted and drank her coffee. The caffeine was kicking in and sharpening her senses.

They drove in silence up I-24 north until the city gave way to strip malls and then finally rolling hillsides. Ramsey followed the winding roads until his GPS alerted him that the address was fast approaching. Melina had to look twice to spot the mailbox covered in thick twisting vines. He slowed and turned into the dirt driveway that wound up a hill.

"This is some property," she said.

Ramsey drove up the steep driveway, maneuvering around the switchbacks with practiced ease. He rounded the last corner, and the SUV suddenly nosed into a circular driveway with a brick house with a wide front porch. The lights were off in the house, and the two rockers on the porch looked as if they had spent the better part of the winter and summer exposed to the elements. The shades on all the windows were drawn. The yard looked as if no one had been there in months.

Ramsey shut off the engine and they both got out. They shifted so that their weapons were easily accessible as they walked up the gravel pathway to the front steps. As she stood to the side, Ramsey tried the front door. After discovering it was locked, he banged his fist on the door.

The sound echoed in the house, rattling around like a marble in an empty jar. She peered between the window frames and the shades covering them. Each sliver of opening revealed views into what appeared to be empty rooms.

"How long has he owned this property?" she asked.

"Thirty years."

"That's a long time."

"Serial killers generally begin with violent fantasies and then graduate to arson and then rape. Out here, he could have had total control over his victims."

"As far as we know, he's killed prostitutes exclusively," she said.

"They are the perfect victims."

She studied the thick front door and then tested the handle herself with a twist. It was definitely locked. "I could break the glass."

"I wish. We don't even know we have the right guy. And whatever you find in there won't be admissible in court."

She peered again through the small gap between the curtain and the edge of the window. The back of her neck tightened just as it had when the Key Killer had approached her.

"Maybe there's a back door that's unlocked," she said.

"We still don't have a warrant."

She turned from the window and went down the front steps. He followed, and the two walked through the tall grass around to the back side of the house. All the windows were covered in thick curtains, and it was impossible to get a good look inside.

Melina faced away from the house, staring at the small open field behind the structure. "Those two women I was looking for have still not been found."

"This killer discarded the bodies of his other victims. It doesn't make sense he would bury a victim on the property."

She stared at the dense line of woods. "He's getting older," she said. "There are more surveillance cameras in the world. It's harder to get away with murder. And I stuck him good."

She walked toward the woods, not really sure what she was searching for. "He dumped his former victims in the woods. If I were older and wiser, I'd definitely stick close to home. He has perfectly good woods near this house."

Ramsey nodded. "What better way to relive the fantasy of killing a woman than to step out on your porch and stare into the woods where she's buried. He's far from any nosy neighbors here."

Several more steps and she caught the first whiff of death's rancid scent. It had been hot the last two weeks, so any creature or human left out here would decompose quickly.

"Do you smell it?" she asked.

"I certainly do," he said.

Both drew their weapons and moved closer to the tree line. Melina was ten feet away when the stench hit her full in the face. She coughed, raised her hand to her mouth.

"There it is," he said. "Do you see it?"

She narrowed her gaze and searched the underbrush until she caught sight of an outline of decomposed remains.

CHAPTER TWENTY-TWO

Thursday, August 27, 4:30 p.m.

Search warrant in hand, Ramsey and Melina watched as a locksmith opened the front door to Mecum's house. A faint sense of excitement churned in Ramsey. This was the closest he had come to this killer, and the idea of catching him now was painfully tantalizing.

The medical examiner had arrived, along with a half dozen marked police vehicles. Yellow crime scene tape had been strung and a tent and multiple tables erected to create a mobile workstation. Agent Jackson was on scene overseeing the search of the woods for more bodies and any trace of Mecum.

The lock turned and the first uniformed cop pushed open the door. That officer and two others entered the house and searched it. They came out ten minutes later. "All yours," the officer said.

Latex tightened against Ramsey's skin as he flexed his fingers. He did not reach for the light switch but waited as the technician dusted for prints. As much as he wanted to search the house, he did not want to destroy vital forensic evidence that would help them nail this guy.

When the scene was all clear, the two walked through the first floor into an outdated kitchen that looked out over a den and a tall fireplace.

She ran her finger over the counter, collecting a thick coating of dust. She opened the refrigerator, which released a stale, musty smell from no use. The freezer was the same.

The two made a methodical search of the first and second floors, but each room was like the last. Dusty and empty.

"I bet he's busy outfitting his new van," she said. "He wants it just right before he hunts again."

"A guy like him might have multiple locations," he cautioned. "There's no sign that he brought anyone inside, so perhaps this was strictly a dump site."

"He's definitely not been inside for a while," she said.

Ramsey considered setting up a perimeter on the property and waiting for Mecum's return. It would only be a matter of time before he came back. But as much as Ramsey wanted to stay in Nashville and see this case to the end, he had a finite amount of time remaining before he had to return to Washington.

As if sensing his thoughts, Melina asked, "How much longer are you going to be in Nashville?"

"A few more days at most. I've got to get back."

"Hopefully you'll be around for the takedown. It would be a shame to miss the party," she said.

"It's been a while since I was involved in an arrest." Again, he flexed his fingers as adrenaline rushed through his body. God, he missed this part of the job.

"I should go back out on the street near the Mission," Melina said. "You said this killer circled back on one of his victims."

"No way."

"If he doesn't know the cops have found this place, he soon will. If we don't catch him now, he'll take his money and fly away."

His phone chimed with a text. "It's from Andy. She has the DMV picture of Mecum."

She inspected the picture, studying it closely. Mecum was attractive. He had dark hair salted with enough gray to make him look distinguished. His face was long, lean, and tanned. He had a patrician nose and stark brown eyes that were so dark they reminded her of a great white shark's lifeless gaze. "It's impossible to tell. My guy was wearing a wig and it was dark."

"How did he move? Did he move like a sixty-two-year-old man?"

"He was strong as hell. No couch potato could have pulled it off."

"We need a solid identification on this guy."

"Is that a yes or a no to putting me on the street? I'd do it myself, but I'm on thin ice with the boss."

"And rightly so." They stepped outside onto the back porch, and he surveyed the property. The forensic team had set up several tents and worktables. They got into the car, and he nosed it down the driveway. Gravel crunched under the tires, and she found herself drawn back to the night she had been left on the side of the road not too far from here.

"I can show this picture around the Bottom," she said. "One of the girls might have seen him out of disguise. I'll also ask Sarah."

"It's a start. And our only play."

"A john with a limp is also memorable."

It was possible but likely a long shot. Only a fool would return to old hunting grounds knowing the cops were canvassing the area. "Okay."

Melina rolled her shoulders as her gaze skimmed the wooded countryside. "While we're out here, there's a diner I'd like you to see."

A grin tugged at his lips. "But you just ate."

She shrugged, unapologetic. "It's true that I'm always hungry. But that's not the reason I want to see this diner. When I was a child, whoever called the police and reported I was on that roadside did it from that diner. Seems plausible that Sonny may have been back to it."

He understood the reasoning behind the visit, but he wanted to hear her thoughts. "Explain."

"Bonnie commented that Sonny was sentimental. Couldn't let go of the past. Maybe that's where he goes to mourn the sister he could not save. Like you said, killers are creatures of habit."

***

Melina and Ramsey arrived at the diner just before the dinner crowd would be coming through. She led the way, reaching for the diner's door seconds before Ramsey.

Growing up as the only child of Detective Hank Shepard, she was basically the son he never had. Her mother had tried to expose their daughter to more ladylike pursuits, but Melina had always gravitated toward hikes in the woods and the garage, where her dad would tinker on his 1974 Cutlass Supreme.

Which was now why she was uncomfortable having a man holding a door or allowing her to walk ahead first. With Ramsey she sensed the moves were automatic. He had been so steeped in old Virginia culture that it was now a part of his DNA.

Ramsey did not seem to mind when she took the lead and followed her and the hostess to a booth in the corner. She slid into the booth as he did, and each reached for a menu. She glanced around and searched for the public pay phone that an unknown caller had used twenty-eight years ago to save her life. There was no sign of it. She had seen pictures of it on the wall by the counter when she had pulled the police report detailing her rescue.

"Have you ever been here before?" Ramsey asked.

"I come about once a year. I always speak to the owner, Pop. He said he was here the night the police received the call about me."

"Does he remember who made the call?"

"No."

The waitress arrived at their table. Each accepted a cup of coffee. He ordered the omelet. She asked for a Big Boy burger with fries. Then she asked for extra fries. The waitress took one look at her slim figure and joked, "There is no God," and turned to place the order.

Melina looked out the window toward the four-lane highway, watching as the traffic rushed past. "Who leaves a kid on the side of the road?"

"You've already met one of them. Sadly, there are many more."

Her mind returned to the body found in the woods behind Mecum's house. "I shouldn't gripe. I wouldn't be here now if not for Bonnie."

"Good way to look at it."

She regarded him, watching as he raised his cup to his lips. He moved with precision, as if he never wasted energy on anything unnecessary.

"I know," she said. "Speaking of evil, is there anyone in the Nashville area who knows Mecum? It's clear that house is not his hideout."

"Jackson's team and Andy are searching for other residences, properties, and possible associates."

Their meals arrived and she immediately picked up a hot, slightly oily fry and grinned. Nervous energy aside, it had been a couple of days since she'd had a real hot meal. And she did not know when she would see the next one.

As they ate, their conversation centered on old cases they each had worked, and she realized their paths had almost crossed several times before. At the end of the meal, he insisted on paying. When they stepped outside and got into the car, she felt a wave of relief wash over her. She was always glad to leave that place.

Her phone rang as he pulled onto the highway. "Andy," she said. "That was quick."

"When it comes to computers, I can do magic," Andy said.

"I'm here with Agent Ramsey. Mind if I put you on speaker?"

"As long as you don't mind Agent Ramsey hearing a few details about your past."

"I'm an open book." Melina actually trusted Ramsey with the details of her past more than anyone she had met in a long time. She hit the button.

"Hello, Andy," Ramsey said.

"Hey, boss. Glad I caught you as well. This might be of interest to you both."

Ramsey started the car but, instead of driving, sat as he focused his full attention on Andy's words. "Ready when you are."

"As you likely know, Agent Shepard provided me access to her DNA account. First thing I did was cross-check her DNA against the sample collected from Jennifer Brown's sink. It was not a match."

She was disappointed and relieved. "Are you sure?"

"Very," Andy said. "I was able to upload it to GEDMatch, an open-source site. Because your DNA is available for access, GEDMatch is able to crossmatch it with its entire database. Any blood relative who has done the same will create a match. From there, a family tree can begin to be constructed. Best hit we had for Melina was a great-grandmother."

"How did my great-grandmother get in the system?" Melina asked.

"One of the many hundreds of relatives you have is likely an amateur genealogist and uploaded it."

"What is the bottom line?" Melina was more anxious than she realized to have something concrete about her past.

"The great-grandmother, Ann Talbot, had a son named Howard by her first marriage. Ann remarried when Howard was only five, and her second husband adopted the boy. His name changed from Talbot to Guthrie."

"Our connection to Bonnie Guthrie," Melina said.

"Correct. Howard and his first wife, Felicia, had two children. The boy, born in 1959, and his sister, in 1960. After thirty years of marriage,

Felicia died. Howard married Bonnie Franklin, now known as Bonnie Guthrie, in 1989."

"Is what Bonnie told me about her late husband's family true?" Melina asked.

"Yes," Andy said. "Lizzie Guthrie, Howard's daughter, was born in 1960 and earned herself a long rap sheet. I know this because Agent Ramsey sent me her name and I did a complete search. Her offenses were mostly related to drugs and prostitution. She's in CODIS and I was able to cross-check her DNA against Agent Shepard's. They're a match. Mother and daughter."

Melina set her head back against the rest and for a moment she drew inward, hearing only the beat of her heart and her rapid breathing. She kept her gaze on the ceiling. "Are you sure?"

"It's a ninety-eight percent chance that she was your biological mother. Lizzie was thirty when she died. You would have been about three at the time, Agent Shepard."

Loss, sadness, and anger collided and then tangled into a tight ball. In a matter of seconds, she had found her birth mother and had just as quickly lost her. Her throat tightened, and she did not trust herself to speak in a calm voice.

Ramsey said, "Did Lizzie Guthrie have any other children?"

"She did. She had a son, who was born three years before Agent Shepard," Andy said. "According to birth records in California, Bonnie Guthrie's account of Agent Shepard's half brother was correct. The boy's name was Dean Guthrie. He does not have a police record."

Frustration ate at Melina as she thought about this dead end. "What about my DNA? Can you find Dean using my profile?"

"I have loaded your DNA into CODIS, Agent Shepard. Your DNA might help us find Dean Guthrie. He can change his name but not his DNA."

"Excellent work," Ramsey said.

Melina remained silent, trying to process what amounted to family information overload.

Andy took another long pause and said, "One last detail. Your original California birth certificate states you were born September 2, 1987, not August 1."

"My parents didn't know my vital statistics. Knowing my mother, she picked the date because it had a sentimental reason," Melina said.

Computer keys clicked on the other end of the line. "When your birth mother died, Howard and Bonnie took custody of you and your half brother. You lived with both until Howard died of a heart attack a year later."

This all fit with what Bonnie had told her. The woman traded on lies, but she also knew when to use the truth. "According to Bonnie, she retained custody of me."

"There is no filing with the California courts regarding a custody order. Bonnie's first arrest was in 1976 and then nothing until 1992. She received a speeding ticket in Tennessee. She was given a court date but didn't appear."

"My dad found me in November of 1992."

"Bonnie was headed east on Route 25."

Melina smoothed her hands over her thighs, letting her mind trip back. A distant audio memory flashed. Gravel kicked up under tires. A car engine roared. She watched the car drive away and in the back window saw a face. The details of that face narrowed into focus. The child, a boy, was screaming and pounding on the window.

"She kept Dean and put me out on the side of the road like a dog." Melina was amazed her voice sounded so matter of fact, even distant.

"It appears so," Andy said quietly. "Bonnie was arrested in 2000. Her arrest record notes there was an underaged boy with her. He gave his name as Dean Guthrie. The pair of them were stealing from an electronics store. As Bonnie was being cuffed, the boy asked to go to the bathroom. He vanished and cops couldn't find him."

"In 2000, Dean would have been sixteen," Ramsey said.

She cleared her throat again. "Do we know anything about him?"

"No. I haven't had a lot of time to look for him, but he seems to have fallen off the radar after Bonnie's 2000 arrest."

"Keep us posted," Ramsey said.

"I would bet money he's here in Nashville," Melina said, her intuition gnawing at her.

"Why do you say that?" Andy asked.

"Because Bonnie came back to Nashville," Melina said. "She didn't come looking for me. She came looking for Sonny."

"Kind of odd that he happened to be in the same town as you," Andy said.

"Not really," Ramsey said. "As he got older, he would have known if Melina had been found, it would have been by Nashville police, and she'd have landed in Davidson County's social services."

She shifted her gaze, meeting his gaze head on. She felt light headed.

He knew as well as she did why Sonny, a.k.a. Dean Guthrie, was here.

"He's here because you're here," Ramsey said.

For more years than she could remember, she had wanted to peel back the veil on her past and know where she came from. But each new layer of history brought with it a new set of problems.

Melina ended the call, doing her best to not show her emotions.

"You okay?" Ramsey asked.

"Sure. Just fine."

"Your nonreaction is more worrisome than any rant."

"This is a lot to take in."

"Have you spoken to your parents about Bonnie?" he asked.

"I've touched on the high spots but not gone into much detail. I don't want to upend their world."

"Something tells me they can handle it," Ramsey said.

"Probably. I just need to process this as much as I can before I get bombarded with questions from them. They mean well, but I can't even answer my own questions, let alone theirs."

"Adoptees have a tendency to hide their true emotions from both their birth and adoptive parents. They become a kind of peacemaker who does their best to not upset the applecart."

"I've read all the psychology books," she said. "Adoptees have lost their birth parents through no fault of their own and consequently fear losing their adoptive parents. They test, prod, probe, all the while expecting and also fearing rejection. And if we do reunite with the birth family, we spend the rest of our lives walking on eggshells so that we don't chase them away." She shifted in her seat as if his scrutiny was too much to bear.

"You've put a lot of thought into this."

"Too damn much. But my observations about adoption and adoptees are not relevant right now. What matters is Elena and finding Sonny."

"The more I consider Jennifer Brown's crime scene, the more I'm convinced Sonny is suffering with serious abandonment and anger issues," Ramsey said.

Melina pictured a young boy who watched Bonnie driving off, knowing his sister was on the side of a deserted road. He must have been traumatized. The fear he had felt as a boy grew into rage as he became a man. "He's killing Bonnie over and over."

"I think that's exactly what he's doing." Ramsey put the car in drive and pulled out onto the main road. For several minutes neither spoke as they wove their way back to Nashville.

All the unknown pieces of her past were falling into place and creating a very sad and dark image. She tipped her head back against the headrest. "New birthday, a birth mother, and now a half brother who is likely a serial killer. So, how's your family doing?"

He shook his head. "You can't pick your family."

"That's for damn sure."

CHAPTER
TWENTY-THREE

Thursday, August 27, 6:00 p.m.

Bonnie was good at figuring things out. Her first stop was the hospital. She knew walking in and asking about the kid was not going to get her anywhere. So she made a quick stop at a uniform store located across from the hospital and bought a pair of scrubs. She pulled around the side of the building and changed into the scrubs and then drove to the hospital.

The success of a con depended on confidence. If you believed your story, the chances of someone else buying into it were good.

She rode the elevator to the pediatric wing. There were several nurses at the central station. They might give up information on the kid, but chances were slim. All the new federal regs made everyone paranoid.

The rattle of the wheels drew Bonnie's attention to an attendant pushing a food cart. Older, with stooped shoulders, he was perfect. She snatched a clipboard from a side cart.

As he loaded a tray with an untouched yogurt and banana beside a plate of meatloaf and mashed potatoes, she came up to him, smiling. "Such a waste," she said. "All that food."

"I hear ya," he said. "Happens all the time."

"Could feed an army on the unopened food alone."

"I know."

She glanced at her clipboard. "I'm here to do a follow-up with Elena Sanchez."

"She's checked out," he said. "Social services came. A foster mom, I think."

"Darn. I was hoping to do a quick mental health analysis. County has implemented a new policy. I'll contact the agent in charge of the case." Again, she glanced at the clipboard as if trying to remember. "Melina Shepard."

"She should know. Her mother took the girl."

Bonnie pretended to write on the clipboard. "Right. The Shepards are good people." She thought back to the article she had read about Melina. There were family details, but she could not quite remember. "Thanks, doll," she said.

At the information desk, Bonnie asked if there was a computer she could use and was directed to a small room reserved for family members of patients. She now had everything she needed.

She searched Melina's name. When she had been in California, all she had had was Melina's first name. But how many Melinas could there be in Music City? Turns out, a few dozen. She had searched each one and come up empty. Then she'd come across an article on Agent Melina Shepard with the Tennessee Bureau of Investigation. The instant Bonnie saw the picture of the young agent featured in a news article, she knew she had found her girl.

Now, as she searched *Melina Shepard*, she skipped all the blah-blah information about her investigative successes and looked for information on Melina's family.

Bonnie found it in an article that mentioned Melina's father was a former detective with Nashville police. Mother was a former schoolteacher. She typed **Detective Shepard Nashville Police.** A few more clicks and there, on the screen, was Hank and Molly's address.

Bonnie scribbled it down and then mapped the directions on the phone she had stolen from Ralph. Outside, she hurried around the building, dumped the clipboard in a trash can, and, in the car, changed out of the scrubs into her clothes.

The drive took twenty minutes, and as she got closer to the residential neighborhood, she followed the street signs until she spotted the one-story brick rancher. She drove slowly by the house and down to the end of the street.

The neat lawns with their neat flower beds and two-car garages irritated Bonnie. A few yards had bikes propped against the side of the house, and others had kiddie pools in the backyards.

It all screamed family.

Shit, Bonnie, Melina, and Sonny would all still likely be a family if Melina had just been good that day. Hell, she had tried to reason with the kid that night in the car. She had given her crackers and cookies and then bribed her with five dollars if she would just shut the hell up. But Melina had wanted out of the car. Bonnie had not enjoyed the three days of nonstop driving, either, but she had been willing to suck it up to get across the country. Sonny had managed fine with the long drive. But Melina kept melting down, demanding to be let out. Finally, Bonnie had granted the little brat her wish.

Bonnie circled around the block and looked toward the Shepards' house. She spotted a woman passing in front of the window, and just behind her was Elena.

Bonnie kept driving. She had confirmed Elena's location, and she knew the address and basic setup of the Shepards' house. She dialed Sonny's number. He picked up on the third ring.

"What the hell do you want?" Sonny demanded.

"I haven't told the cops anything because I don't want them to lock you up," she said. "I really care about you, Sonny."

Silence. "You haven't been quiet for me. You don't want to be nailed as an accessory after the fact."

"I kept quiet for you, not me, baby."

"You always put yourself first, Bonnie." He sounded sure of himself. "You're out of jail. And I know you well enough to know you want to stay out. I got you out. We're done."

She stopped at a stoplight. Up ahead were directional signs to the interstate that could take her far away from all this. "I want to make things right between us."

"There's no making things right."

"I saw the way you looked at Elena. She looks so much like Melina, doesn't she? It's like having your baby sister back."

He didn't speak, but she could hear his breath. He was listening.

"What if you, Elena, and me left town together? What if we kept going east like we'd planned all those years ago? Or what if we went to Mexico?"

"My life is just fine without you."

"Is it, baby? You've developed a nasty little habit, and I bet in your off time you watch Melina, too. Always looking out for your sister."

He didn't respond.

She grinned. "You're in Melina's life, aren't you? Do you watch her through the window of her town house? Watch her feed that little cat?"

"How do you know about the cat?"

Bonnie chuckled. "I've seen where she lives. It was important to me to know she turned out okay and she has."

"No thanks to you."

"Baby, she wouldn't have the life she did if not for me. Putting her on the side of that road was the best thing I could have done for her. You know how she hated the traveling. Elena's the same. She hates the travel. She wants a real family, too."

"That kid is nothing like Melina."

"Not true. Elena's mother died just like your mama. Stuck a needle in her arm. I begged her to kick the habit. You remember how hard it was for Lizzie to stay away from it. She wanted to but loved the dope more than her little kids."

"Shut up."

"I don't want to hurt you, baby. I want to give you a chance to get back what we had before. This time it will be you, me, and Elena."

"You can't do that."

"Of course, I can."

"How?"

"Don't worry about how, baby. I'll get Elena, you can get the key, and then we'll get the money that will set us all up for life."

Silence, and then, "Call me when you have her. Then we'll talk."

The light turned green and she drove past the interstate exit. "Will do, doll."

A smirk tugged at Bonnie's lips. She turned the car around and headed back to the Shepards'. On the way, she stopped at a drugstore and bought a few things for Elena, as well as a blue gift bag. Putting the toys in the bag, she drove to the Shepards'. She parked in front of the neat little suburban house. Time to test the waters and see what these folks were made of.

Out of the car, she picked up the gift bag and, squaring her shoulders, walked up the sidewalk to the front porch.

She rang the bell and widened her smile. When the door opened, the woman stared back at her with open suspicion.

"I'm here to see Elena," Bonnie said.

"Who are you?"

"I'm Bonnie," she said. "I'm like a grandmother to her." Inside she heard a television playing a cartoon. "Elena loves the *Magic Tree House*. She likes the idea of traveling through time."

The woman blocked Bonnie's view with her body. "How did you find my address?"

"I'd like to see her," Bonnie said. "I want to tell her how sorry I am."

"It'll take more than an apology to make amends for leaving her in a wrecked car, Bonnie." The woman tightened her hand on the door as if ready to close it.

Bonnie could feel her temper rising. "Call Melina and tell her I'm here. She'll want to talk to me."

The woman reached for her phone in her back jeans pocket and texted a message.

"Molly?" Elena's voice drew Bonnie's attention back to the hallway behind Mrs. Shepard, and she saw Elena for the first time in a few days.

Bonnie realized how much she really had missed her. She liked the kid. She was quiet, and she listened when Bonnie needed her to distract a mark.

"BB?" Elena asked.

Bonnie heard the excitement mingled with trepidation in the girl's voice. She understood both emotions. People naturally craved the familiar, even when it was not so perfect, and the fear was justified. "Hey, kiddo? How are you doing?"

Mrs. Shepard shifted her stance, blocking Bonnie's view of the girl. "She's doing fine."

Bonnie's smile faltered. "I'd like to see her."

"Over my dead body," Mrs. Shepard said. "Now get off my property."

This wasn't over between them. It couldn't be. She owed it to Elena and Sonny.

A car pulled up in front of the house and she heard a car door slam. She turned. Melina strode toward the house, her face as pale and tight with anger as it had been when she was a little girl.

This was going to be fun.

***

The summer sun was dimming as Sonny walked to the back of the house, where he knew a sliding door fed into a small patio. He had been by the house several times and was familiar enough now with the patterns of the neighborhood to know that after midnight he would not be bothered.

With Bonnie's promises still clattering in his head, he knew he needed to relax. Calm his rattled thoughts and nerves. Bonnie was promising him a family. A sister and a mother he could love.

He glanced down at his trembling hand before he curled it tightly into a fist. He wanted that family so badly. And he wanted to believe Bonnie. But she had burned him so many times. Her promises were always too good to be true.

He hurried up to the back door and was pleased to see she had not fixed the light he had broken a few days ago. He removed a small screwdriver from his pocket, popped the lock, slid open the door, and quickly stepped inside. He did not need a light to make his way through her house. This was not the first time he had inspected the interior. He knew the small kitchen was to the right, living room to the left, and down the hallway was the bathroom equipped with a large claw-foot tub.

He walked down the hallway and entered the bathroom. He switched on the water, running his hand under the hot tap. Steam rose up, fogging his glasses and the mirror. He checked his watch, noting it was almost 8:00 p.m. and she would be home soon.

He had meant to meet up with her last night, but he had been dealing with the bail bondsman. By the time he'd made all the necessary arrangements for Bonnie, his window of opportunity had closed. Maybe it was better that they had not hooked up last night.

He removed the sharp garden shears from his pocket and set them carefully on the counter beside the sink. As he scrolled through his playlist on his phone, he tried to imagine the perfect song for them. All his girls had a song, and Sandra would be no exception.

A car pulled into the driveway. He shut off the water and pocketed the phone. As a precaution, he made sure the small window in the bathroom could be opened. Had not Bonnie always taught him to have an exit strategy?

Bonnie. Fuck. Was there never a time when she was not in his head?

As the night air, thick with humidity, blew in the cracked window, anticipation surged in him. He flexed his fingers, anxious to hold her neck in his hands and watch the panic flare in her gaze and slowly trickle away.

Sandra's laughter, ripe with desire, echoed from the hallway, and he thought for a moment she might be on the phone. And then he heard a man's deep, low voice.

Shit. Shit. Shit.

Who the hell was the guy?

He could stick around. Maybe he could get the drop on the guy and Sandra, but an extra unplanned person created a risk he did not want to assume, especially with Bonnie running around capable of shooting her mouth off.

Moving swiftly, he climbed up on the toilet seat and hauled his leg over the side of the windowsill. He swung the second leg over and dropped five feet to the ground below. But his foot landed wrong and his ankle rolled. He felt a sharp pain and prayed he had not screwed himself. A couple of tentative steps proved it was a serious strain at best. Figuring out how bad would have to come later.

The lights in the house clicked on, and he hobbled toward the small grouping of houses that backed up to Sandra's. Fifty paces ahead, he knew there was another street that fed into the public parking lot of the grocery store where he had left his car.

"Shit. Shit. Shit."

This was all Bonnie's fault. He had been on his game until she came to town. Like all the shit that had happened to him, Bonnie was at the root of it. Until she was dead, he would have no peace.

CHAPTER TWENTY-FOUR

Thursday, August 27, 7:00 p.m.

Melina's nerves were wound tight as Ramsey drove toward her parents' home. They were two houses away when she spotted Bonnie standing on the porch.

Melina unlocked her seat belt and reached for the door handle before the car had stopped. "I still can't believe she had the guts to come here."

"Hold on. Let me stop the car," Ramsey barked as he angled the car near the curb.

"How does she know where my mother lives? Where I *grew up*." Tension tangled with anger and rippled through Melina's growl.

"Remember, this is about Elena, not you," Ramsey cautioned.

"I get that." Her fingers pulled up on the door handle as the tires came to a stop. "Making Bonnie suffer is just going to be a bonus."

Out of the car, Melina marched across the lawn with a hand on her weapon. "What are you doing here?" she demanded.

Bonnie smiled. "I just came by to see Elena. The girl is like a grand-daughter to me. Now that my head is better and I'm processing better,

I wanted her to know I love her. But your mother wouldn't let me get close to her."

"Good for her."

"I have every right to see the girl. I'm all the family that poor little baby has," Bonnie said.

"You have no right," Melina said. "You do not have custody of Elena, and if you did, I would be standing in front of a judge right now getting your rights revoked."

Ramsey came up behind Melina. "Time to move along, Ms. Guthrie. You're out on bail, and I can have that rescinded with a phone call."

Bonnie hesitated. She was a woman accustomed to pushing her luck and dancing on the line separating freedom and jail. "I'm not breaking any laws."

"Try trespassing," Melina said.

Bonnie looked around. "I don't see any signs, but I'm a reasonable person. I don't see why you have to be so nasty."

"You haven't seen how nasty I can be," Melina said.

Bonnie's grin faded and her features hardened. Before she could respond, the front door opened. Her mother's silhouette appeared behind the screen. There was no sign of Elena.

The gift bag dangled from Bonnie's fingers as she sauntered across the lawn toward her car. "I came to do a good deed and check on the child. I'm sorry to have troubled you."

"Don't come back," Melina said.

"I love Elena. I loved you, Mellie."

The nickname sent a quake through her body as distant memories of the endearment surfaced. Bonnie had hit another nerve.

"Bonnie loves Mellie Bellie," Bonnie said in a singsong voice. "I sang that as I rocked you in my arms," she said, eyeing Melina closely. "You remember me calling you Mellie, don't you?"

Melina's shoulders grew even more rigid. "Is it supposed to make me cry or embrace a tender moment we once shared?"

"You do remember. I can tell by your face. You could always hide your feelings from others, but not from me."

Melina shifted to offense. "What is the name Sonny is using now?"

"I don't know what name he's using now, baby. It's been so long since I've seen him."

"Elena says you met with Sonny before your accident."

"She's a little kid. What does she know?"

"We've searched Dean Guthrie and haven't gotten a hit. He's changed his name."

Bonnie reached for the car's door handle. "I don't know where Sonny is, Mellie."

"Who arranged for your bail?" Melina pressed. "Did Sonny arrange it?"

Bonnie opened her car door. "I can get my own bail."

"Who called the cops from the diner after you dumped me on the side of the road?"

For a split second, Bonnie looked confused. The shift was just enough to tell Melina that she had scored a point in this round.

"I don't know anything about a diner," Bonnie said.

The lies rolled off her tongue so easily. "Why didn't you go back for me?"

Bonnie didn't speak.

Melina had a near-perfect bullshit meter and right now it was pinging loudly. "Dean called the cops, didn't he? It had to have been traumatic as hell for a young kid to see his sibling dumped on the side of the road. If you did it to me, it was a matter of time before you ditched him. He must have felt he had to do anything and everything to keep you happy so you wouldn't dump him."

"I never left him," Bonnie said.

"Sure you did. You got arrested when he was sixteen."

"That wasn't my fault. I told him that over and over."

"That arrest report said you were skimming credit cards. It's risky given your record. You must have known you'd get caught eventually and then end up doing serious prison time. He must have known that and begged you to stop."

"You should write fiction." Bonnie's grin dimmed.

"I wish to God it were fiction," Melina said.

A police cruiser pulled up just then. The officer got out and walked up toward Ramsey, who spoke to him in a low tone she could not hear. "He must have been really good at whatever crime he did for you to stay in your good graces. You taught him well."

"You make me sound like a monster." Bonnie looked directly into Melina's eyes. "If it weren't for me, you'd have rotted in foster care."

Melina said nothing. She was a good cop, and a good cop knew when to shut up and let the suspect talk.

"Howard and I were packed and ready to go to Hawaii when we got the call that Lizzie had stuck a needle in her arm for the last time. She was DOA when the paramedics transported both of you to the hospital. Social services was circling and ready to scoop you up. Howard didn't want you at first. Thought you were more trouble than you were worth." She patted her chest. "But I cared. I talked him into taking you. And when Howard died, I still kept you."

"What happened next?" Melina asked.

"You, Dean, and me hit the road. Just the three of us. I was headed to Virginia. I had friends there. I had to stop on the side of the road to pee and have a smoke. When I got back to the car, you were missing. You'd taken off. I looked for you, but I couldn't find you. I went for help."

She supposed if a lie was repeated often enough, it became truth over the years. Maybe Bonnie actually felt guilty about what she had done. "Where's Sonny?" she challenged. She would repeat the question until she got an answer.

Bonnie shook her head. "You always were a difficult kid. You never accepted anything I told you. It was always a fight."

Melina shook her head. "Are you protecting him? Because if you are, it's a mistake. He's not the vulnerable kid he once was. He's been killing women who look like you for years."

"Sonny loves me."

Melina turned to Ramsey, looking for backup. She was swimming in lies that were so emotionally charged that she needed confirmation she was on the right track.

"Sounds like this is more about you, Bonnie, and the guilt you're carrying," Ramsey said.

Bonnie chuckled, her easy disposition returning. "Are you going to fight her battles for her, Mr. FBI man? I bet she's a real firecracker in bed."

Ramsey's steady expression did not change.

Melina imagined the jail cell door closing in Bonnie's face. But if she locked up Bonnie now, she could not lead them to Sonny.

"You going to tell me where Dean lives?" Ramsey said.

"Like I told Melina, I don't know," Bonnie said. "Cops think you can keep asking the same question over and over until you get the answer you want. I don't know where Sonny is!"

"I'm warning you, Bonnie. Watch your step around Sonny," Melina said. "He's a very dangerous man."

Bonnie got into the car and reached for the door handle. "You worried about me, Mellie?"

"You saw the pickle jar," Melina said.

"Don't worry about me," Bonnie said.

Melina did not bother with any more warnings about Sonny. "Don't come back to this house, Bonnie. Or you will be back in jail."

"Yeah, yeah, I get it." Bonnie closed the door and started the car.

Stone faced, Melina watched the car drive away. Only when the Ford rounded the corner did she curl her fingers into fists. The encounter had unsettled her, but she had said her piece.

Ramsey had the good sense not to ask how she was doing.

"Let me check on my mother," she said.

"Sure," he said.

The two walked up the front steps and Melina used her key to open the door. "All's clear, Mom and Dad."

Mrs. Shepard came around the corner with Elena on her hip. The little girl had coiled her legs and arms around her mother like a drowning person did a life raft.

Mr. Shepard hobbled into the kitchen. His hand was behind his back and she knew he had a weapon.

"Mom and Dad, this is Special Agent Ramsey. He's with the FBI. We've been working a case together."

"What case?" her mother asked.

"A missing persons case." Ramsey extended his hand to both of them.

Hank Shepard's grip was strong, and his gaze reminded Melina of a cop trying to read a homicide scene. "How's my daughter involved?"

Ramsey didn't appear surprised that she had not disclosed the details about the Key Killer. "Your daughter has been our local contact on the case."

"Where are you based?" her father asked.

"FBI offices in Quantico, sir," he said.

"Division?"

"I head up a team of agents who work cases all over the country."

"Are you always vague with your answers?" her father asked.

A small smile tugged at Ramsey's lips, acknowledging that Shepard had called bullshit on his answer. "You know the drill. I can't talk about an open case."

"I'm not asking for specifics," Hank said. "Just generalities."

"It doesn't matter now, Dad," Melina said.

"It does matter very much," her mother said. "Agent Ramsey is here to investigate a crime with our daughter."

Melina winked at Elena. "I can't discuss the details, Mom."

"We'll see about that later," her father said.

Her father's eyes burned with unasked questions. Elena was the only thing standing between her and a class-five parental grilling. That would come later when the kid was out of earshot. She owed the kid another bottle of bubbles.

"Where is BB?" Elena whispered.

"She just drove away," Melina said.

"BB doesn't like cops," Elena said.

"They're not all bad, kid," Hank said. "Melina is a cop. I was a cop."

"Some are pretty talkative, too," Molly said.

"Did BB drive back to jail?" Elena asked.

Six-year-old children should not have to ask questions like this. "No. She went to a motel room. But she's not out of trouble yet," Melina said.

"BB's always in trouble," Elena said.

Elena leaned her body into Mrs. Shepard as she stared at Melina with large brown intelligent eyes that all but swallowed up her face. The kid was smart, but life had taught her how to be practical. She might have been relying on Bonnie, but now she had clearly figured out the Shepards had her best interests at heart.

"Don't worry, Mom and Dad. You and I will have a nice visit, and I'll fill you in on all the details. For now, I've got to get back to work. You shouldn't have any more interruptions, but if you do, call me."

"I will," her father said.

She kissed her mother and then her father on their cheeks and held out her flat hand for Elena. "Give me five?"

The girl's eyes softened, and she raised her hand ready to smack it toward Melina's. Just as Elena was about to connect, Melina jerked her hand. "One more time. Be quick this time."

This time the girl's little hand connected with Melina's with a hard smack. "Good job. See you all soon."

"Can we do bubbles?" Elena said.

Ramsey nodded. "I'll get a case of them."

Elena smiled.

***

Melina was grateful Ramsey was driving. Her nerves were shot, and she did not release the breath she was holding until they pulled out of her parents' neighborhood.

"How are you doing?" he asked.

"Outstanding," she said.

"It's understandable that Bonnie upset you."

"I've been living with Bonnie leaving me on the roadside since I was five years old. Don't worry about me."

"On the positive side, I like your parents."

None of the other agents had met her parents. "I've always kept a firm line between my private and professional lives. Now that line is blurring."

"Both your parents look like they can take care of themselves."

"Dad's in his late sixties. He's recovering from a fall off a ladder he had no business being on."

"How's he handling retirement?"

"Getting old sucks, but he's tough."

"Yeah. I could see that. He misses the excitement of the job. He's not worried about going to the mat or pulling his weapon. But he's worried about you, your mother, and Elena."

"I can take care of myself."

"He sees that. But he wants to be needed by you and your mother."

"How would you know? You're the lone wolf type."

He was silent for a moment. "Not by choice, but the job gets in the way."

She was one to talk. She shared her morning coffee with the neighbor's cat. "Does that bother you?"

"It never did until recently."

The car grew silent.

"Your parents look like they're bonding with Elena," he said.

"If Mom has it her way, Elena is going to be a part of their home for good." Melina had been replaced, but in a good way. Her parents needed that little girl as much as Elena needed them.

"You really okay?" he asked.

The stress and adrenaline spike had pricked the underside of her skin. "Hearing Bonnie talk about Elena and love in the same breath churns up memories. When I was a kid, I must have thought she did love me."

"Maybe she did. But self-preservation runs deep in Bonnie Guthrie."

"Maybe she did love me enough to keep me out of foster care. But she's not the kind of mother who deals with a difficult child well for long." This was a conversation she should have had with her adopted mother, but oddly it was easier to share with a near stranger. "Bonnie was lying when she said I got out of the car on the side of the road and ran off."

"She doesn't want a child abandonment case on top of everything else."

"She is a survivor, first and foremost."

"She was surprised when you mentioned the call from the diner," he said. "She recovered pretty quickly, but it was there."

"I saw that, too." She watched as the houses moved past her and the residential road fed into a bigger one. "She's protecting Sonny. And he's still the little boy who wanted Bonnie to love him. Love and need tangled up and knotted in a tight ball with anger," she said.

CHAPTER
TWENTY-FIVE

Thursday, August 27, 8:00 p.m.

Ramsey drove, feeling Melina sink deeper into her thoughts as she sat in silence. He rifled through his best comforting words of wisdom, but they all fell short of the mark. He wanted to help her but did not know how.

Her phone rang and she sat forward, clearing her throat before saying, "Agent Shepard."

He noted a shift in Melina's body language as she tilted her body forward.

"Text me the address. We're on our way."

In a blink, her melancholy mood had vanished, and he was glad she sounded more like herself. "What is it?"

"911 call came in at 7:15 p.m. A woman reported a break-in. The officer who visited her realized this wasn't an ordinary B and E. The intruder drew a warm bath and left behind a pair of garden shears."

"What?"

"Yeah, looks like Bonnie is pressing Sonny's buttons."

Ramsey increased his speed and rerouted to the new address. The home was very similar in construction to the last victim's house. One story. Brick.

"I have Sandra Wallace's DMV picture," Melina said.

He glanced at the picture. Wallace was thirty-eight, blond, and buxom. "Our guy is sticking to his pattern."

"Yes, he is."

Out of the car, Ramsey followed Melina up the front steps and into the house. They were met by an officer at the front door who introduced them to Sandra Wallace. She could have been Bonnie Guthrie's younger sister.

"We came as soon as we heard," Ramsey said. "Can you walk us through the evening? When did you arrive home?"

"It's like I told the other cop. I came in the door with my guy and saw a light on in the bathroom. My friend went to look and found the tub full and the window open."

"Who is your guy?" Melina asked.

"His name is Perry Nelson. I met him at the club last night."

"What club?" Melina asked.

Sandra tucked a curl behind her ear. "Red's Saloon."

"Red's?" Ramsey asked. "On Union Street?"

"Yeah," Sandra said. "I'm a bartender there."

It was not coincidental that their other victim had spent time at Red's. "Have you known Perry long?" he asked.

Sandra shook her head. "No, and after tonight, I don't care if I ever see him again."

"Why is that?" Melina said.

"He got real freaked out when he saw the shears. Thought I had something kinky planned for him. I tried to tell him I had nothing to do with it, but he wouldn't listen. He split."

"Do you have his contact information?" Ramsey asked.

"I know where to find him. He's a bartender down the street at the Boot 'n' Scoot."

"He leaves and then what?" Melina asked.

"I called the cops. Then I sat in my room, cradled a baseball bat, and tried not to lose my shit."

"When did the police arrive?" Ramsey asked.

"Pretty quickly. They seemed interested when I told them about the shears. And I didn't touch anything while I was waiting. Your boys in the forensic van just showed up about a half hour ago. And now I got FBI and TBI in my living room. What the hell is going on?"

"Evidence suggests that a person we're looking for may have broken into your house," Melina said.

"What gave it away, the tub or the shears?" Sandra asked.

Instead of answering, Ramsey fired back with, "Was there anyone else in the bar last night who might have chatted you up or suggested a date?"

"Sure. There are always a few guys each night. Flirting helps with tips, and every so often I do like to spend a little one-on-one time with the cute ones."

"Other than Perry, was there anyone else?" Melina pressed. "Someone who made an impression."

"There was a guy. Real cute. I thought we might hook up. But he didn't come back today."

"Did he have a name?" Melina asked.

Sandra chewed her fingernail as she tried to recall. "I don't remember. It was real busy that night."

"What did he look like?" Ramsey asked.

"Good looking. Kind of tall like you. Strong build."

"Caucasian, African American, Hispanic?" Melina asked.

"He was a white guy. I'd say in his midthirties."

"And this was the night before?" Ramsey asked.

"That's right. The bar has security cameras if that helps."

"It could a great deal," Ramsey said.

"If we don't get a clear picture of him, would you meet with a sketch artist?" Melina asked.

"Yeah, I guess. Who the hell is this guy? I mean, should I be worried?"

"We haven't quite figured that out yet," Melina said. "But we think he's very dangerous."

Sandra looked toward the bathroom where a technician was dusting the doorknob for prints. "What's the deal with the shears?"

"Still working on that," Ramsey said, dodging the question. "Mind if we have a look around the house?"

"Be my guest."

When they had arrived at the last crime scene, much of the water had all but drained from the tub. Now they had a chance to see this killer's ritualistic room setup firsthand.

Both Ramsey and Melina pulled on latex gloves and stood at the threshold of the bathroom. A large claw-foot tub that appeared original dominated the room. Black and white tiled floor, a small pedestal sink, and a mirror that covered a medicine chest set into the wall.

The space was fairly large considering the house could not be more than twelve hundred square feet. There was a window that opened onto a small backyard ringed with trees.

There was no way Sonny would have known about the tub and the room's setup unless he had done some kind of reconnaissance.

"He went out the window," the tech said. "I looked outside and there's a print below. Looks like a men's size ten sports shoe. But other than the shoe impression, there doesn't appear to be much evidence. The shears are old and may give us something. After I've made impressions of the blades, I will pull them apart and see if there's traces of blood."

"Thank you," Ramsey said.

He left the techs to their data collection and walked through the house. It was not a cozy setup. The furniture was threadbare and covered in stains. There were discarded wrappers and used plates on the coffee table and in the kitchen sink. And by the back and front doors, piles of shoes lay haphazardly about. However, the bathroom was relatively clean and organized.

Melina came up behind and the two walked silently out the front door and around the back of the house. Both moved toward the yellow-tented markers indicating a trail of footprints that led toward the woods.

"He was here. He preplanned his escape route," he said.

"A one-level house was a smart play for him. Multiple exit opportunities, especially if in a rush."

"He wasn't expecting Sandra to have company," he said, looking back toward the window. "But his preplanning saved him."

"If Sandra is remembering the right guy, then Sonny made contact with her," Melina said. "But is it unusual for serial killers to have such a short downtime between murders?" she asked.

"Sometimes. Some killers cluster their murders. A trigger sets them off and they kill until whatever is driving them is exorcised or they are caught. This killer's confirmed murders were spaced years apart. Now he may have one confirmed murder with another attempted murder within two weeks."

"If we're dealing with Sonny, and he does have a relationship with Bonnie, her arrival would be a serious stressor," she said. "She's doing her best to turn me inside out."

"Has she managed it?" Ramsey asked.

She tilted her chin up. "Not quite."

"Good." He drew in a breath, glad to hear the brittleness softening in her tone. He needed Melina focused. "If you're a little off your game . . ."

"I'm *not*."

"*If* you were, how would you react to Bonnie's arrival?"

"Anger, fear, and frustration are powerful motivators. If I were a little less controlled, I might have shot Bonnie an hour ago while she stood on my parents' lawn with that shit-eating grin on her face."

Bonnie had the same effect on Sonny, only he followed through on his impulses. "Stress could have pushed him to kill again, and maybe this time he was rushed and wasn't as deliberate as he is normally."

"There was no sign of sexual intercourse with Jennifer Brown," she said.

"Yet the scene we saw at Jennifer Brown's had a sexual component to it."

"We have a killer who's under more stress, and the cooling-off period between kills is shortening," she said.

"This failed attempt cannot be sitting well with him."

"He'll strike again?"

"He may already have," he said.

"Why not just kill Bonnie? Why all the surrogates?" she asked.

"You know the answer. She holds power over him. He kills her and he really is alone."

"Mommy dearest."

"I'd say so," he said.

"What're the chances that he'll leave Nashville?" she asked. "Why not pull up stakes and leave?"

"It's like the Key Killer. The area is familiar. Creature of habit. Like us, they, too, want to keep the stress in check."

"We need to locate the bail bondsman who put up bail for Bonnie. He should have some record of who reached out to him."

***

Sonny stood across the street from the small house, standing behind a privacy fence in a neighbor's yard. He watched as the cops escorted Sandra to her car. An officer placed a suitcase in her trunk.

He should not have delayed taking Sandra. That extra night he had been distracted by Bonnie had nearly gotten him caught.

Stupid, stupid, stupid.

Bonnie had taught him planning was the difference between the pros and amateurs. Prison was full of lazy cons doing it on the fly.

He closed his eyes, pushing down a primal urge to kill. Bonnie had hammered the rules over and over.

And then she had done the unforgiveable. She had gotten sloppy and decided just like that to take a credit card from a regular customer at a bar where she worked. The guy had been too drunk to notice the missing card, until he had sobered up.

She had not even used the card for stuff they needed. Instead, she had gone on a shopping spree that included designer shoes, handbags, and dresses. She'd left such an obvious trail that even the dumbest cop could have found her. She had been taken away in handcuffs five days after she'd purchased $8,000 worth of useless shit.

Only sixteen, he had been so damn scared. Sonny knew she was going to do serious jail time when he arrived at the San Diego Central Jail. As he waded through the people, he tried to crush down the waves of panic crashing over him. When he saw her in the booth waiting to talk to him, he nearly cried.

"How did this happen?" His voice was a ragged whisper.

"Sorry, baby," she said.

"Sorry!" he said.

She frowned, doing her best imitation of contrition. "I didn't think about you. I know that. Did you talk to the bail bondsman?"

"The judge found out about your priors. There are also outstanding arrest warrants out for you."

"I'll beat this."

"You didn't get bail," he said. "The cops mean business this time. No slap on the wrist."

"That's okay. I'll get out. All you have to do is keep that key safe. And when I'm free, we'll get the cash I put aside and go on a real vacation. You can even pick where we go."

"Did you do this on purpose?" he demanded.

"Why would I want to be here?"

"You said yourself you were tired of bartending and going legit."

"I was doing that for you, so you could go to school."

He sat back, staring at her, wishing he could hug her even as he wanted to curse her out. "This is your way to check out of my life, isn't it?"

"That's not true."

The buzz of conversation in the visiting room was drowned out by his pulse thrumming in his temple. His vision narrowed and his palms sweat. Fuck. She was doing her version of leaving him on the side of the road.

It had been a long time since he had felt that raw kind of fear. And shame on him, it was not the last time Bonnie would sweep into his life and make a fool out of him.

Fuck her.

She would not use him again. He would use her and all the others like her. He deserved to be fucking loved.

He inched back from the fence, feeling as if the noose were tightening around his neck. It was not the cops he was worried about, but Melina. She was smart, cunning like him, and no one could possibly understand him better than she. They were cut from the same cloth.

He jogged to the back fence, slipped through the gate, and carefully relocked it before getting into his car.

How many times had he sworn he would never ask Bonnie for help? How many vows had he made to never, ever trust any of her "deals"? And yet here he was, wanting what she was offering.

But this time, it would be different. He was different.

Maybe he could have his clean slate with Bonnie. He was sorry that fresh start would not include Melina. That dream had sustained him for years. But dreams had to change. Life went on.

Getting back with Bonnie and Elena was all that mattered now.

They were his future.

CHAPTER
TWENTY-SIX

Friday, August 28, 1:00 a.m.

Melina's eyes stung from fatigue when she opened the front door of her town house.

The surveillance footage from Sandra's bar had arrived at her office shortly after nine, so she and Ramsey had ordered Chinese food and spent the evening eating stir-fried beef with mixed vegetables, shrimp fried rice, and egg rolls as they watched the footage.

After an hour, she began to recognize the regulars at Red's. Mr. Handlebar Mustache, Mr. Urban Cowboy, and Mr. Baseball Cap, as she now called them. They always entered the establishment around ten or eleven, and all had paid extra close attention to Sandra. Melina was able to grab a clean screenshot of the first two, but Mr. Baseball Cap kept his face turned from the camera.

Both Ramsey and she studied this man. The night Jennifer Brown had last been seen in the bar, Mr. Baseball Cap had appeared briefly, and again he had been careful not to show his face.

Melina dispatched several local detectives to canvass the surrounding retail outlets to see if they had cameras. Mr. Baseball Cap might have been careful in Red's, but sooner or later he would have to let his guard down.

For now, she was glad to be home and have a few hours of much-needed sleep. She locked the door behind her and then placed her keys and backpack on the kitchen counter.

As she laid her weapon on the counter, a tremor slithered along her spine. Instead of releasing the grip, she held on tight and turned on all the lights.

The town house was silent except for the hum of the refrigerator and the whoosh of the air-conditioning. She walked into the living room and noted the three magazines were as she'd left them on the coffee table. Same for the red pillows and the channel selectors. So why, then, did she feel as if something were off?

She flipped on the entryway light and, moving slowly, glanced toward the sliding glass door that fed onto a small patio. Listening, she paused and then followed the hallway toward the bedrooms.

The spare bedroom housed her two bikes and camping equipment. She opened the closet and searched it. Everything appeared in order.

She continued her methodical search into her bedroom and bathroom.

Nothing was out of place. All as she had left it.

And still she felt the very strong sensation that something was definitely not right.

She was more paranoid than the average guy, but she was not average. She was a cop, and the best cops embraced those unexplained feelings they could not shake. Better cautious than dead.

The goal was always to go home at night. And now she was home and still jumpy.

She doubled-checked the patio door one last time, and the security lights her father had installed kicked on as Wild Kitty strolled out of the bushes.

Smiling, Melina holstered her weapon and opened a can of tuna before she exited the door. She set the can on the patio table. The cat jumped up, meowing.

"I know, I'm late." She petted the cat, taking extra time to rub between her ears. It was her favorite spot. Finally, satisfied she had been properly acknowledged, she ate.

Melina stood in the warm night air and stared up at the stars in the sky. "My best friend is a cat."

It was not lost on her that the longest relationship she had ever had, outside her parents, was with a feline that did not even belong to her.

She closed the sliding door behind her, locked it, and wedged the security bar in place. Slowly, she released the grip on her gun, and tossing one more glance around the fully illuminated town house, she returned to the kitchen.

From the freezer she grabbed a double-stuffed-crust pizza and popped it in the oven. She never had the patience to preheat the oven, which meant she was not giving the frozen disc its culinary due.

In her bedroom, she turned on the hot water, stripped, and then stepped into the shower. The liquid heat pushed against her skin, chasing away some of the chill that had settled in her bones. As she dipped her head under the hot spray, her thoughts trailed to Ramsey. Had he collapsed into his bed, exhausted? Or was he reading one of those half dozen case files? Her money was on the files.

She tried to imagine the touch of his hands on her skin and the sensation of his body pressed against hers. Maybe when this case was over, she would ask him up for a drink or, better yet, sex. It had been a long dry spell, and good sex with an interesting man was welcome.

Her phone rang. She shut off the water and grabbed a towel and dried off her hands as she hurried to her bed. She picked up the phone on the fourth ring. She glanced at a number she did not recognize, but that was par for the course when she was running an investigation. "Agent Shepard."

Silence settled on the line. Irritated, she shoved back a lock of thick wet hair. "Is this Sonny?"

More silence and the line went dead.

She tossed the phone on her bed. "Damn it," she muttered as she hurried back to the tiled floor and dried off. Minutes later she was wearing sweats and a T-shirt. Wet hair coiled up, she snatched up the phone. No voicemail.

It could have been a wrong number or a robocall. She rarely got either, but it was possible. She tucked the phone in her waistband. The smell of processed pepperoni and cheese lured her into the kitchen, and after grabbing a hot mitt, she removed the pizza. She divided it into quarters and dragged two hot pieces onto a plate.

Sitting at the small dining table, she took a bite and glanced at her phone. She took several more bites until she had polished off the second slice. Good enough to fill her belly but not tasty enough for the other half.

Melina went to her computer and searched the number in a reverse phone directory. It came back as a burner. Not the kind of news she wanted.

She ran her fingers over her damp hair, heart pulsing in her neck. Whatever hope she had of sleeping tonight had evaporated. The idea of watching television or reading a book had no appeal.

"What to do?" she muttered.

In her bedroom, she changed into jeans, a button-down shirt, and boots. Her gun back on her hip, she was out the door two minutes later.

***

Ramsey was sitting on his hotel bed, a cold convenience store beer in hand, and watching a rerun of a sitcom that was not nearly as funny as he recalled from twenty years ago. Maybe times had changed. He sure as hell had. Either way, the dated costumes and humor were irritating.

As he reached for the remote, his phone rang. It was Shepard. He tossed the remote aside and swung his legs over the side of the bed.

"Shepard," he said.

"What are you doing?"

"Watching a bad show."

"Want a beer?"

He glanced at the half-consumed beer. "Sure."

"I can be there in five minutes."

"Great." He hung up and poured his beer down the sink and stashed the other five in the small minifridge. As he tucked in his shirt, there was a knock on his door.

Habit had him reaching for his weapon on the nightstand and peering out the peephole. Shepard was staring directly at the door as if she knew he was checking out his late-night visitor. She held up the six-pack and grinned.

A smile tipped the edges of his lips and he opened the door. He did not speak as he stepped aside and nodded for her to enter. Her damp hair smelled of roses or lavender, and her skin looked dewy and moist. His mind jerked to her standing naked in a shower.

"I couldn't sleep," she said.

He shut the door. "Why?"

Her shoulders rose in what he now saw as a nervous habit. "Dead prostitutes. Severed fingers. Two killers who haven't been stopped. You pick." She handed him a beer and then twisted off the top of another.

"Do you often have trouble sleeping?" he asked.

"You don't?" She took a pull, and his gaze was drawn to the slim line of her neck.

"I've never slept well."

She dug her finger along the label of her beer bottle. "I had the sensation someone had been in my town house. I searched it top to bottom. Nothing. Then I received a phone call with no one on the other end. It was from a burner phone."

"It upset you."

"More like pissed me off. But after my encounter with the Key Killer, I've been a little touchy." She set her beer down by the television. "And gauging your reaction, I might be a tad paranoid."

"I don't get amped up."

"Oh, really?" She paused, as if choosing her next words carefully. "I'd rather not be alone tonight."

He understood the need to connect, to feel not alone all the time. He set his beer down and crossed to her. "What do you have in mind, Agent?"

His deep tone sparked heat in her cheeks. She cleared her throat. "Three guesses and the first two don't count."

"Say it," he said.

"I want to have sex with you."

His gaze darkened. "Are you sure?"

"Oddly, yes. Very. What about you?"

"This moment has crossed my mind once or twice."

That coaxed a smile. "Really? You were thinking about me?"

"Yes."

"Doing what?"

Instead of answering, he reached for the clip holding her hair up and tugged it free. The damp curls framed her face and brushed her shoulders. He ran his fingers through her hair. "It's as soft as it looks."

"Is that all you thought about doing?" Her voice had grown husky.

"Not all."

"What about this?" She reached for the top button of her blouse and slowly undid two.

As she reached for the third button, he took her hand and pulled her toward him. "Are you in a rush?"

"Depends."

"We're not going to rush this." It was not a request. He was practical enough to know life was going to pull them apart soon enough. He wanted to savor her. He cupped her face and kissed her on the lips.

She leaned into the kiss. Energy radiated through her, and he sensed she was lowering her guard to him. He liked that she had decided to trust him.

He deepened the kiss, savoring the taste of her mouth. He tasted beer. His hand slid to her shoulder and then along her waist. He then realized he was not so different from Shepard. Self-imposed exile for the sake of work and a constant need for justice had also left him isolated.

He reached for the next button on her shirt and carefully unfastened it. "So much for going slow," he said.

"I don't do patient."

His gaze was drawn to her delicate bronze skin, which reminded him of honey. He kissed her naked shoulder and then the hollow of her neck before dropping his lips to the crest of her full breasts.

Melina drew in a breath, threading her fingers through his hair and arching toward him. Neither spoke as they continued to kiss, touch, and strip clothing that dropped to the growing pile on the floor.

Naked, she was not shy and made no attempt to hide from him. She took him by the hand and led him toward the bed. With the goofy sitcom now muted but still playing in the background, she crawled to the center of the bed and propped herself up on both pillows.

Ramsey's grip on his control shattered. All he could think about now was being inside her. He followed her and slowly straddled her. She shifted, moving him to her moist center as he slid inside her.

She drew in a breath, rubbing her hands over his back and then over his buttocks as her excitement rose. He waited as her body adjusted and then very slowly began to move. She arched toward him, wrapping her legs around him and pulling him in deeper.

There were always real monsters in the shadows, waiting for Ramsey to lower his guard so they could claim another victim. He had been warned by a veteran officer that he could not save everyone and to try to do so would be his ruin. He consciously chose not to heed that advice. All could be saved. His duty was to be forever vigilant in the hunt for monsters.

But in this moment, he let his guard slip. He allowed the sensations of pleasure to satisfy the longings and fill the loneliness that had hollowed out his insides.

Shepard closed her eyes, and he knew she was headed to a similar place filled with hungry desire that pushed away all her worries and fears. He gratefully followed.

He moved faster, and her moans turned more urgent. She was here for herself, not for him, but he did not care. She was here, and she would take him out of the darkness and toward the light for just a little while.

When she climaxed, arching her back, he tumbled right after her. For a blissful split second, they were one.

He collapsed on top of her, their hearts pounding in a rapid drummer's beat. She caressed her hand along his back, and he allowed his face to rest in the hollow of her neck.

"Stay for a couple of hours," he said.

She was silent for a moment, as if she did not quite know how to take it. "Are you sure? It's okay if you want me to go."

He rose up on his elbow and touched her chin. He stared into the warm brown eyes that searched his with the same intensity she gave a crime scene. That thought made him smile.

"What's so funny?" she asked.

"You're back to analyzing." He moved a strand of hair off her forehead and tucked it behind her ear.

A lazy smile coiled the edges of her lips. "And you aren't?"

"Maybe a little." He liked having her close and feeling her warmth.

"It's nice," she said.

"Nice?"

"I mean being here. The other part was pretty great. It's been a while. Glad to know all the parts still work."

He chuckled. "Like riding a bike."

"Something like that." She squirmed, and when he rose up to give her space, she slid out from under him. He lay on his back, tucking the pillow behind his head. He was curious about what her next move would be.

She rolled on her side, facing him. She smoothed her hand over his flat belly, drawing small circles. Her fingers moved lower and lower until they skimmed the top of his now-returning erection.

Her smile turned mischievous as she straddled him. After guiding him inside her, she moved up and down. He watched as she cupped her breasts and then rubbed them against his chest.

Once again, he could feel the desire and emotion rise up in her like flames from a pyre. It seemed to consume her, burning into him in a way he had never experienced before. With hands on both sides of her narrow hips, he held on as she rode him hard until finally the heat rushed over him.

She rested her head on his chest, damp with sweat, and leaned forward and kissed him. "Very nice."

"So you're staying?"

"Round three?" she teased.

He chuckled. "How about you lay beside me?"

She regarded him and finally nodded. "Just for a little while."

She nestled her body beside his, and he curled his arm around her waist, taking in her restful breathing. For the first time in years, he did not spend the next hour overanalyzing events. He simply drifted off to sleep.

***

It didn't take Sonny long to find Bonnie. Over their years together, he had learned her patterns cold. He began visiting likely motels, stopping at the front desk, showing her picture and his fake police badge. Three hours into his search, he found her South Nashville motel.

He paid the manager twenty bucks and then knocked on Bonnie's door. Inside he heard a television blaring some kind of game show. Bonnie loved those damn things. When they had been in California, she had put in applications for at least a dozen of them but had never gotten picked. "Just as well," she had grumbled. "Got to pay taxes on those winnings. And never a good idea to hook up with the Tax Man."

The curtains fluttered and he knew Bonnie was looking out the window. Fuck. She could be so smug when he had made a mistake. And he had made a few too many since her return.

The latch scraped free and the door opened. She greeted him with a wide smile. "You've been a bad, bad boy," she said.

He looked from side to side, fearing someone might be watching. "Can I come in?"

"I don't know, baby doll. You weren't so kind to me."

"We have a mutual problem, thanks to that little car accident of yours."

"Shit happens."

Of course, she would be gloating. She never could resist. "If you want to stay out of prison, let me in."

Her smile widened as she stepped back. "You don't have to get all pissy with me, Sonny. You know I would never leave you out in the cold."

He stepped over the threshold, brushing past her as well as her comment. He searched the room, saw a pair of men's underwear.

"Are you alone?" he asked.

"I am now. You picked a good bail bondsman. Full service."

"What did you do to him?"

"Nothing that didn't leave a smile on his face." She grinned. "Don't worry. I took a few pictures. He's not going to say anything. He would end up in trouble with his boss and his missus if the pictures got out."

Ignoring her comment, he locked the door and slid the chain into place. From inside his coat pocket, he removed the pair of new gardening shears.

Bonnie inhaled her cigarette, and as she blew out the smoke, that trademark grin faded. She took a step back but to her credit showed no fear. She carefully stabbed out the glowing tip. "There's no reason for that, baby doll."

"It's long overdue," he said more to himself.

"You think killing me is going to make you right in the head? It won't. In fact, it will drive you over the edge. There won't be enough women in the world to kill if I die."

He advanced on her.

Instead of shrinking back, she took a step forward and put her face within inches of his own. "You've been pissed at me since I left your sister on the side of the road."

The image knifed through him. "Shut up."

"I still remember how she used to scream when she didn't get her way. That kid could shake the bloody rafters with those lungs of hers."

"It wasn't her fault. She just wanted attention."

"Who doesn't want attention?" Bonnie asked. "We all want it. Those first months on the road with the three of us were pretty sweet. We had some good times. Remember that yellow Cadillac we picked up in Salt Lake City?"

Picked up. Bonnie had hot-wired it. But it had been one sweet car. With the top down and the warm air on his face, it was the first time in his life that he had felt free and really alive.

She grinned, staring at him intently. "You remember, don't you?"

"Yes."

"You could have it again," she said. "That freedom and that fun."

The pain that he had so carefully locked away crawled out of the shadows and howled, its doleful sound scratching the underside of his skin. God help him. He had dreamed of those days.

She pointed at him. "And you want it all back, don't you?"

He dropped his gaze, feeling weak and ashamed. Yes. He wanted it.

"All we have to do is get Elena, you give me the key, and I get the money."

"There is no money," he said.

"What?"

He shook his head. "I spent it a long time ago."

She stared at him with narrowing eyes for a long moment, and he knew this would be the moment she sent him away. She held out her arms to him. "That's okay, honey. We'll get more money. We're good at that."

He stepped into the embrace, and she wrapped her arms around him. For a moment he remained stiff with all the anger that had left him rigid. She tightened her hold.

And he relaxed into her. Tears welled in his eyes, and he wrapped his arms around her.

"That's my boy," she said, close to his ear. "Let Bonnie worry about everything, and the three of us will be a family again."

CHAPTER
TWENTY-SEVEN

Friday, August 28, 7:00 a.m.

Sarah had been up since 4:00 a.m., though she really had not slept well in weeks. Two of her charges were missing, and though most of the world did not give a second thought to a missing prostitute, she cared deeply. She thought she'd grasped the evil these women faced each day, but after hearing Melina's description of the Key Killer's van, she wondered if the devil himself now walked among them.

She knew the Lord had sent her a series of tests over her thirty-four years, and she felt like she had risen to the challenge each time. She hoped she could again.

After refilling her coffee cup, she returned to her desk, determined to accomplish something productive today. With some effort, she shifted her mind to the reconciling of the Mission's accounts.

The house was scheduled to wake up in the next half hour, and if she hustled, she could get the task completed.

The doorbell of the Mission rang, pulling Sarah gratefully from the obstinate numbers that were refusing to reconcile. She glanced at the security screens and saw a tall lean man who appeared to be in his early sixties. He was nicely dressed in a gray tailored suit, a white shirt, and polished wing tips. Dark hair was streaked with gray and combed back off his face.

Curious, she rose from her desk, walked down the hallway to the front door to the intercom.

"Can I help you?" Sarah said.

"I'm here on behalf of my client. She would like to make a donation to the Mission."

Although grateful for new donations, Sarah was puzzled. "You're here kind of early, aren't you?"

"You're a mission, so I assumed you're always open. Besides, I have an early-morning meeting downtown. Thought I'd drop this off."

Sarah had a trusting heart but a suspicious mind. And this man made her feel uncomfortable. "You could have mailed it."

The man's grin held little warmth. "My client wanted it hand delivered."

"Hold up some form of identification, please?"

He removed a long slim wallet, pulled out a driver's license, and held it up to the camera. Edward Mecum. Age sixty-two, and he lived in Franklin.

As Sarah started to throw the locks, Mr. Mecum carefully replaced his driver's license into his wallet that he tucked into his jacket's breast pocket. The door opened, and the spicy scent of expensive aftershave wafted over the threshold.

"Sorry for the questions. I have to be careful down here. My name is Reverend Sarah Beckett."

He removed a gold card holder from his pocket, clicked it open, and selected a single card. "As you know, I'm Edward Mecum."

Sarah stared at the card, moving her thumb over the fine linen paper stock. "You said you had a donation?"

"I do." From the same breast pocket, he removed an unsealed envelope.

Sarah accepted it, and in a move that would have made her sainted mother roll over in her grave, looked at the amount on the check. $100,000. She blinked once. Twice. "Wow."

"My client is impressed with your work." Mr. Mecum had a unique accent, but Sarah couldn't place it. It was not a southern drawl, but the way he emphasized the *w* in *work* hinted at New England. Boston, maybe?

"This is very generous." A pan rattled in the kitchen, reminding Sarah that Sam was around if necessary. "Can I give you a tour of the place? The ladies aren't all up yet, but I could show you the library and the kitchen."

Interest sparked in his gaze. "I would like that."

Sarah led Mr. Mecum down the center hallway, digging through her memory files for her canned presentation. She had done over a hundred in the last year, but none of those donors had come close to one hundred grand. "I founded the facility five years ago. We serve women who have worked on the streets or who are addicted to drugs and alcohol. Usually, the two go hand in hand."

"How many women have you helped in the last five years?"

"Over one hundred." Pride came before the fall, but this next statistic always made her stand a little taller. "We have a seventy percent success rate."

"Enviable numbers."

"Yes, they are." Sarah led him into the library and switched on the light. "We put an emphasis on education, vocation, and prayer. This is a multipurpose room where everything happens, including Sunday supper, mass, Bible study, and math lessons, to name a few. I'm working on a brochure for the Mission, but it's still a draft on my computer right now."

Mr. Mecum's gaze sharpened as he walked to a collection of lotions the ladies had made. "Very nice."

"Let me show you the kitchen."

"Of course."

Down the hallway, they entered the industrial kitchen that had been donated by a restaurant undergoing a massive renovation. Sam stood behind the long stainless steel table and was cutting carrots. "Sam, this is Mr. Mecum. I'm giving him the grand tour."

Sam chopped a large carrot in half. "Good to meet you."

"Likewise."

An alarm clock rang from one of the dorm rooms. The house was waking up, and soon the quiet would turn into controlled chaos.

As Sarah led Mr. Mecum back down the hallway, Sam's chops echoed behind them. Sam was rough around the edges, naturally was suspicious of anyone new, but he had a heart of gold. "I'd like to acknowledge the donation with a proper thank-you letter."

"My client wants to remain anonymous. Email a receipt to my address. I'll forward it on to my client. She'll need it for tax purposes. If she responds back, you can simply thank her in a return email."

"Of course. I'll do it this morning." She would be at the bank when it opened. This kind of money would solve a lot of problems. "Bless you and our donor. And thank her for me."

"I will." Mr. Mecum paused at the door. "You have a very impressive operation."

"Thank you."

Mr. Mecum watched as Sarah opened the locks on the front door. "I suppose down here security is a concern."

"It's a rough part of town, but with people like your donor, we're making an impact."

"What made you bring your ministry down here? Your bearing suggests money and education."

She opened the door. "I picked the place with the greatest need."

Mr. Mecum surveyed the asphalt parking lot and the run-down buildings beyond it. "Looks like you've come to the right place."

"Thank you again, Mr. Mecum."

His grip was strong and determined. "The pleasure was all mine, Ms. Beckett."

Another quick nod and he strode toward a dark Mercedes parked in her lot. Sarah quickly looked over the vehicle to make sure the hubcaps and wheels had not been stripped. Down here, a car like that did not last long. Finding it intact, she said a prayer of thanks as she waved one last time and closed the door and locked it.

She dropped her gaze back to the check, making sure she had not read it wrong in her haste. "One hundred thousand dollars. Amazing."

She saw the donation as a sign. Perhaps her fight against evil was not so hopeless.

Sam's chopping grew louder. He had an opinion to share, and the sooner she heard it, the better.

She tucked the check in her pocket and returned to the kitchen. "What do you have to say?"

He dumped the carrots into a pot on the stove. "Big donation, right?"

She pulled out the check and handed it to Sam. "The biggest we've ever gotten."

Sam whistled and handed it back. "That's good."

She reached for a mug in the cabinet and filled it with coffee. "We'll both believe it when it clears the bank."

***

Melina woke to the sound of a coffeepot gurgling and a shower running. For a second or two, she did not know where she was. It wasn't her bed. It belonged to . . .

She closed her eyes, pressing her fingertips to her lids. Awkward.

Her dad used to say, *"Don't mix business with pleasure."*

It was not the first bit of good advice she had ignored.

She rose out of bed, glanced at the clock, and realized it was after seven. Tossing back the covers, she hunted around for her clothes. Most were easy to locate, but the panties remained MIA.

She was feeling too good right now to stress, so she opted to pour herself a cup of coffee. She tore open a packet of sugar and dumped in one of the fake creamers.

She sipped and moved to the small table and chair beside the bed. Ramsey's files were arranged in a neat line. The guy was meticulous. Last night the clear demarcation both had adhered to had been obliterated. But now she was counting on that laser mind of his getting back on track.

She opened the first file and was quickly rewarded with a grisly rural murder scene. The tab was marked Denver, Colorado. She opened two other files with similar gruesome scenarios.

The shower shut off. She crossed her legs and sat back in the chair, sipping coffee that was barely this side of acceptable.

He stepped out of the steam, a towel wrapped around his waist. He had shaved and combed his hair. All he needed was a suit and he would be ready for any boardroom.

"Good morning," he said.

She held up the cup. "Thanks for the coffee."

"There's a coffee shop in the lobby if you'd rather have something tastier."

"This will do just fine. I can already feel the caffeine shaking off the cobwebs."

He poured himself a cup. And for the first time, some of that trademark intense energy had shifted in a way she found really appealing. "We have to be at the crime lab at nine thirty."

"That's almost ninety minutes." She took one more sip of coffee and set her cup down beside the closed files. Again, the warnings demanding distance and the impersonal went silent. "I have a few ideas, but it's going to mean messing up that pretty hair of yours."

He crossed to her and set his cup down beside hers. She rose and reached for his towel, unfastening and tossing it aside.

"I can't find my panties," she said, nestling closer to him.

"That's a damn shame. Better call a cop."

He cupped her naked buttocks and pushed her against his erection. "I just did."

***

The morning school bus was making its rounds in the neighborhood as Bonnie sat in Ralph's car, which she had promised to have back to him by the end of the day. Poor Ralph. Still worried she would out his extracurricular activities.

The little neighborhood children were gathered on the corner, and a couple of the mothers stood post with them. Everyone looked tired, as if they were still adjusting to the school schedule. The excitement of the first days had worn off, and they were all settling into the long grind of another school year.

Bonnie had never bothered with formal schools for her kids. Schools required registration forms, identification, and immunization records that she ignored. She did not buy into the conventional wisdom that kids needed school. Hers had learned well enough. Life was the best teacher as far as she was concerned.

Mrs. Shepard and Elena came out on the front porch and watched as the kids got on the bus and it drove off. Mrs. Shepard was talking to Elena, and together they were waving at the kids on the bus as it passed.

Shepard was probably feeding that girl a line of bull. Telling her about all the fun things she could do at school. Elena seemed to be paying attention, as if she could easily be led to a conventional life.

The two rose and vanished inside, reappearing fifteen minutes later. They crossed the lawn to the car, and Mrs. Shepard hooked Elena into her car seat.

Bonnie could not make her move now, but if she bided her time, there would be an opening. And when it came, she would reach in and grab Elena. Elena, Sonny, and she would leave this damn town for good.

***

A smart fisherman knew the right bait was critical for success. And his little donation was just the kind of lure he needed to access the Mission records, which he hoped had information about Ms. Perky Breasts.

Mecum reached for a cold beer, watching a movie on his computer while he waited for his little fish to take the bait.

The movie was *Pretty Woman*. All the hookers wanted to be Julia Roberts's character, Vivian, the whore with the heart of gold. The young ones might have stepped over the line into prostitution, but they could still look back and see who they had been. The older ones had accepted their fate and no longer looked back.

He watched the computer screen, knowing that he needed to find his Vivian and get her into his van before this damn disease rendered him useless. He had spent the better part of the last twenty-four hours outfitting his van with new restraints so that it was almost a mirror image of the one he had lost.

A small bell chimed on his computer. He turned off the movie just as Vivian was about to see what was in the blue velvet-lined jewelry box. This was a favorite place for him to stop. He loved denying her the surprise and pleasure.

The good reverend had sent an email to the fake address he had given her, offering her humble thanks. Her response immediately created a virtual tunnel that burrowed under firewalls and brought him up in the Mission's computer. He was like a vampire. He could not enter a home unless he was invited. But once the link was clicked, he was over the threshold in a nanosecond, and there was no getting rid of him.

His fish took the bait and issued him his invitation at 9:15 a.m.

"Gotcha."

CHAPTER
TWENTY-EIGHT

Friday, August 28, 9:30 a.m.

Melina followed Ramsey as he drove from his hotel to the forensic lab. As they approached the facility, she took an extra turn around the block so they would not arrive at the exact same time. Neither had suggested a shared ride to the office. As intimate as they had been, showing up in the same vehicle made a personal statement she was not ready to make. First sex, then a car. What would be next? Holding hands? The image made her chuckle as she showed her identification.

"What's so funny?" the guard asked.

"Can you picture me living the white picket dream?"

It was his turn to chuckle. "With who? You're married to your job."

"Exactly."

"What brought that up?" His eyes glinted as if he had caught her doing the walk of shame.

She laughed, catching Ramsey's approach in the corner of her eye. "Nothing. Nothing at all."

Ramsey's stoic features always struck a good balance between disinterested and mildly impatient. He studied human expression and used it to peer into minds, so it stood to reason he was an expert at masking his own thoughts.

Her shoes clicked against the tiled floor as she walked toward the elevators. Raising her gaze to the polished door, she caught a hint of brittleness in her eyes. Those eyes had always held a measure of wariness, but she'd believed hope had tempered it. Maybe not so much anymore. She sensed Ramsey's gaze on her but did not look toward him. Maybe because she did not want him seeing her worry.

They rode the elevator to her floor, and while he headed to the conference room to get situated again, she entered her office. As soon as she set her backpack down, her phone rang. It was Andy.

"Agent Shepard," she said.

"It's Andy. I have an update on your half brother."

"Really?" She sat, not quite sure if she should be standing. "That was very fast."

"I do work magic."

Melina leaned forward a bit, unable to summon a smile. "And?"

"Your DNA was a familial hit to a young man by the name of Dean Guthrie, who it turns out does have a juvenile record. He was arrested for vagrancy and petty theft when he was seventeen. The records were in sealed juvenile courts, which is why I didn't find them immediately. Dean received six months' detention followed by probation. After that, he wasn't arrested again."

"Do you have a picture?"

"An old picture. It was taken about twenty years ago when he was arrested. It should be in your email now."

***

Once Mecum got into the Mission's personnel files, he had access to all the employee and volunteer information for anyone who worked at the Mission. However, the data required that he search each individual,

Mary Burton

and he did not have that kind of time. Then he spotted the draft of the Mission brochure Sarah Beckett had mentioned.

It was full of pictures from everyday life at the Mission. He scrolled through the pages, searching the faces of the women who had been through the doors of the Mission. He looked through each not once but twice, but he did not see his girl. He sat back, disappointed that he had not found her. "Where are you?"

He scrolled to the volunteers' page, not sure what to expect. Midway down the page, he saw her. It was a headshot, and she was staring into the camera. Her lips were compressed into a not-quite-grim line that was somewhere between a smile and annoyance.

"Melina Shepard. Ms. Perky Breasts!" he said.

He scrolled to the next page and saw a group shot of the volunteers. Everyone was staring at the camera except the man standing beside Melina. Instead he was staring at her. As he continued through the brochure, there were more group pictures. Each time this man was in a picture with Melina, he was either close to her or looking at her. The man's name was Sam Jenkins.

He could see Sam had a thing for Melina, so what had she been doing out on the street? Was she trying to help the girls? Was she looking for someone?

He searched her name on the internet and was caught off guard when an article popped with her name and real profession. Melina Shepard. Tennessee Bureau of Investigation.

"Holy shit."

He sat back, feeling as if a lightning bolt had struck him. What had TBI been doing on the street corner that night? He drummed his fingers on his injured leg.

Did they suspect he was in the Nashville area? Had someone actually missed his other girls? Or had it been a fluke? They had to know or suspect something. Random stuff like that did not happen.

He turned to another set of cameras and activated the feeds from his three houses. The first two were as he had left them, isolated and untouched. But the third. "Shit, it's swarming with cops!"

He touched the screen but drew back as more cops strolled into view. He had been on the property two days ago, and it had been perfectly undisturbed.

He rubbed his thigh. He knew the TBI agent had gotten a good look in his van, and he had enjoyed the first blush of fear and panic in her eyes. But then she had stabbed him, and his temper had exploded. He had assumed she was a streetwise whore, not a cop hunting him.

Since the cancer, he had become very aware of time slipping through his fingers and his eventual loss of control over his life. Perhaps because of the cancer, he was less panicked than he would have been a decade ago. His time might be running out faster now, but he still had enough to make his Vivian submit.

He returned to the Mission's personnel files, but Melina, who was not a paid employee, was not listed. However, Sam was paid staff, and his contact information was on file.

"Meh-lina." He liked the sound of the name. Rolled off the tongue. He studied the man's face. "I bet Sam can tell me where you live."

If this man did not know where Melina lived, then the lovely Sarah Beckett certainly did. All he had to do was get one of them alone, and given the persuasive skills of a hand drill, either one would be willing to tell him everything he wanted to know about Melina.

Now the question was, Who could he go after first?

***

When in doubt, set it on fire. Bonnie had used a little harmless arson over the years to create the perfect distractions. Today, she figured she would do the same.

As she slipped into the yard adjacent to the Shepard house, she tried not to think about the money Sonny had spent. Shit. But she should not be surprised. She had raised the boy, and if the shoe had been on the other foot, she would have spent the money.

She kept telling herself that as she opened their trash can. She dumped lighter fluid into the can, stepped back, and tossed in a match. The flames shot upward like a blowtorch onto the adjacent privacy fence.

She walked out the other gate and toward her car, parked across the street. She knew running would draw unwanted attention. Sinking low in her seat, she watched as Mr. Shepard hobbled out of his house with his wife on his trail. Good people were so damn easy to predict.

Mrs. Shepard sprinted as best she could as her husband leaned on crutches with his cell phone pressed to his ear. The water splashed out of the hose, but it was barely enough to contain the growing flames.

When Mrs. Shepard was fully distracted, Bonnie got out of her car and hurried toward the house. Inside the front door, she followed the sound of cartoons and found Elena sitting on the couch eating Goldfish.

"Come on, baby, we got to go," she said softly.

"Where are we going, BB?" Elena asked.

"Ice cream. I promised you an ice cream. Don't worry, Mrs. Shepard said it was okay. She said I just need to have you back in about an hour."

She did not give the girl a chance to answer as she gathered her up off the couch and dashed outside. The difference between Elena and Melina was marked. Melina would have been screaming her head off, whereas Elena was quiet and compliant.

"I don't want to go," the child said meekly.

"It's okay. We'll be back before you know it."

"Why is there a fire?"

Bonnie hustled the kid into the car, which was outfitted with a baby seat. She had stolen the car from a shitty apartment complex late last night. Even if the owner had called in the theft, she figured she had a couple of hours before the cops were really looking. That would be plenty for what she had in mind. The car seat strap clicked in place. Bonnie patted the kid on the head and slammed the car door.

In the distance, shouts and alarms blared as Bonnie punched the accelerator and the two took off. Mrs. Shepard had turned her back on Elena for less than five minutes. But for people like Bonnie, five minutes was a lifetime. Hell, in seconds she could swipe a wallet, pinch a purse, or drive off in a stolen car. She had done all those things to near perfection.

Bonnie glanced in the rearview mirror at Elena's small face, tight with worry. As she drove, she rummaged in a grocery bag where she had stashed a teddy bear. She tossed it toward Elena. It hit the seat beside her.

"I got that for you, baby," she said. "It's like your teddy bear."

"It's not mine," Elena pouted. "And I want mine."

"We won't be gone long enough for you to miss your bear." What the hell was that little creature's name. Jimmy? Timmy?

"Are we really getting ice cream?" Elena asked.

"We are going to see Sonny first," she said.

She angled the car around a sharp corner and then took another quick turn. By now the Shepards would have realized the fire had been a distraction and Elena was gone. Those two were the type to unleash all sorts of hell in her direction. Just her damn luck that all those years ago Melina had been rescued by the Mod Squad.

"I don't want to see Sonny," Elena said. "He has mean eyes."

"He isn't mean, kiddo. He's a big ol' teddy bear, and if you scratch his tummy, he'll laugh." She glanced in the rearview mirror and saw the girl's frown. No matter. She could scream until she passed out for all she cared. It would be up to Sonny to convince the girl he could be nice, and then the three of them could get on with their lives.

Elena sank down in her seat, staring into the smiling face of the toy bear. "I want Mrs. Shepard."

"How can you want *her*, baby? I've been taking care of you for almost a year."

"I don't want to be in cars anymore," Elena said. "I don't like it."

The kid's face scrunched up and tears welled in her eyes. Jesus. Not the tears and the screaming. Some of Melina had already rubbed off on this kid.

"I'll buy you two ice creams, and I'll have them put a cherry on top just like you like."

The pouting lip did not tremble as much. "With sprinkles."

"With sprinkles, baby."

Elena sniffed.

Like everyone else, the kid had her price. Elena wanted sprinkles. Sonny wanted Elena. Bonnie was sure Sonny could scrape together enough money to keep them all happy for a while.

***

Melina anxiously awaited Dean Guthrie's mug shot as her computer came alive. She tapped her fingers on the keys, willing the machine to move faster just as Ramsey stepped into her office.

The home screen was nearly finished populating the icons when her cell phone rang. It was her mother. Her mother was not the type to call in the middle of the day and chat. If her mother called during work hours, she picked up.

"Mom, what's wrong?" Melina asked as her gaze rose to Ramsey's.

"Elena is missing. Our neighbor's trash can caught on fire, and Dad and I went to put it out. I was spraying water on the flames while he called 911. He went back in the house to check on Elena and discovered her gone."

"Did you hear Elena scream or yell?" Melina asked.

She was doing her best to remain calm and to think like a cop, but Ramsey's eyes darkened as he closed the distance quickly. He didn't say a word, but his gaze locked on her like a laser.

"No, I never heard a peep out of her," her mother said. "The television was still on when I came inside, and her cup of Goldfish was still sitting on the end table."

"Was there any sign of struggle?"

"No."

"Could she have gone to a neighbor's? Are there other children in the neighborhood or someone with a puppy?"

"Not that Elena would have known about."

The girl had left the house without a sound, and she was nowhere to be found nearby.

"How long has she been gone, Mom?"

"Ten minutes."

"Have you seen Bonnie again?"

"No." There was a pause. "But I was distracted by the fire. There was so much confusion."

"Mom, I think Bonnie must have her," Melina said. "Bonnie bribed her with something to keep her quiet just long enough to get her out of the house."

"I can't believe I was so stupid. I should have known the fire was a decoy."

"Bonnie's devious, Mom. And she's been conning people for decades. You can't blame yourself for wanting to help."

"Of course I can. I'm not a novice, Melina. I should have had my guard up." Her mother sighed as if she realized now was not the time for berating herself. "What can I do?"

Melina's next words were for her mother's benefit. "Bonnie has a soft spot for Elena. She won't hurt her."

"It's been ten minutes. She could be on her way out of the city or state right now."

"I don't think so, Mom. Bonnie came to Nashville for a reason."

"What reason?"

"Money."

"I don't have any money."

"Someone she knows does."

"Is she going to sell that sweet little girl?" her mother asked.

"I'm not inclined to think so."

"What do I do?"

"Did you call the police?"

"Yes. They just pulled up. Your father is talking to them. We need an Amber Alert."

"Yes, you do, and the officer will take care of it. Stay close to the phone. Does Elena know your phone number?"

"I wrote it on the inside of her shoe and showed her how to call me."

"You did the same with me when I was that age."

"Kids need to know how to save themselves."

"Good. Let's hope Elena gets a chance to call. In the meantime, I'll start a search of my own. Call me if you hear anything."

"You, too."

Melina ended the call and relayed to Ramsey what her mother had just said while checking for Andy's email. "Andy said that my half brother had a juvenile record. He did six months in a minimum security facility and was released. He wasn't arrested again."

"Does he have a mug shot?" He came around the back of her desk and looked over her shoulder.

"Seems so." She clicked on the attachment.

The image that came up featured a young man who had a long narrow face. Like her, he had olive skin, dark hair and eyes. His expression was sullen and his gaze downcast.

"Do you recognize him?"

His face was familiar. She knew this guy. But he was very different now. She leaned into the picture, drawn by a deepening sense of familiarity. And then the puzzle pieces slid together in one of those rare, exhilarating moments.

He was older now and heavier, but she knew exactly who he was.

CHAPTER
TWENTY-NINE

Friday, August 28, 10:00 a.m.

Bonnie arrived at the motel with Elena in tow. She jammed the key card in the lock and twisted the handle. The room smelled like cleaner and air freshener that did not quite conceal the cigarette smoke in the nonsmoking room.

"Can I eat my ice cream now?" Elena asked.

"You sure can, kiddo." Bonnie opened the convenience store bag and pulled out the small container of rocky road ice cream. "Do you have to pee?"

"Yeah."

"Go on then. You know the drill." This kid had a bladder the size of a walnut, and she had learned early on to make sure she hit the head before they went anywhere.

She opened the ice cream carton and fished a plastic spoon out of the bag. The toilet flushed. "Don't forget to wash your hands."

The tap turned on and she heard the splash of water. Elena came out of the bathroom drying her hands on her shirt.

"That's my girl," Bonnie said. "Hop up on the bed while I turn on a cartoon."

Elena scrambled up on the bed. Bonnie handed her the ice cream and spoon. The girl took a bite.

"I got your favorite," Bonnie said.

"It's good." The girl took a second bite. "Can I see Mrs. Shepard again?"

Bonnie pointed the remote at the television, clicked it on, and scanned the channels until she found *SpongeBob SquarePants*. "You sure can."

"I don't like SpongeBob," Elena said. "I want to see *Frozen*."

Bonnie pulled off the kid's shoes. She set them at the end of the bed. Next, she reached for the drugstore bag and dug out the bottle of liquid sedatives. She loaded up a spoon and smiled as she approached the girl. "One big bite of medicine. Mrs. Shepard told me you needed it."

"But I'm not sick."

"This is to make sure you don't get sick. Open wide."

The girl accepted the medicine and winced at the bitter taste.

"Quick, take a bite of ice cream." She nodded. "There's a good girl."

The kid would be sound asleep within ten minutes and would be out for hours. She'd given her adult strength. "Eat your ice cream and I'll look for *Frozen*."

Elena scooted under the covers and settled the carton on her lap. "I like the chocolate best."

"I know. That's why I bought this brand. Now go on and eat."

"Aren't you hungry?"

"I might have some in a bit. You first."

Elena dug into the soft ice cream and took a big bite. "It tastes funny."

"That's just the last of the medicine. Eat another bite and it'll go away." She flipped to the channel that had movies for rent. *Frozen* was not an option, but *Hotel Transylvania 3* was available. Close enough as far as she was concerned.

Elena yawned as the movie's opening scene appeared to string music and a late-nineteenth-century train rumbling through Romania. "Look, the monsters are in disguise like we do sometimes," Bonnie said.

"I want *Frooozen*." She dragged out the word as if it were too heavy to pronounce.

Bonnie sat on the edge of the bed. "Take a couple more bites of the ice cream, sweetie."

She listened and counted the bites. One. Two.

When she did not hear movement, she turned to see the girl had fallen asleep. The ice cream was still in her lap and the empty spoon clutched in her tiny fist.

Bonnie carefully removed the spoon and then replaced the top on the ice cream. She dumped both back in the plastic shopping bag before settling the girl in the center of the bed. Gently, she tucked the blanket up to her chin. "No need to worry, honey. I'm going to get Sonny, and then we'll start our new life together."

***

"My half brother's alias is Sam Jenkins," Melina said. "He works at the Mission." She stared at his picture. "We've worked side by side. We share the same sense of humor, and he's been a good friend." But she had never known the man behind the smile.

Ramsey kept his gaze on the road as he moved quickly in and out of traffic while the GPS directed him toward East Nashville. "I know he's a volunteer. What else can you tell me about him?"

She cleared her throat, trying to focus her thoughts. "His big thing is music, even after retiring from the road. He helped establish the Mission's soap-manufacturing business. He can solve any problem."

"Do you know where he traveled when he was a roadie?"

"All over the world." He had shared pictures of his former life with both Sarah and her, and they had been bedazzled by his who's who list of musical clients. "I can't remember the exact cities."

"Do you know where he lives?"

"No." She had never questioned Sam's motives once. "Sarah will know."

Ten minutes later, Ramsey pulled up in front of the Mission, and the two went inside, where the reverend and a half dozen women were mixing up herbs into some kind of concoction. The room smelled of lemon and sage.

The chance of finding Bonnie anywhere near the Shepards' house was slim to none. What they had to do now was figure out where Bonnie had gone with Elena, and the only other person Bonnie knew in Nashville was Sonny. "Sarah," Melina said.

The reverend, who was wearing a white apron and had pulled back her red hair in a tight ponytail, excused herself and approached them. She removed latex gloves and guided them back to her office. "Have you found the man who attacked the girls?"

"Not yet." Melina heard the impatience sharpening her tone. "We're working on it. I'm here about Sam. Have you seen him lately?"

"Yeah, he was in early but had to leave suddenly. Said there was something going on at home. Is something wrong?"

"Can you tell me where he lives?" Melina asked.

"Why Sam? There is no way he's the guy you're looking for," Sarah insisted. "He was at the Mission the night of your attack."

"We want to question him about something else," Melina said. "He might be connected to another case we're working. Once we've sorted out his involvement, I'll explain it all to you, but for now I need his address. I need to talk to him."

"Sure." Sarah clicked several keys on her computer. "He doesn't live far from here." She rattled off the address and phone number.

Melina typed both into her phone. "That's not far from where Bonnie crashed her car," Melina said to Ramsey.

"Who's Bonnie?" Sarah asked.

"It's part of that long story I'm going to owe you," Melina said as she was already turning to follow Ramsey.

***

Ramsey received the call from Andy as he and Melina were en route to Sonny's house. Melina's body was rigid with tension, and he suspected she was struggling to hold her focus. "Andy, what do you have?"

"I've been in contact with the forensic team working at the Mecum property," she said. "They've excavated three bodies."

He switched the call to speaker so Melina could hear, hoping a shift to Mecum might distract her a moment from Sam and Elena. "Three bodies?"

Melina looked at him, her gaze sharpening.

"Two are fairly recent. The third is much older, maybe even dating back to the 1990s. All appear to be female with significant cranial damage. No identifications yet."

"Keep searching for other properties. This guy likely has money, so he can afford to have other venues like this one."

"It'll take time, but I'm on it," Andy said.

Ramsey ended the call, again wishing he had a better arsenal of comforting words. "You heard most of that?"

"A murder that goes back over two decades. Wasn't that about the time he bought his property and also had his first confirmed kill?"

"He had the land for almost nine years before the first kill in 1999. But men like him often live in a very elaborate fantasy world before they graduate to murder," he said.

"We're getting closer and I want to give the Mecum case my full attention, but I can't until I find Elena." The silence that followed was chock full of emotions. She stared out the car window for close to a minute as she seemed to gather herself.

"Bonnie will not get far."

Melina shook her head, knowing that Bonnie was clever and had survived this long because she knew how to hide. "She did last time."

***

Bonnie parked in front of Sonny's house. There was no car in the driveway. He would be here soon, and they could collect Elena and get on the road.

She walked around to the back side of the house to the sliding glass door. She pulled out a stainless steel knife that she had procured from a restaurant and shoved it between the lock and the jamb. A couple of wiggles and the lock popped.

"Sonny, I thought I taught you better than this."

Inside the house, she walked directly into the kitchen, grabbed a beer from the refrigerator, and pulled out her cell phone and dialed his number. The call went to voicemail. "Sonny, it's me. Come on home and let's get going."

She opened a kitchen cabinet, smiling when she saw the cans of SpaghettiOs. He'd loved those as a kid. She took a long pull on her beer and moved into the living room toward a collection of guitars displayed on the wall. Several were autographed. She lightly strummed the strings on an old Gibson.

Bonnie had to admit the kid had done all right for himself in spite of her. He had made the home he had always wanted. She never could stand being in one place for long. That was not likely to change, but Sonny and she would make it work for Elena's sake.

Behind her, floorboards creaked in the back hallway.

After finishing her beer, she set the bottle on a wooden table and walked toward the living room. "Sonny, baby?"

Mary Burton

Someone came up behind her, and she expected to hear Sonny's voice. Instead, a cord wrapped around her throat and cut off her air. She reached for the cord, trying to wedge her fingers underneath. "Sonny?"

The cord cut into her skin, igniting her strong survival instinct. She dragged her heel down his shin, and when he grunted, she realized she was not dealing with Sonny. She squirmed against him, hoping to break his concentration, but his grip tightened as if he enjoyed her struggle.

Her head began to swim. She gasped, and with the last of the air in her lungs, whispered, "Don't."

Her attacker, knowing she was near death, whirled her around to face a mirror. As the cord slackened, she could breathe and focus beyond her grossly distorted features to the man killing her. He had graying hair, dark eyes, and a smile.

"I'm sorry," he said. "I didn't catch your name."

She willed him to see the desperation in her eyes. Whatever was driving this guy, she was sure she could change his mind. "Baby."

The man snatched her purse and pawed through receipts, coins, a bundle of credit cards that no longer worked, a bottle of tranquilizers, and the motel room key that unlocked the room in which Elena now slept. He grabbed the key. "Is he here?"

Her knees were weak, and it was difficult to stand. "What?"

"Is Sam here? Is he with Melina?"

"Melina? How do you know her?"

"I know all about her. Where is she?"

When she did not answer, he tightened the cord around her neck again. "Where does she live? Where can I find her?"

She grabbed at the cord but could not wedge her fingers underneath.

His temper and frustration were rising, and he twisted the rope tighter. Her eyes felt as if they were going to bulge out of her head. "Are they together?"

The cord's slick nylon edge cut deeper into her skin, drawing blood that trickled down her neck. She mouthed a response but couldn't draw in enough air.

He loosened his hold just enough for her to breathe. "Are they together?"

She had been around long enough to recognize the face of evil. He was never going to let her go. Best she could hope for now was to die fast. She spit in his face. "Bonnie says go fuck yourself."

***

As Mecum looked at Bonnie's bloodied face and her blown pupils, he knew he had screwed up. It had been years since he had really lost control. But the pressure of time was eating at him, and when she had spit in his face, his need to punish her had been visceral.

His window of opportunity to find Melina was closing. He released his grip on her neck and watched her body slide to the floor into a crumpled pile of bones and flesh. He had ruined this chance to find Melina, but he did not have time to dwell on his failure.

He wiped the bloody spittle from his face with his sleeve and then hefted Bonnie's lifeless body over his shoulder. He carried it into the back bedroom, dumped it on the bed, and then covered it with a blanket.

Mecum returned to the living room and picked up the motel key still tucked in the motel's sleeve. Room 132. Convenient. It was not Melina's address, but it was a step closer.

As he crossed the living room, he pocketed the key and the phone. Before leaving the house, he paused at a mirror and inspected his face. His cheeks were flushed but there were no scratch marks. Using his fingers, he smoothed out his thick hair until it was neat and presentable.

He slid into his van, now sporting magnetic signs that read THOMPSON'S AIR-CONDITIONING. His heart raced when he started the engine. He wound through traffic toward the motel in East Nashville. It was not much to look at but fit the woman's personality.

He parked across the lot from the room and watched it closely for several minutes. There was no sign of anyone. He searched the woman's phone for texts. The only person she had texted in the last day had been Sonny. Who the hell was Sonny? The last text read, Baby, I'm coming to your place. The girl is waiting safe in a motel.

Your place. He had found Bonnie at Sam's house. Was Sonny Sam? The girl. Who was Bonnie talking about? Was she referring to Melina? His blood stirring, he took a chance and got out of the car and crossed the lot. He quickly swiped the key and stepped into the darkened, cool room. He saw the small figure lying on the bed and knew it was a child and not a woman. Not his Melina.

He sat on the edge of the bed and carefully smoothed back the child's dark hair. She was sleeping hard, no doubt drugged. In some ways, she reminded him of his granddaughter. Sweet. Innocent.

Sonny or Sam wanted the girl. And Mecum could use the girl to get Sonny to tell him how to find Melina. He might even be able to get Sonny to lure Melina to him.

He typed into the phone: Get the girl. Key hidden in planter to right of door. I will find you in a couple of hours. Cops on my tail. He added the motel address and then hit send.

***

Ramsey and Melina drove to the small East Nashville neighborhood located less than a mile from where Bonnie had crashed her car into the cul-de-sac. He parked out front and the two stood on the curb for a moment, studying the house.

She was still trying to wrap her brain around the idea that Sam was her half brother. Jesus. How long had he known? She thought about all the times she had seen him at the Mission. He was always kind to her and respectful to the residents and went out of his way to make the Mission a success. A part of her wanted to rush up to the house, believing he would not hurt her.

But she was a cop first and cops developed a skill for sizing up homes. Was the lawn cut or the house in order? Were there bushes or trees obscuring the house? Trash in the yard? Shades open or closed? Privacy fences. Locks. Smells. Everything came into play when a cop approached a residence for the first time. All had the potential to be a death trap.

Both Melina and Ramsey checked their weapons as they reached the front steps. Ramsey moved past her. "I'll take point."

"He's my crazy half brother," she said. "He might listen to me."

"Don't count on it." When she opened her mouth to argue, he said, "You take the lead with the next nutty sibling. This one is mine."

Without glancing back, he rapped on the front door. They stood to the side, listening.

"I know this guy," she whispered.

"Apparently not well enough."

The front windows were covered in shades and the curtains were drawn. There were no cars in the driveway. Ramsey tried the knob. It was locked.

"Let's check the back," she said.

Around the back of the house, he discovered the patio door partially opened. Curtains fluttered out the opening, blowing from the air-conditioning.

"He left the air-conditioning on," he said. "Kind of a thing you do when you expect to be back."

"Or you left in a hurry," she said.

"Call in backup," he said.

She called local police and reported a possible link to a serial killer. Cars were dispatched immediately.

Standing to the side, he waited until she was out of the window's line of sight before he further slid open the door. A rush of cool air escaped into the humid heat.

Ramsey pushed back the curtains. The interior of the small house was dark, with no signs of life. He stepped inside, pausing to look left, right, and then up. He motioned her forward and she followed, employing the same search pattern.

Ramsey switched on a light, revealing a neat, organized living and dining room furnished in modern furniture. There was a long credenza in the living room filled with an extensive collection of LPs, and a group of guitars on the wall.

She had seen them all when he had played at the center. She and Sam had fallen into an easy relationship that had never been anything but friendly.

Ramsey kept moving down a center hallway. On the left was what looked like a spare room and an office. The bed was made and the desk clean and organized.

"He got the neatnik gene," she said.

Ramsey regarded her, sensing there was more behind the quip than humor. Silent, he moved to the second door, which led into a small bathroom tiled in blue and white. Again, it was very neat. Mirror and fixtures polished, floor smelling of bleach.

The last door was closed. Each held their weapons up as he turned the knob and pushed it open.

Melina tensed when she saw the figure lying on the bed. The person was covered with a thick quilt from head to toe.

She checked the closet and then under the bed to make sure both were secure before Ramsey reached for the top of the quilt and pulled it back.

She drew in a breath as she stared at the lifeless, bloodied face of Bonnie Guthrie.

Ramsey pressed his fingertips to her throat. "There's no pulse. But her skin is still warm. No rigor. She's not been dead long. Less than a couple of hours."

He pulled the cover back farther. Deep-purple bruises ringed her neck. "She was strangled."

"Bonnie was playing some kind of game. Both ends against the middle."

"And burned the wrong person."

"She was trying to manipulate me when we spoke at the prison. Always scheming to figure out who to play next."

Melina dug deep, wondering if she could scrounge any morsel of sadness for this woman who claimed to have saved her from social services.

She felt nothing for Bonnie. Had she been telling the truth? Oddly, Melina believed Bonnie's story. But she was not foolish enough to accept that Bonnie's motives had been good and pure. For a short time, the woman's interests had aligned with Melina's, and it had suited her to save Melina until she had dumped her on the side of the road. At least Sonny had cared enough to call the cops. She would always be grateful to that boy.

Patty-cake, patty-cake, baker's man.

Memories of her laugher mingled with the boy's. And she knew at some point in her life, she had loved him.

"Is there any sign of Elena in the house?" she asked.

They searched room by room, closet by closet, but they did not locate any evidence of the girl.

In the kitchen, Ramsey searched in the cabinets. He stilled and reached for a penlight. "Come and have a look at this."

"What is it?"

He held up a cleaned mayonnaise jar with a single finger floating in formaldehyde. "It appears to be recent."

"Who is it?"

He shoved out a breath. "I don't know."

She returned to Bonnie's body and pulled back the remaining covers, exposing her hands. All ten fingers were intact. "He didn't cut off her finger."

"Maybe he didn't have time."

"He's in a rush to find Elena."

"Why?"

"She reminds him of me. He wants to recreate what we had as kids."

"It's very possible," Ramsey said.

Melina had taken some comfort knowing that while Bonnie had Elena, the girl would be relatively safe. But with Bonnie dead in Sonny's home, she feared the child was now in the hands of a monster.

CHAPTER THIRTY

Friday, August 28, 1:00 p.m.

Mecum sat on the edge of the motel bed. He glanced back at the sleeping child. He tucked the blanket up around her shoulders.

He heard footsteps approach the motel door, and then a pause to search for the key. He moved across the darkened room and stood behind the door for a moment. Sam stepped inside, confirming he was also Sonny.

Sam looked toward the bed and the sleeping child. His body was relaxed, as if he assumed it was Bonnie standing behind him. He whispered, "Thank God. We're finally together."

Mecum did not hesitate. He thrust the knife directly into Sonny's lower back, knowing he had a direct hit on the kidney. Several more vicious thrusts followed in quick succession. On the last, he twisted the blade for good measure.

Sonny dropped to his knees and looked back. The poor son of a bitch almost looked relieved.

"No, it isn't your woman friend," he said.

Blood bloomed across the back of Sonny's shirt and he fell forward. He caught himself with his right arm. He was already struggling to breathe. "Who?"

Mecum pushed him forward with his boot. Sonny's face now lay flat against the motel carpet. "Nothing personal, pal. This has to do with Melina. That girl owes me a date."

"Don't hurt Elena," Sonny begged.

"I won't. Yet."

"She's just a kid." Sam looked up toward the bed, staring toward the child.

"She's now bait," Mecum whispered as he sliced Sonny's throat. The blood splattered onto the carpet, pooling around his head. The last of the air gurgled in Sonny's throat and then stopped completely.

Mecum crossed the room to the bed and wiped the bloody knife on the spread before closing it and shoving it in his pocket.

He grabbed Sonny by the arms and pulled his body toward the bed and rolled him on his back. He opened the nightstand and removed a sheet of motel stationery and a pen. He quickly wrote a note to Melina. She was a smart cookie, and he had no doubt she would be here soon. Slapping the note to Sonny's chest, he rose.

As much as he wanted to linger and enjoy the intoxicating copper scent of blood, there was no time to waste. Time was the primary commodity now.

He picked up the little girl, careful to keep her bundled in the blanket. Moving from the motel room to the van was tricky, but transitions were a necessary evil.

He quickly crossed the lot and placed her carefully in the back of the van. The child had not moved or stirred. She appeared heavily drugged. It was all the better and easier if she was asleep.

He got behind the wheel and slowly pulled out of the lot. The cops were closing in, thanks to Melina. Chances of him getting out of this alive were slim, but he was not overly concerned. The cancer was going to get him soon. At least he could go to his grave happy knowing Melina was dead.

***

Ramsey secured the area around Sonny's house while Melina called in the local detectives and the medical examiner's office. Within minutes, local uniforms and the forensic team were on site. Several neighbors had congregated at the edge of the yellow crime scene tape, and one news van was parked across the street.

Once the world got wind that they were likely dealing with a serial killer, all bets would be off. The investigation would turn into a zoo as the media stirred up public worries for the sake of ratings.

Melina interviewed several neighbors and was not surprised to hear that Sonny, a.k.a. Sam, was a good neighbor. He mowed and edged his lawn, planted flowers every spring, and had won yard of the month last summer several times. He never had crazy parties or created any kind of disturbance. In fact, if anyone needed a hand moving a piece of furniture or hauling fall leaves, Sam was their man.

Melina knocked on the door of the house directly across from Sam's. The woman who answered the door was very pregnant, and she carried a young toddler on her hip. The mother had dark shoulder-length hair that skimmed her rounded face. Melina guessed the toddler was a boy.

Melina held up her badge, introduced herself, and explained why she was here.

"Sure, I know Sam. He's great. When my husband was sick last summer, he cut our grass. Nice guy."

"There was a woman found in his house." She did not mention that Bonnie had been strangled. "Has he had many visitors lately?"

"He keeps to himself. But a few days ago, there was a woman and a little girl on his doorstep. Sam didn't look happy, and when I stopped the stroller and waved, he didn't seem to notice me. I figured it must be serious because Sam is so easygoing. My Donny and I didn't want to intrude."

Melina pulled Bonnie's picture up on her phone. "Is this the woman?"

"Yeah. That's her."

"Did you hear what Sam and this woman were saying?"

"Sam wouldn't let the woman in the house. She tried to get past him, but he blocked the path. When the little girl came up, he slammed the door."

"How long did they stay?"

"I don't know. We were home by then, and my little guy needed to go down for his nap."

"Did you see the woman again?"

"No."

"Was there anyone else who normally isn't in the neighborhood?" she asked.

"There was an AC repair guy parked across from Sam's house. I'm not sure that really matters."

"An AC repair guy?" The house had been cool, and the system appeared to be working fine. "What was he driving?"

"A white van."

A chill shot up her spine. "Can you tell me what the driver looked like?"

"Kind of attractive," she said. "Tall. Lean build. White guy. Sixtyish."

"Did you see the name of the company?"

"Um, the name started with a *T*. Taylor's or, no, Thompson's."

Melina searched the name on her phone. There was no Thompson's Air-Conditioning in the Nashville area. "When did you see the van?"

"Not that long ago. Maybe an hour or two."

Memories of the Key Killer elbowed their way to the front of her mind. From what they had determined about Mecum, he did not hunt in the daylight nor in suburban neighborhoods. He kidnapped hookers from dark street corners and tortured them to death in his van on one of his remote properties. Bonnie's killer had strangled her quickly and had not tortured her. Mecum's victims took days to die, not minutes.

Mecum, she guessed, had not expected Bonnie. She had been there for Sonny. But why would Mecum be there for Sonny?

Melina had only just learned of her personal connection to Sonny, so how did Mecum know about them?

The easiest answer was money. Mecum had money and resources to find anyone he wanted to find. It was not outside the realm of possibility that he had connected her to Sonny. But why go after Sonny?

Melina handed the young mother her card. "Call me if you think of anything else."

She took the card. The baby reached for it, but the mother held it out of his reach. He began to fuss so she let him hold it. "Is Sam okay?"

"We're trying to determine that right now." When the baby stuck the card in his mouth, Melina handed another one to the mother. "Thank you."

Thoughts of the white van and its promised horrors followed her across the street as she walked toward Ramsey. He was talking to a uniformed officer as they stood beside a blue four-door with Tennessee plates. She pulled him away from the car.

"I think Mecum was here," she said.

"Why here? This kind of area does not fit his profile."

She relayed what she had learned about the van and the man driving it. "He's been here."

The lines around Ramsey's mouth deepened as he nodded to the car. "It's registered to Ralph Hogan. He was Bonnie's bail bondsman."

"Has anyone spoken to Hogan?"

"He called in sick today. I've sent a uniform to find him."

As thoughts of Mecum stalked her, she peered inside the driver's side window and saw a bag of discarded caramel cream candies and a stuffed animal. "Bonnie drove here expecting to find Sonny. Could she have encountered Mecum?"

"Maybe. Or maybe Sonny killed her. We know he's very capable," Ramsey said.

She rescanned the interior. There was nothing that told her where she might be able to find Elena. "Where is Matt Piper?"

Matt appeared with a long thin rod. "I'm here. Hang on."

He wedged the rod between the window and the seal and worked it down until he was able to secure the button that unlocked the door. Inside the vehicle, she immediately popped the trunk.

Melina rushed to the back, praying the girl was not in there. The interior was filled with bags, and she quickly rummaged through them until she was satisfied the contents were just clothes purchased in Lower Broadway.

Melina's relief was fleeting. If the child was not here, then where?

Ramsey's frown deepened. "If Sonny is as obsessed with recreating his family as we assume, he wouldn't have killed Bonnie until he had the girl."

"But Bonnie was the closest thing he had to a mother." Melina understood how complicated and powerful feelings for a lost mother could be.

"Men kill their mothers," Ramsey said. "Way too often."

"And if Mecum was here, he could have Elena." Melina shook her head, trying to slow her racing thoughts even as tension squeezed the air from her lungs. "Bonnie's purse was dumped on the living room floor by the couch. Are there any receipts, keys, or maps?"

"Let me check with Matt," Ramsey said. "I'll be right back."

He jogged over to Matt and relayed what they were looking for. As Melina waited, she stared at the empty interior of the trunk. Frustration coiled around her, making it difficult to stand still. Every instinct in her body told her she should be doing more to find Elena.

"We need to talk to Sarah Beckett," Melina said to Ramsey as he joined her, and they walked to their car.

"Why her?"

"If Mecum found Sonny, he likely knows about the Mission. The one place Sonny and I crossed paths was the Mission. He is looking for me."

"Sarah would have noticed a guy like Mecum asking questions, don't you think? Approaching her would have been a bold move."

"Maybe. But we know he is driven and arrogant." She reached for the door handle. "Either way Sarah might have the missing pieces for us."

Matt appeared at the front door and, spotting them, jogged across the lawn. Ramsey rolled down his window.

"There was a motel receipt jammed in the bottom of her purse. It's dated two days ago. I've dispatched a uniform. We should have an answer about the child in a few minutes," Matt said.

"Good," Ramsey said.

"Elena could still be there," Melina said.

"Thanks, Matt." Ramsey put his car in drive and pulled away.

They had been rolling for five minutes when Melina's phone rang. "Agent Shepard."

"This is Officer Aaron. We've found Sonny at the motel. You better get over here."

CHAPTER
THIRTY-ONE

Friday, August 28, 2:30 p.m.

Melina shook her head, wondering how she could have missed so many red flags. She unmasked monsters like Sonny for a living, and he had been under her nose for almost two years. "What if Elena cries like I used to? Sonny or Mecum will not have the capacity to be kind to her."

When Ramsey pulled into the motel parking lot, the uniformed officer was standing by a short, stocky man wearing a blue jacket sporting the motel's logo on the back. Melina and Ramsey got out of the car and raced toward the room. Flashing their badges to the uniformed officer, they hurried inside. Her gaze scanned the room for any signs of the child.

"Where's Elena?" she asked. "Officer, did you see a child?"

"This is the first we've opened the door," the officer said.

She walked around the bed, past the dark blood trail, to the body by the bed. It was Sam. Sonny. Her brother. His throat had been slashed. His head leaned against the side of the bed. His jaw was slack, open in what looked like an anguished cry.

"Jesus H. Christ." She stood frozen, unable to move a step in any direction.

Attached to his chest was a large note that read: *Melina, I'm not leaving this world a loser. You're my girlfriend now. Join me in the afterlife, or I'll take Elena.* Two dots and a half circle created a macabre smiley face that glared back at her like a wood goblin.

"Mecum has her." Memories of the van's interior flashed in her head. "What is he going to do to her?"

CHAPTER
THIRTY-TWO

Friday, August 28, 3:15 p.m.

Melina's hands trembled and it took all her resolve not to scream out in primal frustration. Instead, she balled her fingers into tight fists as she stared at the body of a man who had been a friend, a brother, and a monster. All her senses went numb. A strong hand banded around Melina's arm, and she felt herself being pulled. "We have to go, Melina. Let the team do its job."

Ramsey's voice cut through the haze. She nodded, quickly falling in step behind him as the two walked back to his car.

Melina pictured Sonny lying in that motel room, his body cut open and bleeding. Mecum and Elena were long gone.

"Mecum called me his girlfriend," she said.

"You two have some very intense history together."

As she began to strip off her gloves, the officer securing the scene called out to her from the motel room. "Agent Shepard. The victim's phone just received a text."

They hurried back into the room and found the officer holding up the phone. "The sender mentions you by name."

Melina looked at the text featuring a video of Elena sleeping in the back of a van. The girl was curled on her side. She searched for signs that the girl was alive, but it was impossible to tell.

"As long as I *think* she's alive, he knows I'll do whatever he says," Melina said. "And he's right."

"Which is exactly why you can't do anything he says," Ramsey said. "He'll kill her and you regardless, if we're not very careful."

Another text chimed. Melina. Date night. Do you think you can find me in time?

She looked at Ramsey. She texted back. Where are you?

You figure it out. Tick tock.

She gripped the phone. Ramsey showed no traces of worry or concern as he carefully took it from her. He was focused solely on the mission.

"I've got to go to Elena," Melina said.

He nodded carefully, and she imagined he was rising above the fray and staring at everyone as if they were pieces on a chessboard.

"Not alone." His tone was hard, unwavering.

"I have to do whatever Mecum demands, for Elena's sake," she said.

Ramsey's expression was unreadable, but his jaw tensed with frustration. "You are not going. He will kill you."

"He might let Elena go," she countered.

"You aren't thinking clearly."

"I have to save her." Her desperation resonated in her tone.

He reviewed the video again. "She appears to be drugged. That explains the turned-down sheets in the motel and why no one reported a child screaming."

"They found liquid sedatives in Bonnie's car," Melina said. "If she dosed the kid, she's been out for most of this."

"And the quieter Elena remains, the longer she'll live," Ramsey said.

Melina rolled her shoulders. "She could be waking up soon. I have to go."

He studied her a beat before nodding. "Okay. You'll go. Tell him you're coming."

"Alone?"

"Yes."

With trembling fingers, she typed the text and hit send.

Mecum's reply arrived a minute later. Can't wait.

CHAPTER THIRTY-THREE

Friday, August 28, 4:00 p.m.

Melina and Ramsey drove to the Mission, and as soon as he parked, she immediately got out of the car and rushed to push the intercom button. "Melina?" Sarah's voice sounded over the speaker.

"Can we come inside?"

"Yes." The door lock buzzed open, and as they stepped inside, Sarah came out of her office. "What's going on?"

Melina updated her quickly, explaining that Sam was dead. Sarah closed her eyes for a moment and appeared to say a prayer.

"Sam did so many good things for the Mission," she said softly. "He was a friend."

"There's another man who could be far more dangerous," Melina said. "His name is Edward Mecum."

"Mecum?" Sarah asked. "I know that name."

"How?" Melina asked.

"He was just here this morning."

"What are you talking about?" Melina asked.

"He rang the bell just after 7:00 a.m. I saw him on the video camera and asked what he wanted. He said he had a donation for the Mission."

"Did you let him in?" Melina asked.

"He showed identification and seemed legit. So, yes, I let him in. He gave me a check for one hundred thousand dollars. The check cleared and I sent a thank-you email with a receipt to his address as he requested."

Melina ran a steady hand over the top of her head. She tried not to think about what could have happened to Sarah. "Did he do or say anything out of the ordinary?"

"No, he seemed pretty normal. Who is this guy?"

"We think he might be the Key Killer," Melina said.

Sarah's face paled as she stared at Melina. "Why would a guy like that give me a check?"

"To get control of your computer." Ramsey reached for his phone. "I have an agent in Quantico who can remotely take control of Sarah's computer. Do you mind if she does it?"

"No. But how could he get my computer? He never touched it," Sarah said.

"The email address you contacted would have sent a virus to your computer," Ramsey said. "You could have inadvertently granted complete access to your computer. Once he was in, he was able to comb through your files and discover Melina's and Sonny's identities."

"But nothing weird happened after I sent the email," she said.

"If he was clever enough, you never would have noticed him poking around. Can my agent do the same?"

Once Ramsey gave Andy the password, she was in the Mission's computer in seconds. Sarah stood back in horror, watching the cursor move on its own, opening files and programs at a rapid pace. Melina walked up and down, and Ramsey knew the waiting was clawing at her insides.

Ramsey's phone rang. "Andy."

"I got him."

***

Mecum had gone on dates with mothers twice before. They had been some of his best. They had a reason to live and to fight. They had a tendency to hold on longer. Melina was not the child's mother, but he would bet his last dollar she had a tender heart and would fight to save the kid.

He looked over at the girl lying on the couch in his cabin. She was starting to stir and would soon awaken. He crushed one of his pain pills into a fine powder and sprinkled it into a glass of water. He sat beside her and smoothed his hand over her forehead.

She blinked slowly, and when she looked up at him, her eyes teared.

"There, there," he said softly. "No need for tears. Drink this, sweet girl."

Obedient, she drank. When she had drained the glass, he gently eased her back on the pillows and waited for her to fall asleep again. Her eyes drifted closed and her breathing slowed.

"That's a good girl."

Melina had seen his text two hours ago. She must be in agony as she wondered if the girl was alive or dead. How frantic was she now as she scrambled to figure out where he was hiding? He could drag this out for hours, if not days, if he had the time. When this was all over, she would know that she had not gotten the best of him.

He took another video of the girl. The viewer could see that she was alive and moving. Poor Melina would be so relieved to know this precious child was unharmed.

He ended the recording and attached it to a text. "Kid, I've kept you alive this long," he said. "No marks or bruises on your little body. That's got to count for something."

He wanted Melina to know, to understand, that he was serious. If she did not join him, Elena would be her proxy.

This time he typed the address of his location along with a warning to come alone. Never killed a kid before. But always a first time. Come talk me out of it. Alone.

He hit send. And waited.

***

Melina leaned against the wall, watching as Ramsey and Sarah stared at the computer screen. Her mother had texted her several times asking for updates on Elena, and each time it had broken her heart to report she had nothing. When Sonny's phone chimed with a text, she braced for the worst before she looked at it.

Drawing in a breath, she glanced down at the display as dread crept up her spine. She opened it and nearly wept when she saw the video of Elena stirring. And then she read the attached words. Never killed a kid before. But always a first time. Come talk me out of it. Alone.

"Ramsey, look at this," she shouted as she rushed to him.

He watched the video and read the text. "You aren't going alone."

An anguished cry rose up in her. She had brought this on Elena, and knowing the child was suffering because of her ripped through her soul like a dull knife. "You can go with me, but I approach Mecum alone."

CHAPTER
THIRTY-FOUR

Friday, August 28, 7:00 p.m.

Melina drove west, pushing beyond the speed limit as she raced toward the address Mecum had given her after she had agreed to see him. She gripped the steering wheel, trying to calm her breathing and regain focus. But each time she thought she had gotten a handle on her emotions, images of Elena popped into her mind.

Andy had traced the address Mecum had supplied and located it on satellite imagery. The land was overgrown with a thick canopy of trees that hid the house. Property records that dated back to the 1980s listed a single-story, two-thousand-square-foot house. There was no telling what modifications Mecum had made since.

"I'm coming, Elena. Hang tight."

Anyone watching would not have realized that Ramsey had ridden in the trunk until they were about a half a mile from the entrance to Mecum's driveway. She stopped, popped the trunk, and watched in the rearview mirror as he rolled out in full tactical gear. He quickly darted into the woods. They were both mindful that Mecum could very well have surveillance cameras on the property.

"Can you still hear me?" he asked.

The voice came through a small earpiece. He barely sounded winded as he ran. "I can."

Agent Jackson had assembled a tactical team that was now gathering a mile behind her in a church parking lot. Ramsey had been dropped off near the base of Mecum's driveway and was moving up through the woods toward the cabin with a long rifle.

"Good. Remember, talk to him. I should be in position in five minutes. Go as slow as you can up the driveway. When you arrive, I'll key off what you tell me."

"Understood."

She drove very slowly toward the twin pillars marking his driveway, searching the trees for any sign of cameras or Ramsey. She saw neither.

She slowed at the pillars and then turned up the long tree-lined driveway that stretched almost a quarter of a mile. When she saw the house nestled against the ground, tension twisted every muscle in her body.

"I don't see signs of the van," she muttered. "House is as Andy described. One story. Windows are shuttered. No shrubs around the house."

"I can see the house," he said. "Mecum has a clear view of the driveway from his porch. You're in a bottleneck."

"I know." She parked and stepped out of the car. She held out her hands and shouted, "I'm here!"

Wind whistled through the trees, rustling the leaves. Branches creaked. The house remained still and quiet. Her skin crawled. Wherever he was, he was watching.

"Be cool," Ramsey said.

She did not respond. Her heart hammered in her chest.

And then the front door opened slowly. She saw Mecum's outline. He did not speak, but she knew the open door was not an invitation. It was an order.

And then Elena stumbled into view as Mecum pulled her forward. The girl looked so small and her face was tight with fear. Tears streaked her cheeks.

As tempted as Melina was to race inside and see Elena, she held her ground. Once she stepped inside that house, her tactical advantage would be greatly diminished.

"Melina?" Her voice was heavy with sleep and brittle with fear.

"I'm right out here, Elena," she said. "Come to me."

"I can't." The child started to weep. "Please come get me."

Melina took two steps toward the house.

"Careful," Ramsey warned. "Careful. I've got a bead on him."

She paused before she climbed the porch's front steps. "I'm not moving until you show yourself, Mecum."

Silence crackled and then Elena vanished from sight and screamed.

Melina pulled her weapon. "Show your face," she growled.

"That's not how this game works." The voice that came from the house was deep and smooth. It sounded more suited to a boardroom. "First, turn the car around and pop the trunk and open all the doors. I want to make sure you're alone."

She slid back behind the wheel and moved the car around. As instructed, she opened the trunk and all the doors. "See, it's empty."

"Very good, Melina. We're going to get along well if you can keep following orders."

"How does it work?" she asked.

"You come inside and visit for a spell."

"As soon as I see Elena. I need to know she's all right."

More silence crackled.

"His tone is arrogant," Ramsey whispered. "He believes he has all the cards. Hold your ground until you see the child."

"Show me Elena," Melina shouted.

"Drop your weapon," the man said.

Melina removed her SIG from the holster and set it on the porch.

"Any knives?" He sounded almost amused.

She removed a switchblade from her boot and set it next to the SIG. She dangled her cuffs from her finger.

"What else?" he coaxed.

"That's it."

"Take your clothes off," Mecum ordered. "I need to be sure."

She didn't move.

"I've all night," he said. "But I'm not sure you do."

"Let me see her."

The door creaked open a little wider, and the little girl stepped onto the threshold. She looked sleepy, her eyes red and her cheeks streaked with tears.

"I had to crack an ammonia capsule to wake her up. She was out cold," Mecum said.

"Do as he says," Ramsey said quietly.

She smiled at Elena. "It's going to be okay."

"I'm scared," Elena said.

"Nothing to be scared of, honey." Melina dropped the cuffs and shrugged off her jacket, and then dropped it to the ground.

"I beg to differ," Mecum said.

Melina concentrated on keeping her expression mild and relaxed as she looked at Elena. She winked at the child and then shifted her gaze to inside the cabin door where Mecum lurked.

"How many?" she said. "How many so-called dates did you have?"

She felt him studying her from the shadows. "Why do you want to know? It's just you and me now."

"Just curious." She began to unbutton her shirt slowly. "I could tell by the setup in your van that you know what you're doing."

"I'm well versed," he said. "But if you think we're going to have a heartfelt conversation, you're wrong. You're not as smart as me, but I bet you're wearing a wire."

When she had first encountered him, he had been looking for a prostitute. He had been looking for sex and most importantly control. She removed her blouse and dropped it to the ground. The warm evening air brushed across her bare skin. "No wire." She reached for the strap of her bra and lowered it slowly to her shoulder.

His gaze shifted to her chest and darkened with an intense energy.

Running her hand over her breast, she toyed with the clasp between her breasts. "See? No wire."

"I'm not convinced," he said.

She knew he wanted to see her breasts, so instead of removing the bra she started on her slacks. She unfastened the top button and unzipped them as she toed off her shoes. "I'll take it all off for you, if you let the girl go."

Elena stared at her, and though Mecum said nothing, she could feel his gaze on her.

"You're a tease," he said.

"You want me to stop?" she challenged.

"Keep going," he ordered.

The pants slid down her legs and collected around her ankles. Slowly, she stepped out of them and kicked them aside so she would be unencumbered by them if she needed to move quickly. She arched her back, giving him a better view of her breasts.

Mecum stepped outside.

He was dressed in pressed khakis and a blue button-down shirt. He was clean shaven, and his hair was neatly trimmed and brushed off his face. He held a very long shiny hunting blade to the girl's side.

"Very nice, Melina," he said. "What else can you show me?"

She narrowed her focus to his face, shutting out Elena's fear. "This is your show. You tell me."

He gently brushed his hand over the little girl's head, pushing back a strand of dark hair. "She's a pretty little thing. She could be your child. Is she related to you?"

"No."

"You care about her a lot. So did Sonny."

"You killed Bonnie and Sonny?"

"I was doing you a favor. This should please you."

"I'm moving on the count of three. One." Ramsey's voice whispered in her ear.

She reached for the second strap of her bra and coaxed it down her shoulder. She took another step closer, knowing the cups of her bra had loosened and her breasts looked as if they would tumble out.

Mecum's gaze dropped to her breasts. He tightened his grip on the knife handle, but the tip eased away from the child as his attention shifted more to her.

"You like what you see?" she said.

"You know I do," Mecum said.

"Two," Ramsey said.

"We'll get this party started as soon as you set Elena free." She knew Ramsey was close but did not dare a glance toward the woods.

Mecum released the girl. The move was not conciliatory, but slightly condescending. He thought he was toying with Melina. "I can be nice."

"So can I," she said. "If you do it my way. I saw what was in your van, and I'm not afraid. I'm intrigued."

He moistened his lips. "You're a tough one. It's going to be a pleasure breaking you. Wait until little Elena hears you cry in pain."

"Draw him out more. I can't get a clear shot," Ramsey whispered.

"Is that a yes or a no?" she asked.

"There's plenty of time for that." Mecum stepped forward, pulling the girl with him. They were less than a few feet from Melina.

The next few seconds played out in slow motion. Mecum stepped away from Elena, edging across the porch toward her like a crouched mountain lion stalking prey. Elena drew back, grateful to have Mecum's attention off of her. Melina held Mecum's gaze. She cupped her breast, feeling more naked without her gun than her blouse. Mecum approached her, moving farther away from the door.

"Three!" Ramsey shouted.

A gunshot fired and Mecum took a step back. The bullet grazed his shoulder. In the movies, bodies recoiled when a bullet entered the body. However, in real life, humans often held steady. Instead of falling, they kept moving forward as adrenaline kicked into high gear.

Mecum did exactly that. He staggered, glanced briefly at the blooming blood on his shirt, and then whirled around, grabbing Elena and dragging her to her feet. He raised the knife, ready to stab her in the chest.

Melina scooped her knife off the ground, and with the flick of a switch, the blade popped open. Mecum gripped the girl's hair and dragged her back in the house.

This close range, she could kill him as quickly with a knife as a gun.

Yelling in fury, he lashed his blade toward Melina, gouging her side. Pain seared through the adrenaline as she raised the knife and drove it into his chest.

Mecum raised his gaze to her, his fury exploding. "Bitch."

She stood, hands flexed, Mecum's blood dripping from her fingers. "Back at you."

Mecum lunged forward, howling in rage, just as Ramsey fired a second and third shot. Pop, pop.

Both bullets struck Mecum in the chest and he fell backward. She raced forward, her gaze on the knife in his hand. As she approached, he jerked the knife forward, but she easily dodged it as he fell back.

Mecum released his grip on the girl and Melina yanked the child free, gathering her up in her arms. She held the child's trembling body close. She remembered the extreme fear she had felt when Bonnie had abandoned her, and then she recalled the sense of relief that had followed when her father had found her.

Melina turned from the door and shielded Elena's body with her own as they dropped to a crouch. She turned from the scene, covering the child's eyes. Elena wrapped her arms around Melina's neck. "Melina."

"It's okay, Elena."

Her side burned and she could feel the blood staining her underpants and soaking Elena's dress. She looked down and knew the wound was deep. Ramsey's hurried footsteps pounded across the yard and up the stairs to the porch.

"You're bleeding," Elena said.

"It's okay," Melina lied.

Ramsey cuffed Mecum before confirming he was dead and called Jackson to move in with his team. He also ordered an ambulance.

"Melina," Ramsey said.

"He cut me," she said. Whatever physical damage Mecum had done to her would most likely heal. Most likely. All that mattered was that Elena was okay.

He tried to pry the girl from her arms, but Elena squealed and held tight. With no choice, he led the two to the edge of the porch and helped her sit down.

In the distance sirens wailed. Melina could feel her head starting to spin, and she blinked to clear her vision. "It's starting to sting a little."

"Elena," Ramsey ordered. "Come to me."

"I want Melina!" she shouted.

"She's hurt," he said. "Can you help me fix her cut?"

"It's okay, Elena." Melina watched as the police car's lights bounced off the trees.

The girl went to Ramsey as the paramedic raced to the porch. Melina fell back against the wood surface, her vision narrowing.

Ramsey pulled off his jacket and balled it up, pressing it firmly against her side. She winced and hissed in a breath.

"Ouch!" Melina's eyes widened as her mind cleared.

"It's bleeding a lot."

"Yeah, I can see that."

He held the pressure steady against the wound. "You take too many chances," he said.

"Not as many this time." She looked over at Mecum's body, knowing how close she had come to dying at his hands not once but twice.

"You scared the hell out of me," he growled.

She smiled up at him. "What a sweet thing to say."

The paramedic came up beside Ramsey, ordering him to step aside. Ramsey hesitated but complied.

"Call my mother," Melina said. "She needs to know Elena is okay."

Ramsey nodded in agreement. "She has every right."

Melina smiled up at him, doing her best to stay calm. "Are you going to make a fuss?"

"Maybe." He cupped her face. "Yeah, definitely."

The sirens grew loud and she heard men shouting. "I think I might be looking forward to that."

EPILOGUE

Melina shifted on the couch in her parents' den and readjusted her earbuds. Her father was currently watching a classic football game—a.k.a. the 1971 Super Bowl. Super Bowl V featured the matchup of the Dallas Cowboys versus the Baltimore Colts. Her father fast-forwarded to all of the eleven turnovers and to the final scoreboard: Colts, 16, and Dallas, 13. In her lifetime, she had seen this game at least a dozen times. As much as she hated watching it, she found comfort in the sameness of her father's habits.

When Dad had keyed up the game, her mother had taken Elena into the kitchen, offering to bake cookies.

Melina tried to rise and follow, but the gash in her side tugged painfully. The stitches had come out yesterday with doctor's orders to take it easy and stay off her feet a few more days. As much as she wanted to rush recovery, a relapse meant more time at home with her parents, whom she dearly loved but who were also driving her as insane as she was driving them.

Easing back on the couch, she selected a podcast. She closed her eyes, refocusing on the narrator's rich voice, which made murder almost appealing.

Instead of losing herself in a long-ago solved case, she saw Mecum's face. He came at her, wielding a knife and cutting her flesh. There was pure, raw delight in his dark gaze. He did not seem human.

She opened her eyes and pulled out her earbuds, shifting her gaze to her father, inspecting turnover number eight. Three to go. Game almost over.

Elena giggled in the kitchen, and the delightful sound chased away the fury and outrage directed at the man who had taken the lives of thirteen women.

Mecum had started killing in 1998, not 1999 as first thought, while he was still living in Georgia. Over the next five years, six prostitutes had been murdered. The bodies were almost completely decomposed, but the medical examiner had noted that each victim had suffered multiple broken bones and the cause of death for each had been strangulation.

Two of those six prostitutes had vanished from Savannah, Georgia, where he had a vacation home. More died in Baltimore and in Wilmington, North Carolina, and the final two died in Nashville during the summer.

Mecum had a type and he never wavered from his profile. Young, under thirty, and with dark hair and pale skin. He had preferred very small-boned women.

Sonny had brought so much evil, but a part of her felt sorry for the tortured soul who had lost so much. Bonnie had spent years manipulating him. When she was arrested and he was left alone, his fears of abandonment had been realized. She understood what that felt like, and there was even a trace of pity in her for Bonnie. Jordie Tanner, the long-haul trucker with the surveillance cameras in his yard, had provided footage that had captured Bonnie racing down the street seconds before she had crashed her car by accident—not on purpose, as they had first theorized.

Whatever tender feelings she'd had for the man she knew as Sam faded as the FBI identified each of the fingers found in Sonny's pickle jar and the one Ramsey had found in his kitchen cabinet. That append-age had belonged to Tammy West, whose body had been discovered in her bathtub.

The women who had vanished in the cities other than Nashville went missing about the time Sonny had been in their cities with one of the bands he managed. Several of the men who had worked with Sonny on the road said that whenever the road crew had a night off, they went out drinking. The one exception had been Sonny, who had always said he had a date with a local girl. One had even produced a picture of Cindy Patterson, who had gotten a backstage pass.

Melina was frustrated with herself and for several nights had trouble sleeping. However, slowly the controlled chaos of her parents' house, now filled with Elena's laughter and growing collection of toys, reminded her she had gotten a few things right.

Elena's and her mother's giggles trailed out from the kitchen. Melina shifted her torso, winced, and pushed up off the couch. She'd had no idea how critical abdominal muscles were until she did not have the use of hers. More core work at the gym was a must now.

"You're supposed to be resting, kiddo," her father said without look-ing away from the television.

"I'm going in the kitchen to see what the girls are baking."

"Turnover number nine is about to happen. Give me a second . . ."

"That's okay, Dad." She kissed him on the forehead. "I'd rather have a cookie."

"Send some in for me, will you?"

She smiled. "Will do."

She had had no contact with Ramsey since he'd left for Quantico over a week ago. In the hospital, he had asked all the right questions, but he had kept his emotions in check. He had looked after her care with the same cool reserve he had mustered in the fight with Mecum. She had considered calling him. Anyone else, she would have dialed the number and called them out. But with him, she could not bring herself to call. She really liked him and, on some level, feared whatever it was they had had was over. She didn't want to hear him say they were done.

She maneuvered slowly, keeping her hand pressed to her side. It had taken forty-two stitches to close up the deep gash that had gone through muscle.

Her mother appeared in the kitchen door. "What are you doing up?"

Melina jabbed her thumb over her shoulder at the television. "I need a cookie."

Her mother watched turnover number nine. "At least there are only two to go."

The front doorbell rang. Melina felt as if the cavalry had arrived. "I'll get it."

Her mother's eyes sparked with amusement. "No fast getaways."

"Got it."

She opened the front door and found Ramsey standing there, dressed in khakis and a button-down shirt rolled up to his elbows. His hair looked in need of a cut.

"Long time no see." Melina was really glad and shocked to see him. She had spent days telling herself she could get beyond him, but now she realized how much she had missed him. As soon as she acknowledged that, she felt a little miffed that he had not called.

A slight grin suggested he'd glimpsed all those emotions in her expression. "How's the injury?"

"On the mend. I can return to work next week. Never thought I'd be grateful for my small office."

"Who's at the door?" her father called out.

She suspected her father had retrieved his weapon from the lockbox beside his chair and was preparing for an attack. God bless her old man. "It's Agent Ramsey."

"Bring him in!" Her dad's voice hitched with excitement.

She stepped aside and led him back toward the den. "Be warned, we are rewatching the 1971 Super Bowl for the millionth time."

"It's a heartbreaker," Ramsey said.

She groaned. "Please do not get my dad started."

Her mother appeared from the kitchen and Elena was a half step behind. They wore matching pink aprons. Her mother's read CHEF and Elena's pint-size version read SOUS CHEF.

"Everything all right, Agent Ramsey?" her mother asked.

"It's fine, ma'am," he said. "I came to give Melina an update." Ramsey shook hands with her father and mother and then handed a brown paper bag to Elena.

The little girl grinned and opened the bag. "Bubbles?"

"In a pink bottle," he said.

"I love pink," Elena said.

"I know," he said with a wink.

Elena opened the bottle and began to blow bubbles.

"We'd all like to hear your report," her father said.

Melina cleared her throat.

Ramsey straightened. "If you don't mind, I'd like to give a recap to Melina first. Keep the briefing official."

"I'm former law enforcement," her father said.

Her mother smiled. "We can wait a few more minutes. Hank, come on in the kitchen and have a cookie."

"I baked them!" Elena said.

"Hank, those cookies smell ready, don't they?" her mother asked.

Her father seemed to sense he had been outnumbered and, grabbing his cane, hobbled into the kitchen after his wife and Elena.

Melina nodded toward the front door. "We can sit on the porch."

"Sure." They retraced their steps through the house, and he opened the front door. He closed it and then made sure she was settled on the glider. He took the seat beside her.

"When's the last time you escorted a girl to the front porch, knowing her old man was on the other side of the door sporting a loaded weapon?"

324

"It's been a while."

"For what it's worth, Dad likes you. So does Mom."

"I like them."

The nine days they had not seen each other had not diluted the absolute connection they had shared when they had worked together to bring down Edward Mecum. Agents sometimes develop a deeper bond when working a case. And more often than not, the relationships that turned romantic fizzled with the case. She feared that was going to be their fate.

"The FBI lab is processing the evidence from Mecum's home, but given what we found, several jurisdictions will be able to close their outstanding cases."

"That's great."

"You did some very solid work, Melina."

"You weren't so bad yourself."

The glider squeaked as he gently moved it back and forth with his feet. "I should have called sooner."

"Probably better you didn't." Still, it was nice to hear him say it. "I've been less than charming the last couple of weeks."

"I wouldn't have guessed."

It irritated her that she had been hoping to see him each time the front doorbell rang. Phone lines worked both ways, so she could have called him. But once her brain had cleared of the painkillers, she hadn't been sure what to say. "They finally going to kick you upstairs?" she asked. "There's no way you can avoid a promotion after cracking this case."

"They tried."

Which meant he'd been in DC full time. "That's great. Wait. Did you use the verb in past tense?"

"I resigned."

He said it with so little emotion that it did not register. "Say again?"

"I quit. I turned in my paperwork yesterday."

"Wow." Never had she considered he would leave the FBI. In law enforcement circles, he was a legend.

"I'm burned out," he said. "Time to shift gears."

"So what are you going to do?"

"For the next few months, decompress. I'll get back into the game at some point. I like the hunt too much to stay away. But if Nashville taught me anything, it was that I like fieldwork more than riding a desk."

She regarded him. "Is that all you got out of Nashville?"

A slight smile quirked the edge of his lips. "No."

"As always, your expressions are hard to read."

"Take a guess."

She swung for the fences. "You're crazy about me."

His expression still stoic, he leaned forward and, resting his hand on her shoulder, kissed her. Whatever self-pity she had nursed the last couple of weeks vanished.

She deepened the kiss, realizing how much she'd missed his touch. "Want to get out of here?"

He chuckled. "Yes, but I suspect there are three humans on the other side of that door waiting for us."

She kissed him again. "Okay. Cookies. Crime update. And then we find a reason to go."

The creases around his eyes deepened when he grinned. "Deal."

ABOUT THE AUTHOR

Photo © 2015 Studio FBJ

New York Times and *USA Today* bestselling novelist Mary Burton is the popular author of thirty-five romance and suspense novels as well as five novellas. She currently lives in Virginia with her husband and three miniature dachshunds. Visit her at www.maryburton.com.